What people are saying about Eleanor Gustafson and *The Stones*...

"We know more of David's life than any other biblical person. But not nearly enough. The tangle of motives and emotions, chaos, and charisma continue to kindle the imaginations of our best writers, drawing us into a story in which we see every detail of our humanity against the epic of salvation. Eleanor K. Gustafson is one of our best."

—Eugene Peterson, author of *The Message*

"Few persons have a more prominent place in the Bible than David, son of Jesse. And few have captured the drama and the grief more dramatically than Eleanor K. Gustafson in *The Stones*. Though these events are very familiar to me after a half-century of teaching and tracing Old Testament details, I found that Gustafson's creative, imaginative, and enjoyable approach brought David's story to life for me all over again. I highly recommend this novel as a wonderful reading experience that will open up new vistas on life and a new portal through which to view this giant character of the Bible."

—Dr. Walter C. Kaiser, Jr., Ph.D.
President Emeritus of Gordon-Conwell Theological Seminary

"In Eleanor Gustafson's powerful narrative, warrior king David's complex character and often ambiguous motivation become not merely legendary but clothed in flesh and blood, in colloquial dialog and a sense of almost physical impact. There is no shrinking back from the brutal facts, the sensual encounters, or the violence of the time. The historical research is impressive and authentic. And there are no cardboard characterizations here; the relationships of David with men, women, and God achieve startling reality. Read between the lines of the biblical record with Gustafson, and discover the story as if for the first time.

—Luci N. Shaw
author, *Breath for Bones, What the Light Was Like*

"High-quality biblical novels are both difficult to write and to 'get right.' Eleanor Gustafson brilliantly succeeds in bridging the spheres of creative imagination and historical reality. In *The Stones*, we meet ourselves in the Bible. We, like Israel's greatest king, are humanly complex and spiritually a 'work in progress.' In this work, Gustafson skillfully takes her readers on an enlightening and absorbing journey into David's world. Like a needle and thread, Gustafson's well-chosen words guide her readers skillfully into the rich and colorful fabric of David's character and the interweaving of his life's experiences. *The Stones* will expand your biblical horizons and is a journey worth taking."

—Dr. Marv Wilson, Ph.D.
professor of Biblical studies, Gordon College

"In these pages, Eleanor Gustafson has brought to life one of the great epic stories of the Old Testament—the life of David. Told from the perspective of Asaph, the author masterfully unfolds the narrative to the reader with a keen eye for detail, yet without ever losing touch with the larger drama of God's work in the life of David and the nation of Israel. Whether you have read the biblical story all your life or this is your first encounter with this intriguing and complex figure, *The Stones* will bring Israel's most famous king to life—I heartily commend it!"

—Dr. Timothy C. Tennent
author, *Christianity at the Religious Roundtable*

"Eleanor Gustafson has given us a beautiful piece of literature that not only allows us to see the flesh and bone in the ancient story, but also guides us through the deeper theological and moral questions posed by the complex and dynamic biblical figure of King David."

—Glenn K. Gunderson, Jr.
senior pastor, Pomona First Baptist, Pomona CA

"The David of Eleanor Gustafson's creative reconstruction and disciplined imagination delights, disturbs, and breathes new life into the master narrative of the Christian story. Enjoy these stones. They may actually turn into bread for your soul"

—Dr. Mark Shaw, Th.D.
professor of historical studies and dean of doctoral programs, Africa International University

"For the serious student of David's life, for anyone who has sought to understand exactly why David is described as 'a man after God's own heart,' Gustafson offers a treasure—biblically-based, penetrating insight into the heart of Judah's greatest king."

—Dr. Finny Kuruvilla, Ph.D., M.D.
writer and health care expert

"You will never read the story of David in the same way again. Gustafson adds color to the biblical account that will make you remember and understand the warrior-poet in fresh ways."

—Laura Kuruvilla
expert in medieval English literature

The
ST NES

A Novel of the Life of KING DAVID

Eleanor Gustafson

THE STONES

By Eleanor K. Gustafson
www.eleanorgustafson.com

ISBN: 978-1-60374-079-1
Printed in the United States of America
© 2009 by Eleanor K. Gustafson

Whitaker House
1030 Hunt Valley Circle
New Kensington, PA 15068
www.whitakerhouse.com

Library of Congress Cataloging-in-Publication Data
Gustafson, Eleanor.
   The stones / Eleanor K. Gustafson.
      p. cm.
   Summary: "Based on the biblical record, this historical novel retells the life of King David from his encounter with Goliath until his death"—Provided by publisher.
   ISBN 978-1-60374-079-1 (trade pbk. : alk. paper) 1. David, King of Israel—Fiction. 2. Bible. O.T.—History of Biblical events—Fiction. 3. Israel—Kings and rulers—Fiction. I. Title.
   PS3557.U835S75 2009
   813'.54—dc22
                              2008038648

1 2 3 4 5 6 7 8 **UJ** 15 14 13 12 11 10 9

To Marilyn Allison,
a representative
of many dear friends
whose prayers helped
burnish the glory of
the Once and Future King.

Alphabetical Listing of Characters

(Parentheses designate fictional names, not fictional characters. More lists are found on page 595.)

(Not all warriors and Levites are listed.)

Abiathar—*high priest*

Abigail—*David's half-sister, mother of Amasa*

Abigail—*David's third wife*

Abishai—*son of David's half-sister Zeruiah and brother of Joab and Asahel*

Abital—*David's sixth wife*

Absalom—*David's son by Maacah*

Achish—*Philistine king*

Adonijah—*David's son by Haggith*

Ahimaaz—*son of Zadok*

Ahinoam—*Saul's wife*

Ahinoam—*David's second wife*

Ahimelech—*high priest at Nob*

Ahithophel—*David's chief counselor*

Amasa—*son of David's half-sister, Agibail, brief career as commander in chief*

Amasai—*Mighty Man*

Amnon—*David's firstborn by Ahinoam*

Asaph—*Levite, chief musician at the Tent of the Ark, narrator*

Barzillai—*old friend from Rogelim*

Bathsheba—*David's eighth wife, mother of Solomon*

Benaiah—*chief of David's bodyguard*

(Boaz)—*first son of David and Bathsheba*

(Caleb and Acsah)—*couple who hid messengers*

Cush—*a Benjamite enemy of David*

Daniel/Kileab—*David's son by Abigail*

David—*king of Judah and Israel*

Dodai—*Mighty Man, father of Eleazar*

Eglah—*David's seventh wife*

Eleazar—*Mighty Man and one of the Three*

Esh-Baal/Ish-Bosheth—*son of Saul*

Ethan—*Levitical musician*

Gad—*prophet*

Goliath—*Philistine giant killed by David*

Haggith—*Daivd's fifth wife*

Hanun—*king of Ammon*

Heman—*Levitical musician*

Hushai—*David's friend*

Ira—*Mighty Man*

Ithream—*David's son by Eglah*

Ittai—*Mighty Man*

Jashobeam—*Mighty Man and mightiest of the Three*

Joab—*commander in chief of David's army*

Jonadab—*David's nephew*

Jonathan—*son of Saul, David's best friend*

Jonathan—*son of Abiathar*

(Joram)—*David's servant*

Kimham—*son of Barzillai and friend of David*

Maacah—*David's fourth wife and mother of Absalom*

Makir—*friend of David*

Mephibosheth—*crippled son of Jonathan*

Michal—*David's first wife and daughter of Saul*

Nathan—*prophet*

Rizpah—*Saul's concubine*

Saul—*first king of Israel*

Shammah—*Mighty Man and one of the Three*

Sheba—*Benjamite insurrectionist*

Shephatiah—*David's son by Abital*

Shimei—*Benjamite gadfly*

Shobi—*governor of Ammon after his brother's defeat, David's friend*

Solomon—*David's son by Bathsheba*

Tamar—*daughter of Absalom*

Uriah—*first husband of Bathsheba*

Uzzah—*Levite whose family guarded the Ark after the Philistines' release*

Zadok—*priest in the Tent at Gibeon*

Zeruiah—*David's half-sister, mother of Abishai, Joab, Asahel*

Ziba—*Saul's steward and guardian of Mephibosheth*

Preface

One day I'd like to sit down and chat with King David. "Did I get it right?" I will ask. "I may have done a fair job with the broad strokes, but how about the finer shading—personalities, capabilities, strengths, and weaknesses?"

It is details that make or break a fictionalized biography. In this novel, I started with the bare bones of the scriptural account and then, by reading between the lines, layered on flesh and blood. A dangerous task, especially with biblical characters. Some, such as David, Joab, Abigail, and Absalom, have clear markers in Scripture, but with others my intuitive GPS had to show the way. Names alone—Benaiah, Asaph, Nathan the prophet, Obil the camelmaster—don't tell much. An author must make people rise and walk. *The Stones*, drawn from a careful study of biblical clues, is my take on the living, breathing people they might have been.

As some characters have been fictionalized, so also incidents have been added to build the rationale for a given character's actions. *That* some characters did reprehensible things is not in question; I need to show *why* they might have done them, or why David reacted as he did in response.

Another aspect of *The Stones* that may need explanation is its moments of brutality. I would rate this novel PG-13—the same as my rating for the Bible itself. David and his men were warriors—*gibborim*—men of blood and violence. That David made it to age seventy amazes me. Furthermore, God gave David the task of fighting and defeating the idolatrous nations surrounding Israel. Indeed, David finished the job Moses and Joshua failed to complete. Before David came on the scene, metaphorical "puddings" made from proverbial "milk and honey" contained idol bits that were hard to digest. After David, though, puddings came out smooth and sweet, and the kingdom expanded its girth from the Negev in the south, up through Syria in the North, and took in Ammon, Moab, and Edom to the east. The Promised Land was now—finally—a feast worthy of the name.

But what about the process? Even more disturbing, what about *cherem*, the God-ordained practice of wiping out men, women, children, and livestock, while devoting the carnage to God? These are hard questions with no easy answers.

God is holy—my starting premise. Humans, however, are inherently evil, some more so than others. For God to separate a people for Himself, He had to carve away the grossly paganized nations that surrounded Israel. The worship of idols included everything from sorcery and temple prostitution to sacrificing children to the fire-god Molech. The Israelites themselves were only a step away from these practices. During these formative years, drastic sin called for drastic measures.

Did the "real" David and Abigail choke on these matters as we do today? I'll ask when I see them.

I have used Scripture extensively. Some passages are verbatim quotes (NIV translation); others are my own colloquial paraphrases. I have chosen not to include Scripture addresses that would pull the reader out of the story. Most passages, in the interest of space and plot flow, have been abridged. My use of the Aramaic *Abba* for *father* is by choice. In Hebrew, the correct correlation would have been *Ab* or *Abi*, but these names just didn't seem to have the same heft to them. Thus, I took the liberty to use the more familiar expression of parental intimacy.

—Eleanor Gustafson

Scroll One

I dreamed of Goliath last night, strangely enough, considering it was Joab, David's general, who died yesterday. Perhaps elation was the link—the Israelites' joy half a century ago when David killed the giant, and mine today when I saw Joab dead on the altar steps.

In my dream, I was trying to question Goliath as I have so many others in compiling this story of David. The picture was silly enough: I, Asaph—all one hundred and forty spineless, Levitical, musician pounds of me, standing eye to navel against this wool-bellied monster who had challenged not only the army of Israel, but the God of Israel, as well. When I talk with people, I try to engage their eyes, but Goliath's head towered high and remote within its crested helmet. The bloated, belch-rumbling bulge of his middle forced me to bend backwards in an attempt to see around it.

Goliath was striding about, his eye on a flurry of activity across the brook. King Saul, tall against his own countrymen but a twig next to the Philistine, was talking with a young lad who had come upon the scene of the face-off. What were they saying? Why was the boy trying on Saul's armor, walking as though to test its feel, then shaking his head and removing it? Watching this, Goliath worked his shoulders under his own scale armor and stamped his legs to settle bronze greaves in place.

"Goliath, my lord," I called. "A few questions, if I may." I trotted beside him, taking five steps to his one. "What are you thinking of in these minutes before your death? I know that's pretty personal, but—"

"Whose death?" A reasonable question, but he said the words absently, his attention fixed on the knot surrounding the king and the red-haired boy.

"I see you're watching David over there. He's the one who will kill you, you know. I know the end of the story."

The giant's shaved jowls hung thick and lumpy, his teeth poked brown and rotten between inch-thick lips. His cropped mane added to the illusion of a naked, weak-eyed pimple atop a furry lump of brutishness. I began to understand that my insolent questions got no answers because Goliath's mind was big enough only to size up an enemy. His left eye circled dangerously. Like another eye I knew.

Joab's eye.

David headed downstream where he knelt by the brook to sort through stones, measuring their heft and smoothness. My dream's eye saw him in simple shepherd's garb, no armor, carrying only his staff and sling. He splashed across the thin stream and faced the giant, intentions clear.

Goliath stiffened, and when his mind caught up with the implications of what his eyes saw, he expanded another foot and turned black with rage. With a mighty whirl that sent his armor bearers sprawling, he spit his injured pride in the direction of the Israelite King Saul, who was watching from his vantage point upstream. "Look a' me," the giant roared, thumping a four-foot chest. "Some sorta dog you see? No, you see I, Goliath. I gnaw warrior bones for supper, but here you serve sticks. By the mighty power of Dagon and Asherah, I will strip feathers and flesh from this stork and feed him to rats!"

"Goliath!" David shouted from below. "Never mind the king." He stood with legs apart and arms akimbo, head cocked rakishly. The first fuzz of manhood sketched red along a face that was fresh, strong, handsome, alive. His voice warbled unpredictably between man and boy.

"That tree trunk of a spear," the lad called. "I wouldn't mind having it or the sword your armor bearer is playing with." His words were light, but his eyes never left the giant.

"Goliath," the boy went on, "you've been a lion against sheep till now. But today I come against you in the name of Yahweh, the Lord of hosts, whom your people say is stuck in a box. The God of Israel will act, and you'll be the one who'll fatten rats. The world will know from this day on that Yahweh saves, not by sword and spear, not by size and fear, but by his power alone. I've killed lions and bears, you know. Their teeth and claws are sharper than yours."

David's voice cracked, provoking laughter. Under its cover David laid aside his staff and drew a stone from his pouch. The Philistine armor bearers danced in anticipation of action at last. Goliath's left eye began circling again. His face darkened, his arms took on the fur and claws of a bear. A snout, round, fur-flanked and vaguely familiar, poked through his facial armor. Now closer to nineteen feet tall than nine, he reared and roared and was no longer Goliath but a bear-like Joab, David's loathsome commander in chief. With weapons carriers and shield bearer tight to him, he thundered down the slope toward the shepherd boy. But the lad, to my alarm, appeared to shrivel even as the giant grew. The Joab bear raised his arms, and the updraft sucked my robe until I felt myself being drawn toward the great beast's maw. David and I both cowered before him. As those claws descended, the armor bearer (whom I also recognized but couldn't name) sprang from under the shield with the giant's own sword. With a mighty, two-handed stroke he cut off the great beast's head. Then he stuck the sword into the ground and leaned on the haft, gasping for breath.

Goliath's armor bearer was Benaiah.

I woke and lay trembling as the desperate intensity of the dream melted into reality. Joab—ruthless commander in chief of David's army—was indeed dead, and Benaiah, David's chief bodyguard, had killed him. The previous evening, I myself had watched Benaiah mount the altar; I saw Joab's blood ooze down those steps, saw his body carried out for burial.

Why should my dream start with Goliath and end with Joab? My questioning Goliath was one of those whimsical twists dreams take. I've talked with nearly everyone else connected with David: why not this giant who played such a pivotal role?

The dream made me see Goliath's brutishness as a thinly veiled version of Joab's. Throw in the giant's awareness of his own power, not just in physical size and strength, but, more significantly, in his strategic importance to the Philistine army. Without Goliath, those enemies of Israel would have had little advantage over Saul and his sons. The parallel was clear: as Goliath was to the Philistines, so Joab was to David. Without Joab—loathsome, loutish Joab—David might well have neither gained nor held his kingdom.

Loathsome, loutish Joab. When Benaiah, David's chief bodyguard, carried out Solomon's order of execution, I for one breathed freely for the first time in thirty years.

It happened yesterday at the Tent of the Ark, where Joab had gone for refuge. Adonijah, another of David's ambitious sons, had made a last, sly attempt to wiggle the throne from Solomon's grasp, but the new king read him correctly and had him put down.

Adonijah's death spelled Joab's doom, for they had schemed together. When Joab got word that the prince had been killed, he came to the Tent, but not in fear. Joab afraid? He would not run from death, but neither would he give his life away. He strolled around the enclosure, measuring each of us in turn. In his eyes, we Levites were fit only for singing and praying and skinning sacrificial animals. He had made my own life miserable on countless occasions, but I took heart that his left eye, subject to circling dangerously, was steady today.

He didn't go to the place of safety until the rattle of arms outside sent him deliberately, without haste, up the steps of the altar, into the swirling smoke, where he touched blood-blackened fingers to the nearest horn of the altar. It didn't seem to occur to him that two vile murders would deny him legal sanctuary. Or perhaps he counted on Solomon not wanting to execute a man at the altar. A precarious perch for Joab, but he had survived all those years on equally slender footholds.

Benaiah, backed by his guard, stopped just inside the entrance. He stared at Joab. When he spoke, his voice was tight. Was he—the most powerful soldier under Joab—was Benaiah ben Jehoiada nervous?

"Joab, come out!"

Joab grunted derisively, a small smile twisting his face. "Maybe I should take orders from you?"

"Come down from there, Joab: the king has ordered it."

"Tell the king to come order it in person. Or better still, tell him to kill me himself. It might give a melon like him backbone!"

After consultation about the propriety of killing even such a man as Joab at the altar, Benaiah and his guard withdrew. Joab straightened, once more surveying the priests and musicians. The breeze wrapped a new cloak of smoke around his tunic. Apart from my nervous fingering of a prayer tassel on my garment, none of us moved or spoke for what seemed hours.

As the last rays of sun faded from the city wall above us, the high priest ordered the lamps lit. With a glance toward the altar, a Levite and a priest turned to the task but scuttled back as Benaiah reentered—with sword in hand. Again Joab smiled, a monster's ugly grimace. Blood-crusted hands rested on the blood-crusted altar, while the blood of innocents cried out for vindication.

"Once more," Benaiah spoke, "will you come down?"

Joab straightened proudly. "I will die here—if you're man enough to kill me."

His eye gleamed, his tone softened. "We've been through a lot, Benaiah, you and I. We go back, don't we? The battles, the exploits. That day of the snow when you landed in the pit and killed the lion… Do you remember, Benaiah?"

We stood rigid under his spell. Light was fading, and the lamps remained unlit. We shivered, mistaking the growing darkness for cold.

"You're no youngster, Benaiah," Joab said. "How long before Solomon puts you out to pasture? You have influence, though. A word from you, and we could put a real man on the—"

"Enough." Benaiah spoke softly, almost with a touch of regret. The two grizzled warriors locked eyes, celebrating one last moment of shared history, then Benaiah leaped to the steps.

I turned away. Tomorrow the altar must be cleansed of pig's blood. But for this day, this night,

> We give thanks to you, O God,
> We give thanks, for your Name is near;
> To the arrogant I say, "Boast no more,"
> And to the wicked, "Do not lift up your horns."
> But it is God who judges:
> He brings one down, He exalts another.

2

To understand David, one must understand his nephew Joab. Perhaps this story is, after all, as much about the general as about the king. Blood runs deep, they say, but the family tie between David and Joab hardly begins to reflect their urgent need for one another.

Joab, son of Zeruiah.

Who but Zeruiah, David's battering ram of a sister, could have spawned a Joab? "The size of her!" my associate Heman once said, his eggshell head wobbling alarmingly. "If it had to, her womb could hold three generals at once; she has but to speak and the gates of Damascus would fall."

Oddly enough, they say the child Joab was pitifully small, unattractive, and full of a thousand fears. Overshadowed by his older brother Abishai and denied the attention the young gazelle Asahel drew, he seemed destined to a lifetime of cruel jokes. The humiliation he suffered from his mother may have been cruelest of all.

No one reckoned on his toughness. One by one, he took hold of his fears, dealing first with lizards. Abishai told me the story. "Lizards are everywhere," he said. "Rocks, shrubbery, inside a king's palace. You pay attention if one gets in your bed. Or your wife's bed. But otherwise, you ignore them. Joab couldn't ignore them, and they didn't ignore him. He seemed to need something to fear, and lizards obliged.

"One day he fell into a dry well that was crawling with lizards. After that, he'd sooner hold hands with a thunderbolt than go near a lizard."

Abishai moved restlessly about the room, an imposing figure with high, prominent cheekbones, a scar crawling across his nose, and a well-trimmed beard that accented a tough, authoritative chin. Then he stopped with that hard look of his and jabbed his middle finger at me, having lost his forefinger. "Asaph," he said, "don't ever underestimate my brother Joab. Once he licked his fears, nothing could stop him."

And lick them he did. When he grew old enough to despise himself for being afraid, he faced first one lizard, then several, and finally a goatskin full, releasing them as moving targets for his half-sized spear.

That was the first step. The next level of self-conquest made my stomach turn—which delighted Joab. "Asaph, have I told you about the first man I killed?"

"Often. And not just one man. An entire family, including women and children. And you only twelve at the time."

"But they were hated Edomites, Asaph. Descendants of Jacob's brother Esau. Edomites, you remember, wouldn't allow Moses through on his way back from Egypt, and God promised that Israel would someday defeat Edom. Wipe them out. *Cherem* on a large scale. My little slaughter was *cherem* on a small scale, against Edomite jackals."

"It wasn't *cherem* and you know it. Did Yahweh command you to kill that family, as he commanded Joshua to kill the people of Jericho? That's *cherem*. Was it a battle in the name of the Lord? No, it was butchery, and I doubt you even thought of Yahweh. Those people had done nothing to you; you simply sneaked up—"

"I hid in the rocks a whole month and studied their tent and flocks and activities. I knew each person, where they'd be at any given hour of the day. My rite of passage, Asaph. If I could kill those people—and the animals. Don't forget them. The biggest nuisance of all, chasing down every last goat. That's *cherem*." He shrugged and gave me a black grin. He might have been handsome enough to start with—a familial trait—with his dark, sharp-angled head, but his face, repulsive through countless woundings, mirrored his nature. His eyes tended toward slits—hard, cold, casting about for potential danger. His mouth was patterned to sneer.

"Some things in life you just have to do. When Mother heard what I'd done, she shoved me against a wall and glared long and hard. I couldn't tell what she was thinking and expected the worst. But she just nodded and let me go. The only time, Asaph—*the only time* she ever approved of me."

He was as cruel to himself as to his victims. He wasn't a natural runner, not like his brother Asahel with his long legs and double portion of energy. In childhood races, Joab often came back slung over the back of a donkey, having tumbled down a cliff or slammed into a tree in a miscalculation of space. Gradually, however, he began returning home ahead of Asahel. Though he could never outrun his brother on the flat, Joab learned to turn obstacles into advantages. Toughness, endurance, and daring made him unstoppable, and iron self-discipline overcame all fear. *"Don't ever underestimate my brother Joab!"*

David knew—and feared—the power of this nephew. Warriors abounded in David's family. While he was still tending sheep, three of his brothers fought under King Saul. In later years, several joined him in the desert, and of course both sisters produced generals: Zeruiah's three, and Abigail's Amasa who, before Joab carved him like one of his hated lizards, seemed slated to become commander in chief of Solomon's army.

But who would have guessed in those early days that Joab the weakling would be a mighty warrior—a *gibbor*? Or that David, popular with hillside shepherds because his songs brightened their lonely nights, would become the man anointed to rule in the fear of God, a man made beautiful under the hand of the Lord?

The crown was not handed to him; he came by it the hard way, even though crowds fawned over him in those early days, not just for his victory over Goliath but for his stunning successes against the Philistines as Saul's chief warrior.

That for Saul was the problem in a nutshell: the crowds now sang louder about David than about him. Saul began looking at his *gibbor* with less than smiling eyes.

David pushed past the doorkeeper, past guardsmen tossing dice, past an astonished Michal (with a wink), past Abner, Saul's imposing general, and into the room where Saul sat, long legs stretched on a footstool in his gloomy, cavernous palace at Gibeah.

Saul's sandals hit the floor. He leaned forward, hands gripping the chair arms. Abner, sword in hand, stared in disbelief.

With an irrepressible grin, David stopped before Saul and bowed low. "My lord the king!" A bag dark and dripping stained his leather tunic from shoulder to knees.

Without another word, he dumped the contents of the bag on the straw-covered floor. Tossing the sack aside, he knelt to separate the bloody mass.

"One, two, three, four, five, six, eight—no, nine—ten, twelve…"

No one spoke. Saul's wife moved into the great room. His younger daughter Michal stood in the doorway, dark eyes flickering between revulsion and laughter.

"Eighty-seven, eighty-eight, ninety…ninety-five, ninety-six…" The pile was now evenly divided. "One hundred five, six, eight, ten-eleven, fourteen, sixteen—the way I'm counting I don't know if this will come out on the nose, but Joab can attest that the total is correct to a man. Two hundred Philistine foreskins from two hundred dead Philistines. Double the bride price you asked and still a fair bargain for a poor man. Twenty-five—"

"Enough!" Saul leaned back in his chair, face chalky and rigid. Taller than most, larger than life, he was once thought impressive. Now he seemed only cadaverous.

Michal sidled toward her mother, eyes crackling, the edge of her robe hiding a smile. Ahinoam signaled silence.

Saul drew a breath and let it out slowly, his face as changeable as cloud shadows galloping across a hillside. Finally, he spoke bitterly. "Yes, you met the price—you and your misbegotten nephew."

"And friends, my lord." He gestured toward the company behind him.

"Yes, yes. Will they help you tame Michal? Perhaps the daughter of Saul will do what the Philistines could not." His twisted smile looked both pained and hopeful.

David looked around, his eyes taking in everything. He never missed a pretty girl and noted more than one here in Saul's heavy-beamed throne room with its smoke-blackened walls. Apart from Saul's chair and stool, the only furniture was a low table and surrounding cushions, benches along the walls, and fire pans for chilly evenings. A thick-walled place of war, not splendor. His gaze took in Saul's counselors; he saw Saul's wife, three of his four sons (noting Jonathan's absence); he saw curious servants gawking at the bloody lump at Saul's feet.

His eyes stopped at Michal, and, when their eyes met, she uncovered her mouth and raised her head. A saucy, seductive pursing of lips replaced laughter, and with a flip of her shoulder she turned and walked from the room with her father's tall, stately bearing.

David smiled, and his eyes flicked to Joab. He, too, had noted the performance.

"Perhaps, sir, you should wash yourself of Philistine blood." Saul's voice cut through the interplay. "Blood is hardly becoming for a king's son-in-law."

David bowed low. "Thank you, my lord! You have honored a poor man and the son of a poor man. May the Lord deal kindly with you."

David and his men, spirits buoyant and invincible, withdrew through the courtyard. Joab clapped him on the back. "A fine day's work, Uncle...I think," he added wryly. "Not for nothing is Saul planting Michal in your bosom. She thinks you're grand right now, but she's Saul's daughter, after all. Better keep knives and spears out of her reach."

"She's just a girl, Joab! She loves me."

Joab snorted. "She loves herself. And you're a fancy ornament right now. Later, when you're out of Saul's favor—"

"What do you mean, 'out of Saul's favor'? I'm too valuable for Saul to turn me out."

"You think you are," replied Joab. "Just because you sing the old man to sleep and take on his Philistines, you think he'd mourn if you didn't make it back from battle someday? Why did he set such a bride price? Not out of kindness to a poor man."

"It's only natural. Fighting's my work, the Philistines my enemies as well as Saul's. It's—"

"David! Open your eyes! He wants you dead. Can't you see that? If you died fighting Philistines, it couldn't be laid against him."

"He'd never—"

"He's crazy as a marsh buzzard, David! You of all people ought to realize that. And he's jealous. Everybody used to sing his praises; now they sing yours, and he doesn't like it. And he looks awful, an overgrown cucumber."

David walked a moment in silence. "He did chuck a spear at me last week, but I—"

"He chucked his spear, and you think he was having an attack of gas."

"Well, it was a bad day. He was prophesying like he sometimes does, only it was like two contrary spirits inside him. No matter how hard he praised and prayed and cried out, the other spirit shook him and twisted his body and mind until he grabbed his spear and lobbed it at some unseen foe. Only I was in the way."

"In the way! Might I suggest you *were* the way? And someday when he's not doing his prophesy thing, he'll pin you to the wall and laugh all the way to Sheol. But in the meantime—just in case you survive his 'prophesying'—we need to get you safely married."

The day of the wedding was dark-hued from the start. Saul had muttered endlessly during the betrothal about losing

Michal to David, yet in the end he not only provided a suit-able house for a king's son-in-law, but a sumptuous feast, as well.

David had wanted to escort Michal from her house to his, but she elected to come to him with her parents, her sister Merab and husband, and her brothers and their wives. Under a yellow, roiling sky, a dozen children wove ropes of flowers in and out of the bridal procession. The entire town of Gibeah gawked at Michal, who had been marinated in oils and spices and adorned with gold and jewels. A tall, stately cypress, she was cool and composed, yet her eyes held a smoky fire that both excited and disturbed.

As David waited for his bride, the air of his courtyard seemed about to combust under a restless circle of dry, silent lightning. Dressed in the splendor of youth and privilege, he drew on the flame-licked sky to infuse the approaching as-semblage with the force of his being.

The bridal company, now swollen tenfold, shifted its atten-tion from weather to the striking couple. Under the enchant-ment of nobility, they ate and drank and sang and danced, and, when everyone had grown mellow, they chanted for one of David's celebrated song-stories. He seldom needed coaxing, especially on such a day. He crouched in a whisper and with a sudden leap and roar catapulted into a dazzling tale of battle and heroism that made children cling to their mothers and clamor for more.

The last golden note of David's first wedding drifted off... but the sky remained sulfurous.

"Jonathan, my brother! Come in!" David drew Saul's son through the doorway. "I've missed you. When you left after the wedding, I didn't think you'd be away this long."

"Are you well?" Jonathan looked David over carefully, taking in his fringed, sash-bound tunic and linen headband that held his thick, auburn hair from total defiance. His body exuded the life and health of a young bull. The "runt" of Jesse's litter had become the most handsome, after all. "And Michal. She's treating you well?"

As they went inside, David looked at his friend closely. "What is it, Jonathan? You're running your hand through your hair—a bad sign. What's wrong? Is your father well? Your mother? Your sister Merab?"

Jonathan looked away. "How's this for 'wrong'? My father wants me to kill you first chance I get."

David shook his head. "You're mistaken, Jonathan. Why would he want me dead? Joab keeps fussing, but—"

"Well, Joab's right. Pay attention to him, David. You're too trusting. No, it's not reasonable for him to want you dead, but he does. He's jealous—that's clear enough."

"Jonathan, a normal person doesn't kill his strongest defender just because he thinks the defender outshines him."

"Kings do."

"Pagan kings, maybe," said David. "Not kings of the most high God. And if they do, something's really wrong."

Jonathan sighed. "I don't know.... Yes, I do," he said decisively. "Here's my plan. Go hide in that field Father just bought.

I'll come along and remind him that not only haven't you wronged him, but you rescued Israel's honor from Goliath's challenge. 'So why, my lord the king,' I'll say, 'would you wrong an innocent man by killing him for no reason?' That's what I'll ask. If he listens, I'll come find you. We'll go back to eating with him, like old times."

David closed his eyes. "Old times…playing, hunting, fighting, eating, laughing…the covenant." He looked at his friend. "Will it ever be the same, Jonathan?"

Jonathan sighed wistfully. "My brother…no, closer than a brother. God has bound us to endure trouble or war, even death. When you're king—"

"Uh-uh, my friend; you first, then perhaps me, if we live that long."

Jonathan shook his head. "No, you'll be king; I'll be your armor bearer."

"Feh! The heir to Saul's throne *armor bearer* to me? If I have to kill every Philistine in the whole of the coastland, I'll see you on the throne of your father. You will be king, Jonathan, I swear it!"

"Did the prophet Samuel anoint me? Whatever my future, being king is not part of it. Israel's hope lies in your hands; I'll do what I can to bring it about. The Lord himself is witness to the friendship between you and me, between your descendants and my descendants forever."

Jonathan rose, ran a hand lovingly down David's beard, and kissed both cheeks. "I must go, friend. Be on guard tomorrow, and I'll speak to the king."

As David watched Jonathan walk away, Michal slipped next to him and played with a red curl. When her attentions got no response, she turned away, annoyed. "Sometimes I think you care more about Jonathan than you do me!" She chased a lizard from the water jars, then moved inside.

"I do," David whispered to Jonathan's shadow in the distance.

"I do...I do...I do...." Those words still play through my mind, a plaintive, haunting melody. David's affection for Jonathan was deeper by fathoms than his regard for me. Jonathan, always Jonathan—seldom Asaph. In later years he talked often with me—perhaps because I was there and Jonathan was not. Strange that he would tell me details of his relationship with Jonathan, but he wasn't the only one willing to bare inmost feelings. It's true that I'm a listener, and people like to talk if fed the right questions. I've sat with high and low, in my house and in theirs, over wine and over brackish water. Of course, I don't claim an infallible memory. I have reconstructed conversations as I remember them, with perhaps here and there the added touch of drama. I've been called a nosy snoop by the likes of Joab, whose least desire was to help me realize my dream of writing out the whole of David's life and its impact on my own, but, by and large, my sources have been cooperative. With so much of my own thoughts and feelings woven in, both good and bad, this personal history may never be read by anyone other than myself, flowing as it does from fierce passion.

I myself never saw Jonathan, but I picture him as gawky; tall people generally are. They say his bearing came from Saul, that he had his mother's almond eyes and curved nose, her full lips and well-tamed black hair. They tell me the overall effect was a strong, sensitive man, a person you could trust. So they say. I can't judge that. I never met him, nor would I likely have questioned him.

A good warrior, a risk taker. He probably copied that from David. The two sang together, but Jonathan was no musician. Not in the sense that I am. Jonathan probably couldn't learn the elaborate rhythms and intervals that characterize David's music. In our early musical sessions, the king seemed surprised and pleased by my quickness. He obviously hadn't had a singing partner who could follow him.

In those dreadful, wavering days of Saul's early obsession, did Jonathan try hard enough to shield his friend? He did gain a stay of execution that next day, but shortly after, when war broke out, David again made a name for himself against the Philistines, and again Saul went grandly mad. This time, after David ducked his spear, Saul sent guardsmen to kill David in his own bed. Michal, though—this was back when she still thought she owned David's heart and attentions—took a *teraph* idol her father had brought home as booty and put it in David's bed with the hair of a red goat at the head. The deception produced a scene with her father, but David escaped and bounced between Jonathan's home and Samuel's in Ramah, trying to figure out how to fix the problem.

The problem, though, was not fixable, neither by David nor by Jonathan. This they learned at the Feast of the New Moon. David had been invited to Saul's table for the occasion. When he hadn't shown by the second day, the Sabbath meal, Jonathan gave a prearranged excuse—and suffered unexpected consequences.

"Son of a whore!" Saul bellowed. "Don't you know that as long as the son of Jesse lives, neither you nor your kingdom will

be established? You've sided with him against me and against your own interests. Now bring him to me. He must die!"

"What do you mean, *die?*" Jonathan protested. "We agreed he hasn't done anything that deserves death. You treat him shamefully, Father!"

"You're the shameful one—my son the bastard lover!" And in one smooth movement, Saul grabbed the spear leaning against the wall and hurled it across the festive spread. Jonathan threw himself sideways, knocking the wine from Esh-Baal's hand.

When he stood, his face was white and his body shook, but his voice remained controlled. "I don't fear your spear, Father. Here—take it. Kill me if you will. I won't be king because you're no longer king. And the only person who cares is the prophet Samuel. He anointed you; he alone of all your people still loves you. He mourns because you're already dead in Yahweh's eyes. David will be the righteous king Israel longs for!"

The next morning, the Sabbath, the golden cord was cut at the stone called Ezel where David was hiding. When he heard the bad news, David fell at Jonathan's feet.

"Don't," Jonathan said, bending over him. "Please. Get up. My heart is breaking. Don't make it hurt more."

Tears streamed into David's beard. "My brother, my lord, and would you were my king. My heart pours out like water because we must part. *Why* does he hate me so? God knows I've tried. I've fought for him, arose countless nights to play away his demons. Has Yahweh really walked out on him? When he went to Ramah to find and kill me, the Spirit laid him out all day, all night. If the Lord is against him, how can he prophesy so powerfully?"

"Prophesy?" Jonathan laughed bitterly. "More likely Yahweh binds him with the Spirit to keep him from killing you."

"Why does Samuel still love him? He refuses to see Saul, but he mourns every day. You think I'm making that up, but it's true. I believe he'd still rather Saul be king. He'd disanoint me in a minute if Saul would just humble himself. I don't compete with him. I just do my job. And now I'm cut off, thrown out, a wild ox cornered for slaughter. Why, Jonathan, *why?*" He bowed low again.

Jonathan knelt and gathered him as a mother would a hurting child. "It's less 'why,'" said Jonathan softly, "than 'what's next.' It's over. Our life together—here, in this place—it's over. My father has killed us both."

They rocked in grief until Jonathan finally pulled David to his feet, wiping his face with the corner of his mantle. "Go, my brother. Go in peace, for we are sworn friends. We have an enduring covenant of blood and laughter and song and the salt of our tears. Go, my strength, my music, my heart; go quickly before Abner comes looking. May God be your Sabbath while we're apart."

Go my strength, my music, my heart.... Yes, my noble David, you were that to many men...to me. You called me friend while you spun tales of battle and booty, of courage. You liked me to sit at your feet when you were full of war and blood. I listened at those times... and yearned. But only Jonathan really mattered. Was he in fact all you remembered him to be? Yes, you fought together, tended each other's wounds, linked arms to dance in victory. But in your moment of calamity, he wasn't there; you had to walk alone.

Nob, city of priests and home of the Tent of Meeting, not far from Gibeah along main walkways, now empty and still in Sabbath repose. A few miles, but the end of David's world. As the sun dipped below the day of rest, he staggered past a pair of grass-roofed dwellings, from which came Sabbath prayers in a cataract of peace that flowed unheeded around his ankles. A thin, reedy-voiced bird piped the "Amen" from a nearby cypress tree.

The leather/skin/cloth-roofed tabernacle, situated to the east of Nob, could just be seen over its eight-foot protective fence. Inside the courtyard, the smoke of the altar etched gold swirls on the eastern sky. Levite gatekeepers patrolling the perimeter stopped, aghast, at the sight of David. Why so distraught? And why had he traveled here on the Sabbath?

David, heedless of everything, pushed through the gate with neither friend nor weapon at hand—not even Joab. Was Joab, even then, no more than David's best sword?

The high priest, Ahimelech *ben* Ahitub and great-grandson of Eli, who had mentored the boy Samuel, was a man old and frail and stiff. He bore an inner strength that grew out of years of burden bearing, of entering into the dangerous presence of God, of measuring out atonement, ram by ram. He was set off from others in the courtyard by four layers of clothing: an undergarment to protect his nakedness when mounting the altar, a linen tunic and sash, a blue robe with gold bells and multicolored pomegranates along the hem, and finally the ephod—a sleeveless garment with threads of gold, purple, and scarlet. On his shoulders he bore the weight of onyx stones with the names of the twelve tribes inscribed on them, and his gold-scribed turban proclaimed him "Holy to the Lord."

Other priests wore simpler ephods and were barefoot, as were white-clad Levites who sang softly in the courtyard while discharging their end-of-Sabbath duties.

Another man, neither priest nor Levite, appeared to worship, bowing repeatedly as the Levites sang, "Hear, O Israel: The Lord our God, the Lord is one." But when David came in, the man hesitated, then retreated to the shadows where lamps had not been lit.

The Tent itself took little space in the courtyard, yet it signified the dwelling place of the Holy Name—the God who is, who acts, who moves. The Ark was at that time at Kiriath Jearim in the keeping of the sons of Abinadab, after the Philistines who captured it found it too hot to handle. Even their god Dagon had unwillingly bowed before it. An outbreak of tumors among the populace had shown the unsettling power in sacred items, and the Philistines got rid of the Ark as fast as they could, before everyone died.

Ahimelech took alarm at David's appearance. He glanced uneasily toward the entrance. "What has happened, my lord? Why are you here at this hour? Are you alone?"

David gritted his teeth against the impulse to run to the altar for refuge or to at least throw himself before Ahimelech. Instead, he drew a breath. "I have come…" he mumbled, beating his brain. "Yes, I have come, charged by the king, on a secret mission. Yes. He told me not to tell anyone. My men…I'm to meet them down the road. Tonight. But I need food. What have you here? There must be bread somewhere in town, but I have no time. I could use five or more loaves. Have you any?"

As he talked, his words came faster and more assured, and he seemed almost visibly to pull himself into the tall, broad, wonder-fighter of Saul's army.

Ahimelech, puzzled, looked him over. David—Saul's champion, chief of his bodyguard, darling of nearly everyone in the country—was dirty and disheveled. He wore no headband, and, most unsettling of all, tear marks rutted his dust-covered face. Sabbath had just ended. Where had he come from? How far had he traveled? What was really going on? "The only bread here is last week's bread of the Presence, which we replaced today. But it's consecrated. I can't give it to you."

David looked down a moment, then resolutely into eyes that had long observed the ebb and flow of human desperation. "I need your help." He spoke with a quiet force that spoke beyond his obvious fabrications. "Ahimelech, will you inquire of the Lord for me?"

Their eyes searched each other, then Ahimelech turned without a word and moved toward the inner court of the Tent to don the breastplate of the ephod with its three rows of jewels that had been used for centuries in making decisions.

When he returned, his face still impassive, he said nothing about what the Lord had revealed. He moved to one of the cubicles lining the outer curtain, tiny apartments that served as living quarters for those on duty and for storage of such things as stale consecrated bread. "I can justify your taking these— on the king's mission," he emphasized the words, "—only if your men have kept themselves from women and their clothing from defilement. Can you assure me of that?"

"Yes." He looked at the priest with pathetic eagerness. "In battle, we hold to the Law's requirements. How else could the Lord bless me?"

"Take them, then, and my blessing as well." Again, he searched the haggard face.

"By chance," David asked softly, stuffing the loaves in his pouch, "is there a weapon? I left in such a hurry...." He looked around. "Hardly a place for swords, but—"

"Oh, but it is!" Ahimelech smiled. "Goliath's sword that you offered to the Lord years ago. I dare say it will serve God's people better in your hand than lying behind the breastplate."

David's eyes lit for the first time. "Yes!" he whooped. "I'd forgotten! Not a sword like it anywhere."

When Ahimelech laid it in his hands, David held it up, testing, weighing, measuring its heft. Satisfied, he thrust it into his girdle.

He turned toward the entrance, then stopped with a frown. "Ahimelech, that man behind the altar—who is he?"

"Who? A Levite?" Ahimelech turned stiffly to look.

"No, next to…that's your son Abiathar, isn't it? Right next to him. He's watching me, and it makes me nervous."

"I see who you mean. Yes."

"I've seen him," David said, "talked with him. But I can't remember…he seems out of place here."

Ahimelech sniffed delicately, raising an eyebrow. "That's Doeg the Edomite, Saul's chief shepherd. He was circumcised six months ago and now comes regularly for sacrifices and vows. He arrived late yesterday and couldn't leave after the start of Sabbath, so he remained the night and appears to be staying this night, as well. Yes, I agree. Out of place. But…an important man. What can I say?"

David shrugged, then turned with new resolve. At the entrance he kissed Ahimelech on both cheeks. "You've been more than kind to me, my father. May God bless you and be gracious to you and your house."

Ahimelech smiled grimly as swirling darkness enveloped David's retreating figure. "May the Lord make his face shine on you, my son—and speed *the king's mission!*"

Doeg, too, noted his departure.

5

The miles between Nob and the Philistine city of Gath amount to little more than a long day's journey, mostly downhill, but for David, climbing Mt. Hermon would have been easier. Alone, on the strength of stale bread and the wan hope that he might find greater safety among pagan enemies of Israel than among his own people, he walked through the shadows of night into his personal valley of blackness.

Until now he hadn't really believed that Saul meant to kill him. Yes, an evil spirit troubled the king. But what was that? Hadn't David himself conquered that spirit with his music? David was used to success, whether in soothing demons, defending sheep, standing against Goliath, marrying into Saul's family, or making himself the nation's military hero.

Now, though, the lion had him by the beard. Neither song nor charm nor prowess could bind Saul's implacable madness. And never, in all his twenty-five years, had he been forced to run away.

Nor was the land of Philistines an ideal refuge. This aggressive people, rising out of the Great Sea, had taken on the despicable practices of the Canaanites. They embraced the whole panoply of Canaanite gods and goddesses, despite having witnessed—through their experience with the captured Ark—the power of Yahweh, the one true God. Here, in the matter of religion, the difference between Hebrew and Philistine was clearly defined.

Also, given the ancient and ongoing hostility between the two nations, the Philistines of Gath would have little compassion for Saul's most able *gibbor*. Nevertheless, their chieftain Achish was known for his generosity. Although a powerful and effective general, his cheerful disposition was proverbial. David hoped this good nature would lead him to trust a proven but little-appreciated Israelite warrior for their mutual benefit. David knew that mercenaries—soldiers in the pay of whatever tribal king would hire them—were not uncommon to other nations. The people of Yahweh would, of course, have no mercenaries; they themselves would fight for the honor of Israel and of Israel's God. But this notion of David's becoming a mercenary in the service of Achish was different, a scheme worth a try. Ignore, at least for now, the specter of actually being asked to fight against Saul or, even worse, Jonathan. In all probability, Achish's trust in David would not go beyond local banditry.

David also hoped for short memories among the people of Gath concerning their champion Goliath. It had been—how many years? Long enough, he hoped, for most people to have forgotten just which young lad had brought down their local hero.

Gath, on the hilly edge of the coastal plain, was one of Philistia's five cities, and Achish was its king. The first thing that assaulted David as he drew near the city gate was camel spit. The second was the rod of the equally ill-humored Moabite camel master who begrudged David's shortcut through his grumbling, groaning caravan.

David's hand went to Goliath's sword but then thought better of it. He bowed his apology and ducked yet another blow.

The city wall rose tall and bright in the early sun. Watchmen patrolling its battlements stood in a knot over the broad gateway, some shielding their eyes against the sun to observe the little camel drama, the rest looking straight down as though expecting some activity. David spotted what he took to be the king's house inside the gate. A heavy guard was posted around it, and two ornate images, Dagon and his son Baal, stood at either side of the doorway, ready to be carried into battle.

David watched as Achish and his strongmen—naked of face and crested of head—left the house and crossed the courtyard. David recognized the king immediately, having seen him strut the Philistine line the day of the Goliath encounter. He noted his smile—a vast exposure of teeth and compelling confidence.

David clambered up a rocky eminence to see why scores of people waited in front of the gateway. They were not disappointed. Achish halted, and one of his armor bearers, some twenty feet away, sent a spear whirling toward him. At almost the same moment, another bearer flipped a sword. Achish, eyeing both weapons, snatched the spear shaft and sword hilt, then faced the crowd with mock fierceness that set the children to screaming. Achish belted his sword and stuck the spear into the ground, then flipped his scarlet-combed helmet high and caught it on his head—to much laughter and cheering. David winced at the thud, but the king seemed unscathed. Achish glowered with pretend ferocity. "You think that's funny," he said to the crowd. "Next time I'll toss up my head, pop it into the helmet, and catch them both on my shoulders. Then will you laugh?" Roaring from the joke, he seized his spear and headed toward the gate, remarking to his nearest aide, "I was brilliant, was I not?"

Achish was brilliant, and in David's eyes right then he loomed larger than Goliath. Though clean-shaven like most Philistines, he appeared rough-hewn and scar textured. His men wore white-crested helmets and short soldier tunics. David looked covetously at the swords in their belts. Swords were scarce in Israel, and these were fine and sharp. For years, Israelites had gone to the Philistines, who alone held the secret of iron, for plowshares, mattocks, axes, sickles, and goads. Needless to say, the Philistines chose not to supply their enemy with weapons. Those had to be won in battle.

A rattle of horse hooves and the appearance of two-wheeled chariots signaled the third part of the morning program. David gawked as three teams circled at full gallop, making the most of their show.

A whistle from above brought the chieftain's eyes up. David could not see the watchman who had signaled, but he saw Achish look in his own direction, back at the watchman, then at him again. His scalp prickled. For better or worse, he'd been noticed and would have his audience with the king of Gath. He set his shoulders and walked toward the gate, hoping that his own demise would not turn out to be the show's finale.

Achish waited between the great wooden doors, wide-set, affable eyes taking in the sword in David's belt, his bare

head, and his gaunt, haggard look. Achish chewed the inside
of his mouth a moment, then nodded discreetly to his chief
warrior.

The king's warrior, flanked by two attendants, moved forward, noting David's beard and fringed garment. "Hold,
Hebrew!" he commanded, with eyes more businesslike than
his master's. David's stomach knotted.

"You have come to this place, Hebrew. Tell us—why are
you here before the gate of Gath?" The warrior's eyes became
slits.

David bowed low. "I have come to greet noble Achish. My
lord's dexterity is astonishing," he added with what he hoped
was a relaxed, friendly smile. "My compliments to him." He
bowed toward the king and with another big breath said, "I
hope to find welcome in his house, having walked all night."

The three examined him closely, and David felt naked. They
could see crumbs from the bread of the Presence in his belly.
They could see the pain of his parting from Jonathan. They
could see Saul's madness and therefore his vulnerability to
attack. The whole of Gath that had watched Achish's entertainment now pressed around him. As he could see the clear
shape of their chins, could they see his bones and veins? The
blood of those veins beat hot at David's temple.

One of the attendants jabbed his companion. "Red beard,
blue eyes."

The other raised his eyebrows and looked at David with
even more interest. He nodded, and David's stomach twisted
tighter.

They looked at Achish. "This is David, a king of Israel. The
one every woman in the land wants for a husband!"

Now Achish raised his eyebrows. "He says this?"

"We know without his saying," said one. "Everyone knows about the women who dance around him, singing, 'Saul has slain his thousands, and David his tens of thousands.'"

Achish chewed his cheek, his smile no longer affable. His eyes glittered, and David's blood turned cold. "An insufferable Hebrew, eh? If what you say is true," the king said slowly, "we have acquaintance of this David. We know him well. How many times have we felt the heat of his sword?"

Not his sword. *Goliath's sword*, burning at his side. Sooner or later they'd notice and ask questions. Despite the blinding smile and clever antics, Achish was a canny, cunning adversary. David had seen the chieftain handle a sword. How many moments did he have before that sword fell on him? *I might fight my way out of this, but….* He was tired, empty, afraid. *Hear, O Lord; answer me. I'm poor and needy. Guard my life. Save your servant. I trust you, O Lord.*

I'm poor and needy. "Poor and needy." Fear stirred cunning, and his voice took on a timbre not his own. "O lord my king, your servant is poor and needy. I've come from far; I've come from far beyond far." Even as he spoke, he noted that exhaustion was aiding his ploy. Words would not be hard to muddle. "My lord king, look at me. Study this head you just tossed in the air. Brilliant, my lord! Brilly, brilly-ant! Oh, that the goats of En Gedi were as brilly-ant as my lord the king!" He went on babbling about whatever his eye happened to fall on, his voice swelling from a mutter to a chant to the cry of a madman. "I'm poor and needy! Save your poor and needy servant! Save your horse. Save your grain jars. Save your dung in grain jars."

He staggered blindly and fell against the gate, then turned to scrabble at it, screeching nonsense until his beard ran white with spittle, his fingers red with blood.

Achish straightened to his considerable height, his eyes contemptuous. "Bah! A Hebrew lunatic! Am I so short of entertainment that I need a madman? He might bring diversion, this David. But he's strong. Strong madmen don't make good house pets. Get him out of here." Achish lifted his heel derogatorily and thrust it toward David.

> Hear, O Lord; answer me.
> I'm poor and needy.
> Guard my life.
> Save your servant, O Lord.

David continued muttering as strong arms detached him from the gate and dragged him off, dumping him next to the smoldering garbage dump. He lay choking in fetid smoke until the chariots clattered off and goat traffic in and out of the city returned to normal. The mournful tune of a passing goatherd underscored his whispered chant. "The righteous cry out; the Lord hears and delivers. You saved me from Achish, Lord, but what now? Hear, O Lord; answer. Save your servant David."

Only after he had pulled himself up and struggled several hundred yards from the dump did he miss the sword. He knew it wouldn't have fallen from his girdle; it had been stolen. He sank to his knees once again. Such a sword, one that was *his* more than any weapon had ever been. Now it was gone. He considered going back but rejected the idea almost instantly. Even with Goliath's sword, he could not take the city of Gath, now that even Achish the benign had turned against him.

The sun, a hard, red eye, glared balefully from a dour sky. David's body throbbed from kicks and blows. He tried not to think of water, but blistering heat compelled him. He knew how to find springs even in desert places, and Gath was far from desert. But this particular hillside promised neither water nor shade, and without shade he dare not lie down for desperately needed sleep. Mouth parched and skin cracked, he couldn't make even simple decisions: Go uphill—toward death at the hands of Saul? Downhill—to more Philistines? North? South? Death lay in every direction.

He walked, heeding mostly the hurt in his heart. He had served Saul faithfully for years: fighting his battles, his giants, his tormenting spirits; serving first as armor bearer, then as captain of his bodyguard and commander of a thousand. He had doubled Saul's bride-price in Philistine foreskins. He'd been patient with Saul's peculiar ways, his mood swings, his "sport" of using David for target practice or sending him off to fight and be killed by Philistines.

And what of Jonathan—that sharpest of all pain? He had given David his robe, tunic, sword, bow, and belt in covenantal exchange. They had lived in Saul's house. Jonathan had shared the pain of being son to such a king, as well as his hopes and plans for the future. He was peerless as a warrior. He'd make a fine king.

Saul had betrayed him, but Jonathan had not. Again and again he'd tried to placate Saul's unreasoning anger, his jealousy. Why would God reject Jonathan because of the sins of his father?

The sins of the father...the sins of the sun. What was the sun jealous of? The great warrior David, running from the sun, scrabbling among stones. Dying of thirst, dying for sleep and food, dying of shame because he had feared Achish, most humane of Philistine sons. *Come, Saul; come find me. Throw my bleached bones on the fires and be at peace, you and Jonathan. Come, O Lord; feed me to dung fires….*

The heat shimmering off the stony hillside gathered maniacal echoes and hurled them at David's head; the dancing landscape grew dark to his eyes.

Is that you, my lord the sun? Or is it Baal…?

The sun was setting when a figure knelt beside David. "Dodai, Abishai!" he shouted to two companions. "He's alive—barely. Bring water."

Abishai felt David's face. "He's cooked. How long has he been lying here?"

Joab grunted. "As long as he's going to. Give a hand."

6

David's passage into consciousness went unnoticed by his companions and only dimly by himself. The gloom inside the cave gave him no clue to his whereabouts, and the chromatic rise and fall of distant conversation revealed no identities. He lay staring inwardly, disregarding messages of pain from his body.

Abishai came with a torch from the fire. "You're awake, Uncle. How do you feel?"

David's eyes flickered to Abishai's nose scar, then resumed their inward focus.

Abishai held a skin to David's mouth and continued questioning but got no response. He called toward the fire. "Joab, Jashobeam, Ira. He's awake."

Seven men rose from the blaze and came to the back of the cave. Abishai spoke softly. "He's awake but won't talk."

Joab knelt and examined David, getting no more recognition than had his brother. Finally, he forced David to look at him. When David's eyes shifted to the side, Joab grabbed his nose and twisted it just enough to make David wince and look up in surprise.

"Enough games. Look at me; talk to me. What's your name?"

David again tried to look away, but Joab had enough hair in each hand to keep the move fractional.

"What's your name?"

David opened his mouth, but only creaking noises came out.

Joab waited, his fingers tightening imperceptibly.

David drew a breath and closed his eyes. "David *ben* Jesse, bastard son-in-law of Saul, king of Israel."

Joab sat back and smiled. "Now we're getting somewhere. How bad do you hurt?" He lifted David's mantle and poked at overlapping bruises.

David yelped and swung angrily at Joab, who caught the arm before contact and laughed. "Well, your fire hasn't gone out. Let's see if your legs still work."

He nodded to Jashobeam and Abishai, and the three lifted David to his feet. Not for long. David's face went white, his eyes glazed, and he began to crumple.

"Okay, okay," Joab muttered. "We'll let you stay sick another day. But then you'll have to sit up and pay attention to your army. You got eight good men here now, and Asahel is rounding up more." He prodded David with his foot. "A king, three stellar generals, and a mobilizing army. All you have to do is get out of bed."

David's body healed rapidly, but mostly he sat near the great rock by the cave of Adullam, looking over the eroded contours of his life. Asahel returned with nearly a hundred men, including four of David's brothers. "Shimeah and Abinadab are coming, too," said Asahel, "and maybe even Eliab. They know Saul sits under his tamarisk tree with a lapful of spears. Every so often he lobs one toward Bethlehem, so the brothers felt moved to get out." Asahel stopped pacing. "Here's your chance, Davi. For once, you can boss your big brothers."

"Let him be," Joab said later when the three brothers were together. "By the time we raise our army, he'll be ready."

"Yes," said Abishai, "but will the army stay with us? Asahel's bunch jumped at the chance to serve under David, but now that they've seen him, they wonder why they're at the cave of Adullam with little to do and even less to eat."

"He needs time," Joab repeated. "Our job is the army. God will see to Davi's job."

David drifted aimlessly through the growing camp. He moved easily among the small flock of sheep and goats, touching some of the animals, but he avoided conversation with men or their families and stayed clear of their tents. Even when his parents and remaining brothers arrived, he spent little time with them. "Not like Davi," Dodai grunted.

"I absolutely never seen him like this," said Jashobeam, gnawing a bone with noisy enthusiasm. "Walk on me, if you want, but he don't even flirt with girls."

Each evening David sat against the big rock, listening to the comforting sounds of mothers and children, night shepherds with their cry of "Hoo-ha-ha-ha!" to soothe the nervous flock. He sometimes plucked a lyre, apathetic fingers sorting through empty intervals that took on a terrible sadness.

Joab and his brothers found none of this encouraging. Joab, of course, had no heart for music—if indeed he had a heart at all. Yet he continued to counsel patience and went out daily to lie grandly to the restless fighting men. He led a number of forays against bandits and marauding Philistines, "just for exercise," he said.

Mostly he waited—and watched David. Although he never crowded him, neither would he allow him out of sight, insisting that someone always stroll along.

Dodai, the "old man" of the band, began to fret. This broad, wonderfully ugly warrior with a warty nose and a coarse web of scars, muttered to his son, Eleazar—who was like him except for fewer scars—"Is Davi getting like Saul? His music playing don't work on himself like it did the old man. Will he start heaving spears?"

Eleazar grunted noncommittally. Next morning, though, he stepped in as David's escort. David paid no heed after a quick glance to see who it was.

They walked through thornbush until the heat of day, neither saying a word. The sun beat down; they'd taken no water along, but still David pushed on. His face showed signs of anguish—whether from thirst or something deeper, Eleazar couldn't tell.

Finally, in a ravine that held the promise of green, David stumbled. He went down easily, almost gracefully, but made no move to get up. As Eleazar bent over anxiously, David began to howl and beat a fist into the ground until it bled.

Eleazar let the storm play itself out while he dug at the patch of green, which finally produced water.

They sat by the tiny spring for three hours, sheltered from the sun by the crumbly cliff above. Grinding a jagged stone into his palm, David began to talk. He told of his sorrow, his anger, his shame. He talked of Jonathan, of Saul, and of Achish, king of Gath. He couldn't be king; a coward neither could nor should be king. Samuel had been mistaken. Saul, with all his failures, was a better king than he'd ever be. And Jonathan would be better than either of them. Even if David did accept the role, he had nothing but a ragtag army who probably wouldn't stick, and he wouldn't fight Saul, anyway. God had made Saul king; God would have to put him down.

Eleazar listened but said nothing. He kept an eye on the passage of the sun, and when David inspected the blood on his palm and hurled the offending rock at the cliff, Eleazar gave David one last drink and propelled him up the incline.

The sun had set by the time they came in sight of the great rock; cooking fires dotted the slope below the cave. As they climbed the hill, a great shout brought their heads up. Men and children clambered on boulders; a double line of welcomers whooped and whistled. David and Eleazar might have been *gibborim*, mighty men returning from a great battle, and, as they drew near a great fire, perplexed and panting, the crowd fell silent. Finally, Asahel stepped forward, his arms outstretched, bearing something. "David *ben* Jesse, future pharaoh of Israel, you've been oiled, you got a name, you got a following. Skinks and desert rats, true enough," he added, "but stupid they're not. And—" He paused dramatically, eyes twinkling. "You got a weapon such as Adam himself would've killed for." He lowered a great sword onto David's hands.

David gasped. "Goliath's sword! They stole it at Gath! Where'd you get it?"

"Jashobeam and I," Asahel said. "The giant and the speeding arrow. Why should uncircumcised dogs keep all the toys?"

With an ear-touching grin, great, bald Jashobeam shambled self-consciously as David looked at him in disbelief. "Well, walk all over me!" said the warrior, not knowing what else to say.

"Look, David," said Asahel. He propelled him around. "Look around you. Look at us—your kin, your friends, your following. *With you as our leader, we can send Saul up his tamarisk tree to bark for his dinner!*"

David threw back his head and laughed, and his laughter swirled through the cave, curled around the Great Rock, leapt across the valley, and skipped among newly lit stars. He flipped the great sword high—higher than Achish's, as high as the intersection of firelight and night—and held his breath. But he snatched the hilt in triumph and danced around the fire, every man, woman, and child dancing with him. Sistrums and timbrels appeared in women's hands. Singing exploded in the night, the rhythm of instruments and feet shaking the foundations of the earth. More than one wept for sheer joy.

Joab leaned against the cave entrance and smiled.

7

There are some—particularly those in the military—
who say that priests and Levites have soft jobs.
They say that priests do nothing more strenuous
than wrestle with unwilling sacrifices, and their livelihood is
handed them on the tithes of the other eleven tribes. Never
mind that they have no tribal territory of their own except for
cities and pastures carved from other tribal lands. But, certain
soldiers would add, they don't have to defend their homes like
everyone else. They're hardly overworked. True, in times of
war, priests go with the army, carrying ashes of a burned red
heifer in a jar to purify those who touch corpses. But mostly
they stay home, light lamps, lay out bread, and offer sacrifices.
They give medical advice and settle religious disputes. They
bang and blow, strum and sing, especially on festive occasions.
And they retire at age fifty.

That's what soldiers think. That's what Joab said many times,
especially when standing near me. But Joab doesn't know. He
doesn't understand that while God chose all Israelites to be
His priests, He set apart the tribe of Levi to represent the nation in the sanctuary.

Levi *ben* Jacob—a curious ancestor in this priestly line. The Levites have a checkered history. At Sinai, when the people melted gold to make a calf idol in Moses' absence, the Levites were right there with all the rest. Yet when Moses returned and called for those who would honor the Lord to step over to his side, they alone of all the tribes responded. Moses then bade them take swords and hack up the rest of the camp. They killed three thousand that day—*Levites* did that. And because of their obedience, God set them apart. "The Levites are mine," he said. "When the firstborn of the Egyptians were killed, I claimed every Israelite firstborn, man and beast. The Levites represent these firstborn. They are mine, for I am the Lord."

God set apart one Levitical branch—Aaron and his sons—to function as priests. The remaining Levites were to serve the priests and the sanctuary. No small job for priest or Levite and especially for the high priest. It's always risky to go near the holy Presence, especially if you don't follow instructions. Look what happened to Aaron's sons Nadab and Abihu and their unholy incense. Uzzah, too. He was struck down just for reaching out to steady the Ark. David was furious with God. But I get ahead of myself.

Enough to say that a high priest develops bad nerves as the Day of Atonement approaches. Consider the word of the Lord to Moses:

> *Tell your brother Aaron not to come whenever he chooses into the Most Holy Place behind the curtain in front of the atonement cover on the Ark, or else he will die.*

The Law lists preparations Aaron must make—bathing, special clothing, animals for sacrifice. But mark this:

> *He is to take a censer of burning coals from the altar and two handfuls of fragrant incense and take them behind the curtain. When he sprinkles incense on the fire before the Lord, the smoke will conceal the atonement cover above the Testimony and protect him from dying.*

You see? The high priest steels himself to step from the safe side of the curtain to the Holiest Place where, if his blood-blackened hands don't shake too badly, he'll spread a thin cloud of smoke to shield himself from the deadly Presence. He does this not once, but twice—the first time with the blood of a bull to make atonement for his own sin, the second with goat blood for the sin of the people.

I was too young to really know Ahimelech the high priest, but he told a story that's etched on my mind. This happened after the Philistines captured the Ark, then quickly got rid of it when it bit them. Even the hapless cows chosen to haul the Ark away were driven by the awful Presence away from their bawling calves and toward Israel, lowing fearfully as they went. The sting of holiness affects more than just men. The Ark was taken by the jubilant Israelites to the house of Abinadab in Kiriath Jearim, where it rested for seventy-five years in the care of Abinadab's sons.

Ahimelech had gone to Kiriath Jearim to celebrate the Day of Atonement. That year the wind whipped the curtains of the Tent, and his incense gave almost no protection. Whenever the smoke thinned, he saw what appeared as purple flame playing over the Ark and felt such intense tingling he could scarcely breathe. The bells on the hem of his garment sounded, even when he stood still. He was sure he would die. Worst of all, he'd neglected to tie the rope to his ankle so he could be pulled out if he did die. "Never again will I fear death, no matter how it comes," he said afterward. "No mere man can frighten me. God alone has power to consume my heart."

Ahimelech did die well, clothed in blue robe and dignity. But may God's judgment consume the man who wielded the sword.

Word of this tragedy came to David on his return from Moab, where he had taken his mother and father for safety. His father, a descendent of Ruth the Moabitess, had relatives there. Gad—the only cheerful prophet I know—sent David back to an area near Adullam where Philistines were stirring trouble.

David and his men had few weapons. Plenty of slings, of course, but swords and spears were scarce. David shook his head. "Only one way to get them—from Philistines. Someday we'll get their secret of iron. But we have bows, javelins, staves, cudgels, a fair amount of armor." He sighed softly, "If only Jonathan were here. He and I alone could beat back a hundred—yes, two hundred—Philistines."

The men were less confident, with stories of Philistine carnage and looting along the border. And when they set up camp in the Forest of Hereth, they found Philistines practically on their doorstep. "At Keilah," Asahel reported. "They've brought uncles, cousins, sheep, fatted giants—the whole farm. If we don't get down there fast, the army will settle in."

David looked at Joab. Their men were best at hit-and-run raids. This would be pitched battle. For an hour, they argued the prospects of salvaging Keilah.

Children's shouts cut the discussion. David shielded his eyes from the sun as a guard approached, supporting a stranger who appeared faint and distressed.

Asahel and Eleazar scrambled down the rocky slope, followed by others. David stayed where he was, concentrating on the stranger, who had fallen yet again. "I know that man. Who is it? He's carrying something."

Joab squinted downhill. "He does have ears, now, doesn't he? Donkey, I'd say. No, his face favors a hare, and his clothing—what's left—well, it seems, gentlemen, that we have a hare in priest's clothing."

"That's it!" David said. "A priest! Abiathar *ben* Ahimelech. I saw him at Nob. Something's happened." He started down, Joab following more slowly.

Ira knelt beside the young man, giving him a drink and emptying the skin over his head. David dropped beside him, noting ashes and tear rivulets on his face. The bundle he held, wrapped in blue linen, brought David's eyes wide.

"Get him to shade. Make way. Gently, now."

They laid him near a tree and tried to relieve him of his bundle, but he clutched it tightly, face contorted and shoulders shaking.

David stroked the mud-streaked head. "Abiathar, you have the ephod. Why? What happened? Tell me."

Abiathar rocked back and forth, his voice in a death wail, his free hand reaching for a handful of dirt.

David, now thoroughly alarmed, tossed a few pebbles himself, then grasped the young man. "Tell us, Abiathar. Who's dead?

What happened? *Hoo.* Be still. We'll mourn with you, but tell us who to mourn." His voice was tight with apprehension.

Abiathar curled even tighter around his emotion.

"I...I must find David *ben* Jesse...."

"I am David. Look at me, Abiathar. Look and see that I am David *ben* Jesse."

Abiathar's eyes were windows of fear and grief and hardship. As though cataloging foes, he marked the circle of faces hanging dark against the sky.

Joab paced and scowled. "Turn the rabbit upside down and shake it out of him!"

Abiathar kneaded his face and moaned, "They're dead; they're all dead."

"Who's dead?"

"The priests. My father. *Ai!*"

"*Ahimelech?* The high priest dead?"

Abiathar nodded. "All of them. Eighty-five who wore the linen tunic."

David slumped in disbelief. The circle of eyes shifted to Abiathar's fine-woven garment, now stained and ripped. No one spoke.

"That's not all. He put the town under *cherem*. Men, women, children...babies, cattle, donkeys, sheep—everyone, everything totally destroyed."

"Who did this?" Rage shook David's voice. "*Who did this unspeakable thing?*"

"Doeg the Edomite."

David recoiled, his face lamb white.

"He...he claimed to be under orders from the king, but..." Abiathar's voice trailed off in a paroxysm of grief.

David rocked in sorrow. Then, shrieking his outrage to the sun, he leaped up and strode to a thicket where he ground dirt into his hair and beat his fists against a tree.

The death wail moved across camp. The only non-weepers—the brothers Joab, Asahel, and Abishai—kept their eyes on David, watching him tear his tunic and pull out his sling to hurl stones toward Gibeah. But they froze when he followed the stones on a dead run, bellowing, "Break their teeth, O Lord; tear out the lion's fangs!" Asahel sprang to follow, but Joab stopped him. "Wait," he said.

Asahel looked up questioningly, then at David disappearing through the trees. The three scarcely breathed.

Gently, Ira continued to question Abiathar. "How did you escape? How did you get the ephod?"

Abiathar closed his eyes. "When word came for Ahimelech and his brothers and sons to appear before the king, I was out...relieving myself. But something told me to stay out of sight. Was Saul having a fit of the Spirit or of madness? Who could tell?"

"So you didn't go with the rest," prompted Dodai.

"I went, but not with them. I went straight over the hill and got there about the same time. I wished I'd taken off my tunic. It's not hard to spot a priest." He looked anxiously at Dodai.

"Go on," said the old warrior.

"You know the tamarisk tree where Saul sits? Well, I borrowed three sheep to get close...well, not to the tree. Someone might..." He looked around nervously.

Eleazar moved in. "Abiathar," he said, taking the young man's hand, "the story. What happened to your father, to the other priests? Doeg the sheepherder killed them. But where? How? At the tree? In Saul's house? In Nob? *What happened?*"

Abiathar swallowed hard. "I will tell you. Yes. Saul was under the tamarisk tree where he holds court. Everyone knew something was going to happen. I mingled with servants and herdsmen. My father Ahimelech was standing before Saul. The others were behind, with Saul's guard around them. Finally Saul spoke. 'All right, you son of Ahitub,' he shouted. 'Why have you and the son of Jesse conspired against me? Don't deny you gave him bread and a sword. You inquired of God for him; you set him up to rebel against me. He's out there this minute, lying in wait to kill me and take over the throne.' Those were his words," Abiathar said. "They're burned into—"

"What did Ahimelech say?" asked Ira.

"My father said, 'No! Who in your entire kingdom is more loyal than David? Your son-in-law, captain of your guard. If you hadn't chased him away, he'd be beside you right now. Everyone, even your servants—' He gestured in my direction, and I was afraid, first that—"

"But he didn't give you away."

"No. He didn't see me. *Ai!* My father!" and again he wept. "I'm sorry...." He struggled on. "'Was that the first time I inquired of God for him?' he asked Saul and then answered his own question. 'Of course not! Why should that be considered treason?'

"Saul blew up. An absolute rage. He stomped and threw things and kicked— He grabbed Abner, his general, and

screeched, 'Kill them! Every last one!' Abner bent forward,
looking puzzled. 'What?' he said. I think he knew what Saul
meant, but he said, 'What?' 'I said, kill them!' roared Saul. 'Kill
them all. They helped David get away. They could've told me
that my son made a covenant with the son of Jesse.' By this
time Saul was raving, his beard ringed with spit. It was awful. 'Listen, you men of Benjamin! Listen to me! Can the son
of Jesse give you fields and vineyards? Will he make you one
of his Mighty Men?' A lad told me he'd done the same thing
earlier. Maybe juice from the tamarisk tree—"

Joab broke in. "You're saying Abner, Saul's general, killed the
priests in cold blood?" His eyes had retreated to slits.

"No. He refused, and I thought Saul would kill him on the
spot. The king towered up, his spear raised. But Abner just
stood there. Eye to eye. He didn't move. How could he do
that? Where does such courage…?"

Joab sneered. "Some are born that way; others are born
priests."

Abiathar looked at him blankly, then stood—a thin reed
amidst hard-muscled giants who creaked of leather, reeked
of war, men who fed off such acts of slaughter. He grabbed
his head and grimaced. "I'm all right," he said with dramatic
pathos. "Saul then told Doeg…to….the priests…sheep milling in a sacrificial pen, trying to get out. And the guard tight
around. It was awful! Doeg looked at Saul, hardly believing
the order, but when Saul nodded, his eyes glittered and…
he smiled! My father…was the first. He…flinched as Doeg
came at him, but he didn't run. O God, he didn't run! I didn't
see much of the rest. I hid among Saul's grapes and threw up.
Women screamed and cried, priests screamed. The guards

wouldn't kill any, but they wouldn't let any escape, either. Oh, my brothers! My uncles and cousins! The house of Eli—gone. I'm the only one left!"

"Doeg the dog!" muttered Abishai.

Abiathar clutched the tree. "He...hadn't even finished killing them before asking Saul's permission to...to put Nob to the sword. The whole town! And there I was, retching on grapes. Finally, I crawled down the row and started running, wanting to warn them in Nob, but I was afraid. Then I thought of the Tent. If Doeg could kill priests, what would he do to the Tent? I hate the scaly toad! My father didn't trust him, but what can a high priest do when a man comes to do vows?

"I could hear Doeg shouting for others to help, so I ran faster, but...too late. The children's screams...they hadn't gone to the Tent yet, though. The ephod...if I could sneak in.... I slid under the side curtain, shaking so badly I dropped the lid of the chest. It made a terrible noise, and someone heard. Someone just outside. I picked up the ephod and ran for the opposite side. Then a thought came. My sisters had tittered about the Forest of Hereth, and I took it to mean that every woman's hero was there. A safe place, maybe.... They're dead, all dead!"

He hunched over his grief. The others stood silent, aghast.

A figure pushed among the mourners. Joab caught the movement and directed his brothers' attention. "What'd I tell you?" His large eye gleamed.

David knelt beside Abiathar with a shepherd's rumbling comfort. "*Hoo-ha-ha-ha!* You're safe now. Things aren't right, but you're safe here. I knew when I saw Doeg at the Tent, I knew he'd tell Saul. I'm the one who brought death to your father, to the house of Eli, and somehow…" He grimaced and gripped the priest's shoulders. "Stay with me, Abiathar. The man after you is after me, too. You'll be safe here. Word of this massacre will spread, and…" His face twisted abruptly. "The final judgment for Eli's sin. The Lord gave the child Samuel a hard word for Eli, and now Eli's descendent bore the thrust of that sword."

David turned to the others, many of whom had also come to him for safety: Jacov, deep in debt with not even a mantle to warm him at night; Ahban whose sons had been killed for a trifling offense in one of Saul's whimsical purges; Rekem, a hothead who chafed at Saul's uneven justice. "You are my friends," he observed. "We're nearly five hundred strong, men without homes, without a king, without a cause."

Uneasy murmurs met his words.

"No cause," he repeated, "but the Lord's cause. We follow where He leads, fight whatever enemies He sends us, eat the food He provides. Our cause is His cause. Though Ahimelech and the others are dead," he went on, a grim jubilance rising in his voice, "God has brought us a priest—and the ephod. Come, Abiathar. You shall inquire of the Lord for us about Keilah."

The Lord's answer came through the Urim and Thummin, but the men didn't like it. How could this ragtag band that huddled with owls fight Israel's most powerful adversary? They were afraid. "Abiathar has never used the ephod before," they murmured. "How do we know he's doing it right?"

Again Abiathar knelt before the ephod, teeth chattering, and again the Lord's answer came back, "Go down to Keilah. I will give the Philistines into your hand."

David's hand punched the sky. "A plain answer. What more do we need? *We—will—trust—God!*" His last word was drowned in a roar of fierce exultation.

8

Keilah—fortified and surrounded by villages, fields, vineyards, olive groves, and barley patches—perched on the top edge of the Shephelah, that north-south band of chalky hills and fertile valleys that lay between Judah's central mountain ridge and the coastal plain. In good times when Israel was strong, they controlled the Shephelah. In bad times, leopards, foxes, and Philistines held it. This was a bad time.

Spring—a time of silver-throated bird song, the seductive scent of flowering vines; a time of grain harvest and hilltop threshing floors spilling out noise and dust. A time for marauders to help themselves to the fruit of other men's labor. The particular band of marauding Philistines now perched beside Keilah were no hit-and-run bandits. They had arrived with livestock, prepared to settle in for the entire harvest season.

The city was walled, but grain fields and threshing floors were not, so a farmer hoping to feed his family had to raise his own army to protect the reapers and threshers.

As it happened, a small army lay a few miles to the northwest. The farmers sent for David's help.

David went. He and his men stood high on a wooded bluff overlooking the enclave and its surrounding patchwork of fields and empty villages, the families having sought protection inside the city. They pretended confidence, but the odds were heavy against them. Along with scattered concentrations of Philistine warriors, they could see a war machine in place for battering the city gate.

Ira and Hurai clambered the bluff, having spied out the Philistine encampment. "Thousands," said Ira, shaking his head. "Seven or eight to each one of us."

Shammah, a huge, dour warrior, grunted. "That all? Ten's about right for me."

"Right," sniffed Asahel. "Your looks alone would ward off a regiment."

"Huh. Beauty's extra baggage; some of us are less encumbered."

After a nervous consultation, David and his men chose a field already harvested as the place for battle—easy to retreat from, if necessary. Philistines seemed to be everywhere, waiting for a call to action. A number of them were harassing a knot of reapers who stood clutching nearly empty sacks. "Easy pickings," murmured Shammah.

"Which—Philistines or reapers?" said Asahel. "The reapers, now—kind of underdeveloped. No question, they'd be easier to pluck—"

Joab, not amused, clouted his brother off the rock. David, on this first move toward the scene below, shrugged. "Good a time as any." He drew a big breath and signaled his two giants. "Jashobeam, you take this side, Shammah the other; the rest of us are the net—a giant sweep."

From the depths of Jashobeam's tree-trunk torso and thick, bulging limbs exploded a cloud-bouncing gust of laughter. "An absolutely *two-giant sweep*—in the name of Yahweh!" He vaulted off the rock after Asahel and set off downhill, his shambling walk suddenly transformed into an efficient, ground-covering lope.

The charge was initially successful. The Philistines were caught off guard, and the watching reapers grabbed cudgels and leaped to join David's fighters. Jashobeam was everywhere, club in his shield hand, spear in the other. He knew his strength and his accuracy, and this kept his humor high.

Shammah, a half head shorter than Jashobeam but more prominently muscled, never wasted energy on laughter. Instead, he focused. Within minutes the field was littered with bodies, and the band paused to catch their breath.

Then disaster struck.

From behind a hill, Philistine reinforcements appeared on a dead run, bristling with swords and spears. David's face went white. "Fall back!" he cried. "To the rocks!"

As Philistines thundered toward the corpse-strewn stubble, David's men scattered. The reapers prudently headed for the city gate.

Shammah, though, did not run. Seemingly heedless of being left alone, he jogged to an adjacent plot of ripening lentils and waited for the Philistines. His jumbled face hardened even more, and his body appeared to expand six inches in all directions. When the clash came, he became two lions, roaring, slashing, thrusting, leaping, whirling—a colossus roused and formidable.

David was first to notice that the Philistines weren't baying like dogs behind them. "Look!" he cried, pointing below. "Shammah's holding them! Joab, you and Jashobeam work toward him with your men. The rest follow me to the left. We'll cut the line. God said fight. We'll fight!"

With the extraordinary help of both giants, they fought to an astonishing victory. Shammah alone killed hundreds of Philistines and gained a sizeable dent in his arm, which he proudly displayed as a worthy complement to a missing ear.

The Philistines left Keilah, abandoning their flocks and herds to David and his men—a good day's wage for the pains of battle.

Keilah—a good place, hard won. David and his men decided to stay there and brought wives and children from the forest. But Saul learned where they were and sought to use David as a bargaining chip for the people of Keilah to exchange for their own safety.

Again, Abiathar's ephod was pressed into service, and, acting on its warning of treachery, David got his people out of town before Saul could move from his tamarisk tree. He left Keilah and passed into the long night of his shaping.

Saul pursued David relentlessly, from desert areas to remote pockets in the hills, to caves and wilderness strongholds—a tireless hunter. As he stepped up his deranged campaign against David, no place—not even arid areas—seemed safe. Every shepherd boy became a potential spy. Even in remote

ravines or sheltered mountain dells where the band felt they
could trust the simple, nomadic folk, Saul somehow found
them out, and David's outposts would appear, out of breath—
the signal to pack and leave.

At first, it was a game for David and his men, matching wit
against wit. They were young and tough and skilled in surviv-
al. When driven into more remote areas, the game wore thin.
The lion stalking from hole to hole wore them down. Food
became an increasing problem as they drew back to places of
little forage. Many took their wives and children elsewhere
for safekeeping, even to Philistine villages where the urgent
rhythm of life kept questions to a minimum.

Often, though, instead of avoiding sheepherders and gather-
ers of firewood, they squatted with them over a bit of bread,
planting bits of misinformation about their own movements.
When the enemy came along, Saul's scouts would follow the
false lead, giving David a scrap of time to escape.

David walked grim and silent during this time, especially if
hardship cost a life. A pregnant woman miscarrying during
flight; a scout slipping from a crumbling outlook and falling to
his death. David took these mishaps as personal failures and
mourned with the bereaved.

He often left camp at night, sometimes with a lyre, sometimes to rage at God, sometimes just to lie under the crushing
weight of stars. Occasionally he came back strengthened, but,
as the endless pursuit wore on, he appeared more and more
haggard.

Two events, though, came as a bit of honey into his life.

9

The first took place at the stronghold of Adullam.
They had returned there early the following summer, thinking that Saul might not sift through old
hiding places. The hope didn't last, but something there fed
his soul.

The day was cruelly hot. David and others had been pa-
trolling the border, engaging in skirmishes with well-armed
Philistine scouts. Returning to the cave, he encountered Ira,
Elhanan, and Hurai, who had observed stepped-up Philistine
activity to the east, in the Valley of Rephaim south of Jebus.
The groups shared reports as they climbed to the stronghold.

Inside the cave, David fell on his bloodstained mantle in utter weariness.

Ira bent his slender frame and looked at his leader's arm.
"You're hurt. That's your blood, not Philistine. Let me see."

David grunted.

Hurai, too, leaned to inspect the wound. Then he stood. "I'll
get water; you get a bandage."

"Yes...water." David licked his dry lips, raised on an elbow,
then slumped again.

Elhanan held out his water bag. David took several swallows, then spat out the last mouthful. "Eechh! Where'd this come from—the Salt Sea?"

Elhanan grinned lamely. "We drank at Bethlehem but—uh—forgot to fill up, and the pool we found wasn't exactly wonderful."

"Tastes like goat water."

"Here." Eleazar brought a bowl from the cave water store. "Try this."

David drank long but lay back with the same sour look. "I'm sick to death of wilderness water! Sick of water that burns, that coats your throat with slime. A pig wouldn't drink this." He threw an arm over his face and sighed. "Oh, Bethlehem! What I'd give for a taste of your water."

Ira murmured an amen and resumed his medical attentions. Elhanan moved off to talk with Hurai. When Ira walked past with bloodied water, Hurai snatched at him, his mouth an upturned bow. "Toss that and come with us. We have an idea."

The brassy sun finally gathered its hot, flowing robe and disappeared behind the lower hills. Cooking fires ignited. David rose, ate, and withdrew to his tent. The entire camp settled to a comfortable mix of talk, laughter, and isolated music, with jackals singing antiphonally in the barren hills.

At the change of guard for the third watch, sleepers were aroused by a warning shout. Men rolled from tents, weapons in hand. Women frantically raked coals and blew on them and soon handed torches to their men. Cries of children weaned on terror dotted the writhing camp.

David's head was slow to clear, but with only a hiss and a grimace, he followed the bobbing lights, sword in hand, to a noisy knot surrounding three men grinning sheepishly in the torchlight.

David pushed through. "Ira and Hurai! Elhanan! What's going on?"

Hurai shrugged. "Well, either we've lost our touch, or our guards are sharper than Philistines. We managed to get through their lines, in and out, without so much as a goat bleating. But try to sneak in here..."

"Through whose lines? What are you talking about?" David asked.

"We went through the Philistines in Rephaim where they're encamped," Ira said. "Elhanan knew how to get around the line of rocks."

David leaned against a rock. "You crossed the Valley of Rephaim, thick with Philistine troops, in the middle of the night. Could you—"

"It wasn't the middle of the night then," Elhanan said. "Just after most were asleep. The best time to cross. What's a little extra noise—somebody out peeing."

"Trickier getting back," Hurai said, "but the first guard was drowsy by then."

David stroked his beard. "Would you mind telling us why you needed to cross Philistine lines this particular night?"

"To get this, of course." Hurai grinned triumphantly, holding up a leather bag. "No more goat pee; here's your water from Bethlehem. We took a good drink, and it was worth the trip just for that."

He held it out to David, who stood stunned, unable to move or speak. In slow motion he belted his sword, reached for the bag, and sank to his knees. He looked first at the container, then into the faces of the three who had brought it. Back and forth he looked, torchlight painting awe across his face.

Ira punched his shoulder gently. "Come on, drink. Our gift to you."

But David shook his head. "No," he said adamantly. "I can't drink it. Far be it from me, O Lord, to drink this! The lives of these men are in this water, their *blood*. Can I drink blood?" He shook his head again. "I cannot drink it." He opened the bag and held it high, tears streaming down his face. "I pour it out, O Lord, a blood offering, a thank offering for these my friends who risked their necks to get this—*for me!*" Slowly, he fed the precious water to the thirsty ground. No one spoke; no one moved under the magnificence of David's act. When the bag was empty, he set it aside reverently, then looked long at each of the three before crushing them in his arms.

The second event came after the group had retreated to the Desert of Ziph south of Hebron, to a small brushy forest called Horesh. Here, on a rocky, scrabbly tor, rose the stronghold Hakilah, a place of respectable defense, if not of comfort.

To this high, austere lookout came two scouts, smiling mysteriously, a third person loosely in tow. David looked closely at this "stranger," then whooped toward him in death-defying leaps. "Jonathan! Jonathan!" The two laughed and hugged and fell and wrestled and slapped backs and laughed some more.

"How are you, my friend?" Jonathan asked, looking David over. "You're thin but tougher than ever, if that's possible. Of course, I keep hearing—hourly—about your treachery and what will happen to me if you're not eradicated. So," he continued with a broad smile, "I'm here to wage war. I'll trot back downhill. You and your men—my, you do have an extraordinary collection," he said, looking around the circle that had gathered. "A bad-tempered lot. Are they starved, or do you beat them every day?"

"They're no more starved than I am. Bad-tempered, yes."

"Well, obviously you trust them, so here's what we'll do. I'll stand against you and these scowlers and eradicate you all. That would please Father—if that's possible these days," he added, his smile fading.

"How is your father?" David asked gently.

Jonathan lifted his eyebrows and shrugged. For a moment he said nothing. "Father is...father." He forced a smile. "He can be his old self one moment—funny, loving, every inch a king—then he turns tyrant, heaving spears at the shadows of his mind. Unfortunately, real people, not shadows, get gored."

"Has he killed anyone?"

"Oh, yes. At least two bodyguards, maybe more. Some have gone missing. Then the half-dozen or so he only wounded. Abner has fits, but his sovereign, right or wrong, is never wrong. But you—tell me about yourself. How are you?"

David pulled Jonathan toward his tent, a patched affair even less respectable than its neighbors. "It's lonely here, Jonathan. A flowerless desert...not even Michal." His mouth twitched. "Can you picture your sister here?"

Jonathan examined a tent rope and ran a hand through his hair.

David saw the familiar gesture. "She's gone, isn't she? Saul gave her away."

Jonathan nodded, his jaw working.

"What's his name?"

Jonathan hesitated. "You really want to know?"

"Yes," David replied gently. "I will not avenge her; I promise you that."

Jonathan sighed. "His name is Paltiel *ben* Laish from Gallim. A harmless oaf, nothing to distinguish him. Father saw to that." He looked off.

"And Michal? Is she happy?"

Jonathan remained silent, avoiding David's eyes. Finally, he shrugged. "I'm not sure. Paltiel is wealthy and can buy her happiness. He dotes enough, but he's fat and soft and stupid and utterly without challenge. She says she's happy."

"Compared to life with her former husband, anyway." David laughed grimly, then turned to search around the tent. "This may be desert, but we can share desert fare. We don't do badly, actually. A few sheep and goats to keep us going and the odd raiding band that happens along. Keeps us in grain and bits of fruit." He rummaged near a pole. "Ah! A date cake. Well," he amended ruefully, "half a cake." He spread his cloak on the ground. "But even a shepherd's table is sumptuous with you here!" He broke off some fruit and settled back. "Tell me about your wife. She was pregnant, if I remember."

"Yes. We have a son. His name is Mephibosheth."

"Mephibosheth. Prince Mephibosheth."

Jonathan raised his eyebrows but said nothing.

They ate and drank and shared stories, Jonathan's eyes probing David. Finally, he leaned forward. "Tell me straight: aside from Michal, how is it with you? You sit here—a desert outlaw on a hill of injustice under my father's shabby treatment. Women adore you, but the man who profited most from your services chucks spears. You have no future, no joy—like a mother whose newborn son doesn't breathe."

David studied his hands. "Those weeks at Adullam with vultures feeding on my heart, I came to realize I still had two things: my love for Yahweh and my gift of music."

Jonathan sat up straight. "David, you taught me to love Yahweh. We talked, you and I, of a shepherd's love for sheep, a man's love for his wife, a mother's love, a boy's for his *abba*. And all the while, I saw these human loves gathering into a thundering, passionate love for God. I saw it in you when we talked of big things, things that make you sing. I see it here. Say what you want about God being hard on you, but your eyes, your soul, are wrapped around a core of love that sometimes leaks out, sometimes explodes like a volcano. Like with Goliath. You pushed forward, a half-grown he-goat, sling in hand: 'I'll put you down and cut off your head so the whole world will know there's a God in Israel!'"

David snorted. "Pure arrogance."

"Not arrogance," said Jonathan. "You saw what was happening. The honor of the God you loved had been violated, and no one would stand to the challenge. So you acted. It's that simple—and that profound. And that's precisely why you're here in the wilderness. *If you cared nothing for God, my father's life wouldn't be worth goat dung right now.* You'd have cut him down and taken the throne, the throne given to you by Samuel—don't forget that part."

David closed his eyes and rocked silently. Finally, he said, "My father Jesse...my *abba*, taught me love. So proud he is of us all. He's old and frail now."

Jonathan was silent a moment, then said softly, "I met your father only once. He was old even then but so caring when he learned who I was—how was my father and did I have sisters and how did they like David and did I know his firstborn Eliab—such a fine, sturdy warrior. I loved him on the spot, and I wished...I wished..." He sighed. "Love doesn't flow out of emptiness, David. Or the other way around: emptiness doesn't produce love. That's the difference between a Saul and a Jesse. And Jesse's son planted love for God in my soul. I have his love, your love, your songs, and I hold them tight to my heart."

David sighed. "Hold them tight," he repeated. "It's all we have. Our priest Abiathar, for all his bloodlessness, does have a good memory, and, between us, the Law has become a strong tower. We study it, speak it, sing it out of our necessity."

"Israel's hope lies in your hands; I know that. You'll be king sooner or—"

David's head snapped up. "Stop! I kept still before, but not again. Get this straight: Saul is king. I'm committed to him as God's chosen. And," he added, his grin returning, "don't even think of joining us. What sort of target do you suppose I'd be if the king's son tagged along as chief goatherd?"

The two walked the brushy slope, talking and even laughing under a pall of sadness that seemed to anticipate a final parting. The sun was heading toward the lower hills when at last Jonathan faced David. The hazy glow washed the emotion on his face, and he closed his eyes, unable to speak. David enfolded him, auburn hair mingling with black.

Jonathan finally stepped back. "Don't forget what we talked about, my brother, my friend. You're in a hard place, inches from death. But no man—not even a king with a sick mind— can lay a hand on you against God's will. You are sheep in this desert furnace, your only shade the valley of death. But God is your shepherd, and you walk a firm path. Pasture and water may be short, but he'll lay it out in his way and time."

He gripped David's arm. "God chose you to be king. Don't lose sight of that, especially now when things are sticky." His eyes twinkled momentarily. "And regardless of what you say, I'm your number-two man! I'll be your chief advisor and— since I do have a sword—head of your bodyguard. We'll let Joab run the army."

They stood awkwardly for a moment, then Jonathan suddenly reached into his pouch and pulled out a small jar. "I almost forgot. But maybe this is the right time, after all. Maybe it has meaning of its own." He worked the plug out, then raised his arm and poured the contents over David's head.

"Oil!" David exclaimed. "Oh, rapture!" He luxuriated as oil penetrated his dusty hair and beard. Jonathan worked it over cracked lips and scaly skin, his thumbs gently smoothing eyelids and crinkled corners. David's nose twitched. "That's no ordinary oil," he said. "Spicy. Almost like—" He stopped abruptly and looked intently at Jonathan.

Jonathan smiled but shook his head. "Don't ask me where I got it; I won't tell. Yes, it's different—a gift. You'll be my king,

I'll be your chief bodyguard—or armor bearer, if you can't find one who can keep up with you."

"Jonathan, this is a heavier anointing than Samuel's—you know that."

"No. I'm no prophet, David. I'm not authorized to anoint anybody, let alone a king. This is...my love for you...and for God. I pour out my love in a sacrifice of..."

He could go no further. The two stood locked in tears until Jonathan broke away and ran down the scrubby hill the way he had come.

A bit of water, a bit of oil—priceless gifts poured on the bitter, lonely desert of David's soul. And timely, as well, for circumstances were becoming even grimmer. The Ziphites— that treacherous, lecherous blot on Judah, perched as they were on their flat-topped hill south of Hebron—could see David's every move.

They spied on David, those men of Ziph, hiding behind loyalty to Saul, but there was more to it than that. A man named Cush, an acquaintance who for reasons I'll note later had it in for David, had been whispering in Ziphite ears, and they obediently became Saul's southern intelligence. As reports were forwarded to Saul by way of Cush, the king deployed troops. Not little detachments. Major armies. To Saul's way of thinking, David was only a shade less deadly than wormwood. From badger hole to eagle aerie, he followed hard. The harried band became rock badgers, clambering up nearly unscalable cliffs to high desert fastnesses, with Saul the lion, stalking day and night, pressing David into places of no escape.

Hear my prayer, O God;
Listen to my words.
Strangers attack me;
Ruthless men seek my life.
Surely God is my help,
The one who sustains me."

10

As a boy, I was captivated, as was everyone, by stories of David and his prowess, especially his encounter with Goliath in the Valley of Elah. I was only twelve or so at the height of his popularity and influence in Saul's court. Although my eyes grew saucerlike over battle talk, I became increasingly interested in David's poetry and music. I went to this or that person who could sing his latest songs and memorized them to write out later.

During the period when David was trying to escape Saul's clutches, few of his songs filtered back, and I was desolate. Oddly enough, one of these few was a wedding song.

As Jonathan had indicated, Michal was out of reach, at least for now, so, after growling awhile, David took another wife, Ahinoam of Jezreel—beautiful, and the daughter of an important tribal leader. Yes, politics—and beauty—drove this choice of his second wife. Some thought he might have looked among his own group for wife material, but, when the women saw Ahinoam dressed as a bride, they bowed before her.

Bathed and oiled and polished like marble, she stood tall, the color-shifting sheen of her raven-black hair playing through strands of gold and pearl. Sunlight skipped across her gold filigree frontlet and along ear and nose rings, a silver necklace, and gold arm and ankle bracelets. Her maidens covered this magnificence with filmy linen, then sang her along to where David waited with fire in his heart to lift off the veil.

The arrangements were, of necessity, simple. David had no home of his own, only his black, goat-hair tent that had been hastily plumped for the occasion. He set up a feasting place outside the village and was able, with the generosity of the bride's family and some anticipatory raiding, to provide a lavish, week-long feast.

Ahinoam expected to be a queen; she made that clear from the beginning. However, life with an outlaw band offered few queenly comforts. An enlarged tent was at best a poor promise of the palace she hoped for one day. In all fairness, it must be said that Ahinoam adapted well to life on the run. She had David's entire attention in those early days, and in turn she fed him and kissed his wounds, having little capacity for much else.

Life settled into a rhythm of sorts. Between times of hasty flight from Saul's stalkers, the group learned to live on the lean side of comfortable. For one thing, they didn't depend merely on raiding for provisions: they made themselves useful.

When David got home one night, Ahinoam asked, "What did you do today?"

"What did I do? First, I made love with my wife." Ahinoam blushed with pleasure. "Then, I set off to exchange peace with some shepherds near Maon."

He described sweeping tracts of harsh, bony land that supported the flocks and herds of widely scattered landowners. "The shepherds spied us from their watch tower and were armed and wary by the time we got there. But words of peace, plenty of bowing, and out comes bread and milk. No problem, once they see I can talk sheep. These fellows had a ewe who'd lost her womb."

"Lost it?"

"Pushed it out with the lamb."

"How awful!"

He shrugged. "I put it back. Whether it'll stay... I'll check back in a couple of weeks. They thought me clever and fed me well."

"You're just out there having fun."

"No, talking with lonely herders pays off. They're beginning to trust me. Plus, I sing for them," said David, grinning. "They're starved for music. There they sit, day after day, never knowing whether bandits or bears will sweep down on them. A tough, lusty lot, yet they're strong, heroic, coolheaded."

David chose his raids purposefully. Strike fast, pursue fast. But he liked to wait to attack until bandits got just close enough for the herdsmen to see and recognize their protector. He then took care to send his greetings to the landowner and thus reaped goodwill and often additional food.

The occasional fool begrudged such gratuities, and, with this sort, David offered no help and sometimes raided the raiders afterward, reaping double measure.

David's shepherd camaraderie often shifted to a relationship with masters. He visited such chief men as Zarbiah and Honaash of Maon, and Tor of Carmel, where his charm and music made him most welcome. He could put almost any man at ease and was equally at home in a large house or a humble tent. He listened and cared and received care in return. Sometimes he talked politics, sometimes sheep. The topic might vary, but his objective was always food for tomorrow and goodwill for the future. He looked for tribal leaders who seemed open to a more formal agreement or covenant of salt.

For all that, David and his band barely got by. Six to seven hundred men, some with families, were a lot of mouths and a heavy responsibility. However, the luxury of a woman in his tent during these anxious days gave a measure of comfort.

One of the aforementioned fools was Nabal; his name says it. No ordinary fool—a God-denying fool. Fat, oily, surly, and generally disagreeable, his only distinction was wealth. His holdings lay in Carmel, where he lived comfortably, eating, drinking, and living out his name.

David saw Nabal as a potential food source. He sent greetings to him at sheep shearing time when food for shepherds was plentiful and a feast expected when all was done. But Nabal, responded, "Who's this David? What have I to do with him? Does he think I'll feed every vagabond who leaves his master and finds himself in want? I have louts of my own to feed! I don't need more."

David turned livid upon hearing this report. Jaw rigid, he strode to the cliff and looked down toward Carmel, then turned and stalked away, the heat of his anger raising whorls of dust. "Useless!" he fumed. "We keep this dog's holdings safe by risking our lives, and what does it get us? To your swords, all of you! May God deal with me, be it ever so severely, if by morning there's a male left to pee against a wall!"

Abigail, long-suffering wife to this Nabal-fool, was outdoors stacking loaves, puffy and fragrant, as they were brought to her from the ovens. Nabal's chief shepherd, a lean, ropy man, approached hesitantly. "My lady," he said, bowing low, "I—uh…"

"Yes, what is it? Please stand up. It's hard to hear people who crumple themselves on the ground. You are Obed, aren't you?"

"Yes, mum." The man hunched uncomfortably before this wisp of a woman, trying to hide the worst of the stains on his mantle.

"Have you a message from my husband?"

"No, mum…well, yes and no. You see—" He stopped and looked worriedly past Nabal's vineyard to the gray hills beyond.

Abigail's mouth set impatiently, but she picked up a loaf not yet settled into flatness and tore it in half. "Obed, eat some bread while it's fresh and hot, and tell me what's troubling you. My husband has said or done something that displeases you?"

Obed received the bread from Abigail with relieved surprise. "Yes, mum, he did."

"You can tell me. Then we'll see what can be done."

"Thank you, mum." He spoke toward the hills as though they were easier to address than a woman. "I don't much mind when he lays into us for not doing what he supposed he said, or when he bats the youngsters for nothing at all. I don't mind, I say. These things happen, and what's the use complaining?"

"But he's done something more serious this time," Abigail prompted.

"Yes'm, he has. By nightfall he could be dead; we could all be dead, if I read things right, and I think I do pretty good."

"Yes, Obed, I trust your judgment—in more than just sheep matters. Please go on."

"Some men came from the hills, men from David *ben* Jesse." He checked for signs of recognition. When her eyebrows lifted, he went on. "They gave us Master David's greetings. 'Long life to you! Good health to you and your household!' they said. But what did Master say? Called 'em flea-whiskered rabbits. Had heartburn over an extra outlay of meat. These men were good to us, mum. Never when we were near 'em did we have to worry about losing our stuff—by their hand or anybody else's. Like a sheepfold, they was, keeping us safe. I been around long enough to tell the difference between these fellows and others."

As Abigail listened, her face grew rigid and pale.

Obed shook his head, again examining the hills. "I tried talking to him—the master, that is—but he turned on me. Called me a rabbit dung gatherer and said he'd turn me out. One less mouth to feed. He's wicked, you might say, when he gets like that. Leastwise, he's got no sense." He seemed to remember himself and looked at Abigail anxiously. "I'm sorry, mum. I shouldn't—"

Abigail smiled stiffly and put her hand on Obed's arm. "Yes, you should. You did exactly right in coming to me. You're an excellent judge of sheep *and* men. Now," she said, turning sharply, "you must help me try to undo this mischief. I've heard of this David. Our friend Tor told us not only of his kindnesses but of his political potential, as well. How many men are with him, do you know?"

"Yes'm. A good number. Maybe six, seven hundred. You seldom see 'em all at once, but I know there's a good many."

Again she raised her eyebrows but said nothing. "Well then, we'll need food for six or seven hundred men. If you'll arrange for—how many do you think? Ten dressed sheep? And donkeys. I'll need my own, as well—saddled, please. I'll see to bread and wine and grain. Raisins and figs might be welcome, too."

She and her servants rose to the emergency, and in less than two hours the little caravan was heading toward the mountains. She saw to it, as well, that Nabal remained uninformed of her venture.

They had not gone far into the twisting ravines when she heard a shout that nearly jolted her from her donkey. Looking up, she saw a cataract of men, several hundred strong, leaping and pouring down the craggy precipice. A few wore helmets and warrior tunics, but most were clothed in blood-crusted skins and makeshift greaves, making them appear more like jackals. Could this be David's band? She hadn't expected a confrontation this soon, and, if she didn't act quickly, they could all be slaughtered before a word was exchanged. With thumping heart, she urged her donkey to the fore and slid off as a formidable man strode toward her, a looming, glowering figure with an unkempt mass of red hair. He was dressed even more disreputably than the others, but his well-muscled frame would have lent elegance even to jackal skins.

For a moment Abigail stood as tall as her five-foot frame would allow, assessing the size and attributes of this white-hot anger she had set out to appease. Then, as he halted, she knelt with her face to the ground.

"My lord!" she cried, taking care to speak distinctly from her "crumpled" position. "Please let your servant speak to you. You have been insulted, and your anger is just. But may your blame fall on me alone. I was busy with matters at home and did not see the men you sent. I should have been there to return their greeting and thank them for their kindness to us and to our men. Please pay no attention to the words of my husband Nabal. He's an incorrigible fool, as everyone knows—and many would say wicked, as well."

David stood silent, unmoving, and Abigail ventured to her knees, eyes carefully lowered. She calculated that he would make up his mind within ten seconds, and a decision based on her face, rather than the back of her head, might be sounder. She displayed for him a low forehead curtained by black hair, a curved nose with a hint of freckles, full lips, and a no-nonsense air. She was dressed simply, her only ornament a fine blue sash at her waist. He also saw beyond her a string of laden donkeys dosing in the afternoon sun.

"My lord," she said, quick to note his shift of focus, "please forgive your servant's offense, and accept this gift for your men. It is but a small token of gratitude for what you've done for us these past months. My head sheep herder Obed—do you know him?" She saw that he did. "He tells me you've been a wall of protection around the livestock."

David nodded stiffly. "Obed's a good man. He knows sheep and a lot more."

Abigail closed her eyes in relief over this small gain. Then she shifted to a new tack. "Do you realize that the Lord our God has restrained you this day from bloodshed, from avenging yourself with your own hands?" she asked, silently praying truth into her words. "I've heard of you from my friend Tor, who believes you'll one day be king in Israel. As surely as the Lord lives, He'll make yours a lasting dynasty because you fight His battles. Even in times of danger, Yahweh will bundle you safely in the core of His being. And when He fulfills His promises and appoints you Israel's leader, you'll be glad not to have this blot, this horrifying burden of needless bloodshed or of having avenged yourself. And please—" Again she used her face to appeal to his. "Please remember when the Lord has brought you success, please remember your servant."

David's stance softened, and he gazed past the caravan to the hazy valley below. As he bent to Abigail, his touch unnerved her even more than his appearance. "Thank you," he said gently, helping her to her feet. "You are kind; you are wise. I praise God for sending you. You most certainly kept me from avenging myself and dishonoring him." A soft breeze of mischief kept hold on her hand and tilted his red head raffishly. "Your words spoke to my heart," he said lightly, "but your gift speaks to my stomach. I accept both with gratitude."

The sun was setting by the time the food had been transferred from the donkeys to the willing shoulders of David's men. David turned to Abigail. "It'll be dark long before you reach home. Will you be all right? I could send some men with you. And will your late return upset the old fool? I don't want you paying for his nonsense."

"Thank you. You are kind. My husband was laying in wine for the shearing banquet. I doubt he'll be in any condition to ask questions or even notice when we get home. My servants will take care of me. If any lions happen along, I'll remind them that they'll have you to answer to if they even look our way."

David tossed back his head in laughter, then bowed before her. "A woman small of body but indomitable in spirit. Go now. Go home in peace. And may God shine His face on you until we meet again."

Within two months, Abigail became David's wife—a radical shift in her life that brought an irrepressible smile to her lips. Finding amusement in the death of her first husband was to her neither seemly nor self-possessed. She fought it earnestly but could not hold back the tide of laughter over her unexpected release from such an ill-suited husband.

Abigail had returned home after her initial meeting with David to find her husband drunk, as anticipated. Though she insisted she overplayed neither his narrow escape nor the part she played in it, her story struck such fear in the heart of Nabal that he went into a paroxysm of wheezing and vomiting and died ten days later. "I did my best for him," she said afterward; "God knows I tried. But God also knows what Nabal put me through."

When Obed delivered the news, David thumped the shepherd and praised God. "He upheld my cause. He kept me from doing wrong. And He dumped the Fool's folly on his own head!"

Abigail arrived at camp with her five maids and bowed before David. "I have come, as you requested, to serve you and to wash the feet of your servants."

David raised her and was again pleased by what he saw. "Yes," he said at length. "They need washing—badly. Tell me—was it hard to leave the fine things of your husband's house? Did you grieve just a little?"

She smiled. "Oh, a lot! I wept all of fifteen minutes. But only for the good people I'd leave behind. Nothing of Nabal brought tears."

"But here you'll have hardship and deprivation, the trauma of pursuit. Will you shed tears over that?"

She smiled wryly. "Can any hardship here be greater than what I've already endured? You, my lord, have asked for me. That is my joy, my happiness."

It was that wedding song, woven of laughter and joy, that blew from the high desert into my thirsty heart. Perhaps if Abigail had not forgotten that laughter outperforms principle when it comes to burnishing love, the song might never have tarnished.

11

*S*ave me, O God; vindicate me. My neighbors put Saul
onto us, repaying evil for good, blaming me for things I
know nothing about. If I'm guilty, if I did rob Cush, then
it's right that I be put down. But I didn't rob him. He accuses me
without cause. LORD, save me...save this poor, shriveled worm....
Can't run...can't get up...."

David lay where he'd fallen for the third time, his heart ham-
mering wasted lungs. Saul was a thin mountain ridge from
David's band, and capture—or death—was minutes away.
Even the indomitable Joab fell and could do nothing but roar
at the others to keep going. Abishai tried to scoop him up, but
Joab bared teeth and dagger. "Leave me! If you have to carry
someone, get David away!"

After David left Saul's employ, Cush cashed in his grudge by
accusing David of a crime. When a leading man of Ziph came
to Gibeah, Saul appointed Cush to talk with him, and David's
activities came up in the course of conversation. The Ziphites
had been neither for nor against the fugitive, but, when the

elder left the palace, anger boiled from a gold goblet he carried that bore the mark of Cush—with the mark of David superimposed. This was a despicable felony in anyone's thinking, but especially concerning a man known to be the king's enemy. The goblet had been found among David's belongings, said Cush, after he had fled to Nob.

Before long, an entire delegation from Ziph arrived at Saul's court, offering aid in the pursuit and capture of the evildoer. Saul responded effusively. "The Lord bless you for caring about me. Yes, your eyes and ears. Any information at all, let me know. We'll get this dog of a rebel!"

When David was confronted with the goblet, he said, "Yes, that's mine. I got it from a Philistine chieftain—fair and square. And that's my mark. But it bore no mark at all when I had it. How did he do that? I don't believe this. Cush is trying to trap me!"

Nothing he could say, no reminders of good deeds would change the Ziphites' minds. When Saul arrived in the Desert of Ziph with three thousand soldiers, David was forced to flee, and the only route to safety lay along the far side of a ridge that separated his band from Saul's army. If Saul got ahead and cut them off, or if he even topped the ridge, they were finished.

David's men stumbled across the chalk, unable to keep up with the galloping Asahel, who ran just below the ridge and sent back periodic signals concerning Saul's progress. One by one, the warriors dropped and could not get up. When less than a dozen were left on their feet, they heard a whistle. "Look!" cried Eleazar, pointing toward Asahel, who had halted above them. "What's happening?"

Asahel stood boldly on the ridge, shielding his eyes from the sun. Then he hopped and slid toward the gasping band. "They're gone! Whoosh! Like that!"

Eleazar and Abishai started up the slope.

"A runner came, whirling and pointing. Saul went livid. He looked toward us, then west, then back our way, belching smoke. He and his general parleyed, both of 'em on fire. I'm guessing some attacker was coming that everyone but Saul saw would eat a bigger hole in their flank than we ever could. O most noble Philistines, we thank you!" Asahel bowed westward. "Abner's garlic outdid Saul's smoke, so the king called off the chase. Would you believe?" He danced and hugged and slapped backs. "They had us trussed and hoisted—and Yahweh made 'em turn and walk away!"

The front-runners backtracked to retrieve the fallen, everyone whooping and joking in the euphoria of escape.

Everyone except Joab and David. Joab nursed a knee and his pride. David sat pale and brooding. "We got away this time, but sooner or later one of them—Saul, Philistines, Amalekites—will get us. Or Ziphites. The whole time we've been here, after all the good we've done, they still believe Cush before they believe me." David curled over, pushing his hands down his legs. "Dogs, all of them, chewing my ankles."

Eleazar, with his mud-flat face and eyes the color of earth after rain, knelt by David and examined an old wound. David felt comfort. These men of his were true *Gibborim*. Mighty in battle, mighty in love.

"Your foot bothering? You fell a lot." Eleazar rubbed dried blood off David's arm.

David sighed and kneaded a shoulder wearily. "Bulls. That's what they are. Fat, sleek bulls of Bashan. And we're mice. Where's Abiathar? I need my priest."

But for all the trouble Saul brought to David, on more than one occasion David had Saul in the palm of his hand—and allowed him to walk away.

After the near-disaster on the mountain ridge, David and his band went to En Gedi—"spring of the kid"—on the western shore of the Salt Sea. A pleasant place in winter, with hot springs and great waterfalls, mountain goats and chamois—pleasant, if you don't find yourself once again on the point of Saul's knife.

The move itself had not been without trauma. No sooner had David collected his families and baggage and started north when a band of Edomites attacked. These ancient descendants of Esau had been enemies of Israel since their king refused Moses passage on the Israelites' way to Canaan. Doeg, who killed Ahimelech and the other priests, was an Edomite, a fact that would endear him to no one but a mad king.

The attack was sudden, deadly, and demoralizing. Four of David's men were killed and several badly wounded. The women and children suffered only minor injuries, mostly scrapes from falling, but Mara, Hurai's wife, went into early labor with her first child. "How terrible it is," said Abigail afterward, "to be pregnant at such a time. If we could have found a cave or even a rock to hide behind, we might have at least delivered her in peace. But what can you do? A baby born dead on a screaming run is better than being ripped open by an Edomite sword."

Not much better. Mara died that evening.

David spent the night outside, arguing at the stars. "God!" he howled. "Where are you? Come here! Defend me against this ungodly, outlaw nation. I run to you as to a stronghold, only to find you've barred the door, shut me out. *Why*, Lord? It seems that every day you give us reason to weep under the heel of our enemies. Give us light and truth, Lord, a torch to guide us."

The next day David split the group, a third of the men taking the families down to the "goat-fountain" oasis while he and the rest reconnoitered the bare, conical hills for strongholds. "Not the best arrangement," David said to Dodai, "but if Saul does track us down, he'll have to dig us out of caves."

Hurai looked at him, his eyes bloodshot with grief. "So you're leaving the families with only old men and boys for protection?"

David's jaw tightened. "Maybe you should stay," he said frostily. "Another 'watch-goat' to stoke a dung fire."

Hurai curled under the insult.

Dodai put a hand on David's arm. "Davi, you got a dagger in your heart, but don't stab Hurai with it. Every man of us'd die for you, and you know it."

David spun to face the warrior, his eyes fiery coals. But the staunch, homely face that bore its own pain made him turn wordlessly to make peace with the bereaved Hurai.

A week later, Saul was sighted again. Having learned that David had gone from Maon to En Gedi, he came down the central ridge from Gibeah and snaked eastward through wadis that channel rainwater to the Salt Sea. His army of three thousand battle-hardened men crawled across the pocked limestone in pursuit of David and his castoffs.

David divided his men. "Fight if cornered, but otherwise keep out of sight. Find caves with hidden entrances, if you can. We've got to hunker down. If they push us downhill, we'll be no more than target practice." After David's intense, hurried prayer, "Have mercy on us, God; have mercy!" the four hundred melted into the hostile terrain.

Stone on barren stone; precipitous cliffs, some over three hundred feet high; narrow, twisted runoffs that spread like fingers down the chalky slope. And heat. Sun playing off white rock sucked moisture from any creature foolish enough to be out in midday. That Saul had left his tamarisk tree to sift through this kind of wilderness pointed to the extremity of his feelings against David.

The cave that David, Dodai, and Eleazar settled on was large, its entrance narrow and almost invisible. Inside, other chambers led from the main vault, and, because of the narrow opening, darkness lay over all but the first few feet inside.

David lay on his face in the cool darkness, his company behind him in adjacent alcoves. He heard nothing but his own heartbeat, Eleazar breathing beside him, and the occasional shifting of the men on their stony pallet. Over and over his silent words became a refrain to which his head unconsciously rocked. *Refuge in the shadow, the shadow of your wings, O Lord. Until disaster passes, I take refuge in your wings; under your wings I hide.*

These images had just become a chaotic prelude to sleep when Dodai jabbed him awake and steered his eyes toward a dark shadow blocking the glare. The shadow squeezed through the opening and stood up. David's heart froze. No one could mistake the tall, powerful silhouette, even in a dark cave. He scanned the entrance for the rest of the army, but no one else appeared.

Saul took a long draft from his water bag and then emptied it over his head. Tossing it outside, he took off his mantle, dropped it close to where David and the men lay, and cinched up his tunic. With a belch that echoed through the cave chambers, Saul settled into a defecatory squat. David looked from Dodai to Eleazar. "This is it!" Eleazar whispered into David's ear. "God's done it! He's dumped Saul right in your hands."

"Get him!" mouthed Dodai.

David squeezed Eleazar's arm and grinned in the darkness. "Don't move," he whispered back. Under the comfortable cover of assorted noises from Saul, David inched forward, knife in hand.

Saul grunted, hummed, cursed the hot sun, cursed his sluggish bowel, cursed David as the principle cause of the rest of his cursing.

Cautiously, silently, David reached for the mantle. He groped the length of material until he reached a fringed corner. Carefully, he sawed at the cloth, then backed into the alcove, Eleazar guiding his feet.

Eleazar was not happy. Neither was his father. "You didn't kill him!" Dodai raged.

"Let me do it," said Eleazar. "He's alone. We kill him, hold up his severed head, and his army will fall apart. Just say the word. I'll take care of it."

David clamped a hand on his wrist, no longer smiling. "I shouldn't have done that much. The fringe burns my hand. This is God's chosen king doing his business in the cool of a cave. *I will not lift my hand against the Lord's anointed!*"

Eleazar turned away, exasperated, then stared at Saul, eyes glittering. David saw and grabbed him. "Don't even think about it!" he rasped. "One sound out of you to force my hand, and you'll be the first to feel it! As surely as the Lord lives—"

"Look!" Eleazar stiffened. "He's done. He's—"

David's hand covered Eleazar's mouth. They lay rigid as Saul stretched and yawned loudly, then pulled bread from his pouch. He wadded his mantle as a cushion against the cave wall and leaned back to eat. He might have settled into a nap if his armor bearer hadn't grown weary on an adjacent cliff and shouted down concern for "my lord the king." Saul groaned and struggled to his feet. He squeezed his bulk through the cave entrance, then remembered his mantle—in intemperate terms—and reversed the squeeze.

David and the others burrowed their faces into the ground and lay without breathing, sure that Saul would see them with his still-dilated eyes. But he squeezed out again and shouted irritably at his armor bearer.

"He's old, Davi," said Dodai. "Old like me. I know how he feels. We could of got 'im, no trouble. We could still—"

David shook his head and rose cautiously. He slipped his sword and knife out of his belt.

"Hold these. And stay hidden unless something goes wrong."

"Where're you going?" asked Dodai anxiously. "What you doing?"

David just shook his head and repeated, "Stay here." With the fringed triangle in his hand, he slipped into the slot and waited for his eyes to adjust before pushing through. Standing with feet apart and knuckles on his hips, he hailed the retreating form of Saul. "Ho! My lord the king!" His voice bounced off the surrounding cliff.

Saul turned with a touch of annoyance, head swiveling from echo to echo to locate the source of the summons.

David waved both hands, then placed them on his forehead in salute to his king and dropped flat with his face to the ground. After a moment he rose to his knees and held the ragged cloth aloft. "Do you see this? From your mantle. Look for yourself. I can see the spot from here. On your right—there—yes. I cut it off in the cave."

Saul held up the corner of his mantle and looked back and forth from it to David.

"Why do you listen when men tell you I'm bent on killing you?" David went on. "The Lord delivered you into my hands. My men wanted me to kill you, but I would not. I will not—ever—lift up my hand against my master, the Lord's anointed. I haven't wronged you or rebelled against you," he went on. "I've done nothing! Who are you pursuing? A dead dog or a flea? The Lord may judge between us and avenge the wrongs you've done me, but my hand will never touch you!"

Saul stood like a stone monolith, and only hot wind soughing across limy rises broke the silence. Then his hands went to his face and his great shoulders bent. "David, my son, my son David! You are more righteous than I. You had my life in your hands but held it gently. What other man would let his enemy go unharmed? May the Lord reward you for the way you treated me today. You will be king; I know that now. But when you come into your kingdom, swear to me by the Lord that you won't cut off my descendants or wipe out my name from my father's family. Will you do that, David, my son?"

"I have already sworn that, my father. But I give you my oath. May there be peace between us."

But even as he spoke the words, he knew that peace between Saul and David would never happen.

O ne of these days…one of these days…." David
stared moodily across the Salt Sea, early rays
glancing off the corrosive boil of the breeze-blown
surface. "A matter of time. Outnumbered five to one—by Saul
alone, never mind others who'd be happy to run us through. If
our enemies should join forces…"

Ira, on the ledge beside him, couldn't think of anything to
say.

David's foot began to jiggle.

"What are you thinking?" Ira asked, drawing up his fringed
mantle.

David said nothing, but his eyes saw less and less of the Salt
Sea, and his body moved to the rhythm of some internal process. He turned abruptly and gripped his companion's shoulders. "Ira," he said, "we'll go to the Philistines."

Ira rolled his eyes toward the heavens. "God save us! He's
gone mad, too!"

"No, listen. We're a line of doves here waiting to be picked
off. Give Saul enough time, and he'll get us. It's that simple.

The men are anxious and restless. They can't even lie with their wives without a sword in hand and their eye out the tent. The women are afraid and tired of eating goat. This place has become a tar pit."

He got up and strode back and forth. "But suppose we go to Achish in Gath. He's a reasonable man, and—"

"If I recall," said Ira with measured sarcasm, "you tried that once."

David turned away. "That was my blunder, not his. If I'd handled it better..." He turned back, energized. "Ira, Achish can be managed, I'm sure of it. Last time, I was alone and a liability. Now there are enough of us to be attractive as mercenaries. Our reputation—and my long-range weapon—won't hurt, either." He grinned. "Achish isn't likely to turn away a bronze bowman and the best fighting force in all of Judah—someone to do his local banditry so he can concentrate on Saul."

"Have you thought of the huge divide between Israelites and pagan Philistines? Or more to the point, will Achish think of it?"

"Yes, he did think of it when I was there. 'Insufferable,' I believe he called us. Sure, we're different, in every way you can think of. We've been set apart by God. But this is strictly a business deal—he gives us asylum, we lend him warriors. We stay away from their gods and let them watch us worship Yahweh. He's not going to be grouchy about it, Ira. He's good-natured. He was like an overgrown boy that day with his sword-and-spear show."

Ira lifted an eyebrow but said nothing.

"I just came across wrong that day. If I hadn't panicked... Anyway, I think we can pull it off. All we have to do is sneak out of here."

"And across the whole of Judah without being seen."

David laughed. "Trust me, Ira. We can do it. Saul will nose around, but even if he does find out, will he attack Gath and the whole of the Philistine army just to get me?"

Achish was indeed surprised when David knelt before him. But after considering the implications, pro and con, of David's request for asylum, he laid out a welcome that astonished them all. David, his war chiefs, and their families were given choice housing within the city gates. The others pegged their tents outside the wall, ecstatic over lush pasturage and abundant water after years of thorns and briars.

For days David did little but eat and sleep. The strain had ravaged him, and Ahinoam fretted over his disinterest in her bed. "Three years married," she complained to Abigail, "and still no child. And you're no better off, even though—" She stopped abruptly and ground her wheat vigorously. "I'm sorry," she mumbled.

"It's all right." Abigail's smile was hard and bright. "There'll be other babies, and most likely you'll bear one before I do. Our business now is to fatten David and see that he rests. Soon he'll sing his 'Dove Among the Lilies' again."

At this reference to "her" song, Ahinoam darted a jealous glance, but Abigail was serenely kneading dough.

Abigail was like that, a woman of great capacity. Quick of mind, practical, efficient, no-nonsense, she dedicated her life to serving David. She also served Ahinoam—preparing meals for Ahinoam to feed David, binding his wounds before Ahinoam would kiss them, giving spiritual uplift when David was down. An astute listener, she grasped political matters as quickly as any man. She planted offhand suggestions here and there but never put herself forward or claimed credit when her ideas worked.

The distress of her first marriage had helped shape her into David's shield and strong tower during those years of exile. It was she who gave comfort when word came of the death of Jesse. David was disconsolate. "*Abba*, my *abba*, I should have been with you, as you were with me. You came to Adullam and offered to tend goats, as you didn't think you'd be much good at fighting. Oh, *Abba*...cut down—a cankered, moss-grown stump."

It was Abigail's astuteness that led them to Ziklag. Like David, all the men appreciated the safety Gath offered, but, while David roamed the hills, many roamed the country's other attractions.

"The land's a sewer," she told David one evening. "A temple to Dagon in Ashdod, with another not much farther. Right in the open—divination with animal livers, broth from goat kids boiled in their mothers' milk and sprinkled on trees and crops to make them fruitful."

"Welcome to Philistia," said David. "That's the scene here. These are pagans. They confuse the god of nature with nature's God. Dagon's son Baal rules the sky and brings thunderstorms. He uses nature and rides the seasons. Our God created nature and rides history."

Abigail's mouth tightened. "Such clever aphorisms!" she exclaimed but quickly troweled over her sarcasm. "It's all nonsense, I know, but the *implications*. I know of at least five of your men—no, I won't name them—five who decided they wanted to wet their feet in the Great Sea. They were drawn off by certain…activities in Ashdod." She bent to pick up David's mantle.

"What activities?"

"Goings-on having to do with Baal's mistress Anath, the goddess of war who fights for his causes. More to the point, she's also goddess of love and sensuality. And Asherah—"

"Hmm," said David, stroking his beard, "a goddess who is both sensual and commander in chief of her lover's army. My dear, could you look into becoming a goddess—only when it fits your schedule, of course?" he added, seeing something less than humor on her face.

"Which aspect interests you most—a whoring mistress or someone who can keep Joab in line?" The flint of Abigail's dark eyes struck sparks in the blue of David's.

"Oh ho!" David reached for her, but she deftly stepped away, the line of her mouth as straight as her back.

"These five men," Abigail went on in urgent disapproval, "came back singing—lustily, I might add:

> Anath swells her liver with laughter,
> Her heart is filled with joy;
> For in Anath's hand is victory.
> Knee-deep she plunges in blood of soldiers,
> Neck-high in the gore of troops
> Until she is sated.

> *She draws water*
> *And washes with dew of heaven."*

David tipped his head and began humming. "She draws the dew of heaven and washes in blood and laughter...lai, lai, lai."

Abigail exploded. "How can you, our 'godly, anointed leader,' joke about things done in the name of gods and goddesses? You should be out tearing down Asherah poles, laying sword to cult prostitutes, invading temples—"

"Now, wait, my little lioness—"

"High places on every side, each for a different god or goddess. Do you have any idea what goes on in those places? And I'm not talking goat's milk. Do you know—"

"You have surprising knowledge about all this. Does it come out of Philistine kneading troughs? Yes, I know what goes on in pagan shrines. Their gods are nothing more than make-believe extensions of their own human muck, whereas Yahweh is real, holy, personal—a God who knows us, who relates to us. But we're guests of the Philistines. How long would we last if I started tearing down their sacred shrines?"

"Your men, then. They should know better. But it's almost like they've come home, returned to their barbarian roots."

David looked at her closely.

"You think that's too strong," she said. "I would guess that a good many of your men would say nothing—they'd welcome Baals and Asherah poles, burn incense to them in the Tent at Gibeon. 'Yes!' they'd say. 'This feels right. This is what men have always done, from Adam on. Yahweh's Law gets in our way.' The proof, my lord, lies in those songs they picked up in Ashdod that slip off their tongues far easier than *Hallels* do. And you off in the hills not noticing. Do you care?"

"Of course I care! They should know better. But a lot of them don't. And yes, a good many turn pagan as soon as they're two shadow lengths away from me. You know what they are. They're with us because it's easier than one-man banditry. Right now, part of the price of freedom from Saul is our having to live among barefaced pagans. Would you rather go back to En Gedi and eat wild goat?"

He circled her, watching her defiant eyes first turn away, then gradually soften.

"I'm sorry," she said. "I have no right—I should keep silent."

David went to her and lifted her face. Ahinoam would have wept at that point, but Abigail willed her tears captive and instead fixed her eyes on David's purple and gold headband. The anger was gone, but a righteous sadness filled its place.

"Maybe…another place, away from…the things here," she said. "Is there no other place?"

Now it was David's turn to stare at her and then at the darkening window. "Perhaps…yes. You may have something. Close enough for protection, yet too far for even a king's eyes to see every move. You're right, Abi. Perhaps a place…like Ziklag." He leaned to kiss her. "My little vixen is a wise woman."

The next day David approached Achish. "If I have found favor in your eyes, my lord, give us a place in one of the country towns to live and raise our families."

"You're not happy here?" asked Achish.

"You've been most kind, my lord, and we are happy. Our children—all of us, for that matter, savor your striking show of sword and spear." Achish wriggled delightedly.

"But who am I and the rest of your servants," David went on, "that we should waste valuable space here? We've lived so long in desert places that we'd be perfectly happy in some out-of-the-way spot—in the Negev, say." He shrugged noncommittally. "Aren't there towns more or less abandoned? Amalekites and all…" David seemed artless, with just a touch of ingratiation, and Achish slid effortlessly along well-oiled skids.

"Hum…yes. There's En Rimmon. Good spring there. And next to it, Ziklag—ah! Ziklag. Has a well. Higher up. Just the place! Amalekites like that area, though. May have to toss them out, but you're capable of that." He squinted at David, then pulled his lower lip sardonically. "Now, suppose some Judaites were camped there. What then?"

David smiled guilelessly. "You give us the town; we'll see to emptying it."

He did meet the resistance Abigail had anticipated when he told his men of the coming move. Beside the entertainment issue, they had no enthusiasm for leaving the fertile plain for the more rugged semidesert conditions of Ziklag. That it lay close to the highway stretching from Egypt to Syria helped some. They'd be far less isolated than in the Judean wilderness. The village on its limestone hill looked across the plain to the Great Sea. Pasture was reasonable, but few cooling winds from the sea reached inland. Nor was the rainy season warm, as at En Gedi. Despite grumbling, though, they settled in, thankful for relief from Saul's vendetta.

They had little trouble securing the town. The few Amalekites bivouacking there sized up the invaders and retreated hastily, not particular about what—or who—they left behind. Abigail commandeered a couple of miserable Egyptian slave girls that Dodai found huddled amid rocks and camel dung.

"They stink, ma'am. No need for you to worry about 'em. I heard Joab say he wouldn't mind taking 'em over."

"No doubt he wouldn't," replied Abigail tartly. "Their bodies will clean nicely, and perhaps their souls are not beyond salvage. Thank you, Dodai."

Abigail found satisfaction in Abiathar's enthusiasm in cleansing the town of pagan objects. He built an altar for the prescribed sacrifices, then went through each street, each house, with incense and prayer. Once again, they were a people set apart, satisfied with the present and the future.

The future kicked in sooner than expected. A band of Amalekites—perhaps some of the very ones they'd dislodged—swooped down on Jashobeam's small flock on the south rim of the communal pasture. One of his sons was killed in a desperate attempt to save the flock—an incalculable loss in terms of the gangly boy's warrior potential.

That night David sat with his nephews apart from the grieving community.

"We have reason, we have cause," said David. "Amalek's been a stench ever since they attacked the Israelites on their way from Egypt. Joshua beat them back, with Aaron and Hur propping Moses' arms through to victory. And if Saul had done what he was supposed to when he captured King Agag..."

"Never mind Saul," said Joab, tapping David's chest. "You do what you're supposed to—wipe out the whole bunch."

Asahel, eyes angry, drummed nervously. "Make holes in 'em. Punch 'em full of holes. Holey. Holy. A new twist to cherem, don't you think?" For once he was not laughing. He turned to Joab. "Achish is sure to hear about this, you know. He won't be happy if you kill off his pals."

"How will he hear?" asked Joab.

"How will he *hear*? How will he *not* hear? He comes often enough. All it takes is one escapee. Achish is no—"

"*There will be no escapees.* I guess we learned that from Saul."

"You talking about Abiathar escaping from Nob?"

"I'm talking about Agag." Joab settled back to watch the impact.

The four sat in silence. David understood that his own anointing as king stemmed from Saul's fatal mistake in disobeying Samuel's solemn command of *cherem*. "Attack Agag and the Amalekites," Samuel had thundered. "The Lord says, 'I will punish them for what they did to Israel on their way from Egypt,' Go in the name of the Lord Almighty. *Spare nothing*; put to death men, women, children, infants, cattle, sheep, camels, donkeys." But Saul had hedged on his commitment. He had kept the best of the livestock—"for sacrifices," he had said—and, most seriously of all, he had spared the king's life. Samuel was livid.

David had met the frail, sunken-cheeked prophet on several occasions after his anointing but never had felt completely comfortable in his presence. The long, sweeping hair of a Nazirite; eyes that exposed his fierce, unremitting will; even his tattered robe, ripped that day by Saul in his desperation— these were constant reminders that prophets mean what they say. But David gave fervent thanks that it had been Saul, and not himself, who had witnessed Samuel's white-hot fury in running Agag through before the Lord. Little wonder that Saul had become unhinged shortly thereafter.

No laughing matter then, nor was it now. "*Cherem*," said David, looking at Joab with growing distaste. "You, of all people, embracing this sort of…obligation to Yahweh. Cheerily wiping out an entire people. On second thought," he added with a touch of acerbity, "killing cheerfully is what you're good at."

"Of course." Joab sniffed proudly. "But consider the political benefits of *cherem*. We get rid of them now, and it's one less troublemaker to deal with when you become king."

"*Cherem* has nothing to do with politics, and you know it. And what about the cattle, sheep, camels, and donkeys? That's a lot to give up, to say nothing of jewelry and—"

"We don't give that up," Joab declared sardonically. "That's legitimate booty."

"Legitimate booty, in a dog's eye!" was what Abigail had to say a week later when the men returned from their raids. "You're attacking Amalekites, killing every living person, and bringing back—"

"We've been raiding Amalekite bands for years. It never seemed to bother you."

"It's not the same. You got them before they got you. Amalek isn't our land; *cherem* doesn't apply. To go out there and wipe out foreign women and children—"

David chuckled. "Ah, yes. Save the women and children and paw through them for possible wife material."

Abigail wasn't amused. "On top of that, you bring back a mountain of goods," she said, pointing to the pile David had dumped on her bed, "plus animals that double our herds, and then tell Achish that your raids are against Judah. Why are you lying to him? He has no love for Amalekites and wouldn't care if you wiped out the entire nation."

"Not so. They're thicker than you'd think, Philistines and Amalekites. And besides, this is the job Saul never finished."

"Did you consult Abiathar and the Urim and Thummim to find out if you're the man to do it? It seems to me you're tearing off on this "vengeance" thing, when it's the Lord's business to—"

"Enough, woman! You have a fine hand on my faults and don't hesitate to say so." The flare died out quickly, and David sighed as he wrung out a cloth and wiped his dusty face. "Abigail, Abigail, you don't understand. We have our reasons. We—"

"You mean Joab has reasons. This was his idea, wasn't it?"

"Yes, and it's a good idea." His voice grew irritable again. "We must get Achish to trust us. Once he thinks we've made ourselves odious to the Israelites... And besides, I thought you'd *like* clothes and jewelry."

"They're soaked in blood. I'd never wear them."

Ahinoam came through the courtyard and into the house. "David, you're here, after all! Asahel's wife saw you sorting booty with the men. From what she said, you got some fine things. Did you— Yes, you did!" she exclaimed, setting down her jar and falling on the goods on Abigail's bed. "Oh, Abigail! Look at it all! Have you gone through to take what you want?"

Abigail set her mouth and turned to the doorway. "The wind off the plain is chilly. We'll need the fire pan tonight."

David raised his hands with a pious shrug of his shoulders. "Lord, I give thanks I was not born a woman!"

13

Ziklag proved convenient for more than just Abigail's reasons. First of all, it was the retrieval of an ancient right. The town had once belonged to the tribe of Judah. Though currently in Philistine hands, it lay close to Judah and near the trade route. A good place, a safe place.

The trickle of followers that had begun years earlier with debtors and malcontents continued to swell, bringing men skilled with spear and shield. The famous Eleven from Gad had found David at En Gedi. The least of these, it was said, was a match for a hundred, the greatest could take on a thousand. Now with David's band established in Ziklag, the flow increased. Some warriors could shoot bows and slings either right- or left-handed. A formidable army.

When a group of Benjamites arrived, David strode forth, suspicious of anyone from Saul's tribe. The leader, who was roughly his own age, bowed low.

"Stand and look at me," ordered David.

The man had a frank, open face and a body like a battering ram, with arms thick and corded and legs black with hair. David studied the stranger. "Your name?"

"Amasai, my lord."

"Amasai, if you've come in peace to help me, you're welcome to share our tents and bread. If you have betrayal in mind…"

Amasai did not smile. "It's we who've been betrayed, my lord. Our father Saul called us to fight, but he's leading the nation over a cliff. We talked with our commanders and even with Abner, but he listened and nodded and sighed and thanked us for coming. That was that. What else could we do but come to you?"

David liked what he saw of this young man. He was not handsome: his nose bent north, and his eyebrows had a look of perpetual surprise. There was, though, a sense of self-assurance, an air of strength and integrity. Something else, too, that David couldn't quite put his finger on. "How is it," he asked, not unkindly, "that you can walk so easily from the service of God's anointed?"

Amasai looked down a moment, then engaged David's eyes. "My lord, I'm ashamed. No, no," he added, sensing a sudden hardening in David. "Hear me out. The Lord's anointed has little attachment to the Lord these days. Ever since he turned Doeg on the priests at Nob—my lord, the report of that deed thrust a knife through us all. At first we were angry, not so much with Saul or even Doeg, as with—" He hesitated, weighing his words.

David's eyes flickered. "As with me," he murmured grimly.

Amasai reached out impulsively. "Yes," he said softly, "with you. The enormity of it! We wanted something obvious, something manageable to grasp. You had fled, and I wanted an explanation. But of course there wasn't one. Your going to

Nob may have precipitated the tragedy, but you never could have anticipated the outcome. The blame is Doeg's, but it's Saul's, too.

"Have you heard," Amasai continued, "that Saul installed other priests and had the tabernacle moved to the high place at Gibeon?"

"I'd heard that, yes," said David.

"He goes there regularly and makes sacrifices as though nothing happened. But inside he's a dead man. That day under the tamarisk tree he gutted his soul, and now he's an embarrassment to those who serve Israel's God. That's why I came," he finished. "I'm ashamed to stay in the service of such a man."

Amasai closed his eyes, then dropped on his face and burst out with a passion that startled David. "We are yours, O David! We're with you, O son of Jesse! Success to you and to those who side with you. God is with you!"

David was unnerved by the power of Amasai's utterance and felt the same indescribable tingle he associated with the ephod and with Saul's prophetic episodes. He bowed. "The Spirit speaks, my brother. You are welcome among us."

These trained, seasoned warriors brought other news, as well: Saul's abortive attempts to counter the Philistine thrust into the midlands, his continuing mental distress, and increasing disunity among the army chiefs. David inquired about Jonathan but learned only that he remained faithful to his father, and that he and Abner were basically holding things together. "Whenever the end comes," said Amasai, "it'll be a rout."

"How soon will the Philistines attack, do you think?" asked David.

Amasai scuffed the dust. "If they knew how bad things are, they'd be out there tonight. But they fear our God."

"They do. Israel's God is a puzzle. When they take the idols of other nations, the armies crumble, and it's easy from there. But we don't have idols—no god but Yahweh to protect us. Drives them crazy."

Within weeks Achish himself had enough favorable intelligence to prompt his move against Saul. He sent part of his army north to Shunem in the rolling hills of Jezreel and then summoned David.

"You want…*us* to help fight Saul?"

Achish's eyes squinted. "Surely you understood when you asked for sanctuary—"

"Yes, of course I understood. Your enemies became our enemies. But this particular…" David shrugged. "I'm just surprised, that's all. Of course we'll go with you."

"We're going with Achish to fight Saul?" Dodai was incredulous at the news.

"You agreed to this?" asked Joab's brother Abishai derisively. "You, who wouldn't raise a finger against Saul, when you all but had him hung on the city wall?"

David shrugged. "What could I say? 'No, Achish. You must realize I can't fight with you. I'm loyal to Saul.' Our heads would be on pikes before we could turn around."

"You could invent an excuse," said Eleazar. "'Pretty awkward, old man. Saul I'd kill gladly, but our own brothers…'"

David sighed. "Something will present itself. And besides, there's nothing we can do about it. We're committed. I'm to be Achish's bodyguard—for life, if I perform well."

"Oh, great!" Eleazar rubbed his head. "From the cooking pot to the fire. Under his nose all day, every day."

When Abigail heard the news, she set her mouth but said nothing. David turned away in anger and strode toward the door. Then he stopped and came back and took her hands. She looked at him in surprise.

"Abigail, what shall I do? The men think we should just sneak off and head back to the old strongholds. But I can't do that; it's too risky. They're watching us. Achish likes what he's seen so far, but he's no dummy. This may be his big test."

Abigail closed her eyes and leaned against him. David held her close until she pulled back and looked at him. "What does Joab say?"

David scratched his shoulder. "Hmph. What do you think Joab would say?"

"Yes, Joab would say, 'Cut down Saul, take over the kingdom, turn around and slaughter the Philistines.' A word not of the Lord." Her nostrils flared disdainfully. "And as you say, to excuse yourself or run away would be disastrous. As I see it, my lord, God is your only recourse. Walk boldly and wait for him to part the Red Sea waters."

David snorted impatiently. "Of course God is our only recourse! That goes without saying. But what exactly do I *do?*"

"You walk boldly and expect the waters to part. David, my lord, listen to me." Abigail pulled him around to face her. "Go out on the hillside, or stay in here where it's cooler. I'll keep

Ahinoam occupied so you won't be disturbed. Sit and listen. Sing. Fix your heart on God who anointed you to serve him righteously, not with tricks or devious ways. The God who brought you safely to this place, through hundreds of tight spots—you can trust this God to steer you around the problem. *He will bundle you in the safe center of his love.*"

David stood silent, staring at the well-swept dirt floor. Then he nodded. "Yes. Listen and sing. Thank you, my love." He kissed her and angled his frame through the narrow doorway.

"And David," she whispered at the figure striding across the torrid square, "I too, like Ahinoam, have a treasure bundled in my belly."

14

I don't recall how the subject came up, but I remember
sitting in the palace on the Feast of Trumpets during
David's fourth year as king in Jerusalem, a year or so after I first met him. We may have been discussing the upcom-
ing Day of Atonement, but, somehow, he and I got talking
about Saul's last days and his appalling burden of sin.

When I told David what I'd learned about Saul's activities
on that dreadful night before the battle, he wouldn't believe
me. "Wrong, Asaph. Dead wrong. I know Saul. My mother
would sooner have dabbled in sorcery than Saul. He wanted
every last sorcerer killed." David put up his hand to stay my
objection. "You'll say we didn't get them all, Asaph, but I know
we did. Someone brought in a witch who did unspeakable
things to children before using their sinews and bones in her
sorcery. She tried to save her neck by naming other witches
and mediums. Many were already dead or had fled south, but
the last one was the last one. I know; I was there."

I didn't want to argue. It's my opinion David preferred not
to believe that Saul would stoop to such an act. But when I
said who had told me—one of the two men who went with

Saul to Endor and saw everything that had happened—he sat quietly, hands twisting his purple headband. At last, he shifted and spoke.

"Asaph, sometimes…a person hates the thing that's darkest in his own life. Saul lived in torment. When I first began playing and singing for him, I tried not to watch his face, it was so awful. But when he began heaving spears, I had to pay attention. I might have been next. When Saul was well, nobody could be kinder, more fun to be with, but when spirits came…" He sighed. "Well, you were saying, Asaph? He found this woman…?"

I told him, but perhaps I shouldn't have. Like Samuel, David never stopped grieving for Saul.

The village of Endor lies southwest of the Sea of Kinnereth and four miles south of Mt. Tabor. Though the town belonged to the tribe of Manasseh, the original Canaanites had never been fully dislodged when Joshua swept through the land four hundred years ago. Even today, a Canaanite presence defines Endor, especially on the perimeter where poorer dwellings are tent pegs that anchor the town to the surrounding hills.

To one such hovel, hardly more than a cave, came three men dressed as common soldiers, though an observer might have wondered at the extraordinary height of one of them. Their "hoy" touched off a calf's bellow to their left, a stream of obscenities from within, and brought forth a thin-faced woman dressed in tatters and annoyance. The threadbare cloth she was settling over her head and shoulders had seen little of water and much of grease and soot. Small, hard eyes appraised her visitors. After a moment she seemed to understand what they were after and began unveiling her loose hair with movements suggestive of something other than sorcery.

The tall soldier brushed aside her advances and said in a thick voice, "No, I'd like you to consult..." He stopped and swallowed. "I want you to consult a spirit for me."

The woman's eyes narrowed to slits. The greasy headgear snapped back into place.

"Consult a spirit! You're playing games. You want me to stretch out my neck to get stuck like a goat for the pot? You don't know nothing about the king if you think I'd put two words together about consulting *spirits*. I'd like to stay alive a bit longer, thank you. Now, you got something else in mind, I—"

The stranger hissed impatiently. "Come, come. As surely as the Lord lives, you won't get in trouble for this. Believe me, I... have influence with Saul."

The woman stepped from the narrow doorway and circled the three suspiciously. "Just who you looking for—just for curiosity's sake?"

"I want you to raise the prophet Samuel."

She stared at him, trying to see through the haggard mask of the stranger's face.

"Is it payment you want?" he asked impatiently. "Sheep, goats, cloth—gold?"

Her eyes glinted. "Gold, you say."

"Whatever you want. Please. I'm in a hurry. Call Samuel for me."

She clutched her headdress and walked around again, opening her mouth with each inhalation, pursing it to exhale, painstakingly measuring risk against gain. She thrust out a clawlike hand, her eyes slits once again. "Gold, you say. No soldier I know gots gold. And you don't carry sheep nor cloth in your bags." Her mouth became a gap-toothed smile, then she jumped as the tall man thumped a rough nugget on her palm. The woman looked back and forth in wonder between his face and the piece she held. She inspected it, shoved it in her mouth for an experimental bite, then, seemingly satisfied, took a breath and motioned them to follow her inside. They crawled through the doorway into a lamp-lit recess that boasted little other than a fire pit and bed in a few miserable feet of space. They remained on their knees in the smoky dimness as she surveyed them suspiciously one last time before preparing her ritual.

With a piece of broken pottery, she scraped a circle in the exact center of the earthen floor, then smoothed it and brushed away loose material. From a shadowy corner behind the fire pit, she drew out a small stone jar. With her scraping shard, she lifted seven coals from the pit and arranged them in her circle.

At this point she began to hum and sway with a professional glance at the men to weigh its effect. Shaking a powdery substance from her jar, she sprinkled it ostentatiously on the coals. The odor rising from it became overpowering, and the two companions turned away, almost retching. Their leader remained rigid.

The woman again took to swaying and humming in a practiced manner, working her voice to a pitch, patently contrived for the occasion. "She should've stuck to harlotry," my informant told me. "She was bad at make-believe."

Suddenly, she screamed and scrabbled backward, obviously terrified. "You lied to me!" She pointed her finger. "You're no soldier. You're the king. You're Saul!"

Saul waved in a placating gesture. "Please...don't be afraid. What do you see?"

"Get away. Get away from me!" She pushed herself against the bony scarp that was her back wall.

With difficulty, Saul persuaded her to continue.

She looked at him doubtfully, then went on. "I see..." Her voice trembled uncontrollably. "I see an old man...long hair, a robe. The robe has...a rip to one side."

Now it was Saul's turn to cry out. "Samuel!" He bowed wretchedly, face to the ground.

A voice spoke, as though from miles beneath them. "Why have you disturbed me?"

The men could see no form, but they heard the voice and agreed afterward it wasn't trickery on the woman's part. She huddled in terror as far from the circle as she could get. If the men hadn't been blocking the door, she would have been outside.

Saul raised his head cautiously. "My lord, I...am in great distress. The Philistines...their army is like a great flock of sheep across the plain. I'm alone. God has turned away. He no longer speaks to me. Prophecies, dreams—nothing. Only you can help. Please, my lord Samuel...please tell me what to do."

The heap against the wall that was the witch moaned in terror. An answer did not come immediately, and the tension mounted. When the voice spoke again, its tone was sorrowful, heavy. "If God is your enemy, do you expect me to be otherwise? You disobeyed Him—by your own decision. You chose not to carry out His wrath against the Amalekites, and now the Lord is calling your debt. The kingdom has been torn from your hands and will be given to David. Tomorrow at this time Israel will be in the hands of the Philistines. You and your sons will be with me."

Saul gave a fearful cry and threw himself full-length on the floor where he convulsed with a violence that sapped all remaining strength. The two men dared not approach him. The woman lay trembling until she was certain the spirit had left, then drew on her experience with men and crept toward the king.

"My lord," she said tenderly, "You asked me… I'm sorry. I wish…" She laid her hand hesitantly on his shoulder, as though he might yet turn on her. "You're shaking. You need food, love. I'll get a little something that'll give you strength."

Saul shook his head. "No. This morning…a vow. I will not eat before the battle."

One of the companions gave an explosive "Puh! That's what he does. When you most need food, call a fast."

"Can't fight on an empty stomach, can you, love? I got a calf fattened. I can—"

"No! I will not eat."

The two looked at each other and at the woman. One man shrugged and edged closer. "My lord the king, listen to her. Without you to lead us, we don't have a prayer. And without strength, you can't lead us against the Lord's enemies. Let the woman fix what she has, and we'll all be the better for it."

After much coaxing, Saul allowed himself to be helped to the woman's couch with its suggestion of luxury in keeping with her primary profession. There he sat, unseeing, unmoving, until the woman had stoked the fire and readied the pot, butchered the calf—a gift, one would assume, from a customer—and baked bread without yeast. In little more than an hour, she set the steaming kettle before the king and his companions.

In silence they tore off pieces of bread and scooped out stew meat till they'd eaten their fill. With scarcely another word, the three walked from the house into a darkness that sucked them toward an unseen vortex.

15

Yellow dust plumes drifted east from the column of horses, chariots, and soldiers marching in units of hundreds and thousands. An army large enough to worry local farmers had already advanced north and was mobilizing at Shunem, a small town rooted in the rich soil of the Valley of Jezreel that bisected the northern hills. In later years, the town of Shunem would produce the beautiful Abishag to warm King David through the winter of his death, but on this day townsfolk were scurrying to secure their cattle and sheep, removing them beyond the reach of hungry Philistines.

The Israelite army, camped south of Shunem at the spring of Jezreel near the base of Mt. Gilboa, eyed the gathering horde and rubbed yet more oil on their leather shields as though to forestall disaster. Saul, by now more scarecrow than king, sent scouts scrabbling up Gilboa for news from his top general Abner, who was watching troop movements from the summit. Between reports, he trailed after his son Jonathan, who circulated among the troops with a joke or word of encouragement. Jonathan tried to interest him in food or in some detail of military preparation, but Saul would not be diverted.

"They keep coming," he said hoarsely. "They're after me. They can see me."

Jonathan tried to smile and patted the talons gripping his arm. "You're tall as a cedar tree, Father, but I hardly think they'd spot you this far away."

Saul shook his head stubbornly. "Abner thinks it's hopeless."

"That's not what he said a couple of hours ago."

"He doesn't say it, but that's what he thinks."

Jonathan did not reply, his cheerful mask sagging. He sighed, then straightened. "The God of Israel is our God; we're in his hands. May his will be done." He turned, muttering, *"Even to the cutting down of cedar trees."*

"It's the Gibeonites," Saul whispered, a new tentacle of fear clutching his throat. "The ones I didn't kill are in league with Achish."

David and his men marched at the rear of the Philistine column. Six hundred mercenaries were in units under Joab, his brothers, and Jashobeam, Shammah, and Eleazar. They took care to cloak their misgivings about Israelites fighting Israelites, especially when Achish himself drove alongside, chatting affably.

They had just negotiated the narrow, rocky pass at Megiddo and were fanning out on the plain of Jezreel when a cluster of chariots bearing Philistine commanders approached Achish. "My lord the king," they said, "a word with you. Privately," they added, looking pointedly toward David.

Achish raised his eyebrows and studied David as though to read in him the reason for this consultation. Achish gave the reins to his charioteer and said to David, "Take a short rest, my boy, but keep your men close. We want to make Shunem by sundown."

David watched Achish closely as he stood listening to his subordinates. "Something's up," he muttered to Eleazar. "Achish is chewing the inside of his cheek."

"Yes. They don't want us, after all, maybe." Eleazar said hopefully.

The king was arguing with his generals. He gestured and pointed and shoved chests. The men stood firm, however, and finally the king turned angrily and strode toward the Israelite mercenaries. He clasped David's shoulders affectionately. "David, my son," he said, "when you came to me two years ago, I wondered what was in your heart. But from that day till now, I've found no fault in anything you've done. I see no reason why you shouldn't be with me in this battle, but my men— they feel differently. You know how generals can be before battle. Touchy as women in labor."

"I wouldn't know about that," said David. "Yet."

"What?" Achish roared. "Your age and no sons? What have you been doing?"

David shrugged lamely. This was hardly the time to rattle off his activities.

"Well, son, now's your chance. My generals want me to send you home."

David's heart leaped, but he struggled to manufacture a look of disappointment. He thought, oddly, of Abigail kneading bread, praying for—or perhaps willing—the waters to part. "You mean we can't fight with you against the enemies of my lord the king? Why, my lord? What have I done?"

"You've been as pleasing to me as…as an angel of God, like you fellows say." Achish flashed his broad expanse of teeth. "But my men…they're nervous, you know. You have a reputation. Even our soldiers know the song of your people: 'Saul has slain his thousands and David—' you know the one. Now they're afraid you'll turn against us at the last minute to get back into Saul's good graces." He gave David a fatherly pat. "I know you wouldn't, but the stakes are high. Turn back now; go in peace." He consulted the late-afternoon sky. "On second thought, camp here for the night and start back at first light. You'll be with your wives in three days. Then you can get cracking on those sons!"

He gave David another affable squeeze and with no further ceremony catapulted into his chariot and whipped his forces toward Shunem.

Three days did get them home, but, as they topped the last hill and whooped their arrival, they stopped and stared uncomprehendingly at the far side of the valley. Smoke rose, but not from ovens or cooking fires. Women were not at kneading troughs. Children were not playing games. Ziklag lay a burned gash along the limestone hillside.

Sheba *ben* Bicri, a Benjamite, was first to move. With a high, keening wail, he crossed the valley, stumbled and rolled, but got to his feet and scrabbled up the slope.

The men searched feverishly among the rubble and charred timbers, some of which still smoldered. "They're not here!"

cried Dodai with a small measure of relief. "They weren't killed outright, anyway."

"But they're not here," said Sheba bitterly. "My wife and sons are *not here!*" He turned on David. "This is your fault. If we'd stayed home, if you'd had backbone enough to stand up to Achish…." He thrust his fists at the sky, weeping and raging.

David, blank and staring, seemed hardly to notice and wandered aimlessly. But a short time later he was forced to take heed. Joab pointed to a group of men Sheba had assembled. "They've got stoning on their minds," Joab said. "In case you're interested."

"Stoning! They think this is my fault, that I'm to blame? They think—" He stopped abruptly and shuddered. "Oh, Joab…" he said, clutching his hair with both hands and sinking to his knees. "It is my fault. We shouldn't have—"

Joab was on him in two strides and yanked him to his feet. With his left eye circling and his face inches from David's, he hissed, "Mourning is a luxury you can't afford right now. Put iron in your backbone and act like a man. Are you going to let these sons of whores get the upper hand?"

David stared back hard, his hair gray with ash, his tired, dusty face lined with rivulets. He closed his eyes and took a long, shuddering breath. "Fight for me, God," he muttered. "Come to my defense. I'll talk to them."

Joab released his arm. "You're a king; don't forget that."

David nodded wearily and turned away. As he moved toward the rebels, he sorted through the faces. Most were men he could have predicted would rally to the likes of Sheba. His heart smote him, though, when he saw Hurai next to Sheba.

Grief upon grief. Having lost his wife and firstborn in the desert, Hurai had recently taken another wife. All of them were enraged animals, bitter as gall.

An eerie silence, broken only by the lament of wind, lay over the land. No sheep or goats, no children shouting or crying, no comfortable chatter of wives over cooking fires. A hundred pairs of bloodshot eyes watched David's approach.

"We've been dealt a bitter blow," he started, rather satisfied with the inadvertent quiver in his voice. "This was our home for two years. Our families, our livestock, our belongings—all gone. We—"

"We lost sons and daughters," cried a voice. "What do you know about that? Our sons and daughters. What would it have taken—fifty men, maybe, to protect them?"

"Two years, you say," cried another. "What about the other years? Does Ziklag erase hunger, thirst, thorn bushes? What about those years, David?"

David closed his eyes, those years burning his gut like water from the Salt Sea. He straightened and, with tears on his face, walked into the group with a hand on this one or that, speaking the name of a wife or son.

Sheba struck his hand and spat on David's beard. "You will not dirty the name of my wife!"

David froze, a red haze spreading under the ash on his face. Jaw clenched and eyes blue columned, he seemed a storm about to hurl lightning.

Behind David, a group perhaps twice the size of Sheba's gathered quietly, some with swords and staves. Joab and his brothers, along with Shammah, Amasai, Eleazar, and Ira formed the vanguard. Hardly a sound could be heard among the thousand. David and Sheba edged around each other, two angry dogs, stiff legged with hackles raised.

Finally, David spoke, his voice even and hard. "I'm sorry you did that. I could ask you to wipe it off—and you would—but instead I will say I'm sorry for what my decision brought on us all. We should have left protection. I can see that now, and I take the blame. But I had no choice about going. They were watching. Achish trusted us, but his chiefs didn't. They would've been on us in a minute if we'd tried to sneak away.

"No," he continued, gathering confidence, "we were right to go with him, to believe that God would somehow work it out. He did. Right at the Megiddo Pass. At the last minute. The battle probably started the day we turned around. God turned it around for us, and he can turn this around, as well. Where's Abiathar?" He turned from Sheba as though ending a chat about the weather. "Abiathar!" he shouted. "The ephod."

It was a calculated risk. The ground held an infinite arsenal of rocks for stoning. A signal from Sheba—the mere lifting of his heel against David—would touch off a bloodbath. David, though, pushed through his adversaries and headed toward the high priest.

Abiathar, pale and starting, pulled the ephod from its carrying pouch. He laid it on the ground and straightened the breastplate pocket. "You...want me to put it on?"

Without answering, David squatted before the linen garment of blue, purple, scarlet, and gold. He ran a finger over the names of the twelve tribes engraved in onyx at the shoulders, along the rings and chains and blue cord that held the folded breastplate. When he came to the rows of gems on the breastplate itself, he passed his hand over them cautiously, closing his eyes at the tingle that enveloped his arm. Satisfied, he grabbed an egg-sized stone as though he needed something solid in hand. He watched distantly as Abiathar struggled into the garment that seemed far too weighty for any man to bear. When the priest was ready, David cried out in anguish of soul.

> *Who is like you, O Lord?*
> *You rescue the weak from the strong,*
> *the poor from those who rob them.*
> *Our enemies laid their nets;*
> *they came like lions stalking prey.*
> *Our hearts are carried off,*
> *our eyes run with tears*
> *as though weeping for our mothers.*
> *How long, O Lord, will you look on?*
> *Rescue us; restore to us our wives,*
> *our sons and daughters.*
> *I will give thanks to you before your people.*
> *My tongue will speak your praises*
> *all day long.*

Gripping the stone, David bowed low, his face to the ground. Then he nodded to Abiathar, who wiped sweaty hands down the sides of his robe. David prayed again. "O Lord, God of Israel, shall I pursue this raiding party? Will I overtake them?"

Abiathar swallowed several times, then reached into the breastplate for the Urim and Thummim. Hands trembling, he withdrew the sacred objects with a grimace of pain, held them high until his arms could bear it no longer, and then inspected them. "The Lord says…" His voice cracked. "The Lord says, 'Pursue! You'll overtake them and rescue your wives and sons and daughters.'" Relief strengthened his voice. "So *says the Lord!*"

16

The six hundred traveled south over rough, barren land, tracking signs of recent passage. Food and water were scarce among them, for most had calculated closely their requirements for the return trip from Megiddo, expecting plenty at home in Ziklag. A search through the ruins had turned up little; the raiders—most likely Amalekites—had been thorough.

They reached the dry brook Besor in the heat of the day. Some searched for water, but many collapsed at the edge of the wadi—quivering, leather-lipped ghosts too far gone to negotiate the steep descent and opposite climb. David moved anxiously among them.

At Asahel's whoop of "Water!" David called back, "Bring some; we need it here."

Alone, Asahel labored up the slope with three skins full. "If their mothers were dying of thirst," he fumed, "not a one of the bastards down there would carry a drop."

David ignored his complaints. "Give me one, another to Ira, and then go to the weakest. We're in trouble. Dozens are down. We could start losing them in minutes."

Joab called from the opposite bank. "Where are you? What's the matter?"

David hissed in exasperation. "Men are dying. Bring water. Or send somebody if you're too lazy."

He went back to distributing water but looked up a short time later as men, grumbling and swearing, poured out of the wadi, some with water skins, most without. He saw Joab driving the last of the troop into the ravine like so many sheep.

"Joab!" he thundered. "What are you doing?"

"Just showing my lord that your servant isn't too lazy to get you a drink."

Furious, David threw himself against the surge of men. "Stop, all of you! We don't have strength to throw away. If you brought water— Ahimelech, take your skin to the right. Shammah, to the rear. Check the trail to make sure no one fell before we halted. The rest go back across. Find shade if you can. Take a nap."

"A nap!" Sheba snarled. "Maybe we should erect tents while the slugs recover?"

Livid, David strode to Sheba and with his face inches away, pointed silently across the wadi. Sheba stared back for a moment, but his eyes wavered, and he turned grudgingly.

Ira stood beside David. "Most of these fellows can't go on. What do you say we leave them here—maybe with some of the baggage."

David nodded slowly, his eyes following Sheba. "Good idea. We'll move faster with less to carry."

After an hour of debate and rearranging supplies, four hundred men pushed on. Not far along, Eleazar jogged back to David. "A man lies ahead—alive but just barely."

When David reached the place, the man, face shriveled and tongue blackened, lay limp and unseeing. Ira lifted his head and dribbled liquid into his mouth, with no response. They poured and rubbed his chest until he began to respond, licking hungrily, choking, swallowing great drafts.

They sat him up, with Sheba muttering all the while about wasting time "raising the dead."

When he had revived enough to talk, David squatted beside him. "Who are you? Where are you from?"

"I'm—Egyptian…Amalekite slave. Three days…got sick. Master left me. We…raided…through the Negev, the Kerethites, the territory of Judah…Ziklag…"

The circle of men leaned closer.

David grasped the man's arm. "Can you lead us to this raiding party?"

The Egyptian looked at his swollen feet. He sat silently, considering the implications. Finally, he said, "Swear…before your God…that if I take you, you won't…kill me."

David's eyes narrowed. "Of course I won't kill you."

"Or hand me over to my master—same thing."

"I swear to you I will not." He crossed his fingers over the mood of his men, should the rescue attempt fail.

The man was weak, but with help he led them across washes and down wadis until at last he raised his hand in caution. In the distance they heard the bleating of sheep and the ill-tempered protests of camels.

David and his lieutenants crept to where they could look down on the Amalekite camp spread across the valley. "There they are." Ira pointed to a miserable group huddled under the eye of several guards. "No tents, no shade. Dogs!"

"Dogs, bogs!" Asahel hissed toward the encampment. *"Servants of goatherds, dung pickers, emitters of foulness!"*

Joab studied the lay of the land, the sounds of revelry, the defense arrangements. "Drunk," he grunted with satisfaction. "And stuffed to their eyebrows. Time and nature will put them in our hands."

"Time we don't have," David said. "We aren't drunk or stuffed. We're tired and hungry. And before they sleep they'll be on our women; you can bet on that."

Abishai looked at the sun. "An hour before dusk. What can we do in an hour?"

"Nothing," Joab said. "Drunk or no, they'll see us the minute we poke our heads over the brush. We either wait for dark and fight on empty stomachs or get some sleep and hit them at dawn—with stomachs emptier still."

They lay silent and grim, watching a few young men drift toward the penned-up women and children, pointing at this one or that.

"All right," said Asahel, his eyes burning, "we've got an hour. Let's get closer to the prisoners, then attack. Lightning out of a dark sky. My son Zebadiah's down there...." He stopped, jaw working.

"All right," said David, "let's do it. Asahel, take your pick of men and work around to the other side. Plan your strategy, but wait for the signal."

Asahel grunted. "My strategy includes picking off a few emitters of foulness along the way." He crawled off as David gave orders to Joab, Ira, and Abishai.

When the sun went down, all were in place—a thin circle around the Amalekites. Under camouflage of dusk they began their painstaking descent and got within yards of the revelers before an alarm sounded and Joab blew the trumpet. Fueled by rage and hunger, David's men tore into the disoriented raiders, slashing with sword and spear and javelin. Asahel's band quickly surrounded the prisoners and drove their guards into the panicked camp. Asahel himself fought from one campfire to another, stooping neatly between thrusts to snatch a bit of bread or meat. Between mouthfuls and spear thrusts, he murmured thoughtfully to his victims, "A hole for you…and a hole for you. Holes for the holy. Be holy."

The Amalekites were unable to organize defensively, even though they outnumbered David's men ten to one. But when darkness fell, the attackers were forced off to avoid killing each other. They moved the women and children away from the battlefield, the latter weeping from joy and fright. The odds were plain, even to a child.

Few of David's men had been as resourceful as Asahel in finding food, a point that exasperated him. "We find Amalekites with food spilling from every tent, and you stand around whining. Do I have to go kill a fatted calf for you?"

In the end he did just that. With a few good men, he sneaked into the Amalekite camp toward the first available provisions and, with a protesting goat under each arm, strode off, leaving his men to handle the token reprisal.

The next day's battle produced more serious fighting. The Amalekites, no longer drunk, had regrouped. But so had David. With iron in their hands and eyes, his men swept systematically across the encampment, killing every Amalekite, young and old.

Only one blunder marred their conquest. Four hundred Amalekites on camels broke through Dodai's line and escaped. Joab railed furiously. "What were you doing while they mounted up? Holding their bridles?"

Dodai leaned on his spear, head down, eyes closed, face lined with fatigue.

"Old men!" Joab spat the words. "Old soldiers make mistakes."

David strode to Joab and hissed, "I hope you live long enough to remember those words."

They started home the next morning, carrying as much as they could and driving herds before them. When they came to the Besor and the two hundred men they'd left there, Sheba muttered around a bandaged cheek. "Must we divide the spoils with cabbages? We took the risk, did the fighting. The booty is ours. They should be happy enough for their wives and children."

Dodai told David about the murmuring. "Maybe Sheba's right," Dodai said, his voice dragging in weariness. "At least… those who didn't make mistakes…I don't deserve…"

David put his arm around the old soldier. "Dodai, my friend," he said, "We're tired, all of us. We pushed as hard as we could, those who stayed, those who went. We emptied our jars to the last grain. The Lord put our enemies into our hands, and we'll share equally in his bounty. And," he added as an afterthought, "if I ever have a say in such things, this is the way it will be, a statute and ordinance for all Israel."

Even before they finished cleaning Ziklag, David sent gifts throughout the region where he and his men had run from Saul, and to key men in Abigail's home territory. "You never know," he said to her with a twinkle. "A few small gifts now... payback later."

17

Over the years, I've talked with survivors of that last, terrible battle, men from both sides, such as Onam, who saw but couldn't stop the Philistine archers who were descending on Saul, and Ittai, at that time a capable Philistine strategist. Innocent sufferers: Jonathan's son Mephibosheth, whose nurse dropped him in her panicked flight; Ziba, a servant of Saul; Abner's wife. I've tried to fathom their deepest thoughts. Snatches of conversation, an expression of terror—these are at best crumbly bricks for building a reliable history, but we can, perhaps, come close to the passions and pathos that lie beyond the facts.

The armies were in place. Sheer numbers alone depicted the stark contrast between the two forces. Add to that the spiritual decay of Israel's leader, and the outcome was virtually predestined.

Saul slept poorly, if at all. His mind—what was left of it—seemed to be on his early call and anointing by the prophet Samuel. He was once again the long-legged, bashful lad. His father Kish, brother to Abner's father, had sent him after some missing donkeys. In the course of the search, Saul was directed to the prophet's house. "The leg," Saul the king muttered as he meandered toward his last battle. "Samuel made sure they gave me the leg—his own portion of the sacrificial lamb. He pushed it on me. But look at the leg now. The leg has walked into the lion's mouth."

Those listening to these deranged ramblings heard in them the trumpet of doom.

Achish, too, was up and prowling. Not with anxiety. No, he felt confident in his own strength, in his army, in his superior equipment, in the glitter of his gods that stood ready to be carried into battle. His only provocation for cheek chewing was the unpredictability of Israel's God, that divinity who refused to take shape and be carried around. What might this Yahweh God do when the sun came up?

Abner, Saul's general, slept soundly. He knew the cause was hopeless and had worked out his own strategy for escape and for salvaging what troops he could. The king would die—that was a given. Along with him would go three sons, Jonathan, Abinadab, and Malki-Shua. Jonathan would be an incalculable loss. The other two… At least Saul had failed to persuade his remaining son Esh-Baal to join battle. Not that his quick demise would be a bad thing. Not at all. This way, though, Abner could fight with one less boulder around his neck.

Jonathan. His thoughts were the hardest to trace. He too knew hopelessness. But unlike Abner, his duty lay in fighting till God ended the battle for him, one way or the other. Surely he prayed. Surely he thought of David. Surely he ran a hand through his hair.

I have thought of David, too, in that regard. Had Jonathan lived, how might he have stood between David and me? May God forgive the trace of gratitude in my heart over a good man's death.

An Amalekite approached Ziklag. Despite torn clothing and dust on his turban, his air was far from mournful. Had he known of the recent raid on that town, he might have weighed the prudence of an Amalekite showing himself in Ziklag. As it was, he saved himself a beating only by declaring he had an urgent report for "David the almost-king." With studied timing, he pressed hands to his forehead and fell to the ground, writhing piously before David.

David, sweaty and sooted from salvaging half-burned roof timbers from the wreckage, was little inclined toward hospitality. "Who are you? Where are you from?"

"O my lord who is to be king of all Israel and of all its surrounding nations, O most exalted David, I am the humble son of an alien, an Amalekite. Two days ago I escaped from Mt. Gilboa, from up north." He shifted his eyes to assess the impact of his words.

"Did you, now?" David spoke contemptuously, but he leaned forward with ill-concealed eagerness. "What happened? Tell me."

"O lord, may you live forever. May your enemies be as the Israelite army this day—dead or scattered to the winds. Like arrows from ten thousand bows, whole towns are fled before the Philistines. And, O my lord—" He looked up again, sharp eyes calculating. "The greatest of your enemies, Saul himself and his son Jonathan are dead. His sons Abinadab and Malki-Shua, too. And his chief armor bearer." Here the Amalekite risked a bit of levity. "Good fortune for you, who once bore Saul's armor. Had he not conferred the boot upon you years ago, you might have been..."

The rush of words trailed off as a wave of red mounted alarmingly to David's face. "How do you know all this?" David's voice was hard and tight.

"O most reasonable lord..." The Amalekite shifted uneasily. The conversation wasn't going as planned. "I happened to walk the mountain at the time, and—"

"You 'happened'! Ha! Robbing corpses before they hit the ground!"

The Amalekite's eyes widened righteously. "My lord! May my mother lie as those corpses if what I say..." David's eyes reduced the remainder of his sentence to a confused rattle. He tried to improve the image of fear and solemnity in his face. "I happened to the king, O my lord. He was on a high place, on his spear but not dead. Philistine chariots were charging uphill. They'd flutter on him in minutes. He solicited me to kill him before they got to him. 'I'm dying,' he cried out to me, 'but not briskly enough.' Arrows had gored him, and his blood was—anyway, did I have a choice, O most kindly of sovereigns?"

David said nothing.

The Amalekite, not encouraged by what he read in David's face, dug into his bag and withdrew two items. With the eagerness of a merchant displaying wares, he laid out an armband

and a metal helmet, its sole ornament a small horn. "I am sorry for him, so bad off he was. I killed him out of pity. And so you'd know your enemy really is dead, I brought Saul's very crown and bracelet. They're for you, my lord; may all your enemies lie as King Saul! May the strength of the mighty God of Israel, the inexorable, the irresistible, make your sword and lance." Again he bowed in pious subservience.

David knelt to finger the items. His shoulders hunched, and he began to weep.

With this first bit of encouragement, the Amalekite felt moved to improve his costume with additional rips and motions of dust throwing.

In a lightning move, David yanked him to his feet. "Why weren't you afraid to kill the Lord's anointed?"

The Amalekite hung shriveled and terrified in David's hand. "My lord," he squeaked. "I—"

"Your blood be on your own head. You came here thinking I'd reward you for killing Saul. My guess is that you didn't kill him at all; you don't have the liver for it. You were there, though, and got to his body before the Philistines did. Nevertheless, your own mouth condemns you when you confess to killing the Lord's anointed. Joab! Drag this uncircumcised dog out of my sight and strike him down."

Without a word, Joab stepped forward, grabbed a handful of oily, black hair, and hauled the man behind the nearest remaining wall, screeching and beseeching.

David stayed in the hills that night and much of the following day. In the evening he called an assembly. Entire families gathered silently in the open space near the village well. David sat at the edge of the well, harp in hand. Marks of mourning were upon him, but he remained composed, saying nothing until all had arrived. Then, without preamble, he positioned the harp and fingered a plaintive melody. His listeners closed their eyes and swayed to a haunting sadness that stirred within them, not because of Saul's death—they'd often wished him dead—but in response to life's many deaths. They felt it gather—a small death, perhaps of a stillborn infant—then rise to encompass heaven and earth and mysteries beyond the grave. When David began to sing, they hardly noticed the seamless transition.

> *Your glory, O Israel, lies slain on your heights.*
> *How the mighty have fallen!*
> *Saul and Jonathan—*
> *In life they were loved and gracious;*
> *In death they were not parted.*
> *They were swifter than eagles, stronger than lions.*
> *Jonathan lies slain on your heights.*
> *I grieve for you, my brother;*
> *You were dear to me.*
> *Your love for me was wonderful.*
> *How the mighty have fallen!*
> *The weapons of war have perished!*

David had one final word before dismissing the assembly. He had, it seemed, been thinking of more than his lament while roaming the hills. He pulled several smooth stones from his pouch, selected one, and held it up. "Israel's strength is slings and spears," he said, "but Philistine arrows brought down Saul. If we're to defeat the Philistines, we've got to out shoot them. Our expert bowmen who can shoot with either hand must instruct us. And as the men of Judah learn, they'll sing this song, this 'Lament of the Bow.' We'll build new 'weapons of war.'" He hurled the stone westward, toward Philistia. "*Our gibborim, our mighty warriors, will avenge the death of Saul!*"

S hall I go up to one of the towns of Judah?" David
inquired.

The Lord said, "Go up."

"Where shall I go?"

"To Hebron."

Hebron, highest of all cities in Israel, straddling the north-south trade route. Hebron, the town where Abraham and Sarah lay buried, the city given to Caleb on his defeat of the Anakim, that fierce race of giants. To Hebron David brought Ahinoam and Abigail—just in time for the first of two babies to be delivered. His loyal band came with their families, feeling at last that they'd come home—a settled place, a safe place. And to Hebron came the elders of Judah to formalize their agreement with David in the eating of bread and salt, and to anoint him king over the house of Judah.

A solemn, proud occasion. They hardly knew how to act, those desert-hardened warriors fresh from pools of gore. As David and his chiefs assembled behind musicians conscripted for the occasion and walked a long corridor of the leading men of Judah, all bowing as he passed, he began to sweat. No one spoke, no one cheered. Coarse-clad herders, vinedressers, potters, field hands, as many as had two feet to carry them, stood on tiptoe behind festal-robed landowners. Women watched from the hillside, following the slow, stately procession. Trumpets alone broke the silence. *What am I doing here?* David asked of himself. *Samuel made a mistake, anointed the wrong brother, and now things are twisted, upside down. I'm a usurper; Jonathan should be here, not I.*

But a glimpse of his brothers now bowing to him pricked his last hope of escape. David could imagine how they would testify to his calling: *Yes, Samuel did pour oil over the lad. We saw it; we were there.*

No, they'd never allow him off the hook.

And neither would Joab, impelling him from behind. Joab and Jashobeam and Ira and Eleazar. His friends, the mightiest of his *Gibborim*. If he was to be king, these men had brought him to the moment. Now they prodded him toward his anointing.

The road seemed long to the high place above the town, the place chosen for worship. Abiathar and perhaps twenty underlings led the way. No shortage of priests in Hebron, that Levitical City of Refuge. After years of makeshift dress, the high priest at last wore a new, complete outfit as befitted this mediator between God and man. A blue robe trimmed with pomegranates and bells, over which lay an apron-like ephod stitched in blue, purple, and scarlet with the old jeweled breastplate in front. On his forehead a crown of gold proclaimed him "Holy to the Lord," a designation even more solemn because he was bearing, on behalf of the worshippers, the guilt inherent in the sacrifices themselves. He carried a gold flask containing a special blend of anointing oil. He had gone to great lengths to procure this oil from the only perfumer he could trust. Formulated of liquid myrrh, cinnamon, fragrant cane, and the finest olive oil, the compound imparted holiness to whatever person or object it was rightfully applied. Few pagan nations anointed their kings. Samuel, though, had seen the necessary connection between Israel's holiness and its political strength and had separated out both Saul and David as representatives of the holy liaison.

When at last they reached the high place, the trumpets ceased. Other instrumentalists took over with harps and lyres and cymbals to lead the singing. Heman was among them, playing his harp—nervously. While his status as grandson of Samuel qualified him for the task, it did nothing to calm him.

Hidden deep within his protective high-priestly gear, Abiathar found his mouth almost too dry to speak the words of prayer and coronation. He thought back to his flight from Nob when he had demeaned himself in abject fear. From that day, David had been his protector, his superior in every way. Abiathar had, of course, served him as high priest, but as a man among men he was nothing. Now he had somehow to draw from within himself the courage to make a king. Why could not Samuel have lived to do this?

David drew a deep breath and looked to Abiathar for strength. He saw the man's terror, but behind it he saw the office. He, Abiathar; he, David; they, the tribe of Judah; all of them stood before Yahweh the I Am in weakness, humility, and faith. With trembling hands, he passed his headband to

Ira and knelt against that frightening backdrop of silence to receive the unction of royalty.

The tension broke slowly. At first came the stiff, awkward homage of the immediate participants to their new sovereign, followed by the even more awkward obeisance of the *Gibborim*, those men who had tended his wounds, seen him at his worst, spilled oceans of blood in the effort to bring him to this place. It was more than David could take. Eyes twinkling, he leaned close to his kneeling men and whispered, "Get me out of here; even kings have to make water."

Ira and Eleazar dropped hands from foreheads and looked up quizzically, but, seeing David's bemused expression, they began pounding him. David leaped and bellowed and whooped, then grabbed his exuberant companions and danced arm in arm downhill toward town, all of them singing at the top of their lungs. Women with timbrels and sistrums sang and danced in the eddying swirls of this magnificent, ruddy, sovereign presence. "All those months, those years of running and hiding, of cooked lungs and thirst. It's over, and I'm *king!*" whooped David. "How long since Samuel yanked me out of the pasture? Fourteen, fifteen years? Long enough. King at long last!"

One of David's first official acts was to commend the men of Jabesh Gilead on the east bank of the Jordan for their kindness to the dead king and his sons. An old friend told him of the opportunity.

"My lord the king." A round lump of a man with a flat nose and an honest, companionable face bowed before David, who was sitting uneasily on the seat of power at Hebron's city gate. "My lord," the stranger repeated, looking up quizzically, "do you remember some sheep that escaped the hand of a very young shepherd?"

"Hushai!" David sprang from his chair and pounded the man's back. "Remember? You saved my life! The bastard who took my animals saw easy pickings from a scrawny kid whose sheep wouldn't follow his '*Taa! ho, ho.*'"

"What were you—nine or ten?"

"Something like that. You thumped the bully while I grabbed the closest sheep and got out of there."

David looked his old friend up and down. An Arkite. Canaanite by birth, Israelite by conviction. He saw quick, clever eyes and a mouth ready to laugh, but beneath was the staunchness and sympathy that the past had already established. "Hushai. Friend of my heart. I would never have recognized you."

Hushai laughed. "A friend gone soft," he said, patting the plumpness around his middle. "Linen merchants sit a lot and eat. But look at you. Shepherd boy to king. I've been watching, you know, following your ups and downs. And now that you're king, I made bold to come. Not for myself, mind you." His chin tilted proudly. "I came because you loved Saul and Jonathan. Have you learned what became of their bodies?"

"No. I've asked everywhere, but no one could say. I assume the Philistines took them."

"Yes. To Beth Shan on the Jordan River. Saul's head went to the temple of Dagon, his armor to Ashtoreth. The bodies were hung on the wall. The people of Jabesh Gilead learned of this, then crossed the river at night to get the bodies."

"Jabesh. Of course!" David thumped the arm of his chair. "They'd do that. Before Saul was recognized as king, he rescued their city. Did you know?"

Hushai shook his head.

"Ammonites had come against them and offered a treaty—in exchange for the right eye of each townsman. Saul got word of this while he was plowing. On the spot, he butchered his oxen and sent pieces all through Israel. 'Your oxen will look like this if you don't follow Saul and Samuel,' the message said. It got their attention. Over three hundred thousand from Israel and Judah mustered under the fear of Saul and God—in that order." David smiled. "God delivered Jabesh Gilead, and the people made Saul king. And now...after all these years, Jabesh didn't forget." He stared through the gateway. "Where are they buried—Saul and his sons?"

"They burned the bodies and buried the bones under a tamarisk tree—appropriately. Then they fasted seven days."

David nodded. "Jabesh did not forget Saul; I will not forget them. Hushai, thank them for me and then come back. Forget your linen trade; I need a good man at my side."

Other good men came to David at Hebron, including Jehoiada, leader of the family of Aaron, himself a priest. He brought nearly four thousand men to help David fight against Abner, who now represented what remained of the house of Saul. On their arrival, Joab muttered about "'Tent boys" pretending to be warriors. He was particularly annoyed by Jehoiada's son Benaiah, a lad large in zeal and strength but small in discretion. "A hyena cub tripping my men," he fumed. "I threw him in the dump ashes last night, and this morning he came with five spears he had salvaged and remade. Damned, big-eared nuisance!"

David laughed. "Don't forget, I was a nuisance at that age—and nuisances sometimes kill giants."

Zadok was another new arrival and perhaps the only priest who ultimately forced grudging admiration from Joab. The twenty-two trained officers he brought sweetened the pot, but, in the beginning, the commander kept a close watch on them all, mistrusting any son of Aaron or Levite who claimed to be soldier material. Zadok was young and adroit, but it was his zeal for the Lord, glowing like burnished bronze, that caught David's attention.

Everything about Abigail's pregnancy had been hard. Months of nausea, weeks of threatened miscarriage, and days of fruitless labor before she finally delivered a pallid, sickly infant. David, after his first disappointing inspection of the child, named him Kileab—"restraint of father"—and seldom looked in after that. Abigail called the child Daniel—"God who judges"—and vengefully poured herself into keeping the boy alive.

Ahinoam tried to soften the edges of Abigail's bitterness, but the presence of her own son Amnon, a husky, healthy five-month-old, was an affront she could neither conceal nor restrain. A beautiful baby with the black hair of his mother, he kicked and crowed and won the heart of his doting *abba*.

For months, Abigail kept to her chamber whenever David was around. He inquired after her dutifully, but, being busy negotiating a new wife, he gave Abigail only perfunctory attention. The situation changed on the arrival of Maacah, daughter of Talmai, a notable chieftain in Geshur across the Jordan. The political advantage of this wife would be considerable. Both Abigail and Ahinoam knew this and worked hard to prepare the bridal chamber. The bride's virgin friends would bring flowers and spices, but the two wives wanted nothing that would reflect on either their housekeeping or their goodwill.

The wedding feast had to be seen to, as well. Expectations would be high. Of the two wives, Abigail had had the experience of Nabal's household, but the perfectionist pressure she put on herself made her irritable. Kileab, too, was cranky, and, after an explosion of women and babies, Abigail scooped her son and ran through the courtyard to the street.

Composing her face as best she could, she walked briskly toward the weaver's house in an attempt to appear occupied. She paused, though, by the well where a knot of Levites and others clustered around Zadok, the young warrior priest, recently arrived. His wedge-shaped face was mostly beard and frown lines, with piercing eyes that served as windows to the fire within. His rare smiles were measured in white, even teeth. He sat on a low wall and spoke animatedly.

"David can make all the alliances he wants—marriage or otherwise—but political power comes from the Lord. He knows that. David is a horn of strength—not just for Judah, but for all Israel. Saul turned from God, and his throne crumbled. With our help, David can pull the nation together and become a ruler stronger than Saul ever thought of being. Why? *David loves God.*" His finger jabbed each word.

"*Yes, yes!*" whispered Abigail, forgetting her "weaver" errand.

An older Levite spoke. "But there's Abner. And Esh-Baal."

"Esh-Baal's a jackass!" came a contemptuous voice. "He wouldn't fight alongside his father and brothers: what sort of king would he make?"

Zadok shrugged pleasantly. "A jackass of a king. But you're right: Abner's the man to reckon with. He's loyal to the house of Saul, so Esh-Baal will undoubtedly be part of the picture. But Abner's got ambition. He'll set up Esh-Baal as a front, but where? The Philistines will pick him off if he stays at Gibeah. Across the Jordan, maybe?"

Abigail's face throbbed with excitement. She shifted the baby to still his mewling and tried to appear interested in something spilled on the edge of the well. How foolish she'd been to keep David at arm's length these past months! She hungered to be privy once again to this sort of talk. Her mind leaped to the possibilities: Ramoth in Gilead? Mahanaim? Had David himself been thinking of this Transjordan territory when he commended the men of Jabesh Gilead? Or, for that matter, with his betrothal to King Talmai's daughter Maacah? The gratification of airing hurt feelings had cost her dearly, and now she'd have to wait till well after the wedding before she could mend walls. She could do it, though. But she'd have to get back into David's good graces before other women came along—and they would…they would.

An enterprising wall mender, not only did Abigail not wait until after the wedding, but the day of the wedding itself became her opportunity. She needed time to accumulate materiel, but she put her strategy into action only a few days in advance. "My lord," she said, "your wedding day is just a Sabbath away. Have you given thought to personal preparation? I've gathered fine spices and perfumes—nard, stacte, aloe—" She noted David's sudden interest but hurried on to forestall questions. "I also have a small basket of mandrakes."

David laughed. "Do you believe I need a love potion?" he asked lightly.

A good sign, she thought. "No, my lord," she replied with a tiny smile, "but Maacah might." His belly laugh heartened her even more.

"My lord, I'll gladly give these ointments as my gift to you and your bride, but I would be honored if you'd permit my hands to apply them."

He replied with equal gallantry. "My lady, it would be my pleasure to accept such a gift from your hands."

The day of the wedding arrived, and Abigail took careful account of the room in which she would anoint David. It must be fresh and clean but with no unwitting symbols of a competing love. It must be private but not completely so. She had her compounds and vials arranged in the order she would use them—an alabaster container of nard, a precious ointment she had brought from Nabal's house against just such a situation. She would massage it into his entire body as a base for other perfumes—the stacte and aloe, along with the more common sweet cane and myrrh. Her touch must be sure and competent, yet relaxing, non-threatening. She would talk but not of politics. Focus on Maacah—yes, on her beauty and charm, her thick, lustrous hair, the garments she would wear when she emerged at twilight from her house. The daughter of a king would be well-attired, but David would equal her beauty, if she had anything to do with it. His clothing would be perfumed, his red hair and beard would glow with oil. She'd make this the finest wedding a king's wife could ever expect. And—she would be welcome in David's presence from the start. Time enough then to suggest he pay attention to Ramoth Gilead or Mahanaim as a competing seat of power.

19

David's greatest asset was Joab, and Joab was his greatest liability. Esh-Baal's greatest asset was Abner, his greatest liability, himself.

Now that Saul was dead, Abner could breathe. He could expand his sizeable chest and inhale winds of possibility. True, he had poor material to work with. Esh-Baal—or Ish-Bosheth, "man of shame," as he was later called—was by all accounting little more than a hollow gourd stuffed with chaff. He was weak, but at least Abner knew the size and shape of his weakness and could prop him appropriately.

Where to establish his man, though? The homestead in Gibeah was out of the question. Philistines would be on him in a minute. No, the king must be positioned away from Philistines, somewhere across the river. Perhaps in Mahanaim of Gilead, on the north slope of the Jabbok River. Distant, yet strategically close to the important action. There he would establish his pawn, prop his throne with pillows, and pump him full of high-sounding phrases—to fool the puppet king himself, if no one else.

With his figurehead in place, Abner could then set out to reestablish the house of Saul. He had regrouped what was left of the army, instilling heart through tough discipline and lavish praise. Abner expected much, and they gave it willingly.

For two years, nothing much happened between David and the house of Saul. Abner drilled his army, and David built his power base. Then the war began.

A young man, wild-eyed and gasping, lurched into the dark courtyard of David's house at Hebron. He shouted hoarsely, clinging to the doorpost to keep from collapsing.

At first, only his own tortured breathing broke the silence. Then Shammah appeared. "Who is it?" He pried the lad from the doorframe and tried to make out his face. "Bring a lamp," he called toward the house. "Give your name, boy."

The lad gasped, "Benaiah."

"Benaiah! What is it? What happened?"

"Asahel's dead. Where's…David?"

"Dead! *Asahel?*"

Again the boy nodded, holding his chest. "David…?"

"He's not here. Where've you come from?"

"Gibeon east. Wasteland. A battle. After the pool."

"What pool? Speak plainly, boy."

"A face-off. At the pool."

"The pool of Gibeon? A one-on-one at the pool of Gibeon. And Asahel was defeated? I don't believe it! Who—"

"Not then. Later. Twelve pairs…killed each other…touched off battle."

Hurai came with a light, and Abigail followed. She moved to the boy, saw the state he was in, and put her arm around him. "Don't question him out here," said Abigail. "He's exhausted. And bleeding. Take him inside."

Benaiah's shoulders hunched, and he gave way to tears. "He's dead...."

"Come," said Abigail. "Something to drink, then you'll lie down."

The story came out in bits and pieces. In what was evidently a trial sortie for Abner's new army, he had set out from Mahanaim and crossed the Jordan with a sizeable force. David's scouts had discovered the move, and Joab and his brothers were dispatched to head them off. The groups had met at the Gibeon pool.

After some posturing, the generals and their top men sat down on opposite sides. Abner sauntered forward, bronze accouterments glinting in the sun. "Joab," he said. "I've some young men here who've been training hard. They'd like to test themselves against your boys. What do you say—twelve face-offs? We'll see which tribe is the stronger—Benjamin or Judah."

Joab looked at his brothers. A corner of Abishai's mouth flicked upward. "What's he trying to do—weed out incompetents?"

The three consulted, then Joab shrugged and turned to respond. "We've got twelve who can match any warrior you select. Pick your men."

Abner's men, it seemed, had already been picked. They stepped forward smartly. Joab sized them up. Behind him, three platoons hummed eagerly to be chosen to represent Judah. He turned to his brothers. "Four from each group—expendables. Not hard to figure how this will turn out. When it's over, we're on them, and it won't be an exhibition."

Joab was right. When the signal was given, each man grabbed the other's hair and thrust his dagger into his opponent's side. In seconds the mass duel was over.

Scarcely waiting for the combatants to fall, Joab gave the signal, and the three units leaped over bodies with a vengeful yell. The battle was on.

It turned out to be more of a clash than Joab had anticipated. Abner had trained his men well, and they fought fiercely, but Joab's superior force and experience began to tell. Hundreds of bodies marked a trail toward the east as Abner was pushed toward the river. Finally, his trumpet sounded retreat, and the Benjamites fled.

Most of Joab's men stopped to catch their breath. Asahel, though, saw his chance for a coup. If Abner were out of the way, Esh-Baal would collapse, and David would rule the entire nation. As a warrior, Abner was without question a match for any of them, but he'd fought hard this day, and he was no longer young. Asahel, on the other hand, was young and fast— a gazelle unparalleled in either Judah or Benjamin. Though Abner had a head start, Asahel would catch him and cut him down.

"I started to follow," said Benaiah, "but it was over before I got there. I learned what happened from a wounded Benjamite soldier."

The wounded soldier heard Abner rasp, "That's got to be Asahel."

"Yes," Asahel replied. "A leopard on your back."

Abner said, "Stop, for your own good. If you have to prove something, pick one of the young fellows. Take his weapons." Asahel would not stop, and Abner spoke more pointedly. "Go back! I don't want to kill you. How could I look your brother in the face?"

Still Asahel kept on, the gap narrowing.

Suddenly, Abner stopped abruptly. He thrust the butt of his spear toward Asahel, most likely to ward him off and gain a momentary advantage. But with their speed and the force of the blow, the spear, sharpened for sticking in the ground, went in Asahel's stomach and out his back.

Every man stopped when they came to where Asahel had fallen, and the roar of their breathing turned to hoarse weeping. Joab and Abishai pushed through the knot and bent over their brother, whose glazing eyes held a look of surprise. His lips moved. The two leaned close but could hear just two words. "Hole…*holy*."

Joab sat stunned as Asahel's eyes fixed. Then grinding fistfuls of dirt into his hair, his cry raged against the hills. "*The son of Zeruiah will be revenged! For this you will pay, Abner ben Ner! I will walk in your blood!*"

The bereaved brothers did not waste time mourning. Within minutes they were on their feet and running. Benaiah, ever seeking Joab's approval, had loped alongside.

The sun was low as they approached the hill of Ammah. Joab raised his hand and halted. There on the hill, the sun shone red on a formidable line of warriors—bows, swords, and spears at the ready.

"Joab!" called out Abner. "Your brother—does he live? I struck with the butt of my spear. He fell, but—"

"Zeruiah's son is dead!" Joab raised both fists in anguish.

On the hill, Abner appeared to slump. "I'm sorry. I warned him. He was young and trusted too much to his legs. I begged him to turn back. Not because I was afraid. I fear no warrior. I fear no battle. But as David would not kill my cousin Saul, so would I not deliberately kill his nephew Asahel. I only tried to stop him. Joab, listen to me. Must the sword devour forever? This can only end in bitterness, brother against brother. Call it off, Joab. Now."

Was it grief that turned Joab around, or was it Abner's army taking its stand? Joab sank to his knees, head bowed. Finally, he stood. "Yes, Abner," he said. "Bitterness. As surely as God lives, if you hadn't spoken, we'd have chased you till dawn." In the silence that followed, he muttered, "Till dawn, another dawn, any dawn…I can wait to walk in your blood."

The sun set on Joab's trumpet blast.

20

On the day Absalom was born of Maacah daughter of King Talmai, David took Haggith as his new bride. Maacah was furious. So was David. Her labor shrieks, amplified by spite and moderated only slightly by distance, dampened the festivities, despite Abigail's best efforts. She too was angry. As usual, she had poured herself into this wedding and was pleased. David looked fine. The design of his robe, his filigree crown, and the scarlet silk sash he wore only at weddings made him look every inch a king-groom.

Abigail tried to have Maacah removed to the far side of town, but the laboring queen would have none of it. Even after the baby was born, she insisted the child be presented to its father, effectively disrupting the singing and dancing. David, irritated to his limit, was about to create a scene, but the bride's maidens clustered around the swaddled infant that was fresh washed and salt rubbed. "Such a handsome child! And the hair!" they said, glancing at the infant's father. "No need to guess whose child he is!"

David turned to Haggith with an exasperated shrug. "My love, you shall have a son like that; I promise you."

That night, in a bed redolent of spice, Adonijah was conceived. And when he was born, his hair bore the same rufous tinge as his brother's.

Red hair. I wanted red hair because my hero David's hair was red. Mine was not black and hardly even dark; I saw it as ugly brown. And fine. That was perhaps the worst part. Fine hair, Levite hair—not coarse and thick and…*warlike*, like David's. It's painful for me to confess this, even so many years later.

This childish covetousness prompted the one genuinely courageous act of my life, an act that still stirs my soul to awe—until the idiocy of it sets fire to my face. My desire to look like the great warrior-poet drove me to creative measures. Never mind that three of me would fit in his body, and that the weight of his sword in my hand would probably tip me over. I would become like him in whatever way I could.

How could I make my hair red? I was smart enough to understand that colored wool did not come from colored sheep and thus began to explore the art of dyeing. I questioned a purple-fingered woman who lived near us, and she told me that red dye came from worms. "Worms!" I exclaimed. "A *tola* worm. Like this," she said, fishing a reddish grub from a jar. Then she told me, or at least I understood her to say, "You eat them. Of course, you've got to find dozens to make fine reds, different shades and all, and then—"

I'd heard all I thought I needed and grubbed at the base of oaks until my pouch held the required number. Then my nerves and stomach began asking hard questions. I squirmed under the weight of my longing. Big breaths alone kept my stomach from rejecting the very sight of the writhing maggots. I sat looking at them a long time, then took one last breath. How I actually brought myself to swallow them, I can't say, but I did and then promptly fell into the sin of pride, though not for long.

Each day I examined my hair for signs of red, then went back in despair to my dye expert, only to learn that the process involved *heating* the tolas, not eating them. Though bitterly disappointed, I was conscious of at least one boon: vermilion on the fine hair of this Levite would not have sat well with my father.

An act of foolish pride that pains me in the telling, but the courage it required gives me some small understanding of what a warrior such as Abner must have drawn on for perhaps the most courageous act of his life.

Five years they fought. Abner was good—a clever strategist, a general who cared about his men and won their loyalty—but the remaining sons of David's sister Zeruiah were better. Fearless, ruthless, using David's popularity as leverage, Joab and Abishai took advantage of every means—fair or foul—to strengthen the king's hand. Some battles they lost to Abner's sheer genius, but the setbacks only fueled Joab and Abishai's single-minded lust for power and vengeance.

Abner, too, was ambitious. Many suggest that his ultimate goal was the throne. Build the army, establish political allies, and, at the right moment, a quick knife jab through Esh-Baal's flab would make Abner a fitting successor to Saul. To support this theory, his detractors pointed to Rizpah, Saul's concubine.

Esh-Baal created a dust storm by accusing Abner of lying with Rizpah to secure power. (As we learned only too painfully years later, he who lays the king's wives and concubines sits on the throne.) Perhaps he had reason for his suspicions, perhaps not. Perhaps he felt Abner's breath on his throne and wanted to force him back.

No one really knows. Esh-Baal claimed one thing, Abner another. Abner was an honorable man, Esh-Baal was...Esh-Baal. Abner denied the accusation—strongly. "Am I a dog's head? For seven years I've held you upright, put you on the throne, and trained your army. I fought the house of David. To this day I've stayed loyal to the house of your father Saul. Yet you accuse me of bedding Saul's concubine? Me—the only friend Saul had? May God stick it to Abner if I do not give the Lord a hand in crushing the house of Saul and establishing David over Israel and Judah from north to south, from Dan to Beersheba. Esh-Baal—or Ish-Bosheth, man of shame—you jabbed the wrong bull this time!"

Esh-Baal said not another word, being just clever enough to measure Abner against himself.

Abner fumed only a few days before making his move.

Early in the month of Ethanim, David called together chief men from the towns to the north and south of Hebron. On thick, woven mats in the cool heart of the palace around massive bowls of fruit, these clan chiefs discussed their defensive needs with David and his military advisors. Loudly. Emphatically.

David listened patiently. Because of their kindness to him and his men in those early years of flight from Saul, he wanted them to feel safe—and grateful. He listed off the garrisons he had posted. "Some of my best men are out there—" He broke off as a young man came through the doorway. "What is it, Benaiah?" Annoyance tinged his words.

The young man bowed nervously. "A runner is here, my lord. He will not say—"

"Later. If it's important enough, he'll wait. An interruption of this sort, Benaiah—"

"My lord." Benaiah understood the precipice he stood on, but something drove him to the edge. "He's come a long way, a two-day run—most likely from the northeast."

"Then give him two days' worth of food and let him sleep two—" He stopped and looked more closely at the young man. "You know more than you're saying, Benaiah."

"I don't *know*, my lord, but I *think*—"

"You're thinking perhaps a message from Mahanaim, which is northeast. From Esh-Baal or Abner. Is that what you're thinking?"

"He will not say—to me, at least."

"But your bones tell you…"

"Yes, lord, my bones."

David looked back at the chief men, then at Benaiah with a fierceness that shook the lad. "All right, get your bones out of here and fetch this runner. If the message turns out to be of little consequence, keep your bones out of my sight."

Benaiah knew he'd won his gamble when David sized up the spent runner. The soldier bowed, then stood with an air of pride. This was no common messenger. Although slight of build, his intelligence, alertness, plus the scars and muscles of his arms spoke of his competence as a warrior—perhaps even an uncommon warrior. He had the severe, almost unsettling air of a man whose every effort would be dedicated to the performance of duty. David glanced at Benaiah and raised a whimsical eyebrow. "Our court nuisance judges well," he murmured to no one in particular. He addressed the runner. "You come from Abner." He did not make it a question.

"Yes, my lord." His eyes met David's with the same confidence.

Those eyes were joltingly serious, and, almost in self-defense, David took his arm. "Come sit down. You've traveled far and carry words heavy with importance. A bit of a wash first, then something to eat." The king snapped his fingers, setting in motion a cadre of servants bearing water and towels and a jar of oil. After offering fruit to the runner, David drew him apart from the still-arguing tribal leaders.

"Now," he said, "what word has Abner for us?"

The *gibbor* bowed formally, then recited his message. "My lord the commander acknowledges the long, bitter struggle between Israel's factions. 'And after all this shoving back and forth,' he instructed me to say, 'just whose land is it in the end? We've accomplished little but the spilling of blood. But now,' my lord Abner says, 'if you'll make an agreement with me, I'll bring all Israel over to you.'" The runner bowed, then stood tall and looked David in the eye.

David's eyebrows arched at this. He stood silently, measuring this fearless soldier. "What's your name, young man?" he finally asked. "You'll either be a formidable enemy one day or a powerful friend. Either way, we need to become acquainted."

"I am Uriah the Hittite."

"Uriah the Hittite, while I talk this over with my friends here, Benaiah will take you off for something more than figs and a nap to carry you back to Mahanaim."

David sent the visiting chiefs off to eat, as well, and he and his men stayed in the room to discuss this new development. Joab paced the perimeter of the group, growling occasionally but refusing to say what ailed him. David eyed him suspiciously.

In the end he sent for Uriah. "Tell your master yes; I will make an agreement with him to join all Israel into one nation. One thing I demand, however: I want the daughter of Saul back as my wife. She cost me a hundred Philistine foreskins, with an extra hundred thrown in. Do you know how much blood that involves, Uriah?"

"Yes, my lord, I do." The young man did not flinch.

"You're made of stern stuff, lad. Stern enough to tell Abner not to even think of coming to me without Michal. Now, Uriah." He put his hand on the young warrior's shoulder. "Take that message to your master, and repeat it to Esh-Baal, as well. After all," he said, turning and grinning at his companions, "he's the man in charge, isn't he?"

Except for an acknowledgment that the message had been received, David heard nothing from Abner for months. For one thing, Michal's remarriage to Paltiel *ben* Laish complicated the matter of giving her back to David. Michal herself drove off the first emissaries from Abner with fire and spit. After that, Abner placed the affair in the hands of Esh-Baal. "She's your sister. Now do your part."

Esh-Baal squirmed and protested but eventually ordered his personal guard to take his sister away—with Abner in attendance. This gave him the small satisfaction of not having to speak to her personally, and the larger satisfaction of annoying Abner.

The removal required a small army—one platoon to secure Michal, another to fend off the distraught husband. Finally, after three miles of listening to the loud laments of Paltiel, Abner placed his own formidable face in front of the man. "Enough! If you follow us beyond Bahurim, I'll throw you across the Kidron Valley to the Jebusites. Now go home. Michal was David's before she was yours, and a king has every right to his wife. Although why he'd want a lioness in his bed… Go, Paltiel. Go back home. Take a wife you can handle. The daughter of Saul is two sizes too large for you."

Abner had a few other chores and an interruption to tend to before he could return to David. The interruption came in the form of a sullen-looking visitor.

"Yes?" said Abner impatiently.

"My lord, I am Sheba *ben* Bicri, a Benjamite connected with David's army."

Abner could make only flitting contact with the young man's cold, elusive eyes.

"I'll come straight to the point. Rumor has it you may abandon the house of Saul. If you do, what would become of Benjamin? A small tribe, convenient only for David to wipe his feet on. And even more to the point, what would become of Israel? You're cousin to Saul and legitimately in line for the throne. If you would hold on a bit longer, my lord, time and David's enemies will again lift up the house of Saul."

Abner examined this hood-eyed insurrectionist and his beard-parting scar. "I presume you consider yourself one of David's enemies. And you want a preferred seat in this new house of Saul?"

Sheba met Abner's appraisal with a directness that was sharp as flint. "I am for the good of Israel, my lord, not the good of Sheba. And I have infinite patience." With that, he bowed and turned away.

Abner watched his deliberate, unhurried step. "If Sheba *ben* Bicri remains in David's army," he murmured, "David had better look to his life somewhere down the road." He then shrugged off the intrusion and returned to the problems at hand.

Tribal elders from all over Israel came to Mahanaim—heads of tribes, heads of families, long and white of beard, heavy with wisdom. They came to the palace, a building more impressive than Saul's house in Gibeah but not as grand as Esh-Baal would have liked. The pillows Abner propped him with were austere at best. The elders filed into the great room, smoky with wall sconces and fire pots. Abner greeted them with his advisors, military leaders, and personal guard arranged impressively behind. To his right and left stood Baanah and Recab, chiefs of his raiding bands.

After the protocol of hospitality, Abner got down to business. "Many years ago," he said, "some of you wanted to make David your king. You saw his military skill, the quality of his leadership, his loyalty to God. You argued that Saul's weakness would become Israel's weakness. Perhaps you were right. David has grown. He's demonstrated his ability to defend the nation and to govern its people." He looked each man in the eye. "He is, after all, Saul's son-in-law and wants to be re-united with his wife Michal. This, in effect, realigns him with the house of Saul, giving us the best of both political spheres." Heads nodded; Abner straightened.

"David's time has come, my friends. The Lord himself promised, 'By my servant David I will rescue my people Israel from the hand of the Philistines and from the hand of all their enemies.' I urge you now to seize the moment and make David your king."

The elders were more receptive than Abner had dared to hope. One obvious question arose, however. What would become of Esh-Baal?

Abner snorted. "Esh-Baal will continue being Esh-Baal—if he minds his own business." He looked at Baanah and Recab. "I can't imagine him doing otherwise."

After discussion that was basically pro forma, the elders gave Abner authority to pursue the matter with David.

As the meeting ended, Abner drew aside the elders of Benjamin. Arguably, they had the most to lose, as Sheba had suggested. Because the seat of power had already moved from Gibeah of Benjamin to Mahanaim across the Jordan, this new shift of governance from Israel to Judah could bring at least indifference and perhaps disgrace to Saul's tribe. But the elders of Benjamin had lost patience with Esh-Baal. They knew only too well just how flimsy the throne on which the "man of shame" sat.

Satisfied, Abner turned his face toward Hebron. He now had his arrows trimmed and in his quiver. He was ready to approach David.

21

So, Joab." David turned from a lengthy conference with two chief counselors—Ahithophel and his uncle Jonathan—to address the taut impatience that had been wearing a track around the perimeter of the room. His general did not wait gladly.

When David spoke, Joab spun angrily, tripping over his armor bearer Naharai, who had been napping beneath the window. David's irritation matched Joab's. "Must you prowl my walls like you need to pee? Who are you raiding today?"

"We'll be lucky to get out of here before dark."

"The sun's been up all of an hour. If you wanted to leave before dawn, why didn't you talk to me last night? How many men have you got?"

"About three hundred. And Abishai."

"That's all?"

Joab's jaw flexed. "I should need more?"

"Where are you headed?"

"Downhill."

David smacked the paneling next to the window, and Naharai scrambled for cover.

"All right, all right," said Joab petulantly. "I'm heading for Jebus. That nest of jackals in their thick-walled den annoys me."

"You expect to bring down an inaccessible fortress with three hundred men, hmm? Well, don't forget pack animals this time. The last raid—"

"That was incompetence, and I won't say whose. I don't take pack animals. Jebusites have pack animals. Enough for all the booty and more besides."

David did not ask how he planned to get more booty than "all."

Mid-morning the next day, the watchman on the Hebron city wall called down a small dust in the distance. At the same time, a runner arrived to say that Abner with twenty men and assorted servants were approaching Hebron. "And," he added, "a lady rides a chair."

The news galvanized David. With a hurried apology to visiting musicians (one of whom was Heman), he ran through the house, roaring, "Abigail! I need you!"

By the time Abner actually arrived, three animals had been butchered for a feast. A small army of servants waited inside the cool antechamber with water jars, basins and towels, and a vessel of oil for parched skin and hair. David greeted Abner warmly, then moved outside to assist the woman from her canopied chair.

"Michal," he said, his voice husky and unsure. "You are welcome in my home."

Michal said nothing, and only when she lost balance getting out of the chair would she accept his hand. He could see little of her veiled face. Her haughty stiffness, though, gave a clear message, and David was happy to turn her over to Abigail at the door.

I myself met Michal only once, some fifteen years later. I talked with her at length, largely because she would otherwise have had to talk with David or Abigail, neither of whom was acceptable just then. She was no longer young at that time, and dye hid strands of gray. She bore the proud mark of Saul with fitting elegance, but her eyes held the hardness of Saul's latter years, without the madness. In many ways she was David's opposite and equal, and thus they could not talk. No one would disavow her dark, spicy beauty. But beauty or no, David's loyalty to Saul and his house seldom extended to that particular bedroom. Whether they ever again had relations I cannot say, but Michal bore no children, and I believe that to be the hand of the Lord.

David welcomed Abner and his chief men and ushered them to a room less formal than the one in which he normally received delegations. It was comfortably appointed with two chairs for the principals and assorted cushions and skins for the others. Bowls of fruit were brought, along with choice meats and skins of wine.

"You have come." David smiled at his guest. "With Michal."

"Yes. With Michal." Abner's mouth twitched. "A hornet for your lambing pen."

David laughed. "So. You have felt her sting."

"I happily turn her over to her rightful place. I'd as soon bed a viper."

David listened closely to Abner's report of his meeting with the elders of Israel and of Benjamin in particular. "You have done well. What about Esh-Baal?"

Abner snorted contemptuously. "As long as you keep food in his trough and dancers in his bedroom, Ish-Bosheth won't be a problem. I'm guessing he won't last long. No, not by my hand," he replied to David's sharp look. "I'll make every effort to keep him alive, but…" He shrugged ambiguously.

"You've laid the groundwork. What's left to do?" asked David.

"I'll assemble all Israel so they can make a compact with you. They're ready, eager, and nothing should prevent you from ruling over all that your heart—and your army—can manage."

The afternoon was spent feasting and dancing. David sang songs full of joy and praise and hope for the future of Israel. Abigail had seen to a munificent table, with course after course of the finest food and wine she could command. She also found room for all to bed down, and, in the morning, a pleased Abner and his men prepared to return to Mahanaim. "Go in peace," said David. "We two have eaten bread and salt; next step, doing the same with the assemblage in Israel. Safe journey."

Just after Abner's departure, Joab and Abishai returned with their raiding party after two nights away, in high spirits and toiling under booty beyond what their stolen pack animals could comfortably carry.

"What've you got?" Benaiah was first to greet the victorious raiders.

"Gold! Ivory! Fine robes! Not from Jebusites, may they rot in Sheol, but from—" Joab broke off on hearing music from inside the king's house. Hooded eyes noted servants in festive attire hauling out the remains of revelry. "What's going on here?"

"Abner came with his chief men. They just left. Didn't you pass them?"

"We weren't on the road. What was Abner doing here?"

"He brought Michal back."

"Oh, did he?" The words came out viciously.

Benaiah, ignorant of the implications of Joab's left eye, spoke only of matters impressive to a young lad. "A lot of talk, and the food! They ate bread and salt, exchanged gifts, and the king sent him off in peace."

Joab looked at his brother Abishai, then wheeled and headed for the palace door. He found David dancing arm in arm with assorted comrades.

> *Restore our fortunes,*
> *O Holy One of Israel.*
> *Let Jacob rejoice and Israel be glad!"*

Even the stately Ahithophel swayed perceptibly.

From the doorway, Joab deftly captured David and pulled him into an adjoining room, making no effort to disguise his wrath.

"Abner was here, I'm told. In your hands. Right here. And you let him go!"

David, flushed from dancing, turned wine red with anger. "Of course I let him go. He came in peace. He brought Michal back. He's done everything needed to turn all Israel over to me. Isn't that reason enough to let him go?"

Joab strode up and down. "I go off on a raid and come back only to find that Abner *ben* Ner slips in and out without a hand lifted against him. Have you no sense? Abner is out to deceive you. He brought Michal back, but why not? She's not exactly an asset to anyone. I suppose you told him my movements, your talks with clan leaders. You might as well've handed yourself over." He stalked to the window, then spun around fiercely. "He was *here*, right here! Now he's gone!"

David was too angry to speak, and, after a moment, Joab stalked from the house and roared, "Benaiah! Zebadiah *ben* Asahel is at the gate. Get him." He made a visible effort to lighten his tone. "I want the two of you to go after Abner. He can't have gone far. Tell him—"

Benaiah stared. "You're sending Zebadiah after the man who killed his father?"

"Abner's a general, and generals kill. That's their job. Zebadiah better get used to it. And I want him here. David forgot to explain something crucial to the arrangements. The rest of the retinue needn't return. This won't take long. Bring him back in less than an hour and you'll have your pick of the booty. Now, hurry!"

Zebadiah had his father's speed, as well as a couple of years on Benaiah, and the latter pushed hard just to keep him in view. In no time, they caught sight of the group gathered around the well of Sirah, a mile and a half beyond Hebron's city gate.

When Abner returned to Hebron, Joab met him at the gate and grasped his beard to kiss him. "Sorry I was out when you got here. We were out rounding up Amalekites."

"So I see," said Abner warily, one eye measuring the plunder being unloaded on the far side of the square, the other Joab's frame of mind. "You hit a good caravan."

"Yes." Joab laughed and listed the more unusual pieces they'd taken.

"So." He looked directly at Abner and spoke agreeably. "The war's over at last, eh? I understand you brought the lioness back. How'd you manage that? The question is, what can David possibly do with her, now he's got her?"

"His problem—now happily off my hands. Between her and Esh-Baal—"

"Ah, Esh-Baal! The second mouthful of hot soup for David to swallow."

The two laughed, and Joab leaned toward Abner with a conspiratorial air. "Esh-Baal—or does everybody call him 'man of shame' now? Tell me, what should we know about this bleary-eyed, slobbering, pink-faced turnip?" Eyes twinkling, Joab drew Abner toward one of the defensive chambers flanking the gateway, as though to allow for a frank answer. And there in the shadows, congenial smile still camouflaging his intentions, Joab drove an ivory-handled dagger into Abner's belly.

Abner's eyes swelled in comprehension as he slumped slowly. Joab's face, convivial mask stripped away, followed Abner's to the ground. "Brother Asahel is avenged!" he whispered.

I've always felt cheated. I did have the satisfaction of seeing Joab's dead body on the altar steps, but even that could never match the lyrical sweetness I might have experienced in watching him walk with torn sackcloth in front of Abner's bier. The grand finale of humiliation. The one time in his nefarious career when Joab was totally in check.

Joab should have been cut down on the spot. His brother's death at Abner's hand was clearly an act of self-defense in the context of battle; Abner's death was outright murder. David had executed other men for far less. Joab, though, had calculated carefully. He knew that David's ambitions rested almost solely on the genius of his commander in chief. At that moment especially, on the brink of political union with Israel, Joab was not dispensable. He would live to kill again.

When David was told of Abner's untimely end and at whose hand, only his uncle Jonathan was bold enough to remain in the room. Benaiah was there, too, but he was not standing against David's fury. He lay on the floor in a corner, broken. It was he who had run after Abner, he who had unknowingly led him into a trap. He'd heard Joab's joking tone, watched the two men turn to the cubicle; he'd observed Abner crumple, seen the bloodied ivory in Joab's hand. His brain, however, couldn't process the components. That Abner had been murdered finally registered, but, instead of turning on Joab, whom he could in no way affect, he had seized on Zebadiah *ben* Asahel, who was drinking from a borrowed skin, oblivious of the turn of events. "You killed him!" Benaiah shrieked. "You killed Abner as sure as if you held the knife! When Joab sent us after Abner, you knew he'd do this, and because Abner killed your father, you let it happen!"

Zebadiah turned white, his eyes glazed. The world and the sudden horror Benaiah had thrust upon him retreated to a point far in the distance. He knew only his own raging grief over a dead father, to which had suddenly been added a mysterious new dimension of personal involvement. He lay where Benaiah hurled him, writhing in silent agony.

Benaiah hurried to David. He knew how the king would react, and he wanted—he needed—to be assaulted by a fury greater than his own. David's anger seemed somehow to atone for his own complicity. The king's words—along with chairs and pottery—thundered off the walls and beat around him like sling stones ricocheting off trees. The storm moved away as David exploded through the courtyard toward the city gate. Benaiah lay alone in the clotting silence that sought to staunch his emotional wound.

Word spread, and people from all over the city ran toward the gate. They saw Joab, the gore on his arm signifying less than the gore on his legs. "*I will walk in your blood!*" he had roared that day of the face-off as he bent over his brother's body.

He had his blood and now stood silent and stony as David, backed by Jashobeam, Ira, Shammah, and Eleazar, addressed the people. "Abner." His voice was stiff with anger. "See him lying there. Look at the blood. Feel it. Smell it. It's not ordinary blood. That's the blood of Abner *ben* Ner, cousin of King Saul, brought down, not nobly in battle, but by treachery. Noble blood made vile, wretched.

"Look at this man, covered with the blood of Abner *ben* Ner. What he's done can never be washed away. These stones will be stained until his own blood cleanses them. *This act of treachery is not of my doing.* I and my kingdom are forever innocent before the Lord concerning Abner's blood. May the full weight of that blood fall on the head of Joab *ben* Zeruiah and on his house. May Joab's house never be without running sores or leprosy or disability or sword or famine. *Joab, may you not die in peace!*" The stunned silence that followed this dreadful curse was in itself appalling, and David was not quick to break it.

Finally, though, he gave the order for Abner's body to be prepared for burial, then turned once more to Joab. "You will tear your clothes and put on sackcloth and walk in mourning in front of Abner." He moved to within an inch of Joab's face. "*You will do this.*" No one doubted that this command would be obeyed.

Within two hours the body had been washed and clothed in the garb of a victorious warrior, hands and feet wrapped in linen cloth and another cloth over the face. The men waiting for Abner at the well of Sirah had been informed and brought back. When all was in readiness, David bent and selected a stone as though that were part of getting ready, as though a stone might arm him against a foe as yet undefined. He then gave the signal, and the bier was hoisted on eight shoulders. The entire city moved out, wailing like jackals, a thousand sistrums emitted their ghostly rattle of bone against bone. Joab walked alone in front of the bier, David behind, followed by those who had accompanied Abner to Hebron. Joab did as he'd been instructed, tearing sackcloth, beating his breast, scooping up dust to coat his hair. His face, though, remained a mask, his movements wooden. Abishai stayed as close to his brother as propriety allowed, his own eyes smoldering coals. Had he a hand in Abner's death? No one could say for sure, but he showed no surprise when told the news.

Hard by a vineyard with its thick, cumbrous aroma of ripening grapes, a tomb appropriate for a *gibbor* had been prepared, and as the body was laid within. Carefully and almost as an afterthought, David placed his stone at Abner's right hand and wept aloud. As the tomb was closed, he sang this lament:

> *Should Abner have died as the lawless die?*
> *Your hands were not bound,*
> *Your feet not fettered.*
> *You fell as one falls before wicked men.*

He drew a wordless, rich-textured improvisation out of the nascent wine of grief and vine, his own emotion playing off that of the mourners. In a way only David could accomplish, the lament pulled nearly everyone into mass weeping, naturally and without manipulation. At that moment it could not have been otherwise.

The leaders of Israel approved. David's response to the tragedy had been right and good. This heartfelt act of mourning the death of a fine general and nobleman did more to endear him to the hearts of Israel than any other bit of diplomacy. Within weeks the kingdom was ratified, unified, firmly in hand.

23

"They're too strong for me, Benaiah. These sons of Zeruiah are too strong."

David had sent his men from the room. He wanted to be alone. Whether he had not noticed Benaiah hunched in the corner, or whether the young man was too inconsequential for him to care about one way or the other, Benaiah had not been asked to leave.

"Do you understand, Benaiah, that a prince and a great man has fallen in Israel this day? Can you grasp that?"

"Yes, my lord."

"Tell me what it means."

For a moment, Benaiah wished he'd left with the others. Still sore from his own hand in the death of Abner and from his unwarranted treatment of Zebadiah, he wasn't hankering for a quirky conversation with the king right now. He'd rather just hurt in silence. He rubbed his ears. What could he say? What should he say? Yes, Joab was a scoundrel? David should have opened Joab's belly in retaliation? Did David expect a reply, or was he simply thinking out loud? Benaiah chewed his lip. He decided on something general, a truism. "May the Lord repay the evildoer according to his evil deeds."

David looked at him as though to fathom such an obvious statement. "May the Lord repay the evildoer according to his evil deeds," he repeated. "Yes, Benaiah, but who is the evildoer? Joab? Or am I the evildoer for needing Joab, depending on him, for not wanting to put him down? Look what he's done. He's put the fear of God into Moabites, Edomites, Amalekites, and even Philistines. None of these are in our pouch yet, but now, with the whole nation coming behind us, it's a matter of time. And sooner or later, we'll get the Ammonites and Arameans. But that's *with* Joab. He's sheer genius, Benaiah. Abner was a great general, but Joab's extraordinary. Abner could stand up to him, but he couldn't beat him. He gave it all he had but then bowed to reality."

"But there's you," said Benaiah. "You're not exactly ordinary in battle, my lord. You know just where to move, how to attack, and it works. All the men say so. It's not just Joab."

David nodded. "Perhaps so," he replied slowly. "I am a good warrior. God has trained my hands for battle, put strength in my arms. Have you ever tried to bend a bronze bow, Benaiah?" He chewed his lip. "It's the two of us working together. As a team we're three times as good at making war than either of us alone. And conceivably, with that combination, we could bring down every nation this side of the Great River in Mesopotamia. But what does it all hinge on? A rotting sling instead of a bronze bow."

Benaiah watched the king's restless energy drive him around the room, heedless of cushions or stray bowls. "My lord," Benaiah said finally, "just before the others left, you said you were the anointed king. When Samuel chose...anointed you way back, what happened? What did he say?"

David stopped pacing and drew a sharp breath as though he'd been hit. Then he snorted. "You know Samuel...no, you didn't know Samuel. Be grateful for that. A white, testy lion. God's man, and other men feared God in his presence. The day he came, he went through my brothers and waited while someone dragged me from a far pasture. At first he saw only the runt, but then with something like astonishment he opened his vial and poured the oil. I don't recall his actual words—some ritualized blessing—but I remember the spicy smell. And I got the message: from then on, the focus of a dusty, smart-mouthed youngster needed to shift from tending sheep to tending a nation—a remote, nebulous responsibility I couldn't begin to comprehend."

"That was it? Nothing else happened? He didn't give you anything? You just went back out to the sheep?"

"I went back, but not *just*. I didn't understand the calling but felt that Samuel knew what he was doing. All that night I stayed awake, feeling God sort through my muscles, my bones, my head. Almost as though I were being rebuilt to make room for His Spirit. I'd been set aside for a special role, but how it would work out I had no idea."

"So you felt God in you right from the beginning."

"From that day the Spirit was on me. I had power. Not the sort that runs in my family. Most of my brothers were as strong or stronger than I'll ever be. I could *do* things, *feel* things, *know* things they'll never know. The face-off with Goliath, for instance. A clever bit of action on my part, yes. But I *knew* just what to do. My love for the Lord was so powerful right then, I couldn't have done otherwise."

"Do you feel that love now?"

David stopped pacing and looked sharply at Benaiah. Then he stared out the window. Finally, almost as though he were ignoring the question, he said, "I was anointed king of Israel. I was to shepherd God's people. How many times did I doubt that? Those years in the wilderness, running till I coughed blood, tired, hungry, desperate, responsible for six hundred men and their families. No, I didn't feel much love for God at those times. But I did it. I did what I had to, and somehow God gave me strength to get through."

"You did what you had to."

Again David looked at him. "Yes." An odd look came over his face. "I did what I had to." He stepped toward Benaiah and, wrapping his arms around the young man, began to weep. In later years, Benaiah tried to describe to me the sudden warmth that flooded his body under this embrace, as though his blood had been removed and heated in the sun and then put back in his veins. "I felt God in David's arms, Asaph." Under this and the emotion of the day, he too wept.

"Thank you, Benaiah. I have need of you." David stood back and cupped his hands around the lad's head. "I want you to leave me."

The boy started to pull away, but David held him.

"I want you to go wherever you want, for as long as you want, and become a man of discipline, of loyalty, of strength. I want you to pull together a unit of men you can trust and work with. Then I want you to come back and serve me." He watched

Benaiah's eyes widen. "I am as certain of this as I was of God's Spirit on the day of my anointing. You will be my right arm, and you will help me keep Joab in check. He's ruthless. He'll stop at nothing to retain his position. He'll deny it till he dies, but I know that Joab's fear of losing his position—not blood vengeance—was what killed Abner. And by all that's holy, if another Abner comes along, Joab will be out of work."

He turned the boy around. "Go, Benaiah, and may the Lord be your power until we meet again."

It has often been said that Ish-Bosheth's response to any crisis was to take a nap.

By nightfall, word of Abner's death had gotten back to Mahanaim. Ish-Bosheth had already bedded down, and Baanah and Recab, whom Abner had left to guard the king, could not think of a single reason why he should be awakened. If he was able to sleep through the wailing throughout the city, then he definitely needed his sleep. Morning would come soon enough.

Morning did come, and Ish-Bosheth, on hearing the news, could do nothing more than alternately run panic-stricken through the palace or cling to Recab, a quivering mass. The palace, of course, could not contain such a show, and soon all Israel became alarmed. Abner was dead. The king was reduced to yogurt. An accord had not been fully negotiated with David, and now what would he do?

Baanah and Recab were probably the only two men in the countryside who were not concerned. They were brothers, sons of Rimmon from the tribe of Benjamin. They knew how each other thought—and they had a plan.

They knew Ish-Bosheth; they knew that when his frenzy ran down, he would take to his bed. They had not long to wait.

Normally on entering the palace, they would have no cause to go beyond the outer rooms, but they invented a need for some wheat and carried a bag upstairs as though headed for the storage room on the roof.

They didn't go to the storeroom, however. They slipped instead into the bedroom that was lending Ish-Bosheth the last bit of comfort he would have in this life. A battle-callused hand over his mouth, a quick stab to the region of his heart, and Ish-Bosheth joined his father and brothers.

Baanah and Recab did not dawdle over sentiment. They separated head from body, stuffed it into the bag along with their own bloodied cloaks, then sloshed water over their hands before walking calmly from the "storeroom" with their bag of "wheat."

They traveled all night by way of the Arabah, that desolate, lion-infested valley of the Jordan and Salt Sea. They arrived at Hebron before David was even up, but their wait was easily borne in anticipation of the king's good pleasure. When finally given audience, they bowed and said, "My lord, we bring a gift—the head of Ish-Bosheth, son of your enemy Saul. This day the Lord has avenged my lord the king against Saul and his offspring." They drew their grisly offering from the bag and held it high in pride.

David sucked air, his face stone hard. He walked around the display. "Am I correct in assuming you did this?" he asked them. "You and no one else?"

"Yes, my lord. Yesterday at midday while the king napped." Their chests swelled.

David kept his voice even as though explaining a simple matter to dullards. "I don't think you understand. A man came to me at Ziklag to tell me Saul was dead. He thought he was bringing good news. I had him put to death—his reward."

He increased the pace of his circling. "And now you come, expecting reward. As surely as the Lord lives, who has faithfully delivered me from trouble, you killed an innocent man in his own house and on his own bed. Esh-Baal was utterly incapable of posing a threat to anyone, yet you killed him. How much more should I now rid the earth of you?"

Pride dissolved in Baanah and Recab. They had little time to regret their deed, however. David nodded to his guardsmen, and the two were taken out to be killed. Their hands and feet were cut off and their bodies hung by the pool to the east of the spring so no one would even suggest that David had anything to do with the death of Saul's son. They buried Ish-Bosheth's head with honor in Abner's tomb at Hebron.

During the week of mourning, life in Hebron stood still—waiting. David refused to meet with diplomatic envoys; no raiding bands went out. Joab remained in disgrace, his future as David's commander in chief in jeopardy. The Mighty Men kept to themselves, not out of pique but with a quickening sense that something akin to birth was about to happen.

It did. At week's end, the watchman on the wall cried out the approach of a large body of men, not military in nature. The city awoke. Within minutes, David appeared at the gate attired in his most regal, purple-trimmed robe, made by Abigail for just such occasions. Tribal representatives from all Israel, their servants bearing gifts of gold and leading fine breeding stock for David's flocks, approached the king and bowed low.

This was only the beginning. Men armed for battle appeared by the thousands from every tribe—Dan in the north, Reuben, Gad and half of Manasseh east of the Jordan, and the other tribes in between. Day after day they streamed in, all of a single mind.

A grizzled man of Benjamin, clothed in stripes and scars, stood forth to speak for the vast host. "My lord, we are your flesh and blood. You grew up among us. While Saul was king, you brought victory to Israel in military campaigns. You gave us music, you gave us laughter, you gave us hope that our sons and daughters would no longer be carried off by Philistines or Amalekites. Through the prophet Samuel the Lord said to you, 'You will shepherd my people Israel; you will become their ruler.' And God made you king.

"But now, my lord, we beseech you to rule beyond Judah. We, the men of Benjamin and Naphtali and Simeon and of all Israel, offer ourselves as liege subjects. Be our king, too, O lord, if you will."

David, in all solemnity, looked into the eyes of the tribal leaders, one by one. Then he bowed with his face to the ground. When he raised himself, still on his knees, he said, "I will. As God prepared Moses to lead his people out of Egypt, so may he give your servant grace and strength to establish his chosen land." He leaped to his feet and with a dazzling smile embraced the startled elders.

The next day, they met to iron out the details of the compact before the Lord and to eat the bread and salt. The following day, Abiathar again poured the sacred oil, anointing David king over all Israel. Samuel's twenty-two-year promise had at last been fulfilled.

Great joy erupted, and for three days they feasted and sang. At long last, he was *Hamelech David*—high king of all Israel, nourished by the blessing of God and the love of his people!

Hebron had been an ideal capital city for Judah, perched as it was on the north-south highway that traced the spine of the hill country. It seemed less appropriate, though, as capital for a united Israel. "Jebus," said David. "That's the place."

"Makes perfect sense," said his friend Hushai, "especially if you want to whittle down your army by half. Nothing like a good bloodbath now and then. And what'll you have in the end after you've paid the price? No city. Ask Joab. He's prowled Jebus time and again. The Millo fortress is untakable."

"I don't ask Joab anything," growled David. "Jebus is the place. More centrally located. On the border of Benjamin. Doesn't belong to either Judah or Benjamin, so neither Judah nor Israel will feel slighted. And it would be highly defensible."

"Once you get in. David, you can't *get* in."

"If it's the right place, Hushai, we *will* get in. Sure, it's a viperish nest of Canaanites, and they've held the citadel for who knows how many hundreds of years. Up to now, no one's thought it worth the price of knocking down their door." He sat back and smiled. "Now it's worthwhile. We'll get it, Hushai. It's the place."

A dust-covered runner bowed low before Achish in the Philistine city of Gath. "O my king," he said, "I bring word that David has been anointed ruler over all Israel. Abner is dead, Esh-Baal is dead, the elders of the tribe of Saul and the other northern tribes have struck palms with David. He—"

Achish shook the table with a mighty whack. "By the gods of land and sea, I'll carve out his liver! Double-dealing blackguard! Achish fell for his charm once, but he'll feel the thrust of Achish's sword before the month is out. Before he has a chance to test the weight of his crown, he'll lack a head to rest it on. How long since the anointing?"

"I'm not sure. I got my information third or fourth hand. I ran all the way from Keilah, that there be no further delay."

"Well done." The thickset, battle-scarred monarch stalked the perimeter of the room, mouth pulling his cheek within chewing range. "We must attack, of course, as soon as possible, before he builds strength. He's got an army and a half already—damn him! And throw in Abner's men…" He swung around. "Yes…what's your name? We've got to stop him immediately. Will he move his capital from Hebron? Well fortified, but too far south. Maybe Gibeon…or will he take over Mahanaim now that Abner's of the picture?"

"Or…Jebus?"

"Jebus! Last place in the world. Ideal if he could get in, but…" He narrowed one eye at the flat-bellied, tightly ordered, inordinately handsome runner who moved with the ease of youth and inbred authority. "Why would you suggest Jebus?"

The man shrugged. "My source didn't actually mention Jebus..."

"But you heard something."

"Yes...something." He drew a nervous breath, understanding that he could be either making his career or shortening it precipitously. "An unlikely source, but...sometimes the unlikely...."

"Yes, yes. Get on with it. What have you heard?"

The runner took another breath. "*Rumor* has it that David will try to take Jebus. Just casual conversation, mind you. My informant said the Israelite god would deliver the Millo into David's hands. Look what their god had already done, he said: got them out of Egypt, razed Jericho, pushed Canaanites back to places like Philistia and Jebus." The runner prudently left out the part about David outsmarting Achish. "Maybe he was making it up. Who knows?"

"Faugh! Obnoxious Israelites and their pesky god. There's no pleasing them. What we think is holy they say is despicable. They fuss about what they eat, what they touch, what they wear. And try to get them to fight on the last day of the week, uh...your name again? You think the Israelite god will tear Jebus apart?"

"What I believe doesn't matter. What does David believe? The name is Ittai, my lord."

"Yes. Ittai. From where?"

"Right here. From Gath, my lord."

"Yes. A bright, good-looking young lad like you should be in my army."

"I am, my lord. I command a regiment. I dressed as a civilian to escape notice. And to strike up conversations."

"Commanders send runners; they don't carry messages themselves."

"This was important, my lord. I run well."

Tension knotted the army when word went out about the offensive against Jebus. With Joab in disgrace, everything was out of joint. Abishai and his men were sand in everyone's eyes. Where would the other generals line up? David himself would lead the assault, but exactly how would the army rank behind him?

The most level heads belonged to the Three—Jashobeam, Eleazar, and Shammah. They circulated among the troops, putting out fires. The Three consulted long with Uriah the Hittite, whom David had specifically enlisted after Abner's assassination as a possible addition to his elite cadre of Mighty Men. Uriah had once dwelt among Jebusites and knew their ways. "They're coarse and cruel," he said. "They sometimes force cripples to the top of the wall. They torment them, get them screaming, then holler down at the invaders, 'See our fierce defenders!' Above the north gate, they say, is an obscene Baal idol with a huge pearl at the end of its penis. Represents a man's seed, they say. Fertility. The idol watches over the city, presumably squirting seed on every woman who goes in or out."

When Ira heard the Baal story, he felt drawn by its obscenity. "Maybe, Asaph," he said to me later, "the only difference between us and pagans is that we know how bad we are and walk the path to the fire with our bulls and lambs to ask God's forgiveness."

By dawn, the entire army, some ten thousand strong, was lined and ready when David strode to the fore. His bronze armor was burnished to challenge the rising sun; his sword and sling hung at his belt. His armor bearers held the great and small shields, bronze and regular bows, quivers, and spears. David was in his prime, fully alive. As he leaped onto a rock to address his men, the sun struck fire off his thick hair. He stood looking over the assembly in one of those magic, hold-your-breath moments, then lifted his face and plunged, trumpet-tongued, into a song of battle.

> *O Lord, the king rejoices in your strength.*
> *He trusts in the unfailing love of the Most High*
> *and will not be shaken.*
> *Be exalted, O Lord, in your strength;*
> *On the day of battle,*
> *we will sing and praise your might.*

He paused and looked across the vast army. Then, his arms piercing the heavens, he bellowed,

> *The Lord reigns forever;*
> *He has established his throne for judgment.*
> *He will demolish his enemies' strongholds!*
> *Rise up, O Lord;*
> *Rise up like a lion for the service of the Lord!*
> *May your enemies be scattered;*
> *May your foes flee before you.*

A roar went up. The Lord was in charge of David, David was in charge of the army, and they could dislodge whatever nest of vipers they found in whatever rocky fortress.

David had one more thing to say. "Whoever breaks through to the Jebusites first will become commander in chief of the army of Israel!"

Joab, who day by day had prowled the encampment—though with remarkably little to say—bellowed back, "Does that 'whoever' mean whoever?"

For just a moment the light dimmed, but the ebullience of the day prevailed, "Yes, Joab, *whoever*. But in your case, toppling that idol over the gate would help. Now—*to Jebus!*"

"*To Jebus!*" roared the troops. The trumpets sounded, and the noise echoed down the stony slopes to the boulders below. The assault on Jebus had begun.

Abiathar, carrying his awkward bundle, felt deflated. "He might have consulted the ephod—for the sake of formality, if nothing else," he grumbled. The ephod *wanted* to be consulted; he felt sure of it.

A figure, cloaked from the heat of the day, slipped casually down a rocky slope until he was sure no one was paying attention. Then he ran. When he reached the hills east of Keilah, he threaded his way among dung-cooking fires until he reached a spear-bannered, black-skirted tent. Ducking inside, he bowed. "It's begun, lord king. David is headed for Jebus. He has prayed to his god, and none in Hebron doubts he will gain entrance."

"Thank you, Ittai. Well done. We'll give him more of a challenge at Jebus than he bargained for."

25

At Beth Zur they saw them, the Philistine army, a vast swarm of locusts. David went white. "Achish! I should have known he'd call his accounts sooner or later."

Abishai grunted. "He's had seven years. What's he been doing all this time?"

"Why shouldn't this be his time? New king setting off on a fool's quest. It's what I'd try in his sandals. Now what do we do? It looks like three, maybe four to one."

"We're on high ground, he's low. That helps some."

"Come, come, Abishai! Just sit here on the bare ridge waiting to be picked off?

"Well, what's your solution—run back to Hebron?"

David shook his head. "There's got to be another way. The wilderness, maybe…the old stronghold above En Gedi. It would give us time to plan." *And to consult the ephod,* he thought gloomily.

He turned decisively and began barking orders. As the army shifted direction, he called after Abishai. "Post a watch. I want to know if they'll follow or encamp somewhere else. I'm guessing Achish likes the desert even less than Saul did."

The Philistines settled southwest of Jebus in the Valley of Rephaim. It gave them excellent stance against David, should he decide to engage. If David didn't engage, then they could strut on whatever ground they wished. The army filled the slopes and overran two small villages.

David sat before the Lord in the hostile Judean wilderness. He had been careless. Caught up in the attack on Jebus in the pride of his strength, he had not observed the basic precaution of posting eyes and ears along the Philistine border. And he had not consulted the Lord concerning Jebus. He had assumed, and he had been wrong.

He sat long, the old heaviness of those fugitive years pressing hard.

> *Lord God, I plead for mercy.*
> *Trouble surrounds me.*
> *Sin plucks the strings of my heart,*
> *My heart drums holes in my chest.*
> *Lord, save me! Yahweh, help me quickly.*
> *May your love and truth be a wall around me.*
> *May this king who seeks my life*
> *Be shamed and confused;*
> *May he turn back in disgrace.*

He called for Abiathar and the ephod. Bracing himself against the unsettling tingle, David asked, "Shall I go and attack the Philistines? Will you hand them over to me?"

Abiathar bent trembling over the ephod. The answer came. "Go. I will hand the Philistines over to you."

David remained on his face, not moving. Abiathar began to wonder if he'd heard. But David sat up, an incipient calm working through lines of fatigue. "Get ready, Abiathar. Tell Abishai what the Lord says. He'll know what to do. I'm going to sleep."

At nightfall they moved out across the treacherous terrain, and before dawn the army was poised on the southeastern edge of civilization, ready to attack.

The scheme worked. The lightweight force posted by the Philistines where they least expected attack was easily breached, and the Israelites fell upon the main body like a flood. The surprise and fury of the attack touched off wholesale retreat, the Philistines abandoning even their war idols.

David did not go on to Jebus. For one thing, both Eleazar and the giant Shammah had been wounded. David himself got a nasty slice on his leg, and with the emotional drain of the unexpected Philistine offensive, they decided to wait at least a week before going out again. "Besides," said David, "I don't trust Achish. We don't need him driving chariots up our backs just when we're ready to take Jebus."

His instincts were right. In less than a week, Achish was back in the Rephaim Valley with an even larger force. This time, when David inquired of the Lord, he received a puzzling answer: "Do not go straight up, but circle behind and attack in front of the balsam trees. The sound of marching in the tops of the balsams is your signal to move quickly. It means the Lord is in front of you, already striking the Philistines."

Knowing that Philistine scouts would be watching this time, David sent a small force into the wilderness as though the army would duplicate its earlier maneuver. The major body split off and circled around Jebus until they came to the balsam wood near Gibeon. David and Abishai crept to where they could observe the Philistine army. "It's working!" David breathed. "They're down valley, waiting for us. Let's get back to the woods," he said, grinning. "We don't want those treetops to march without us."

Abishai grunted derisively. "Treetops! A crazy—"

"Look!" David pointed, his voice tightening. "The treetops *are* marching; the men are grabbing arms and shields! And here comes Hurai on the run. Abishai, my spine has lizards running up and down!"

The attack was perfect. Again, the battle turned into a rout, and this time they pursued the Philistines from Gibeon all the way to the Philistine town of Gezer.

Achish was killed in that second strike. Joab informed David but was careful to add, "Be assured, my lord, that he didn't die by my hand." He deliberately left the report sketchy, omitting details of his own dogged pursuit of Achish's crippled chariot. The king's horse had been wounded and fell at last, leaving both driver and monarch isolated and at Joab's mercy. That Joab brought Achish to the ground, that his armor bearer Naharai struck the final blow—at his instruction—he did not bother to report.

David said nothing. He stared at the sun setting over Gath, at the dazzling display of a master showman. The scarlet-combed helmet tumbled up and up and up… "You think that's funny," Achish had said to the crowd, "but wait'll I throw my head up, pop it into the helmet, and catch them both on my shoulders. *Then* will you laugh?"

David could not laugh…not now.

26

Jebus. By anyone's assessment, a challenge. A fortress on a high, rocky tongue jutting into the Hinnom Valley. Three sides dropped off sharply; a tall, thick, earth-filled bastion called the Millo guarded the only approach, from the north.

For centuries, Jebusites had made their home within its walls. Joshua's efforts to dislodge them had failed, and hardly anyone had bothered after that. Why should they? A small piece of land—twelve or so acres—with the Jebusites more or less minding their business. For all its strategic potential, no one really wanted it that badly.

Until David set his mind on making it his capital.

As David descended the valley west of the city, his generals who had scouted the area briefed him. In the golden glow of late afternoon, they rounded the southern tip of the fortress and started up the Kidron valley on the east, keeping out of arrow range from the wall towering above. Derisive shouts rang from the battlements. "Ho, small king of Israel—little finger high! You think to bring us down? Ask big King Saul how easy it is. Ask Joshua or his friend Caleb. If Hebrews two hundred years deep couldn't take us, what gives you hope, *King David*—little finger high? Our lame and blind could push you off, so run home to Caleb's city. Stay where it's safe; play your king game there."

"Lame and blind nothing," said Eleazar, limping from the first Philistine encounter. "Women and children could hold this place. As poor shape as I'm in right now, *I* could hold it!" He sighed. "It does look hopeless. The slope is sharp, the walls high. And the only access has that monstrous fortification."

David said nothing, but his eyes took in everything. He listened to all they told him, occasionally asking a question.

A noise behind brought their heads around. Joab and Abishai, with Uriah trailing, climbed the valley toward them. They said nothing and stopped an appropriate distance away, examining the fortifications. David resumed his walk.

"Watch your step," David said as the ground sloped sharply away. "A brook. Source of the Kidron, maybe? Where do they get their water, anyway?"

"Right here," Eleazar said. "They reamed a well in the cliff, making a fair-sized reservoir. Behind those boulders." He pointed.

David nodded. "I see it. There must be a shaft or tunnel that gives access from inside." He clambered over the rocks and disappeared, then came out, beard dripping. "Tastes good, and plenty of it."

They crossed the brook and continued up the valley to study what they could see of the terraced Millo. Watchmen threw down occasional torches to make sure no one was trying to climb the embankment. The city rang with raucous songs.

David and his men turned in silence and headed for the encampment below.

When they came to the spring again, he stared at the dim boulders. "That water shaft," he said finally, "might be our door to the Jebusites. From what—"

He broke off at a familiar buzz over their heads. "Arrows! We're talking too loud."

They ducked out of range. "Let's get some rest," said David. "We've got a city to conquer tomorrow."

That same night at the start of the morning watch, a figure slipped from among sleeping soldiers and eased up the Kidron valley along the base of the fortress. Finding the entrance to the spring was easy enough, but, once inside, not even a star's worth of light broke the blackness. He came to the well more quickly than expected, and an unnerving splash made him freeze. When he was certain no one above had heard, he pulled back to a concealed cleft until daylight began to filter into the hollow.

David too was up before dawn. He ate parched grain and figs with his three chief officers, then consulted with the division chiefs. The plan was simple—the only option open to them: They would surround the city and hurl large sling stones and a barrage of arrows over the wall in hopes of whittling down the number of defenders. Rammers would try to batter their way through the Millo fortress on the north, but that outlook was dim at best. They had a double gate to ram, plus whatever resistance from warriors between the doors. Then too, as shielding on their rams was virtually non-existent, archers on the Millo would target the bearers. Victory was hardly a sure thing.

David, though, felt certain something would develop. At the time of prayer and with Abiathar and the ephod standing by, he ran his eyes over the assembly and addressed the troops. "Look up, all of you, to the hill above Jebus. Mount Moriah. Abraham brought his son Isaac from Beersheba to this place to sacrifice him in obedience to God's command. He stood right where you're standing now. He looked up in dread, yet set foot to the mountain, confident that God—somehow, in some way—would provide. And He did. As Abraham raised his knife, the angel of the Lord stayed his hand. So shaken he could hardly stand, Abraham looked around, and, there in the thicket, caught by its horns, was the sacrifice God provided in place of Isaac.

"Abraham called the mountain, 'The Lord will provide,'" David continued, "and we'll hold to that word today. We'll climb Mount Moriah, and there *Yahweh will provide*. Here, in the name of the Lord, we claim that miserable shelf called Zion. It shall be cleansed of Jebusites and be forever known as Jerusalem, Mount Zion, the Holy City of God.

"Moses instructed our forefathers. He said to them, 'You're to seek the place the Lord will choose, and there he'll put His Name for His dwelling. To that place you must go. Bring burnt offerings and sacrifices, tithes and special gifts, vows and freewill offerings, the firstborn of your herds and flocks.'"

David's voice became white hot. "This is the Lord's command—*for us*. The past presses us forward; the ephod presses us forward. We will build a place for His Name to dwell. May He strengthen our arms to enter His city on this our day of victory!"

The warriors shouted, they sang, they prayed, the trumpets blew, and on that crest of emotion the entire force moved out. Within minutes their barrage of arrows and stones began. Cries from within the fortress testified to the effectiveness of the strategy.

Several divisions armed with spears and swords began the ascent of Moriah by way of the Kidron valley. Although they marched within range of Jebusite archers, their own sharpshooters kept return fire at a minimum. The three ramming poles had a hard slog up the valley, but finally they reached that formidable, ironclad barrier that had withstood countless years of attack.

The figure inside the spring of Gihon faced a double threat. He was as wary of being seen by his own side as by the city dwellers. He knew, too, that as the day and the battle warmed, trips to the spring would become frequent. He needed to hide by starting up the shaft. Would he even fit through the opening? He wasn't large, as David was large, but his shoulders were broad, especially with the armor he'd need if he did in fact make it to the top. He'd need water, as well. He stripped to the bare essentials: helmet, leather tunic, metal belt, and sword. His leg greaves would stay behind, as would the big shield. He'd take the small shield and "borrow" a large one once he got up there. What he couldn't wear he'd tow on a rope.

After burying superfluous equipment outside the tunneled well, he filled his small water bag, attached it to his belt, and with a final look around began his ascent.

Right away he got into trouble. The shaft was smoother than he had expected, with projecting stones scarce. He could find neither handholds nor purchase for his feet. After only a quarter of an hour's effort, his body dripped sweat into the pool below.

Then from above came an ominous sound: a jug scraping against the shaft signaled a call for water. He was blocking the way. How long before someone began asking questions about the sudden dryness of the spring? He studied the spring activity for a long period, noting that it was drawn nearly dry at intervals throughout the day and stored in a reservoir above. Climbing could be done only during the intervals between draws. But war thirst would establish a different rhythm from normal water usage, making the heat of the day a poor time to climb. Perhaps at night after the final draw. What's time, after all? A hunter stalking prey will lie for hours, if necessary. The important thing is to be ready to move fast, silently, and with no impediments. Even a leather tunic would make the tunnel too narrow. He'd have to climb naked. After considering all this, the climber took a long drink, then hid in a recess and settled for a nap.

Toward evening, a second man approached the spring. He stepped cautiously inside, then crouched defensively at a noise overhead. He listened for a time, then smiled and set about roping his excess armorage in imitation of the sounds above. Not knowing how narrow the tunnel was but assuredly of slighter build than the first climber, he left on leg greaves and a woven leather vest to protect his back. With rope tied to his belt, he began his climb, hiding his own movements under the grunts and clatter of the man above.

Ira leaned over David. "Let me see your leg. Is it still bleeding?"

David lay back wearily in the soft glow of Ira's lamp. On the hill behind them, cooking fires lit courtyards and houses that had been appropriated by soldiers. The looming shadow of the Millo rose just below. "A scratch. How many men did we lose?"

"Not many. A dozen, maybe."

David grunted noncommittally.

"Discouraged?" said Ira.

David sighed. "Not really. Disappointed that we didn't get in today. Angry at their taunts about the 'lame and the blind.' But we'll get in. There's a key to this place, I feel certain. Ira, who have we got that's small and agile?"

"Well...let me think. There's me. Skinny enough and wiry— if you're thinking what I think."

David pressed Ira's arm. "I'm not putting you in there. You're too valuable."

"Well, how about Joelah and Zebadiah? They're small—and ambidextrous."

"With bows and slings. I need swordsmen."

"Joelah's good with a sword. So is Ahimelech the Hittite."

"Yes! Ahimelech. Not easily daunted. Get him and Joelah and maybe four others. Make sure they're fed and watered, and meet me at the Gihon spring as soon as you can. Swords and small shields only."

Progress up the shaft was slow. It was tight for even the second climber, without the shoulder mass of the first. They stopped to rest frequently, the second being careful not to give his presence away—not even when the man above urinated on him. Air could not drop through the shaft, and the closeness became oppressive.

After hours of creeping upwards, they began to hear watchmen calling back and forth. "Good!" muttered the first. "At least it's still night."

Sounds from above canceled sounds from below, and neither climber was aware of new scrabblings below them.

David and Ira listened with satisfaction up the shaft. "We'll need to be ready at the gate in case this happens to work," David said. "Get back to your men. Ready them to attack on signal. We don't want to tip off the 'lame and blind' that we're up to something. And Ira—" He chucked the other man's elbow. "This could be the Lord's key!"

Suddenly, he was in fresh air. Not out, but nearly so. He stopped, breathing hard, gritting his teeth against the sting of sweat on what was left of his back and arms. He'd made it. He'd escape this stony Sheol, after all...but what then? He'd collapse, leg muscles stretched beyond function, his back bloodier than a morning sacrifice. He was towing armor but could never bear to put it on. Leather on raw flesh... He'd gotten up, but to what purpose?

He moved up the last three feet, then sprawled across the shelf between the shaft and the reservoir. If anyone came for water now, he was dead. He could not lift a finger. He lay unmoving, his rope dangling in the face of the second climber. That man, too, was exhausted, his legs quivering blobs of fire. He regretted wearing his greaves. He could only brace himself and pray—and hope that life would return quickly to the warrior above.

After a few moments, the upper man pulled himself to the edge of the reservoir and bid his trembling hand fetch a drink. Finally, he dragged at the rope and silently untied the armor, considering what, if anything, he could bear to use. His helmet. His sword, of course. His small shield, but only until he could swap it for a bigger one. He needed all the protection he could get. He could not wear his leather shirt, but perhaps the metal belt that protected his lower body. Down below, he had reluctantly slipped a bit of bread and a few figs into his bundle. Now he was thankful. It might make the difference.

Life began to flow through his veins, but was it enough to accomplish his goal? Would it get him to the gate and to the sacred pearl from the idol that guarded it? He picked up his sword and moved through the darkness, allowing his hidden companion to haul his tortured body across the shelf.

27

My husband wants to be David's commander in chief. He has a chance, you know. Just before the troops left, David told them, 'Whoever breaks through to the Jebusites first will become commander in chief of the army of Israel.'"

Abigail didn't know. "Are you sure of that?" An eyebrow arched skeptically as she surveyed her visitor. She had assumed this to be a purely social call, but now she wondered about the woman's motive in coming.

"Yes, I'm sure. I heard it myself. At the staging area when I waved good-bye to my husband."

Abigail stared at her guest, aghast at the picture of an enormous muster of troops, each man totally disciplined, totally focused on the impossible task of conquering Jebus. And somewhere on the fringe, a woman. Indignation starched Abigail's backbone. This young woman of fragile beauty, thick, lustrous hair, and unsettling, smoky eyes, seemed to lack all common sense. Abigail had seen her at the well and had talked with her once or twice, and the woman had seemed bent on pressing Abigail with her husband's merits and position in David's army.

"I was close enough to hear everything, and—"

"Soldiers don't appreciate the sight of a woman at such a time," Abigail said tartly.

Her caller seemed not to notice. "He said it—I mean, about becoming commander in chief. He said what he said right after he prayed, and all the men cheered. I looked at my husband, and I knew right away he was going to try for it."

"But he—he didn't tell you so himself."

"No, but I could tell from his face—"

"You were close enough to read his face among so many soldiers?"

"Well, he was quite near the king."

"You were *that* close? My dear, do you realize how fortunate you are that the king did not see you? He's very particular about such matters. I suppose you'll tell me next you had relations with your husband before he left you."

The woman looked shocked. "Of course not! The king doesn't allow it, and my husband...he..." She stopped, then drew herself together. "My husband is loyal—to his king and to the Lord. He's not an Israelite, and some say I shouldn't've married him. My father Eliam—one of the king's *Gibborim*, you know..."

Again, Abigail didn't know.

"They say my father should've thrown this Hittite out when he asked for me. But my husband *loves* Israel's God. He's a skilled warrior who *always* does more than he's asked. And now even my grandfather—it was even harder getting his approval, you know."

"Is your grandfather one of the Mighty Men, also?" Abigail's mouth twitched.

"Oh, no!" The woman looked shocked. "My grandfather is Ahithophel, one of the king's chief counselors. Surely, you know my—"

Abigail's eyebrow arched. "Yes, indeed. I know Ahithophel!"

"He was hard to win over, but now he thinks my husband shows great promise. He wants to become a *Gibbor*...my husband, that is; not my grandfather."

Abigail struggled against laughter—the lordly, manicured Ahithophel among the Mighty he-goats! "After he's made commander in chief? Your husband, that is."

"Oh, no," the woman answered blithely. "If he were commander in chief, he'd be above the Mighty Men, and that's even better."

To gain composure, Abigail studied her servant girls, who were grinding grain and stoking bread ovens in the courtyard. After a moment, she could again address her caller. "My dear, if I were you, I'd go back home and tend my household. Stay away from places where women are not welcome. Do you have children?"

"Not yet." Again she looked uncomfortable. "My husband... well, he's strict about...well, he's always going off soldiering. War is worship, he says, and you can't do it beforehand, and when he's home, then I'm unclean, and well..."

"I see." Abigail's eyes softened for the first time. A young wife, a husband zealous for the Lord and ambitious. Or was it the wife who was ambitious? She reached out her hand with sudden warmth and offered words that would return to haunt her. "Bathsheba, my dear, you will have a child. Your husband will not always be soldiering. He will come to you."

One man. Two men. Eight men. A walled city restless with torches and unaccustomed fear, watchmen looking inward, as well as outward. The task of climbing the steep street to the inner gate of the Millo would be formidable, even at night and in the darkest of shadows. One man might do it, but eight?

The inevitable happened. A hand reached from the dark and grabbed the foot of the first of the water-shaft climbers. He fell heavily, and the agony of raw flesh could not keep silent. He was up in a flash, however, sword in hand, and his detainer paid full price.

He had perhaps a minute to speed toward the gate before the Jebusites reacted. The others, too, seized the fleeting opportunity. By this time, gray light was filtering over the east wall, both helping the runners and revealing their presence. The first man met resistance, which he hacked through, stopping only long enough to yank at the large shield of a fallen Jebusite. The dead man, however, had too firm a grip, and this break in stride opened the Israelite to mortal danger. He was immediately surrounded, and with only a small, badly damaged shield—doomed.

The second runner saw what was happening and hesitated as though weighing the death of his chief competitor for leadership against the good of the newly formed kingdom. He found the same shield, hacked at the dead man's hand, and in one smooth movement tossed the shield to the front-runner. The battle at the gate began in earnest.

By this time, the trailing six had fought their way to the inner gate, and the eight together, more than a match for "lame and blind" Jebusites, roared their challenge. Six covered two who worked the bars of the gate. Once opened, however, the cage within held more armed and howling Jebusites. Another pair of Israelites moved in to polish these off, and the outer-gate bars, weakened by the previous day's pounding, gave way.

David was first of the massed, furious-faced warriors to push through the gateway. He came in, great sword flailing, and nearly chopped one of his own men. "Uriah!" he exclaimed. "How did you get in here? You weren't among the six—"

"The water shaft—but I was not the first, my lord; not the first."

The force of the storming army pushed the two men apart, and they turned to relish the final moments of conquest. In less than half an hour the fortress was secured. "Jebus is ours!" whooped the king. "Jerusalem! Zion! City of David! City of God!"

Wave after wave of soldiers poured in and climbed to the top of the walls, singing and dancing against the blast of exuberant trumpeters. They had taken the city. They'd done the impossible.

The grand stroke, the bold move—the most effective, both strategically and politically, of David's entire career. Not done alone, of course. Were it not for those eight brave warriors, David might never have breached the walls. But his was the vision, his the faith that God would "part the waters," as Abigail might have said.

Nor was it accomplished without cost. Abishai bent over the body of his brother, taking in the dirt clotting his raw, naked back, the arrow in his shoulder, unprotected arms and legs hacked to the bone. The eyes of this mangled mess were fixed and staring. Shrieking rage, Abishai hurled his spear at the wall, not caring who might be in the way, then fell to his knees with a grimace of pain that trivialized any physical wound. Then he raised his head, sat on his heels, and hurled dirt with a keening wail. "Two brothers! Asahel, Joab! O God, he's dead!" he cried, his voice strangling. "Joab is dead!"

Without so much as a twitch, the "body" mumbled, "Not dead. Commander in chief." Painfully, he willed his fingers to open.

In his palm lay a large pearl.

28

David's first chore when he entered Jerusalem was to rid the fortress and its surrounding villages of Jebusites. The second, more difficult chore was finding a place to live. Six wives, six sons, a scattering of daughters, assorted concubines and their offspring, plus an army of servants to maintain the king's harem in courtly comfort. He knew what he wanted, but until he could devote time to think it through, makeshift quarters would have to serve.

And makeshift it turned out to be. The most suitable dwelling, which had housed the Jebusite chief, was the obvious starting point, but most of David's wives made it clear that living in one house with their growing families was simply out of the question. Each, of course, preferred to be alone with David in the fine house, with the others going to auxiliary quarters. Michal and Abigail were the exceptions. Abigail would gladly escape the press of other wives with their sharp tongues and brawny sons who made Daniel's life miserable. David, though, valued her managerial skills and would not allow her to leave.

David was quick to make his mark on the fortress. He rebuilt the area around it, from the supporting terraces inward, repairing the damage done to the north wall and Millo. He liked the city, its height and perspective, its defensibility, its potential for the future. He walked through the ancient jumble of dwellings, deciding which were usable and which should be leveled. He knew where he wanted his palace and kept the area as tenant-free as possible, allowing only his *Gibborim* to stay there.

The City of David. "Abigail, I'm here. I've arrived. King of Judah, king of Israel. The Philistines have been put down and won't challenge us from here on. With my generals and an army weaned on thorns and privation, we'll expand our boundaries and make this a nation among nations, a power to be reckoned with. So what if Joab ended up in charge? He earned it. Only he could have pulled off such an incredible coup. If you could have seen him, Abigail, you—"

"I did see him, my lord. I helped his wife clean his back, endured his screams and curses. I stitched sword cuts and—"

"Oh."

"And furthermore, when the young man holding him fainted, I—"

"I should have assumed you'd be on hand for stitchery. Did I thank you properly, by the way, for the new robe you made?"

"Yes, you did. You made a gracious speech."

David moved to a window and looked out on the houses of his *Gibborim*. That was the site, on the promontory, where his palace would rise, white and gleaming. He sighed. "This place doesn't look like much, but it's a far cry from Saul's cramped, gloomy palace."

"Whereas your house emanates light and life from the moment you rise each day." Her mouth twitched slightly.

David stepped to her and planted a kiss on her mouth. "Abigail, you're good for me. No pretensions allowed. The things you've done for me all these years, starting when you kept me from acting against that husband of yours." He released her and whirled away with a quick-step dance. "Achish is dead, the Philistines vanquished. The Amalekites know our swords. The Moabites and others may soon bow down and cry, 'O exalted ruler of north and south, may you live forever!'"

"If they do not, my lord, you may be sure that I will." Again her mouth twitched. "But might I suggest, O lord who lives forever, that you not count your lambs before they are birthed. Many a monarch has fallen before the snapping jaws of foxes and jackals. Your sons, if you're lucky—"

She stopped suddenly, the quirky smile fading. Almost in shock, as though seeing him for the first time, her eyes widened, then filmed with tears.

"What is it, Abigail? Did I say something wrong—again?"

She shook her head slowly, almost sadly. She reached out toward him but then withdrew her hand and sank to her knees. "Your son, my lord...but no, not Daniel—"

With a shock, David detected the familiar lizards on his spine, down his arms. For an instant, it produced only annoyance. Why couldn't God stick to normal channels of communication, like prophets or ephods? Why did his Spirit rest on such odd agents as Saul or this most difficult of wives?

"...the Son of the Most High," she was saying. "The Lord God will bless him. He will sit on your throne, reign over the house of Jacob...." Her body trembled, her eyes fought against such a takeover of her normal self-control. "Not just for his lifetime…My lord…" Again she looked through his soul to some outer region of the universe, her voice dropping to a whisper. "My lord, through your son, you will live forever! The bundled treasure kept for eternity…."

David bowed low before the Lord, but still he was irked. A good word to hear, but…his wife! Had it come from Balaam's donkey, he could have taken it more gracefully.

That may have been the last truly civil conversation David and Abigail ever had.

Scroll Two

A top tumbled pasture land west of Jerusalem, a silhouette writhed along the sinuous curtain of heat
that descended from brassy skies.

*A man was running—but why at midday? Was something
wrong? What reason did he have for being far from the usual
paths? A shortcut?*

In the gulch below, a band of men pondered these questions
from their patch of shade. The traveler dropped below the
horizon and appeared to be angling in their direction. They
hunkered into invisibility—and waited.

To separate chaff from grain, threshing is done in windy
places, places broad enough for the comings and goings of
grain carts—or for the odd chariot race.

Here, above the gate of Jerusalem, on the well-flailed expanse belonging to a young Jebusite named Araunah, two
war-scarred chariots drawn by equally damaged horses ca-
reened around a track of sorts. With neither driver adept at

charioteering, the horses went at will through the byways of upper Jerusalem.

For one of the drivers, the exercise was deadly serious. Body plastered with horse lather and dust, he sawed the reins with grim determination. Naked from the waist up, the man's back was a blanket of scabs and scarring, healed so tenuously that small trickles of blood seeped onto his belt.

In contrast, the opposing charioteer was simply having fun. He whooped and laughed at his mistakes but gave no quarter to his companion.

The inevitable crash came when one team popped a trace. The chariot skidded sideways, shearing a wheel from the other vehicle and tossing its driver safely out of the mêlée. The first driver caromed into the tangle of wreckage and panicked horseflesh. As the dust settled, he peeled himself off the stone path with a resounding curse and crawled toward a skin of water. For him, any challenge worth his trouble usually required more than a single try. The set of his face announced that he would drive again.

A scattering of sheep, blending into the craggy hillside, spooked at the runner's approach and became a gray cataract drifting from his path. The forty men in the thicket below remained still, invisible against the dry, dusty floor.

As they watched the runner, their eyes caught the approach of three travelers from the opposite direction—Moabites, from the cut and design of their clothing. The runner continued toward them, and the two parties met, affecting a wary sort of prior acquaintance. No warm greeting, no friendly banter; perhaps a business transaction. The runner removed his headgear and wiped sweat from his face, smoothing his beard as by habit over a pronounced scar on his left cheek.

The leader of the hidden onlookers stiffened. His eyes, brown and alert, scrutinized the runner. "The scar...Sheba *ben* Bicri," he whispered to his nearest companion. "I'm sure of it. One of David's men."

"Sneaking around with Moabites?"

"A troublemaker from way back," said the leader. "What's he up to? There. He's handing something to the Moabites. Cloth."

"A tunic, maybe?"

"With matching headband. Yes, that's it. When David first went to Hebron, he had Abigail design servants' uniforms with purple trim. 'A king's servants,' he said, 'should dress royally.'"

The leader paused, pondering. "Sheba...a rotting fig. Sheba plus Moabites...stinks even more. That nasty business last week near Gilgal came out of Moab. What did they hope to gain by provoking David? He's been on decent terms with them. His great-grandmother Ruth was a Moabite." He shook his head. "What did they intend to prove at Gilgal? It doesn't make sense. Did they think David would ignore it? Feeling for a hole in his armor? Maybe—"

He stopped as Sheba bowed curtly and turned toward Jerusalem. On his departure, one of the Moabites, hair and beard trimmed in Hebrew fashion, took off his outer garment, put on the tunic Sheba had brought, and then donned his robe again. The Moabite trio followed Sheba as the rocks of the gulch became men who headed toward Jerusalem by another route. "We need to check this out," said the rangy leader. "It won't do on my first day back to kill someone David was expecting."

David and some four hundred soldiers toiled up the hill, having just returned from the raided village near Gilgal. A hard, heavy excursion. The palpable horror that hung over the town still lingered over him. His nephew Amasa, son of his half sister, Abigail, had reported the massacre, but before mounting a major offensive against Moab, David wanted to investigate the matter himself.

Now, hot and tired and nearly home, he came upon the chariot debris. One of the horses had to be killed; the others staggered about in various stages of nervous collapse.

"What happened here?" David growled at Eleazar, who had come to greet the king.

"Joab happened."

"Oh? How so? Last I heard, he couldn't even walk."

"That's why he was driving. 'If you can't walk or fight,' he said, 'learn something new.'"

David grunted with annoyance. Joab had advised him to take along a larger number of men so he could retaliate immediately. That his nephew had been right didn't set well. "Maybe you should've sliced Joab's throat along with the horse's." He nodded toward the carcass. "Something to be said for the practice."

Eleazar laughed. "He's by the gate, waiting for the bleeding to stop. His wife decreed that blood and other loose parts would not be welcome on her clean floor."

"How bad is he?"

"He'll live. It might set him back a week."

David turned toward the gate where Ira was sponging the grimacing general.

"Not a word, Davi," Joab growled. "Not one word!"

"Feh! Far be it from me to interfere with your amusements." He moved toward the gateway.

The long climb from the river plain had emptied almost every water bag. David's face was lined and dirty; his eyes focused inward. He did not notice the unusual number of strangers in the gate area, some carrying firewood or talking with beggars. Once again, with practiced ease, the forty men had made themselves invisible to all but the most discerning observer. Their own eyes were alert and focused; they were particularly honed in on a Moabite who had similarly blended into the bustle. As David came into view, this man separated himself, covertly slipped off his robe and headdress, and shoved them behind some jars. Now wearing the purple headband and purple-banded tunic that declared him to be a servant, he stepped out boldly and approached David with a deferential smile. One hand bore a silver bowl of water; the other was tucked unobtrusively in his belt.

Other servants came forward as well, carrying assorted bowls and jars to service David and the Mighty Men. When they saw the strange servant, they stopped in surprise, trying to process his sudden appearance.

The eagle-eyed leader did not hesitate. Muscling David aside, he thrust his short blade through the Moabite. His men moved to back him but kept their swords out of sight to arouse neither the palace guard nor David's companions. Cool brown eyes bent over the dying man; a Moabite dagger was extracted from the "servant's" belt and held before the startled David. "If I were you, my lord, I'd either teach my servants better manners or hire a better bodyguard. May we offer our services?" Benaiah and his forty men bowed low before the astonished king.

J erusalem—the city on a hill. Her days were purposeful, busy, buoyant. Her jeweled nights danced to irrepressible music. The old had been cleansed; the new gleamed with light and life. Few lived within the actual confines of the Jebusite fortress—David and his Mighty Men, the bodyguard, his administrators, priests, and officials. Everyone else lived on the surrounding hills or the valley slopes, comprising a vibrant, pulsating metropolis, the new heart of David's expanding kingdom.

The genius in David's choice of Jerusalem for his capital city was obvious to all and was indeed one of the factors that defined the greatness of his reign. In one stroke he had stitched together the fragile peace between Judah and Israel, established an impregnable base for future kingdom expansion, and begun the long process of reshaping the pagan aura of Zion into a place where God would be exalted.

The palace had been built at last—the fulfillment of a dream. After David's conquest of Jebus, King Hiram of Tyre sent emissaries, and David himself journeyed to Tyre to forge a lasting friendship with architecture and artistry as the common bond. Soon after, carpenters and stonemasons appeared in Jerusalem, along with cedar logs from the mountain forests of Lebanon. The result was more than David could have hoped for.

Surrounding the palace on its central prominence were the homes of his Mighty Men. Benaiah, Eleazar, Shammah, Ira, Jashobeam, and Uriah—appointed as a result of his water-shaft bravery—were in the first ring; others filled the perimeter.

The city had taken shape.

Benaiah and his band of Kerethites and Pelethites supplanted the old bodyguard. "Benaiah's Boys," they were called. Benaiah himself had gone away a boy and come back a *gibbor*, a mighty warrior. Though now bold enough to stare down David, his love for the king imbued him with courage and responsibility, bringing a new dimension of security and order in the city. David had chosen well.

The rest of the military was a well-bonded, well-structured war machine. The generals—scar-stitched warriors such as Jashobeam, Shammah, Dodai, and his son Eleazar—had long, colorful histories of valor, which in turn generated confidence among their troops. Wherever these "bulls of Israel" went, enemies dissolved out of fear. Or perhaps good sense. Better to surrender and work out a settlement than face defeat and death.

David had sensible advisors with whom he met frequently. His Uncle Jonathan, mid-forties and still handsome, bore with humor the family air of authority. An insightful counselor, he served as scribe at these meetings, recording various kingdom events.

Ahithophel—father of Mighty Man Eliam and grandfather of Uriah's wife Bathsheba—was a man of order and uncommon sense. He lived as he dressed: well-groomed, well-trimmed, excellent in every way; perhaps the only man in Jerusalem whose every tooth remained in his head. He was objective, never swayed by personal loyalties. It was this very strength that David sometimes found difficult, but in the end, he knew Ahithophel always had the kingdom's interests at heart. What was best for the kingdom was best for David—not the other way around. Ahithophel seldom laughed and never joked. Though invariably polite, he held definite opinions—and was almost always right.

Jashobeam, Eleazar, and Shammah—"the Three"—were under Abishai's leadership. Among them, they counted fewer teeth than Ahithophel's alone. These men of valor and integrity formed the hub and mainstay of the military.

The same could not be said of Joab—or at least not the integrity part. Valor, yes. Lifeblood of the kingdom, yes. Integrity, no. One may have thought they knew Joab as well or better than the Three, but they would be wrong. No man knew Joab—not even his brother.

Joab's brother, Abishai, was chief of the Three, as well as an agile, quick-thrust spearman and valued advisor. Hot-blooded and hot-headed, he could be counted on to see the dark side of any situation—a valuable service, provided cheerier eyes were there to balance him off. He could also be counted on to dole out correction with his sling, as mood dictated.

Amasai, the warrior of startled eyebrows and a nose that bent north, had come to Ziklag with the Spirit's fervor upon him. Although he was not numbered among the Thirty, David made him their chief, as Abishai was over the Three. A wise move. *Gibborim* don't always agree on which direction to pull the plow. Amasai not only could clarify the direction, he could make everyone else think it was their own idea.

All in all, David and his advisors worked with a driving, harmonious rhythm. They knew what they had achieved; they knew what they wanted. The professional army was in good shape, and a monthly militia rotation was being developed to augment it as needed. With this pool of reserves, a large force could mobilize quickly for major offensives. Amasai had chosen Amasa, another of David's nephews, to handle the militia. Years later, many saw this as Amasai's one misjudgment.

As a newcomer, Benaiah had to scrabble for respect from those who had known him as "The Nuisance." Fortunately for him, Joab's injuries kept him from physically challenging the guardsman to challenge Benaiah. Joab lost no opportunity, though, to jab him verbally. Benaiah parried with humor, and only after Joab's wounds had healed enough to get physical did the newcomer decide to draw a line in the sand.

David saw what was going on but said nothing. If his new bodyguard couldn't handle Joab, he wasn't worth his keep in olives.

Joab acknowledged the line and laid plans to cross it.

The night before a military sortie, he drafted his nephew and companions to help dig a man-sized pit close to the road they would be taking. Zebadiah *ben* Asahel had never really forgiven Benaiah for hurling blame at him for Abner's death.

On their way the next day, Joab began baiting Benaiah. The guardsman quipped back but refused to be drawn into a fight. When they neared the camouflaged trap, the baiting could no longer be ignored, as Joab had designed. The pit diggers squared off around it.

Benaiah took in glances that tended toward a particular spot. First he tried ducking out and picking his own place of battle. When howls of cowardice forced him back, he faced Joab, the two armed only with staves. Benaiah drew first blood with a blow to Joab's shoulder. Back and forth. Whacks and grunts. Though not young and quick like Benaiah, Joab was wily. He used the corner itself as a weapon. Benaiah slipped out time after time. Finally, in a maneuver that sucked away every man's breath, he took a blow that sent him straight toward the pit, yet somehow he dropped just short of it. With astounding agility, he tumbled to Joab's weak side, planted his staff between his opponent's legs, and tripped him into his own trap.

To his credit, Joab used the hand Benaiah extended to climb out of the pit.

That night, when David heard about the duel, he sang a song, tongue-in-cheek:

> He who shovels a hole and scoops it out
>   himself falls into the pit.
> The trouble he causes snaps back in his face,
>   and violence pours on his head.

The new regime outlined out its political and military agenda. The Philistines were down but not altogether out. They still had a top general, Ittai the Gittite. After the death of Achish, Ittai retained power, largely because of his brain. But he had doubts. It seemed inevitable that David would batter the Philistines into either nonexistence or utter submission. In either case, Ittai preferred not to be on the losing side. He was proud but also practical.

Despite the panoply of Canaanite gods the Philistines had carted to Mt. Gilboa for the battle against Saul, their great victory had only uncorked the irrepressible David. At Rephaim, where they caught him on his way to Jebus, he should have been put down once for all. David not only had escaped, he had won a decisive victory and killed their king. How had this happened? How much was due to David's obvious ability and how much to the Israelite god who could not be carried around?

The battle of Metheg Ammah became Ittai's personal moment of truth. Would he continue to fight for the Philistines or come to terms with the Davidic juggernaut?

He satisfied his dilemma by fighting as hard as he could while there was still something to fight for. As anticipated, David came across the Shephelah like a bull against a flea. When Gath fell, Ittai put his brain to work. He wanted to survive; he wanted to be on the winning side. He could have run like most of his men and quite likely would have escaped. Instead, he fought his way close to David and pulled out the special scarlet crest that Achish had worn on his helmet. He attached it to his own and made sure David saw it. Having thus drawn attention, he pulled out a second artifact, a purple and gold braided headband that David himself had lost while in the service of the Philistines. Achish, having somehow gotten hold of it, had given it to Ittai.

Now, with full attention on him, Ittai signaled his desire to talk. He approached David and threw himself down. The first words out of his mouth were, "Please tell me why your god is stronger than ours." It worked. David recognized an honest question when he heard it.

The Amalekites were hardly worth mentioning. David had demoralized them during his years at Ziklag. Thus weakened, these nomadic bandits were quickly subdued.

Still, there was Moab.

The first of many documents that came into my hands in the compilation of this history was a clay tablet with a list of military objectives. I don't remember how I obtained it, and it contained nothing noteworthy, but that tablet was, for me, the gateway to a fabled city, a sip of wine from an ancient skin, a breath of Mt. Hermon in a desert place.

I became, in that moment, more than just a musician—I became a historian. At the time, I could not have defined the term, but I knew that I had begun to be defined.

I saw history not just as a record of events, but as blood coursing through fossilized bones, bringing to life the feel, the smell, the taste of the past. It is arms elbow deep in earth, coming out with a lily in one hand and menstrual rags in the other. It is the lovely, tumbled hills of Judah etched on heart-wrenching blue. It is a boil of unspeakable savagery that erupts in places like...Moab.

Moab—the land of Lot east of the Salt Sea. A land whose mountains stretch like a wall against the caustic waters. A land whose bounty was credited to fertility cults and the sacrifice of children to the god Chemosh. A land whose recent indiscretion brought David's wrath hard upon them.

Moab—one of the names on the clay tablet.

As Benaiah had noted, the two nations had been on reasonably friendly terms for years. Not only did Moabite blood flow through David's veins, but he had taken his parents there for safety from Saul.

Yet Moab had seriously miscalculated the caliber of Israel's new king with an unprovoked massacre on a village near Gilgal on Judah's side of the Jordan.

"With no wall and no watchtower," Amasa had reported to David, "the villagers hadn't a chance. A handful of farmers against...," he bit his lip. "If I'd gotten there a little earlier...." Though hardened to atrocity, this one knifed him. "Exactly two-thirds," he said. "Cold-blooded calculation. Two-thirds of the town's children."

"Why that number?" said David.

"Who knows? But they herded all the youngsters into the square—thirty or forty of them...well, it wouldn't have been forty...thirty-nine, maybe. The people kept saying exactly two-thirds, as though a perfect number might somehow ease their pain. When I got there, the Moabites had just left, and the parents had just pulled their children off the sharpened stakes. Most were dead, but some were not."

David's face settled to steel as he strode around the room.

"Even worse...the one-third forced to watch. And the parents." Amasa stared out the window, the pall of dust and blood and agonizing death heavy upon him. He turned suddenly. "*Why?* Why that village? Why children? Why two-thirds?"

"No one else was killed?"

"A couple men and, I think, one mother. And half-grown boys. I almost forgot them. They were rounded up and counted off. An arbitrary number, but close to two-thirds. They weren't killed outright, only their genitals cut off. Most will probably die."

Added to the assassination attempt that Benaiah had foiled, this equaled one enraged king.

Moab paid.

The attack was quick and effective. In less than three hours the entire Moabite army had surrendered. As the dust settled, the stench of war squelched any victory song.

Fingering his sling, David grimly surveyed his mass of captives. Abishai came over, not pleased. "They're happy, you know, these hinnies sitting here. I can't believe you wanted captives rather than corpses."

"Corpses don't recognize justice, Abishai. These 'hinnies' will have an hour longer to ponder the meaning of the word. I want you to make them lie side by side in long rows and lick dust. Take a cord—this sling, maybe. It's long enough. Measure the rows. Put every two lengths to death; the third length lives. Moab will need them to help raise the tribute I intend to impose—silver, gold, lambs, wool, pottery, and slaves to carry it all."

Abishai not only smiled. For once he laughed.

The conquest of Ammon—the last name on the clay tablet—is another story altogether.

4

Part of David's anger was due to a nasty back wound he sustained in the battle with Moab. He had taken a javelin thrust that first seemed little worse than getting the wind knocked out of him. The tip, though, had penetrated his leather armor, and, by the time he got home, he was burning with fever and roaring for Abigail to take care of him.

Of all his wives, only Abigail would have entered his room that evening. The others would have fled the smell, if not his uncleanness. Even the servants delivering oil, wine, and other medicaments retreated hastily with their noses covered. Abigail took one look at David, laid aside her robe, and settled in. This healing would be long.

After trying to bathe him herself, she called for Ira. "He fights me. He thinks I'm trying to assassinate him. If you could just hold him. Yes, the smell is bad, but once I get the wound cleansed—"

"My lady, I know the stink of wounds well enough."

The next hour emptied that entire section of the palace. Wives, servants, and slaves all found reason to sleep elsewhere.

When quiet reigned at last, Abigail looked across the bed at Ira, face dripping and clothing spattered with blood. Eyes wide against weariness, she seemed wobbly. Ira sprang to her side. "My lady! Sit down. Shall I call for your maid?"

Abigail stiffened resolutely. "Thank you, Ira. I'm all right. I would like to wash my hands, however." But as she turned toward the bowl, she staggered and went white. Ira led her to a chair, then wrung a cloth and gently wiped her face.

Abigail's days and nights were long and hard for a full week. She would not relinquish her place, however, even to Ira. "He seems comfortable with me. I'm not the assassin anymore; you probably would be. Today it's Cush."

"Huh!" Ira said. "Cush wasn't the first enemy to accuse him and won't be the last. They swarm to a king like flies to a carcass."

Abigail looked through the doorway at the sleeping king, compassion and longing in her eyes. She knew David. She knew his hurt under liars like Cush or traitors like Sheba. She knew his fears. She knew how to comfort and support him in such circumstances, but a wall of her own construction had risen between them that she could no longer work her way through. He used her in times such as this, but she wasn't deluded into thinking they'd ever again be soulmates. She sighed.

Ira saw her sadness. "He's lost flesh, but he seems better, don't you think? The fever's down."

"Yes. He's well enough to contemplate why he got wounded in the first place. The wrath of God is on him, he says; God's arrows did him in. Sin caused it all." She smiled. "I offered to help remind him of specific sins, but he didn't appreciate that."

Weeks passed before any song passed David's lips, and even then, the words spoke of inner torment.

> O Lord, do not rebuke me in your anger,
>   or discipline me in your wrath.
> My guilt has overwhelmed me
>   like a burden too heavy to bear.
> My wounds fester and are loathsome,
>   my back is filled with searing pain;
>   there is no health in my body.
> My friends and companions avoid me because of
>   my wounds;
> My neighbors stay far away.
> Be not far from me, O my God.
> Come quickly to help me, O Lord my Savior.

During the hours that David was out of his mind, Abigail sat stroking his head, rubbing his arms and legs to will health into his body, not minding that he called her *Abba* instead of his usual *Abi*. If she napped while David slept, he sometimes woke to see exhaustion across her features. Once again he saw how unequivocally his strength rested on hers. *Abigail is my shepherd....*

While he drifted in and out of consciousness, his other wives paid reluctant visits—regal wraiths that floated toward him from beyond bedroom walls. Michal, the dusky beauty he'd wrested from Saul with his bloody bag of a bride price. Had she come now to scratch out his eyes? Or was she now Saul—strong willed, all dignity and royalty, no sense of the spiritual? Her second husband Paltiel was pulling at her and David couldn't reach the hand she wouldn't hold out to him.

He was king now. Had he wanted, he could've taken Saul's wife and concubine for his own. They were peering at him, too—old and used. Ahinoam had mothered Jonathan as well as Michal. And Rizpah with her sword-point eyes. Both women had endured Saul; why would he want these living testimonials to madness?

No, now it was his own Ahinoam standing by him. Beautiful...vapid.

Ahinoam always had Abigail to take care of the slack. But Abigail doesn't approve of Ahinoam's son.

"Amnon always gets what he wants."

Is that you speaking, Abigail, or have I just heard you say it so often?

"Ahinoam doesn't want the boy crossed."

"Keep in mind, my lord: the eldest son usually succeeds to the throne."

"What would become of your kingdom under Amnon?"

Oh, Abigail of Carmel, my industrious little scorpion. You could have birthed a Joab or an Abishai, but instead you brought forth a long-eared hare, Kileab. "Restraint of father." The irony. His continual mewling and puking calls for every ounce of restraint within me.

David struggled to his side. If he could untie his arms and legs, lie on his back, maybe his wives would walk on the ceiling instead of bending to his whirling eyes.

I see you, Maacah, but a flashing sapphire hurts my eyes. Later... bring Absalom, bring Tamar and her pet bird. You were raised by

*a king, Maacah, and know what kings do. I want you to stand
on a pillar and say, "David, you're a king. What a king wants, a
king gets." Say that, my love, and I'll think about what you want
for Absalom.*

"Absalom is as selfish as his mother but cleverer at conceal-
ing it."

Oh, Abigail, you see too much.

"Yes, I do. I see sweet talk, an ingratiating smile. A born poli-
tician. A schemer who never forgets a wrong. Cross him and
he'll wait. Years, perhaps. Such patience and perseverance—
all in service of himself! His sister Tamar, though—a good
girl."

*I hear you, Abigail. You like girls, but not boys. You'd like the
boys to be girls like your son, leading pet birds.... Haggith, my
dear, shouldn't you have clothes on? I can see right through your
head. And your son Adonijah...he is Absalom's shadow. He tries
to copy his brother but never gets it quite right. At least Absalom
is effective and capable in his perversity—and doesn't crack his
knuckles. Put Amnon, Absalom and Adonijah together...*

"David, you've got to do something about those boys. Already
they're arrogant, drunk on their own beauty and charm. What
will they grow into?"

*You've come, Abital, with little Shephatiah. Beautiful and con-
tent to sit like a jewel on a cushion.*

"Abital is a poor parent. She and Eglah want privilege for
their toddlers but not a program to make them into men."

David stirred and turned toward the patient caretaker,
Abigail, sitting at his bedside. Were the visits of his wives real?
Had he been talking with Abigail all this time? He was unsure

of everything. All he did know was that the wraiths had departed and reality was sitting beside him.

"Dare you say that, Abigail, mother of Kileab? Why do you say the boys are being coddled? They're still children, after all, some just babies. The oldest is what? Ten? Eleven? The older boys are being trained for warfare."

"Yes, but they'll never fight. You feed and water Joab for that purpose, so they'll never really learn. They know only mischief. Already there's talk. But you never scold. You were not parented that way. Your father—"

"Yes, *Abba* would scold. But he was kind, gentle, and that's what I try to be."

"But what comes of it? Your children bow and say nice things to your face, but look at what they do. The beggar boy and his pet monkey, for instance."

"That. The little tramp probably stole it."

"You don't know that. The boys certainly didn't. Yet they grabbed it away from him and pulled it apart—in front of Daniel, just to make him scream. Is that what you want your sons known for, my lord? From such children come other children."

"Oh, Abigail, boys will be boys. You're angry because Kileab threw up. You're overprotective. Let him be with the other boys. It'll put some starch in the lad."

"I want no part of that sort of starch. Just yesterday, Amnon sidled over to Daniel and whispered that men and women don't couple like sheep and goats. More like dogs, he said."

David guffawed, then grimaced in pain. "Abigail, that's just boy talk, from Cain on down. It doesn't mean anything."

"I won't have my boy talking that way. He may not be strong, but he can and will be civilized. My lord, in my heart I believe you stand in great spiritual danger."

"If only I *could* stand," he said peevishly.

"*Listen* to me!" She stopped abruptly and turned away. David said nothing. After a moment she turned back. "I'm sorry, my lord. I shouldn't speak that way. But these past weeks I've worried over you. I worry that your passions and parenting will scuttle Yahweh's calling and ultimately the kingdom."

David drew an angry breath. "Abigail, from the time each could talk, I've led the children in '*Shema yisra'el adonai eloheynu adonai ehad.*' 'Hear, O Israel, the Lord our God, the Lord is one.' I've taught them, questioning them regularly on what they've learned."

"And if they learn next to nothing, what do you say? 'You'll know it better next time.' That's all. I've heard you. I've seen your girl-watching proclivities. Six wives and eight concubines aren't enough to keep your eyes in their proper place. Oh, David, God made you his king. What will happen if you betray that trust? I care deeply about that." She closed her eyes and fought for control. "I care deeply...about you."

David might have held out his hand at that moment, but he resisted the urge. Instead, he lay on his side, eyes closed, face gaunt and hard.

Abigail walked stiffly from the room.

5

David's life had four specific pivot points. The first was his encounter with Goliath. That great victory over the Philistine giant not only thrust him and his talents into public view, more importantly it helped define the inner purpose of his life. No one in that crowd—soldiers, brothers—could see what was really at stake in that face-off: the honor of Israel and the power of the living God. God had helped the shepherd boy put down lions and bears; would He not help him put down a Philistine dog? Perhaps even then David saw the shape of his calling as shepherd of Israel.

The second pivot point came when he fled from Saul to the tabernacle at Nob and begged the high priest for the bread of the Presence and for Goliath's sword. That cut him loose from Saul and a kingdom on the point of collapse.

The third was this particular wound, a bubble of time that forced him to look backward and forward, inward and outward, and to study both conquest and worship.

We have not yet arrived at the fourth. More of that later.

As he lay in bed, David saw battle and conquest consuming his life, with time for little else beyond food and wives. Yes, he had good generals to run his wars, but the king who leaves such things totally in the hands of other men is a fool. The fulfillment of his dream depended on his own vision. And the security of the dream depended on his keeping at least one eye on the ambitions of the brothers Zeruiah.

The dream involved more than conquest, however. A major part of David's nature had lain dormant during the kingdom-building years, slipping out on emotional occasions that drove him to song or to the contemplation of glory. It found voice, of course, on Sabbaths and the great festivals, in burnt and sin offerings. He thanked God daily for such basic bounties as grain, new wine, and oil. But there remained in him a ravenous appetite for spiritual food. Now, lying in bed, he had time to think, plan, and prepare for things beyond kingdom building. He had time to feed on God and define the spiritual focus of Israel. The Ark was a major concern. It was a small box, yet it had played a crucial role in Israel's history. When the Philistines overran Shiloh and took the Ark, it was said that Yahweh's glory had departed from Israel. The Philistines found it too hot to handle and quickly let it go, but only now was the glory beginning to return. The Ark had suffered benign neglect during Saul's reign. The high priest, of course, visited it once a year on the Day of Atonement, entering its tent with his protective incense to sprinkle blood for himself and for the people. But it was worthy of a permanent home.

Moving it, though, would be formidable and complex. For instance, should the Ark go to the Tent of Meeting at Gibeon, or should it, as David felt strongly, come to Jerusalem to serve as the center for an entirely new style of worship? And how could he get it there? It would be unthinkable simply to hire someone to haul the sacred object to Jerusalem. The move it-self would be a major event. The Ark had been in exile for some seventy-five years and its entry into the city would occasion pomp and rejoicing. The logistics alone—who should be invited, food for thousands, transportation decisions—these were no small matters.

David's mind kept coming back to a new worship center. Creative liturgy. Levitical personnel, not simply menials to serve the priests, but to lead prayer and music. This new place wouldn't be large enough for the major festivals of Rosh Hashanah, the Feast of Weeks, or the Feast of Tabernacles. But later, perhaps a permanent structure—a temple—could be built. He saw it rising tall and gold in the morning sun... columns, capitals, porticos. A great altar in the courtyard with a river of blood from sacrifices. And salt, symbolizing the strengthening and preserving quality of the nation's covenant with God. Salt in a wound stung unbearably—much like the ephod's holiness—but salt on a grain or blood sacrifice was the agent of transfer: purity for corruption, righteousness for sin.

David's friend Hiram king of Tyre would help build this temple. David already had a modest store of gold, bronze, and silver from gifts and tribute. And as nations were subdued during the next few years.... Yes, a temporary tent in Jerusalem would be appropriate before the Lord, with a permanent house for his Name soon to follow. Now he needed to consult with Abiathar...and Zadok.

This time of reflection, coming during Passover, led to a different sort of prompting. Passover took David back to celebrations in Saul's household when he had observed the sacred meal with Jonathan. The slaughtered lamb, blood of protection on the door posts, bitter herbs of remembrance—solemn symbols harkening back to Israel's great deliverance from Egyptian slavery—now brought back images of holy friendship, of a covenant bond more powerful than death. Then, too, Passover brought to mind his own deliverance from the hand of Saul.

What had happened to Jonathan's family? David knew he'd had a wife and at least one child. What had become of them on that dreadful day of Saul's defeat?

"Hushai, you're good to visit a grouchy invalid day after day."

David's flat-nosed companion chuckled. "My lord, if I announce a sudden need to pee and don't come back, you'll know you've gotten too grumpy. Or I can tell you to shut up. A friend can do that. Advisors and soldiers have to be diplomatic."

David sighed. "You're good for me, Hushai." *Like Jonathan was,* he said to himself. Hushai, not having heard the comparison, wondered at David's next rambling monologue about Saul and Ish-Bosheth, injustice, and life on the run.

David stood with a grimace and walked stiffly around the room. "Hushai, will you do me a favor? Find out who's left of Saul's family, particularly his son Jonathan."

Hushai's mind leapt to retribution. *Is his pain turning earlier suffering into anger? Kings often annihilate an enemy's dynasty, and David is a king. What should I do? What should I say?* He decided to follow through on the request and see what came of it.

Hushai rummaged around Gibeah, talking to old linen clients and anyone else who might know something. He learned that besides Saul's four sons by his wife Ahinoam—Jonathan, Malki-Shua, Abinadab, and Esh-Baal—he had had two by his concubine Rizpah—Armoni and Mephibosheth. Of his daughters Michal and Merab, only the latter had children—five sons. As David had said, Jonathan had a wife and son; the child shared the name of Rizpah's Mephibosheth.

After Hushai had collected this information, he decided to dole it out to David from a different angle, hoping to learn the king's mind in the process. He preferred not to be responsible for a bloodbath if he could help it. He would start with Ziba, a servant from Saul's household.

When the old man heard Hushai's suggestion that he appear before the king, he too considered David's motive.

"Don't worry," said Hushai. "I doubt that the servant who emptied Saul's chamber pot is a political threat to the king. I'll stand by you, and if he tries to kill you, he'll have to kill me first."

David was on his throne, his robe pulled wide to hide the pillows behind him. "Ah!" He reached out his hands to the leathery, sharp-featured Benjamite. Hushai took heart and shoved his trembling charge forward. "You are Ziba?" asked David.

Ziba's voice wouldn't work on the first try. Swallowing a few times, he finally said, "Yes, my lord. Your servant."

David held his hand longer than Ziba would have preferred. "I remember you. I'd come in hot and tired, and you'd have water."

"Yes! And Master was hardly ever pleased to see you."

David snorted. "You might say that. Anyway, you understood and were kind. I remember. Please sit down, Ziba. Hushai—" He motioned vaguely.

But Hushai, greatly heartened, already had a cushion for the old man.

"Ziba, I've been thinking a lot. God has made me king over Judah and Israel. He's helping me subdue my enemies. He's restoring my health. Perhaps you heard..."

"Yes, my lord. Praise be to God for sparing your life. Thanks to—"

"Yes, yes. I am grateful. Now, do you know of anyone left in the house of Saul to whom I can show God's kindness?"

Hushai let out his breath and smiled.

"For instance," continued David, "I know Jonathan had a son. What became of him? Do you know?" He leaned forward eagerly, then winced and sat back.

"Yes, always one for Jonathan, you were. A good man, Jonathan."

"An excellent man. Is his wife still living?"

"No, she died soon after her husband, birthing his child—a daughter, I believe. But his son lives, though he is crippled in both feet."

If Ziba was nervous over his audience with the king, Mephibosheth was mutton broth when Ziba brought him to the throne. Only a boy, fourteen at most, and with sticks to prop him, he came expecting the worst.

This time David was able to bend to the lad. "*Hoo-ha-ha-ha!* Don't be afraid. I loved your father, and I'll do right by you.

Your father was proud of you when last we spoke. Come sit beside me. Let's talk. How were you injured?"

Mephibosheth swallowed hard and looked desperately at Hushai, then Ziba. They nodded encouragement. "I—I don't remember much...that day. My—my mother screaming, tearing her clothes. Everything was packed, but when we went out, it all got left behind. I wanted my mother, but she was heavy with child and made me go with my nurse. She was crying, everyone was running, and then...I only remember my feet hurt bad."

"The nurse tripped and fell, my lord," said Ziba. "Landed on the boy's legs. A big woman. They were broken too badly to be fixed. Couldn't walk at all for two years and poorly now, as you can see."

"I'm sorry," said David, "sorry that Jonathan's son will never run like his father. Where have you been staying?"

"In Lo Debar near Mahanaim, with Makir *ben* Ammiel."

"Ah yes, Makir. He's good to you? A friend of my friend Barzillai; he mentions Makir often. And you were close to your Uncle Esh-Baal for a few years."

The boy nodded.

"You're not a warrior, of course. Do you sing like your father?"

The boy shook his head.

"Do you make poetry?"

The boy looked blank.

"Well—ah...Mephibosheth, let's see what we can do for you. For the sake of your father Jonathan, I'll restore your grandfather's land to you. Also, stay in Jerusalem and eat with my own sons, like I did at your grandfather's table. Will you do that?"

Mephibosheth bowed low, trembling hands pressed to his forehead. "My lord...a dead dog like me...?"

David smiled and turned to the servant. "Ziba, I hear you have a big family."

"Yes, my lord." He straightened proudly. "Fifteen sons and twenty servants."

"Well done. You'll have help, then, to farm Saul's land and provide for the boy."

Ziba's face lit, but still he was wary of the king's motive.

David took his hand. "I can't bring Jonathan back, but I can serve his son. It's my privilege."

When they had left, David slumped in his chair. A rumble of thunder gave definition to the gloom inside and out. Rain patterned the dust on the windowsill.

"You're tired, my lord," said Hushai.

David shifted but didn't reply right away. "Did I do the right thing, Hushai? I can't read either one of them. Mephibosheth is certainly no Jonathan. His name—'from the mouth of shame'—is too close to his Uncle Ish-Bosheth's, the 'man of shame.' And Ziba..." He lapsed again into silence.

"Right or wrong," said Hushai with a grin, "what you did certainly beats separating heads from bodies."

David smiled crookedly. "You were thinking that?"

"It's what kings do," said Hushai.

"Not this one. Well, sometimes...when it's needed." He sat absorbed in his thoughts, then roused himself. "It's a step in the right direction, Hushai. Let's go look for Ahithophel and start the Ark on its journey home."

6

Two things on that day are forever etched on my mind. The first was my initial encounter with David, his passing touch and the three words he spoke: "You play well."

The second was a man on the ground, struck dead by God himself.

David and his Ark committee had planned out the details of the move. Every logistical eventuality had been thoroughly considered and provided for—or so they thought.

A new tent had been erected inside the palace compound. Although daily sacrifices would continue at Gibeon, the tabernacle had been duplicated on a smaller scale in this center of worship, and sacrifices would be made in both locations. The differences with this tabernacle would be the presence of the Ark and more provision for music. At the time, no one had an inkling of David's concept of worship, but his genius later became apparent, and all of us marveled.

Invitations went out to all the tribal leaders in Israel. The political significance of this event could not be underestimated: the nation's spiritual and political interests were fused in the Ark.

The military also was utilized. Not every soldier, of course, but the bodyguards, Mighty Men, and commanders of thousands and hundreds would serve as power on display.

Musicians especially were sought, and you can imagine my thrill on receiving an invitation to participate.

With thousands to feed, food was, of course, a major concern.

The spiritual significance of the event was clear: David was king, but Yahweh was in charge of the king. Just one thing slipped past everyone, including David: the Ark could not be reduced to numbers and arrangements. Who could have foreseen the dreadful outcome? In retrospect, we all identified clues. But at the time?

For seventy-five years, the Ark had rested at the home of Abinadab in Kiriath Jearim. Abinadab's oldest son Eleazar had been consecrated to guard the Ark, and upon his death, other sons had taken over. Now just two remained: Ahio and Uzzah. To them, the Ark was a familiar presence; they'd never known a time when it had not been in their family's care.

The day of the move dawned crisp and clear. From his "eagle's nest," the highest room of his palace, David surveyed the sea of tents that stretched as far as the eye could see. Important people were in those tents—priests and Levites by scores and thirty thousand tribal leaders from the whole of Israel.

And Nathan.

The day before, a stranger approached the palace requesting audience with David. He gave neither name nor business. If

I had seen him, I would have said immediately, "This man's a prophet." Nathan had the look of a prophet: harem-scarem hair, deep-set black eyes that seemed capable of touching off wildfires, a hawk-like, unyielding aspect, and a loose-jointed recklessness about his body and clothing. He appeared friendless, but only by choice. In offering himself as God's mouthpiece, he had cast off the pleasures and demands of civilized society to become a genuinely free man. Only the prophet Gad seemed the exception to this rule, but he had intensity of a different sort.

Nathan was younger than David but bore a mature agelessness. Even now, years later, he seems no different than that day when he first appeared at David's court.

When he did gain access to David, he seemed uncertain about what to do with it. David, after being looked up and down to the point of awkwardness, was about to throw the fellow out when Nathan said, "I will be needed here," and again his eyes searched out David's liver and kidneys. David had known Samuel, and in that short sentence, Nathan's voice struck him an almost physical blow. His eyes opened wide, and he bowed before the prophet. "I am honored that you have come," was all he said.

I was twenty-five at the time of the Ark parade, but already I had a reputation as the most promising son of my father Berachiah, himself a noted musician. The anticipation of finally meeting the musician king was almost unbearable. Dressed in my finest Levitical robe—thick and full to lend substance to my short, slender frame—hair trimmed painstakingly and adorned with my father's gold headband, I still felt naked. The king would certainly point his finger at me:

"You, there! Dressed so fine yet bereft of talent, a mere boy, a dabbler in music. Give me one reason why you should stand before the Ark of the most holy God. None, eh? Seize him; drag him away!"

But when I actually saw David as we gathered at Kiriath Jearim, glory surged through my soul. All I'd heard of David's personal charm, his musical ability—every bit was real. I could hardly stand when he came to the musicians at the head of the parade, moving from one to another with words of appreciation and encouragement.

I don't know why I was surprised—overwhelmed, even—by David's size. I suppose the story of Samuel choosing the runt of Jesse's litter had led me to think of David as small. Plus, most musicians aren't noted for their superior muscle. Taller than I but shorter than Saul, he nevertheless had the cut of a king. Part wild ox; part aesthete. I was in awe.

Samuel's grandson Heman knew David and had played the harp at the Hebron coronation. In this event, he and I, along with Ethan, were to sound the bronze cymbals and sing; others would play lyres and harps. Singers under the direction of the Levite Kenaniah would number in the hundreds.

The scene at Kiriath Jearim was chaotic. Men in festal robes and flower garlands shouted and jockeyed for position while women sang and danced around the edges, adding to the confusion.

Uzzah, Ahio, and other Levites had placed the Ark on a new cart drawn by a team of young oxen. A square of fine linen, woven with priestly colors, covered it, and flowers had been heaped around; even the oxen wore garlands on their horns. Ahio walked in front of the cart and Uzzah at the side, both with ornamented prods for the oxen. They, of all Israel, seemed out of sorts. Did they regret the transfer of the Ark from their charge, or did they somehow sense what was to come?

At last all was ready. Trumpets, harps, lyres, tambourines, and cymbals all played. A mighty sound rose from the singers. We stepped toward Jerusalem.

Although David's place was in front of the oxen, he circulated among the musicians, leading the singing and shouting. The effect was galvanizing, and with the Presence in the Ark stirring us, we praised God with our entire beings. Behind the cart came all of Israel, a swelling and constricting parade that stretched for miles.

Then, at the height of land, on the threshing floor of Nachon, it happened.

A simple thing. An ox stumbling. No obstacle, no unevenness to cause it. Maybe a misstep. The hand of God, perhaps. Whatever it was, the ox stumbled, the cart lurched, and without thinking, Uzzah put out his hand to steady the Ark.

What happened next I doubt anyone can ever really know or understand. I was far ahead of the Ark and saw nothing. The noise we were making drowned out everything until the shock buffeted us. But others saw.

From all reports, Uzzah seemed to swell and then deflate as though he had popped, as though his body tried but could not contain such a strong infusion of life. Those walking near the Ark were thrown down, yet they felt strong and alive and were startled to find death in their midst. A scent—not exactly of fire or death or incense—moved in an ever-widening circle, touching off coughing and breathing difficulties.

For a full minute, none of the immediate spectators moved. David's face went deathly white, then red. Then, dragging a wheezing, constricted breath from deep within, he howled. He raged against the heavens, against the Ark, for this outbreak against Uzzah.

It seemed clear in retrospect what had gone wrong. The only Levites in immediate attendance had been Ahio and Uzzah, to whom it had 'belonged' these many years. The high priest Abiathar had been little more than an observer. He had prayed beforehand, but no one had consulted the Lord concerning the matter.

Uzzah obviously had not thought carefully about what he was doing, nor did he have in mind the restrictions concerning the Ark. He had been raised around this object. When the ox stumbled, he had reached out to steady it. A reflexive act. His last act.

The Ark of God, the holy God; the Ark called by the Name, the name of the Lord Almighty; the Ark of the Presence that can kill.

7

The parade stopped there atop the hill. Clouds billowed; a smattering of rain plopped sullenly on threshing dust that lay decades thick. After the initial outcry, no one in the immediate area moved or made a sound. I could hear the shock as it rippled through the crowd behind the cart. Ordinary noises came from Obed-Edom's spread below—donkeys and goats and sheep. Obscenely ordinary, given what lay on the ground.

Joab and several Mighty Men lurched forward, then stood frozen by what they saw. No one wanted to go near Uzzah's body, least of all Abiathar. David was transfixed, studying the flowers, now blighted and dripping from the cart. He drew dangerous breaths. Zadok the warrior priest approached Uzzah and touched him cautiously to make sure he was dead. Perhaps he was making sure the body itself was not an agent of death. I remember thinking how brave he was. If touching an ordinary corpse made a person unclean, what sort of uncleanness—what sort of judgment—was Zadok taking to himself here in the shadow of the Ark? And what could possibly purify him?

David closed his eyes, the color gone from his face. "We can't go on, Zadok. I don't want the Ark in Jerusalem. I don't want it anywhere near me. It's not safe." He drew stricken breaths and stared at Ahio, bent weeping over his brother's body. "The ephod is bad enough. Just your arm gets eaten away. The Ark, though... I want to leave it here, Zadok, in the middle of the road; I want to run away." He threw an arm over his face as though to shield it from a noisome mist rising out of the ground. "God broke out against us here. *Perez Uzzah*— outbreak against Uzzah."

No one knew what to do. By now a crescendo of mourning enveloped the nexus of death with upwards of forty thousand people wailing. The domestic animals below stared silently up the straw-strewn hillside.

Amasai, chief of the Thirty, worked his way through the crowd with a small man in tow. "My lord," said Amasai, "this is one of the doorkeepers—Obed-Edom the musician. He has something to say."

With garment torn and dust on his head, Obed-Edom bowed before David. "Your servant, my lord!" he said. Shaken by the paralysis of those in charge, he looked at David's runneled face. "My lord, your servant's house lies just below." He pointed across the threshing floor. "Would my lord come to your servant's house to rest or to decide what to do? I'd take the Ark myself, if that would help. Yes." He nodded at the new thought. "My lord, I offer myself—for destruction, if that's what comes of it—in the service of the Ark." He bowed again.

Zadok looked on with pained wonder. "Obed—servant. Appropriately named."

"Is there an honor higher than dying for the Ark?" asked Obed-Edom. "I can't think of one."

At that moment, David couldn't quite see the honor, but he made arrangements with the Levite and began the trek back to Jerusalem. He stalked the middle of the road, saying little to his companions—Hushai, Zadok, Abiathar, and myself.

Uzzah was, of course, the focus of what went wrong. Yes, he had touched the Ark in an unauthorized way, but with a ferocity that rattled me, David turned on himself. "This is my fault, but I don't know how. God knows I care. I cared when Goliath insulted us and our God. I had to defend Yahweh's glory and honor. My brothers thought I was just a dumb, stupid brat."

Abiathar jumped in hastily. "What you did that day, my lord, was certainly not dumb or stupid. It was—"

"Don't be a toad, Abiathar," David snapped at him. "I don't need that. I was stupid and arrogant—a half-grown he-goat."

"My lord, I only meant—"

"Go 'mean' elsewhere. I'm looking for answers, not sheep bleeting."

Abiathar withdrew, pained and embarrassed. I was glad I'd withheld my bit of flattery. In the awkward silence, I made bold with another approach. "My lord, is it true that no one inquired of the Ark in the days of Saul's reign? You, at least, tried to honor it after years of neglect. One would think your honorable intentions might cover mistakes or perhaps informality—"

I stopped, regretting the last word. David turned sharply as though noticing me for the first time, and my heart quailed.

"Informality," he said. "God is not pleased with informality. Be specific—what's your name? What is 'informality'?"

I breathed again. "Asaph, my lord." My small smile didn't work, so I hastily erased it. "Procedure, perhaps? As I see it, Uzzah's motives were good; his procedure was wrong. Did anyone else ponder whether or not—I don't mean to imply," I added hurriedly, "that Abiathar didn't do his job."

"You're right. We didn't consider procedure, we didn't consult the ephod, and I'm to blame. Abiathar may have had procedural thoughts, but he doesn't stand up well to his king. I set the tone; the fault lies at my door."

"No more than at mine," said Zadok. "And I'm not afraid of you."

David almost smiled.

Hushai shook his head. "No one questions your zeal. But you're—shall we say—creative? Evidently, God doesn't like creativity. Not that kind, anyway. In music, perhaps, but not with the Ark."

The set of David's jaw alarmed me. "It's not enough," he repeated savagely. "A good, honest offering isn't enough. Yahweh supposedly looks on a man's heart, not on the outward appearance of things. That's what he told Samuel. True, I didn't examine the Law of God; I didn't consult the priests. But still," he went on, "Yahweh shouldn't blast good intentions."

"Oh, shouldn't he?" said Zadok. This boldness among David's close associates surprised me, especially in such a context. This was my first taste of the king's inherent humility.

Zadok started ticking off his fingers. "When Moses built the first tabernacle, God said up front, 'Get close to the Ark in an unauthorized way and you die.' As plain as that." Next finger: "When the people started complaining—one might say justifiably, considering their hardships and skimpy diet—God breathed fire on them." Third finger: "When Moses struck a rock to get water, instead of speaking to it as God ordered, God barred him from the Promised Land. And look what happened with genuine rebellion, immor—"

David raised his hands. "Enough. You've made your point: we have no excuse." His face, though, remained hard.

The entire nation mourned. Many of the visiting dignitaries went home, but some stayed to see what would follow this extraordinary turn of events.

The Ark of the Testimony. The atonement cover. The dwelling place of the Name, the Lord Almighty, *Yahweh*, enthroned between the cherubim. "There," said the Lord Almighty to Moses, "above the cover between two cherubim, I will meet you and give my commands for the Israelites." A chest so holy, so deadly, it was hidden behind a thick curtain for the sake of mortals. None but the high priest dared look at it—and that only after a detailed routine of sanctification, both before and after exposure. Even so, he needed smoke from his censer to protect against that dreadful Presence above the atonement cover.

Kohathites of the sons of Levi were responsible for the Ark. When it was to be moved, priests were to cover it with the shielding curtain, along with seal hides and a blue cloth. When the Ark set out, Moses would say, "Rise up, O Lord! May your enemies be scattered; may your foes flee before you." When it came to rest, he would say, "Return, O Lord, to the countless thousands of Israel."

How could something so integral to every man's spiritual training be blithely disregarded by those who should have known better? Why, for instance, did only a thin square of linen cover the Ark? Why weren't Levites carrying it on poles instead of following the Philistines' example of hauling it on a new cart? To our shame, we had followed a pagan nation rather than the instruction of Moses. This much was clear: God had His fist in our faces as if to say, "You will not treat the Lord your God lightly." We were chagrined.

Especially David. He spent hours staring out the window. Then reports began filtering back about the blessings Obed-Edom was experiencing—an extraordinary fertility rate among his stock, bumper crops, the birth of twin boys. "Coincidence," said Michal contemptuously. "It's been less than three months. Did twins pop fully developed into the womb the moment Obed-Edom got his hands on the Ark?"

Despite his wife's cynicism, David was encouraged to try again. It was, after all, the right thing to do. The Ark must no longer remain on the fringes of national attention; it must be given a place of prominence to serve as the heartbeat of God in the new capital.

This time, however, each person—not just worship leaders—would undergo a scrupulous three-day sanctification procedure: ritual washing of bodies and clothing, abstinence from sexual intercourse, and avoidance of other ceremonial defilement. Inner cleansing would be sought as well. David helped plan the music. "I know it's hard to sing joyfully when you're scared to death, but that's what we'll do," he said. "Keep in mind, I'm more frightened than you!"

The cart had been burned outside the city. Levites would carry the Ark this time, its long, ornamental poles resting on their shoulders. And it would be covered properly. We felt better about that; the wonder remained that *only* Uzzah had perished.

The day arrived, much like the first, only warmer. Overall, this parade would be sparser than the first, more dedicated to the specific task at hand. We were assigned precise places in line. Heman, Ethan, and I were in front with the bronze cymbals to establish the rhythm for the singing. Behind us were seven singers with lyres and another rank of six with harps.

Kenaniah would walk behind the instrumentalists. His powerful voice would gather our fear and lift us through curves and cadences we could never have achieved on our own. Behind Kenaniah were Elkanah and my father Berekiah, serving the Ark as gatekeepers, followed by seven priests with silver trumpets. Then came the Ark, with Obed-Edom and Jeiel positioned behind as trailing gatekeepers. Last in line was the king with his retinue of elders and military captains. David wore a fine robe of purple and gold with a priestly garment underneath. It seemed fitting that the king, as head of a priestly nation, should take a priestly role in this highly dangerous operation.

Every eye was on the Ark itself, its poles shouldered by Levitical bearers. Would there be another outbreak—"Perez Asaph," or "Perez David"?

Nervously, David stooped and picked up a rounded stone, quite like a child just learning to sling, arming against some nameless, shapeless foe. He looked at it for some time as if drawing on it for meaning and strength.

Our launch was shaky at first. After only six steps, a bull and a fatted calf were sacrificed. All along the route, clusters of priests held animals to be sacrificed at regular intervals as we inched toward Jerusalem.

Having survived the first couple of stops, we gave a collective sigh. Lightning had not fallen a second time. The move was going well. David's spirits improved, and his fervor grew. He shed his colored robe for the white priestly linen beneath and began to sing, tentatively at first.

> *He restores my soul,*
> *He leads me in paths of righteousness.*
> *May Yahweh see our distress;*
> *May the Name of the God of Jacob protect us.*
> *Remember our sacrifices;*
> *Accept our burnt offerings.*
> *O Lord, save the king!*
> *Answer when we call!*

His confidence grew. He raised his arms, holding his stone skyward, closed his eyes toward the heavens, and burst forth with a shout of praise. The people responded. This continued antiphonally, the singers carving out their part in the festal shout. Rams' horns sounded, the silver trumpets sounded, Kenaniah sounded his magnificent voice, and we rode the tonal wave with all the fervor we could muster. By this time the king was dancing. I've seen David dance many times since that occasion, but never again did he seem so resplendent, so powerfully inspired. He was out of himself, beyond his role as king. In that moment, David *was* the nation's passionate love for God, the flame on its altar. And the nation responded with an increasing crescendo of worship.

We climbed the last hill, and the Ark was installed—with great care on the part of the Levites—in a pavilion rich and ornate on the southwest corner of the palace compound. Here on the new bronze altar, priests offered the final burnt and fellowship offerings. David looked again at the stone before slipping it into a pouch on his belt.

By that point, I had expected that everyone would wander off to savor the day. To my surprise, David came to me and put an arm around my shoulder. I began to tremble. "You play well." He drew me to face the crowd. "Look at this man!" he shouted. "A master musician!"

The people roared their approval, and my head began to spin.

"Asaph has done excellently this day, he and his fellows, and he'll continue before the Ark from this day on. I offer him a song of thanks to the Lord."

He stepped away and was quiet a moment, drawing notes and gratitude out of his heart. Then he began to sing.

> Give thanks to Yahweh, call on His name;
> Make known among the nations what He has done.
> Sing to Him, sing praise to Him;
> Tell of all His wonderful acts.
> Glory in His holy name;
> Let the hearts of those who seek Yahweh rejoice.
> Praise be to Yahweh, the God of Israel,
> From everlasting to everlasting.

When he finished, the people stood stunned, then exploded with "Amen!" and "Hallelujah!" I wept because I couldn't help it.

After seeing to the distribution of a loaf of bread, a cake of dates, and a cake of raisins to every man and woman, David went home to bless his wives and concubines and their children. He found his first wife Michal armed for battle. "Well, my lord," she said brightly. "How the king of Israel distinguished himself today! Leaping and cavorting half naked." Her words fell like toads from her mouth. "As subtle as a camel boy. The three slave girls of my servant Rivah stood giggling on the terrace. They enjoyed your fool's show."

Dark lashes veiled her arrow-tipped eyes, but the contempt of her heart threaded back to her father's house with its dank, secular atmosphere. Saul had neglected more than the Ark. Michal had received little nourishment from him even in the cultural requirements of the Law. She understood dignity and royalty, and David's dancing had diminished this. David the warrior she admired; David in a priest's ephod she despised. She could destroy the priest, though, by making his behavior somehow indecent, lascivious.

David stiffened. His voice held the crackle of ice. "A fool. Yes, I became a fool for God. And I would become even more foolish. Yahweh made me king, demonstrating to the world that God blesses those who bless him. I glory in humiliating myself before such a God. In case you've forgotten, God rejected your father and chose me because your father lacked the zeal you hate. What you despise, though, will be my greatest honor. In whatever way and with whatever lack of dignity, *I will worship the Lord.*"

Eyes smoldering, he moved toward the door, then turned back. "Those girls you mentioned… Humiliation before God is one thing; dishonor in the eyes of a slave is quite another. See to their backs at day's end."

Abigail was ill from exhaustion and unable to receive his blessing.

8

S ome months later, Nathan the prophet went to bed. It had been a good day with a pleasant tiredness to cap it off. He stretched out on his thin mat, reviewing his conversation with David. They had sat in David's "eagle's nest" high in the palace, directly above the king's living quarters. Broad windows scooped in winter sun and summer breezes. This day brought a breeze. Inside, sipping fruited drinks on a linen-draped daybed, Nathan had accepted luxury.

The king was euphoric. His wound had healed and his immediate enemies had been subdued. More battles lay ahead, but for now he could enjoy a tiny oasis of rest. The second attempt to move the Ark had gone well, and the chest now rested in the palace compound with Abiathar as high priest. Zadok, the acknowledged tribal leader of Aaron, had been washed, dressed, and anointed in a splendid ceremony to serve as priest at Gibeon. To my everlasting joy, David had made good on his promise that I should be chief musician before the Ark—a first, radical step toward the new worship he envisioned. Heman and Ethan would minister similarly with Zadok at Gibeon and would join me on special occasions.

David glowed as he talked with Nathan. His mood was expansive, yet he moved restlessly around the room. Finally, he turned to the prophet. "Nathan, look at this house. A palace of—how many rooms?—all cedar. Smell the wood. Look at the grain. A man couldn't ask for a finer dwelling."

"It is fine, my lord." Nathan peered about with a vague look of disengagement concerning material things. David seemed not to notice.

"The Ark, though, sits in a tent. A tent well-made but hardly finer than a wealthy Amalekite's. You know, Nathan, as I read about the Ark in preparation for..."

The word *Ark* abruptly blanked David's voice from Nathan's mind and sent him digging through the recent debacle. He had suffered considerably prior to the first attempt to move the Ark. His digestion was normally sound, but for no apparent reason his stomach had begun to burn and roil and ruin his sleep. He had suspected the cause but had chosen not to leave his room and confront the king, especially in the middle of the night. Now, more than four months later, sourness still tainted his breath. David's voice drifted back.

"'You haven't reached it yet,' God told Moses, 'but when you cross the Jordan and settle your inheritance, I'll give you rest and safety from your enemies. *Then*'—and this is the important part, Nathan—'Then I'll lead you to the place I've chosen as a dwelling for my Name. There you'll offer sacrifices, tithes, and special gifts. There, you and your family, your servants, and the Levites will rejoice before the Lord your God.'

"Nathan, *this is the place*." David jabbed his forefinger toward the floor. "Right here. Jerusalem, Zion, City of David. God brought me here and has put down my enemies. Think of the past, Nathan. What I went through to get here. Then consider the prospects. *This is the place for the house of God; I'm sure of it."*

He squatted before Nathan, eyes smoldering. "Nathan, there are times when I feel I might die like Uzzah. Not from touching the Ark, but from just holding out my love to God. Love can be dangerous, Nathan. A fire is consuming my heart, and if I were to articulate that fire, I'm not sure I'd survive. It needs an altar." He shifted to one knee and faced the prophet squarely. "Nathan, I want to build a house for the Ark of the Testimony of the Lord, the glorious footstool of our God."

Now he had the prophet's full attention. Nathan was amazed and excited. A temple. His mind leaped ahead. The house would tangibly show the presence of God in the midst of his people; it would symbolically underscore the peace of the kingdom.

And David was the man to do it.

His military superiority would give them space and time for such a project. A building to serve the Presence, not a big, expensive monument in Yahweh's name. In addition, it would provide an appropriate setting for David's musical genius and liturgical sense. The project wouldn't happen overnight, of course. It might take a lifetime. But David was still young—little more than forty.

Now, as Nathan mulled these things in bed, a familiar sensation came upon him. Not the sour stomach of four months ago. Something different. He could not accurately describe it.

The closest he could come was climbing Mt. Hermon on a sleety day, feeling the sting of ice crystals on hot, naked flesh.

Thus the word of the Lord came to Nathan.

He didn't sleep that night, but he was used to that—the occupational hazard of his calling. In the morning, he pulled himself from bed, humbled by a new perspective. He needed to talk with David but wasn't sure how the king would take it. Nathan was not bold as, say, Zadok was bold.

He approached Ahithophel for an appointment, then wished he hadn't. Nathan and Ahithophel were not a comfortable match.

The king assumed Nathan's desire to talk would hark back to the previous night's conversation, but a look at the prophet's haggard face told him otherwise. He went rigid.

At first, Nathan tried—awkwardly—to smooth the way, then gave up. Prodded by the Lord, he delivered the message exactly as it had been given to him.

> *Go, speak to My son David. Tell him,* "You talk of building Me a house. Are you the person for this? Do I even need a house? Think back. From Israel's days in Egypt until now, did I ever ask for a permanent dwelling place? I traveled as you travel, dwelling in a tent the same as everyone else.
>
> "I want your heart. I took a boy from sheep pens to shepherd my people Israel. I trained a man of war to carve out a secure place for my people. I will cut off your enemies and bring rest to my people.
>
> "You are a warrior, a shedder of blood, assigned to plow peace for your descendants, not to build a house for my Name.

"I must first build your house, and then your son will build a house for my Name. As I am your Father, your son will be my son. When he does wrong, men will punish him, but never will I remove my love from him as I did from Saul. Your name, your kingdom, your house, your throne, my son David, I will establish forever."

David sat pale and shaken as Nathan finished speaking. "A covenant, Nathan!" he whispered. "A covenant of blood!"

David's mind snapped to Jonathan, to a particular supper that had started normally with the ritual killing of an animal for the meal, or "cutting a covenant," as some called it. But with great solemnity Jonathan had halved the lamb and laid the pieces on either side of David. Then he had stepped between them, dipped his hand in the gore, and clasped David's hand. "I swear by the most holy Name of Yahweh," he said, "that your enemies shall be my enemies and your friends my friends." It had shaken David to the core, this impulsive covenant of blood. It was after that meal that Jonathan gave David his robe, tunic, sword, bow, and belt in covenantal exchange. From then on they had been blood brothers.

Abraham had known such a covenant. God met the patriarch between assorted animals, also laid out in halves. But Abraham had been a man of peace, whereas David knew only war. What was the connection? Was the Lord, through David's obedience as a warrior, somehow bringing life from death in an eternal covenant?

David thought of Abigail's portentous words when they had first settled into Jebus. "Your son, my lord.... Through your son,

you will live forever! The bundled treasure kept for eternity..."
He shivered again as he had that day.

He wandered the room aimlessly, the point and counter-
point of the word he had heard coming together in thunder-
ous polyphony: *No, you can't build me a house. Yes, I will build
your house.* David grabbed the prophet and dragged him toward the door. "Come with me."

They jogged to the Tent, Nathan panting more than a little.
After speaking to Abiathar, the two went inside. Nathan prudently stayed near the entrance, but David went as close as he
dared to the altar of fragrance in front of the curtained-off
Ark. There he lay before the Lord God, in whose Presence
even the smoke of incense bowed down. David sneezed.

For a long time he remained silent. When words came, he
spoke wonderingly.

"Who am I, O Sovereign Lord, and what is my family that
You should look on me with such grace and favor? You've
traced the future of my family, not for just one generation, but
forever. For the sake of Your word, You've done this mighty
thing.

"There is no God like You, a God of ancient covenants. You
gathered a people for Yourself; You gave us a name and redeemed us from slavery through great and awesome deeds.
You brought us to the land of our inheritance.

"And Lord God, today You place me, not just *melech*—
king—on an ordinary throne, but *hamelech*—high king—on
an enduring throne. My dynasty will last forever, my name
will forever hide in Your great Name.

"O Sovereign Lord," David's voice dropped almost below
Nathan's hearing, as though on the verge of sacrilege. "*Abba*

Father…bless the house of Your servant, that it may continue forever in Your sight. With Your blessing, the house of *Hamelech David* will indeed be blessed."

With that expression of spiritual strength, David went out to establish the kingdom of God, to serve the Sovereign Lord as a man of war. But as it turned out, at least some of the blood that spattered his hands was less than holy.

9

Twelve barefoot men stumbled across the edge of night toward the Jordan River. Ammonite jeers fell behind them, as had stones, slung at their departing figures. Most of the twelve wanted to rest, but Hushai, his soft body prodded by sheer will, pushed them on. "We'll be safer if we keep going. Then we can stop and find covering."

Dawn unmasked their humiliation—feet raw, cuts dripping blood, buttocks bare and striped from being driven like goats, faces disfigured by half beards and utter shame. The group had little left with which to hide their nakedness. They crossed the river and collapsed on the bank where passing herders found them huddled in ignominy.

When the runner arrived at the throne room with the report of the Ammonite outrage, David's angry bellow caused a new slave girl to shrink in terror.

Like Moab before the massacre, Ammon had been on relatively good terms with Israel. King Nahash had mellowed since the days of Saul when he had threatened the men of

Jabesh Gilead with right eye removal. When David became king in Hebron, Nahash had asked for a treaty.

Hushai had gone with a delegation to meet with Nahash. "A wily old buzzard," he had told David afterward, "but re- alistic...calculating. He knew he'd have hot tar on his hands if he didn't make some sort of peaceful gesture. 'The young Israelite king may be a green fig,' he told me, 'but he's not short on chutzpah.'"

Now Nahash was dead, and his son Hanun had plopped himself on the throne. Feeling benevolent after Nathan's prophecy, David had responded with a gesture of sympa- thy. Once again, Hushai had been dispatched with a delega- tion, this time one that was neither political nor threatening. Nahash they had known, and Hanun's younger brother Shobi was a friend who had twice given aid to David in his flight from Saul. Hanun, however, had been an unknown. Was he going to be ornery like the youthful Nahash, mellow like the old king, or affable like his brother? David had packaged sym- pathy with optimism—a mistake, as it turned out.

After his beard and disgrace grew out, Hushai came from Jericho to report to David.

"Once inside the door, we knew we'd stumbled onto a snake pit. Guards everywhere. Thick-necked, gussied-up minder of goats on the throne. Rat-eyed henchmen gulping wine from silver bowls. The smell of fools makes me gag."

"Who was in charge?" asked David. "King or henchmen?"

"Feh! The cronies played on the king's stupidity. *Spy* was the operative word. They whispered and guffawed, plucking our nerves like a lyre."

David's eyes narrowed. Hushai went on.

"Hanun talked civilly, but when the nobles started mixing with the guard, I began to sweat. Twelve figs against forty or more warriors. We saw it coming but couldn't do a thing. They grabbed us, held us down, shaved half our beards off, and cut our clothing just above our genitals. Yes, yes. It could've been worse, as I kept telling the others. I want you to know, David: each man bore the insult well. Not a word, not a howl, even after they banged us around. They took our sandals, then drove us with sticks through the streets of Rabbah, shouting, 'Hebrews like to be different; look at them now!' Up and down they paraded us until we were beyond exhaustion. Fortunately, the river was downhill all the way. Thank you, by the way, for permitting us to stay in Jericho until our shame was covered."

David gave a deprecating wave. "Hushai...I'm sorry this happened. If I'd had an inkling—"

"How could you? You made a peaceful gesture; why would Hanun pull such a stunt? Madness."

"Yes." David touched Hushai's bristled beard. "This means war."

Even Hanun came to that conclusion—too late. The fun was over. He had the ingredients for a major conflict in his kettle, and suddenly his appetite was gone.

He was not altogether without resources. He knew his father's friends and debtors. Along with his own considerable army, he called in twenty thousand Aramean mercenaries from the northern sovereignties of Beth Rehob and Zobah, the Syrian bailiwick of King Hadadezer, and twelve thousand from Tob, an Aramean principality north of Gilead. The king of Maacah in Aram reluctantly agreed to help but showed up with only a thousand men.

From his citadel in Rabbah, Hanun surveyed the plain and plotted his moves, but his knees began to tremble when he saw his own grave in the distance.

10

Spring had come, the month of Abib when kings go out to battle. David, however, took off with a peaceful agenda, visiting small kings up and down the coast who were eager to become vassals and ward off annihilation. He wanted, too, to call on King Hiram in Tyre. Although the temple project was not David's to carry out, his head was bursting with ideas, and Hiram would know what materials he should collect for his son.

Joab, then, was left to take a sizeable army—roughly thirty thousand—to Rabbah, the capital of Ammon that straddled the headwaters of the Jabbok River. The citadel itself, an impregnable fortress, sat high on a mountain ridge in the northwest quarter, gleaming in the late-afternoon sun as Joab approached the Ammonite stronghold.

The next morning, the army awoke to find Ammonites outside the gate preparing to attack. If that wasn't enough to give Joab heartburn, Uriah jogged in to report that Aramean mercenaries were bivouacked five miles away, ready to pounce. "If we attack the city," said Uriah, "the Arameans will be on us. But if we go after them instead, the Ammonites will attack."

Joab swore and kicked a stack of shields. The Israelites had marched right past the hidden troops, and now the Arameans were in a position to flank them.

He prowled the ranks, then made his plan. The cream of his army, led by Jashobeam, Eleazar, and Ittai the Gittite, would turn back with him to face the Arameans. The rest would fight on at Rabbah under Abishai, with the help of Shammah and Amasa.

Abishai drew him aside. "You're taking the Gittite?" he asked. "Achish's right-hand man?"

"Ittai's all right. He's admirable, loyal—and," Joab added wryly, "after seeing what happened to Uzzah, devout."

Joab's strategy was simple. Uriah would scout and deploy help to whichever force got into trouble. This was a gamble, Joab knew. He and Abishai would both be grossly outnumbered, and under these adverse circumstances, he had an attack of piety. "Stand fast," Joab said to Abishai. "Do your best for our people and the cities of our God. The Lord will come through for us."

Pious words don't always spell piety. True, Joab observed the law—outwardly; David wouldn't have it otherwise. But he seldom talked about God unless it suited his purposes. Or when he'd been shaken. The business of Uzzah and the Ark shook him. I saw his face go white that day. I believe his face was still white when he went off to fight the Ammonites. Here at the height of Joab's strategic powers, he faced the longest, toughest campaign of his career. Perhaps he knew the shape of things to come and, for the first time in his life, was moved to apply to God.

Joab had reason for concern. The Aramean mercenaries he faced represented thirty-seven tons of silver, the best force Ammonite money could buy. They had horses, chariots, and foot soldiers by the tens of thousands, not to mention capable generals.

With luck, he might be able to sneak up on them. But he'd need time. "Delay the attackers as long as you can," he told Abishai. "Messages back and forth—whatever you need. Try to give me three hours."

When they reached the distant overlook and surveyed the army below, Joab decided to split his thin force even thinner to double the attack points. Leaving Jashobeam, Eleazar, and Ittai with their men, Joab and his battalion made the danger-ous crossing to the far side of the valley, crawling with extraor-dinary patience across the gray hardpan. At a place where ex-truding boulders narrowed the valley, they spread out and crept into place, covering the better part of the opposing army.

They hadn't long to wait. A horseman galloped in with battle news, and almost immediately the Arameans galvanized with shouts and rattling armament.

Joab and his men lay hidden and still until the chariots and horsemen moved out. Then, responding to little more than a finger raised in signal, a hundred archers released their bows, and dozens of men crumpled on the valley floor. Chaos erupted among the Arameans as another volley, coupled with a similar assault from the opposite side, sent them into confusion. Joab relied on bows until the opposing generals organized an as-sault. Even then they waited until Aramean soldiers scrambled up the slope before rising with swords and spears that imme-diately ran red.

By this time, the chariots had circled back and were milling uncertainly. Ittai and his band of sea people went to work on the closest. Before long, the few still mobile took off in a dead run, followed by the ragged remains of the infantry.

"After them!" shouted Joab. "They mustn't regroup with Hanun's army!"

They needn't have worried. The Arameans didn't so much as pause to check on their employer. The entire body of mercenaries headed straight north, and when Hanun, watching from the citadel, saw the rout, he pulled back his own men to the safety of the city.

Joab shrugged and returned to Jerusalem. "Nothing lost, nothing gained."

He'd no sooner gotten there, however, when word came that the Arameans had regrouped, this time under Hadadezer, the mighty king of Zobah, who controlled most of the northern territory as far as the Euphrates River, and Shobach, his commander in chief.

"This wouldn't have happened if you hadn't let them walk away," said David.

"Sure," said Joab. "Chase Arameans while Abishai broils on the Ammonite spit. You should maybe come out and blow the trumpet."

David rested his chin on his fist for a moment. "Shobach's a general I wouldn't mind having on our side. Like Ittai." He sighed, then straightened, "We'll need the militia for this, as well as the army. Get Amasa to muster all Israel."

All Israel mustered within the week, farmers and tradesmen ready to fight. I've said it before: Hebrews are not like other nations. They are a holy people. They live differently, they dress differently, they worship differently, and are ready to arise at a moment's notice. Their king is committed to righteousness, a concept enemies seldom take into account. They say Hebrews are flesh and blood like all other men; why should they be harder to defeat?

War is their worship. With a clear cause, a sense of proprietorship over the land given them by Yahweh, they rally willingly to a call to arms. They also carry into battle the Ark of this God who cannot be seen. Bottom-line respect for them by enemies often comes too late at the mean end of Hebrew spears.

David went first to Mahanaim to set up a base of operations and a supply depot, then led the host to Helam, Shobach's chosen battle arena—a flat plateau, ideal for chariots. They stared across the arid field at numberless chariots and thousands upon thousands of bowmen, spearmen, slingers, swordsmen. The flags of Hadadezer's army rattled urgently against the wind. Their own banners seemed limp and pitiful. David and Joab looked silently at the array, then at each other. David swayed to some silent tune deep within, then began to chant:

> *For those who fear You,*
> *Your banner is our shield.*
> *Save us, help us;*
> *Deliver those You love.*
> *We look to You against this foe;*
> *Man's help is worthless.*
> *Give us victory, Lord;*
> *Crush our enemies.*

Joab pursed his lips, then said, "Let's go."

Levites lifted the Ark and priests sounded trumpets, not just asking God's help, but expecting it and giving thanks in advance. Units of tens and hundreds and thousands marched out. Slingers and bowmen in front with their round shields. Regulars, each with two spears, a sword, and large shield. Commanders and generals with individual armor bearers. The king would fight close to Joab, both keeping an eye on the overall battle.

The initial shock came on the crest of a roar, and slingers settled to the task of felling as many opponents as possible. They were good—accurate with missiles the size of plump figs. Hours spent in practice and contests gave them a proficiency that made even David's score on Goliath seem almost mediocre. They would keep their own tally and later boast— if they lived, if they won.

Sword on sword, spear on shield; the roar of rage and pain quickly swallowed the initial snap of bowstrings and sibilance of ten thousand arrows. The sweat of terror soon melded with the stink of blood and spilled guts. Battle madness escalated as horror-eyed bodies became a grotesque mosaic on the plain of Helam.

Shobach was formidable, the size of his army daunting, and he used his resources well. He tried to wedge through David's troops while simultaneously attacking both flanks. David, Joab, and the *Gibborim* had to do all they could to keep up with his rapidly deploying tactics, let alone try to outmaneuver him.

The battle seesawed over two days, but superior training and endurance among David's warriors began to pay off, and the slaughter began. Forty thousand foot soldiers killed, seven hundred charioteers, and seven thousand horses.

As David and Eleazar stood surveying the killing field, Joab came toward them, smearing an arm over sweat and blood on his face. "Shobach's dead," he announced.

David looked at him with almost reflexive hardness. "Your hand, I suppose."

Joab shrugged. "Actually, he'd been hacked pretty good, but I gave him a chance to surrender. Told him you wouldn't mind a good man like him on our side. He didn't think much of the idea and went for my throat. What was I to do?" His face took on an aggrieved expression.

The outing brought more than victory. David collected the gold shields Hadadezer's officers had carried, as well as cartloads of bronze. Tou, king of Hamath in the far north, sent his son to congratulate David with even more articles of gold and silver and bronze. In David's mind, every ton of these materials translated to so many temple articles.

When other vassals of Hadadezer heard the outcome of the battle, they lost no time in giving themselves over to David and treating for peace. David established garrisons in the Aramean kingdom of Damascus and exacted tribute. "This is heady stuff," he said to Eleazar. "Not only is our kingdom nearly doubling, we're getting booty far beyond anything I expected!"

For all intents and purposes, Aram had been hamstrung. Hanun the Ammonite could no longer look to the north for help. But Rabbah itself still gleamed in the setting sun. The Ammonites would fight another day.

11

"Asaph, I'm exhausted."

Only twice had I ever heard Abigail say those words. On both occasions they were addressed to me. Other times I had seen her weary to the point of collapse, but always she would stiffen her back, compose her face, and carry on. Why did she admit her limitations to me, of all people? Perhaps I was removed enough from her sphere of activity to be safe. A haven of refuge, a hiding place. I like to think that. She knew I would listen without interference. She knew I saw the selfless love she bore for her husband. She knew her words would stop with me.

My wife had just gotten some fresh camel's milk. I poured a bowl for Abigail and settled her in a bit of shade. She took a sip and closed her eyes to savor this tiny pleasure. I didn't push her. As sometimes happened, she might say nothing at all and simply go her way with a nod of gratitude and firmer step. But after a long silence of drinking, she looked at me with startling directness.

"Asaph, please explain to me why God allows concubines."

Thank God she handed the bowl back before speaking, giving me an excuse to return it to the house! A dozen steps in, a dozen steps out—time to think. Where was she going with this? I knew she disapproved of the harem David was stockpiling—nine already, in addition to seven wives. But as Maacah took pleasure in reminding Abigail, concubines—women not suitable as wives—were a king's privilege. Most of David's collection were daughters of soldiers or tradesmen, but one had been a slave girl, another an Edomite virgin captured years ago. They lived apart from his wives, and their children had few rights other than a life of ease and splendor. Everyone knew this motley collection was a trial to Abigail, but what in particular had irritated her today?

"My lady," I said finally, "we know, of course, that concubinage was not God's original design for men and women."

"Nor were third wives," came the tart rejoinder from David's third wife. A reminder for me to walk carefully.

"The Law provides for, but does not condone, the weakness of the flesh, my lady. The Patriarchs indulged before the Law was actually written, and it was left to Moses to make the best of it. The Law doesn't allow men to toss wives and consorts into the street at whim. The practice now seems largely contained to kings. We can be glad for these strictures, for the sake of society at large." This was becoming uncomfortably stuffy, but then the subject was equally uncomfortable. "In your instance..."

"Yes, in my instance." She fell silent and studied a bit of hyssop that had muscled through the adjacent wall.

"David's harem is troubling you, my lady?" I suggested.

"David's harem is a blot on David's judgment," she said, so fiercely I jumped. "They're an undisciplined, irresponsible lot, their whelps even more so. Asaph, if I were five people, I might be able to keep the palace operating smoothly. These women are expected to work, but unless someone stands over them, they mount any excuse and ride off. If I were five people...but I'm only one. I cannot monitor them every moment. I cannot be everywhere to keep shame out of public view."

Her words poured out. "Liliah's a trollop, by anyone's definition."

"Perhaps excepting David's?"

"Excepting David's," she agreed. "He chooses to think the best of his women—all but his third wife," she added tartly, "and his sons can do no wrong—excepting his second son. Liliah isn't even subtle with her flirtations. Adah, on the other hand, does her work in dark corners. This morning I found Daniel moping about, not wanting to look at me, obviously distressed and ashamed over something. Finally he allowed that Adah had had a 'conversation' with him. I don't need to spell it out, Asaph. I lost most of the morning trying to repair the damage she'd done the boy and then had to work twice as hard on housekeeping because no one else had done anything. I have reason to believe that both Liliah and Adah have done some serious entertaining while David has been away, but of course my word means nothing."

"My lady! That's a serious charge!"

"Do you think I make it lightly, Asaph?"

"No, you wouldn't. What will you tell the king when he comes back?"

"I won't even mention it. His women hide their tracks well. And David isn't the jealous sort. He'd simply brush it off, telling me I've been peering under too many bed mats."

The word *jealous* clicked in my head. "If he were concerned, there is a test...." Was it wise to even mention such a thing?

Abigail frowned. "A test?"

"For unfaithfulness. In the Law. It's seldom used these days, but not unheard of. In fact..." I kneaded my chin nervously. "I heard recently that Saul commanded the high priest Ahimelech to do a jealousy test on Ahinoam early in their marriage."

Abigail's lips pursed. "Why do I not find that surprising, knowing Saul?"

"A solemn action, nonetheless," I said. "And one not pleasant for a man like Ahimelech."

"Yes, please tell me. I seem to remember an old aunt speaking of such a thing when I was young, but I hardly knew what she was talking about. I remember wondering at the time whether any other nation's gods required such a thing."

I drew a breath. What had I gotten into? "The Law states," I said slowly, "that a husband who suspects his wife of unfaithfulness may take her to the priest. The priest then takes her before the altar and places in her hands a jealousy offering of barley flour. He removes her headdress, allowing her hair to fall—"

Abigail nodded. "A symbol of judgment. She would expect judgment."

"Exactly. And while she stands there considering her sins, he puts holy water into a clay jar, then adds dust scraped from the floor of the Tent. Finally, he speaks the words of the curse. 'If you've slept with no other man while married to your husband, may this bitter water of the curse not harm you. But if you have gone astray and defiled yourself by sleeping with another man, may your abdomen swell abnormally and your womb be barren.' Then the woman will say, 'Amen. So be it,' and drink the water."

"That's dreadful!" said Abigail.

"Oh?" I had expected her to nod approvingly.

"Of course. Such treatment would most likely kill her, guilty or not."

"Only if she is in fact guilty of adultery."

"Or if she has a weak constitution that can't handle dirty water."

"She stands there in God's hands for Him to judge. If she hasn't done the thing accused, nothing will happen. The God of the Ark, the God of the ephod, is the God who knows her heart."

Abigail tightened her lips. "*Yahweh* makes me nervous," she said.

I laughed. "Well, presumably in Ahinoam's case, God adjudged her innocent, for she bore four sons after that."

Just then, Absalom *ben* Maacah bounded into the courtyard. He loped toward us with his affable smile. "Ha! A double surprise!" he said. "My father's songbird and his commander in chief. How are you?" He kissed first Abigail, then me. A handsome lad of fifteen, his hair was his defining mark, so thick he seldom needed turban or headdress. Bound by a gold band that could scarcely be seen for the thicket it contained, the red and black of his parents' hair merged in a rich, glorious russet. People noticed Absalom. He of all the king's sons had the potential for equaling his father's size and strength, plus charm and appeal. Abigail, however, was not swayed by his appearance. She sat straight and composed her face into pleasant blandness.

One could not help liking the lad. I knew Abigail's concerns, of course, but personally had seen nothing more than high spirits cloaked in exceptional politeness. I'd heard more than one person express regret that Amnon, not Absalom, was first in line to succeed David. Amnon was blatantly self-serving and had other failings. Abigail's son Daniel, second in line, while an intelligent, well-behaved child, was hardly kingly material, and she prayed daily for Amnon's health and reformation, that Daniel be spared the honor.

"I was passing by," said Absalom, "and wondered if you were here and had time to sing that song my father asked for last Sabbath. I liked it. I'd like to hear it again."

I glanced sideways. Surely Abigail's opinion would rise at such a request. Her expression did not change, however.

"Which one was that? 'We give thanks to you, O God, we give thanks'?"

"No, not that one. The one that goes, 'I will watch my ways and keep my tongue from sin.'"

My backbone went rigid. Was he toying with me? Or was this some sort of performance to impress Abigail? "You must be mistaken," I said stiffly. "That's the psalm your father presented to Ethan."

He laughed disarmingly. "Oh, the very one I'm trying to push out of my brain! It keeps plaguing me. That's why I wanted you to sing yours to replace it. The one about instruments and singing."

I relaxed. "Oh, yes: 'Sing for joy to God our strength; shout—'"

"That's it! Sing it all—and rescue me, please."

Please, indeed. Pleased, I sang.

> *Sing for joy to God our strength;*
> > *shout to the God of Jacob!*
> *Start the music. Bang tambourine,*
> > *strum harp and lyre.*
> *Blow the ram's horn at New Moon,*
> > *when the moon is full, on the day of our Feast;*
> > *The God of Jacob has commanded it.*

A command performance for the king. What more could a musician desire? When I finished, Absalom took my hand and bowed low. He looked me in the eye and said, "Thank you, my father. You sing every bit as well as my own father." And with another bow to Abigail, he turned toward the gate, detouring just enough to hike up his robe and leap over the open cistern in the center of the courtyard.

12

As if Ammon and Aram weren't enough of a plateful for David, Edom chose that moment to rear up on its hind legs, horns cocked for battle. The scout who brought the report to the battleground at Helam wished he'd been less quick to volunteer. "Damn Edom!" David roared, scattering donkeys and chattel about, the messenger having scurried out of reach. "How *dare* they challenge us!"

Edom—Israel's ancient enemy in the mountainous region south of the Salt Sea. The land of Esau, whose name became Edom after he traded his birthright for a meal. The land that refused Moses passage on his way from Egypt to Canaan, forcing him into desert regions to the east. A land of variegated rocks, abrupt cliffs, and deep ravines. A land of terraced hillsides that yielded abundance and prosperity.

Now the Edomites wanted more. They had reached the southern end of the Salt Sea and were heading northward.

David stopped snarling and turned on the unfortunate messenger, pounding him with unaccountable glee. "I've got it!" he shouted. "Balaam's prophecy! Where's Zadok? I need Zadok. Get him here. Tell him to bring the Fourth Book of Law."

Zadok gloried in battlefield duty. Each priest served a month at a time—eternal to most but all too short for Zadok—before returning to duty in Gibeon. The din, the clash, and the intense exertion of battle fed his inner fire, and for him, as for Uriah, war was simply a different form of worship. He himself did not fight; he dutifully sacrificed, purified, prayed, and sang, all the while drawing war into his lungs.

Five minutes later, Zadok appeared with scroll in hand. "My lord the king," he said with some amusement.

"Zadok, I may have unlocked the mystery of Balaam."

"Ahh! The Aramean soothsayer. Maybe you'll have better luck with him than the king of Moab did. Balaam was supposed to speak an incantation against Moses as the Israelites mustered on the border of Canaan but couldn't seem to pull it off."

Zadok searched the scroll. "Here it is—Fourth Book of Moses, fourth oracle:"

> *The oracle of Balaam son of Beor,*
> *the oracle of one whose eye sees clearly.*
> *I see him, but not now;*
> *I behold him, but not near.*
> *A star will come out of Jacob;*
> *A scepter will rise out of Israel.*
> *He will crush the foreheads of Moab,*
> *The skulls of all the sons of Sheth.*

"Here it is," said Zadok, moving his finger to the spot. "Pay attention."

> *Edom will be conquered;*
> *Seir, his enemy, will be conquered,*

but Israel will grow strong.
A ruler will come out of Jacob,
and destroy the survivors of the city.

"Ha!" This time David pounded Eleazar. "There it is! Written. 'A ruler will rise.' That's us. And '*Edom will be conquered.*' You heard. God's word to us. Now, do it. Abishai. Take some generals and head south."

Within a week, Abishai's army advanced on Edom and struck down eighteen thousand soldiers in the Valley of Salt, a wadi off the Arabah. One part battle, six parts slaughter. And as David had done in Damascus, Abishai posted garrisons throughout the country.

Edom had been conquered...by the star and scepter of Jacob.

Soon after my courtyard conversation with Abigail and the unexpected appearance of Absalom, nasty rumors began circulating through Jerusalem—rumors that would ultimately endanger David's life. Any public figure attracts gossip and intrigue, but most can be ignored. David's own record was his best defense, and although gossip bruised his pride, never before had it posed a threat to his life.

This time, so it seemed, David's enemies were not behind this. Ordinary men were generating heat, and leading men began calling for abdication or even death.

The actual charge wasn't that serious, but it was tied to Saul and his weaknesses, so it stirred emotions beyond reason. And because of our courtyard conversation—which seemed linked to the matter—both Abigail and I felt squarely in the middle. Anything we said, however, only made matters worse. I believe the impact of this episode shortened Abigail's life by several years.

It boiled down to the following preposterous charge: David suspected his first wife Ahinoam of infidelity and had questioned everyone in the palace without uncovering hard evidence. He therefore had proposed a jealousy test to determine the truth of the matter. He hadn't actually gone through with it, but the detailed description of the process had reduced Ahinoam to yogurt.

This charge—a total fabrication, let me make clear—planted thistles in the minds of men and women alike. Yes, the Law could not be set aside, but certain parts that had by long custom been neglected now seemed barbaric.

To complicate things further, Ahinoam had been guilty of a minor indiscretion, and David had reprimanded her rather harshly. He also had criticized his wife Eglah when she had refused him after he joked about her inedible honey cake. "Bad enough that my wives are unclean the same time each month," he snapped, "or short on doves and pigeons for their atonement. But shutting me out over a honey cake that tasted like rabbit dung...!"

The bare facts seemed almost funny—if you ignored the implicatons. How little fuel to ignite a bonfire! But more serious than the gossip was the mystery of its becoming public. The two Ahinoams, David's and Saul's, somehow became linked. People looked on Saul's chronic jealousy as a noxious fever that ultimately destroyed the nation. David was becoming like Saul, they said. Ahinoam was not the only wife who was suffering. Look at his differences with Abigail. And his rage over Eglah—that most sheeplike of wives. *"We will not have another Saul,"* they trumpeted. *"David must die!"*

Who spawned this nonsense about the two Ahinoams? At first, I assumed Abiathar had publicized his father's story about Saul's Ahinoam. I pressed him hard on this, but he hotly denied telling the story. That left myself, Abigail...or Absalom.

None of this had been spread to anyone beyond those directly involved—chiefly wives and concubines. Absalom, though he may have heard our conversation with its mention of Ahinoam's test, could hardly have heard other details. Such matters were simply not talked about within children's hearing. Only women would talk....

"It has to be Liliah or Adah," said Abigail, her face drawn. "With the work they manage to escape, they've had time enough to construct any number of schemes."

"But they're nearly hysterical over what might happen to David."

"Why shouldn't they be? If David falls, they fall, too. They've been busy behind his back—I'm certain of that. But someone is using them. I'm equally sure of that."

By late fall when David was due back from Ammon, the matter reached a pitch that even Ahithophel could not defuse. Many of us felt that when David did return, he should come not at the head of his army but surrounded by it for protection.

Until winter rains halted their campaign, David and Joab continued to poke at Hanun in Rabbah with minimal success. Aram and Edom had been dispatched, but Ammon remained a bone in their throats.

They dragged themselves home. "Time to beat olive trees instead of Ammonites," said David. "It's been a long summer, Joab. We're getting old...well, most of us," he added, watching Benaiah vault over his armor bearer in some exchange of high spirits.

Joab's eyes retreated deep within his head, one of them circling ever so slightly.

The weather turned nasty, and as they dropped off the heights, snow stung them with the intensity of a blizzard. The men scattered to hunker under trees or rocks. Joab paused on the rim of a sinkhole. Although he might find shelter there, the climb out might be more trouble than the cover was worth. He started to turn away, but movement in the pit caught his eye. He stared, then smiled maliciously. "Where's Benaiah?" he said.

Benaiah heard. "Who wants me?"

"A good place here." Joab drew Benaiah toward the pit. "As still and dry as Sheol against that wall. I've got some parched grain we can munch. A little tough getting out, but we'll help each other. Watch your step; it's slippery."

He held Benaiah's arm as though to keep him from falling. At the same time, he contrived a fall himself that tripped Benaiah and sent him tumbling into the pit.

Joab lay where he fell and moaned convincingly but otherwise kept silent. He could see the scene below and was rewarded by the flurry of activity he'd anticipated.

Benaiah did not lie still, having fallen almost on top of a lion. His yelp of surprise and the lion's defensive roar brought a scramble of men to the edge of the pit. Benaiah leapt to his feet, knife in hand. He hunched off his cloak to free his movements. Man and beast circled and feinted.

On top, Joab continued to moan. He had tried to keep Benaiah from falling, he told questioners, but slipped himself and hit his head.

Benaiah waved off help, never taking his eyes from the lion. The lion slashed viciously, drawing red streaks on the warrior's leg. Benaiah could not get close enough for a knife thrust.

His chief lieutenant called down. "Want a spear? A club?"

"Neither. I'll—"

The lion, in a lightning move, leaped to a boulder and then to Benaiah's back. They crashed to the ground with dreadful cries and roars. Benaiah rolled and stabbed backward and somehow managed to separate himself. The lion was bleeding too, and the spectators could see a broadening ring of color on the snowy floor of the pit.

They went to circling again. Both were tiring, and the onlookers grew tense.

David shoved to the fore, shrugging off his fur robe and preparing to drop into the pit. "I'm coming!"

"No!" said Benaiah. "My fight. Stay there; keep out of trouble."

"No! I'm coming down."

"He doesn't want help," said Eleazar, holding him back.

"But I've fought lions. I know what it's like."

"By now he knows, too. Besides," he added, glancing at Joab, "this is more than just a lion scrap."

David ground his teeth, eyes fixed on the desperate, panting contest.

Suddenly, the lion lunged at Benaiah's throat. As they both went down, Benaiah drove his knife into the animal's belly and ripped upward. The lion's teeth parted in a terrible roar and, after frenzied writhing atop Benaiah, melted into red stillness.

With a shout, the men spilled into the cauldron and hauled the beast off their comrade. David bent to mop blood. Benaiah returned a weak grin. "I'll take Ammonites any day."

Joab was inscrutable the rest of the trip home. David looked on him with loathing but on Benaiah with more than awe.

13

"Ahithophel won't listen to me, Hushai." Abigail sat on a fleece-lined chair near the firepan with eyes closed and a stiff hand over her mouth. "David's safer fighting Ammonites right now than he would be in his own home, and Ahithophel either doesn't care or knows something I don't."

The set of Hushai's mouth showed exasperation. "You've tried and I've tried. It's not like Ahithophel to ignore the weather. The king will walk straight into a den of vipers."

Abigail's face contorted, but she took a deep breath and concentrated on a fold of her robe. Hushai took her hand. "My lady, there are snakes around your feet, too. Two weeks now! You're less notorious than Ahinoam, but lies are buzzing—"

"Gossip, Hushai; not lies. There's a difference." But the qualitative difference evaded her right then, and she clutched Hushai's hand.

"Please, my lady, let me send for some wine. I'll find a servant." He rose and went to the sitting room door just as I rushed up the corridor.

"Hushai!" I shouted. "News! I was told my lady Abigail was here."

Abigail rose, her face pale. "What is it, Asaph?"

"David's on his way home. A runner's been dispatched—finally—to tell him what's happening. Ahithophel says, what with Ammonites, Arameans, and Edomites, he didn't want to worry David with matters he couldn't do anything about. He's right, but why didn't he say that days ago?"

"Thank God!" Abigail clasped her hands in enormous relief. "In you I trust, O my God. Don't let my husband be put to shame."

Two days later, trumpets announced the returning army. It also signaled an ugly band of men who gathered at Araunah's threshing floor and marched through Bahurim to confront David. Far from the happy celebration that ordinarily greeted returning troops, the mood was sour on both sides.

David, as usual, led the way up the incline. Warm from the long climb, he had tossed his thick mantle and headgear to an armor bearer. A heavy tiredness from the summer's campaign sucked at his limbs and rivuled his face.

Although forewarned, he stopped in surprise at the angry mob descending on him. At first he was inclined to club his way through. Joab and Abishai, however, backed by the guard and the *Gibborim*, moved in, war in their eyes but appeasement in their voices. "Brothers," said Joab, addressing the throng, "is this the way to greet your king? We've had a season of victory, defeating the Arameans and the Edom—"

"David is not our king!" A small man, mighty in wrath, thrust out his bearded chin at the commander in chief. "A man who cannot rule his own household is not fit to rule Israel!

We won't have another Saul; we won't have a man who acts despicably toward his wives. This is not what *Yahweh* wants, and I lift my heel against you!" With that, the dissidents, to a man, thrust a contempt-clad foot toward the king.

David's beard bulged at the insult, his eyes fiery columns. Joab again turned to the crowd. Eleazar moved close to David. "Don't say anything," he said softly. "We don't know enough. One way or another, we'll get inside, shut the gate, and find out what's going on. Then we'll talk—on our ground. This could touch off a massacre. That may be what they're after, but it would hardly make you popular."

Joab started on a new track. As though he'd been nothing more than an admiring spectator, he described Benaiah's contest with the lion, boasting of the strength and courage of the guardsman. He pointed to where Benaiah sagged, more dead than alive, against the horse he'd insisted on dismounting. In a different context, David would have knocked Joab down for such bald-faced hypocrisy, but now he could only bite his tongue.

Even hypocrisy failed, however, and in the end the army formed a phalanx around David and forced their way into the city. The closing of the gate did not set well, but the army imposed peace by taking the leaders of the rebellion into custody until the matter could be investigated.

The palace, however, knew no peace. "This is idiotic!" roared David. "If it's been going on so long, why wasn't I informed? How can I possibly defend myself? I'm left looking like a jackass while my noble commander in chief spews sanctimonious twaddle. Where's Ahithophel? I need somebody to sort this out."

Abigail came into the great room to extend her relieved welcome. As he turned to her, she bowed. "My lord," she said, her face aglow, "I'm glad you're here at last! And safe." She stopped, seeing a tiredness behind his anger that shocked and silenced her.

David, misinterpreting her look, turned on her. "Yes, my lady, I'm here. And I'm told my third wife herself has become part of this stench. Have you managed to muck up my entire household while I was gone?"

Ahithophel made his entrance just then, and David turned from Abigail, who stood stunned and bloodless amid a dozen men who could not for the life of them think what to do or say. She finally willed her feet to exit the room with at least a minimal degree of starch.

"Ahithophel, will you please tell me exactly what is going on and why I was not told of it sooner?"

The two, along with Uncle Jonathan, moved from the great room to a side chamber. There Ahithophel detailed the stories currently circulating and defended his inaction with the reasonable observation that two weeks' delay wouldn't matter that much and that, in his estimation, the difficulty was not serious enough to cut short a major military campaign.

Later, when David was with Zadok, Abiathar, Heman, and myself, we talked over the legal aspects of the problem. "The Law is the Law," said Zadok, "regardless of what anyone thinks of it. Just because nobody has invoked the edict on jealousy for who knows how many years doesn't alter what God said."

"I agree," said David, "but the Law isn't the issue. It's how people are twisting it into something I supposedly did. I'm not

Saul! Why would I imitate a mad king? I guess I know what it's like to be on the short end of jealousy!"

"Yes," said Zadok soothingly. "You know, we know, most of the people in the city know. But how do you still a storm of mischief?"

"We can *say* the Law's the Law—and it is," I said, "but this particular ordinance is upsetting. Can you blame people for not liking such a law? Isn't that the real problem? If I had to choose, I'd rather see revulsion over an obscure law than to have them twirl it like a sling and howl for blood."

I'd been looking at Zadok and Heman as I spoke and was startled off of my cushion when David thumped my back. "Asaph, you've got it! That's just what I'll say...with sling in hand," he added, grinning slyly. He sobered instantly. "Above all, we want to be just, yet merciful, before God. I can relate to that, and they will hear me."

They did. With sling and stone in hand, David spoke eloquently in defense of himself and his wives. He spoke of Saul and the colossal differences between them, of the Law and its role in determining justice. Before he finished, people everywhere were weeping and praising God for such a man as King David.

Almost everyone. A dozen or so still murmured and met in dark, dank places where their deceits could breed unchecked. This would go on year after year, a relentless drumming. What started as a ridiculous misunderstanding became a monster that stalked David the rest of his life. Often he'd come to me, soul in shreds, crying, "Asaph, if I had wings, I'd fly from this maelstrom and just sleep."

"Trust God," I'd say, for want of anything more comforting, and then he'd blink the way he did in his later years. "Yes, Asaph," he'd reply. "Sing it with me. We need it, you and I."

> *Cast your cares on the Lord*
> *And He will sustain you;*
> *He will never let the righteous fall.*

After matters were at least tentatively settled, I talked with David and described my conversation with Abigail, telling him about the "coincidence" of Absalom's visit, as well as of Abigail's heroic effort to serve the truth. He quickly saw that the rumors against her were false. He would have left it at that, had not Hushai and I both reminded him of the deep distress his words had caused her.

"What words?" He looked at us in exasperation. "What did I say that would bother Abigail? I say all sorts of things to her. She never gets mad."

"Not mad, David," said Hushai. "Hurt. Even a tough lady like Abigail doesn't appreciate being cast publicly as a stench in her husband's nostrils."

"I never said that!"

"Words to that effect. And other choice ones, besides."

David took a breath and straightened. He hunched his shoulders. His jaw muscles worked. His eyes blinked convulsively, which may have been the start of that particular nervous spasm.

"All right, I'll apologize." His tone indicated he'd far rather face Ammonites in the dead of winter. "But I want you both here as witnesses."

Abigail came in, pale, but chin high. She bowed formally before the king, who rose to greet her. For several moments

David held the hand she courteously extended, his face inscrutable as they studied each other. What did he see? A stallion's energy in a tiny cumin seed? Or a woman worn and old before her time? Did he see the staunch loyalty and love she'd borne her husband and his high calling? Or did he see only the nettlesome shape her love often took?

Finally he spoke, obviously uneasy. "My lady...Abigail, it has—ah—come to my attention that I may have... That my words may have caused you distress when I first came home." He tried a smile, but it turned to blinking instead.

Abigail's face did not alter as she responded quietly. "Yes, they did, my lord."

"I've since been informed of the things you suffered on my behalf and of your efforts to set things right. I am, of course, grateful to you."

"Thank you, my lord." Her head dipped slightly.

"And I am...sorry I spoke in such a way before getting the full story. I was tired, you know." His speech picked up pace, like a child trying to divert parental wrath with a story of personal woe. "A long summer, a miserable hike home, then to find—"

"Oh, yes, my lord. I was shocked to see you in such a state. In fact, even as you were speaking, my mind was busy with possible remedies—a warm bath, a hot drink, a massage with hot oil." Her chin and one eyebrow tilted fractionally.

David's eyes flickered but returned resolutely to his task. "Will you forgive my thoughtlessness, my lady? I spoke evil against you, but you had only my good in mind."

"I forgive you, my lord, and will continue to have only your good in my...heart." With another stiff bow to paste over this sole chink in her armor, she walked away, a queen every inch David's equal.

David dropped into his chair and rumpled his hair. "Why can't my most valuable wife wear the face of love?" he asked peevishly.

Benaiah's lion wounds kept him in a palace bed for over a week. Although he could hardly be there without sensing something afoot, David and his men maintained a conspiracy of medicinal silence. Finally, though, Benaiah dragged himself from his bed to stand nose to nose with David. "You will tell me what is going on."

David made a face and turned away. "Your breath is a menace. Go back to bed."

"No. My breath is the sword of illness; I'll use it to get what I want. Now tell me."

David sighed in resignation. "All right. But sit on the far side of the firepan." He began to explain the matter.

Benaiah demanded detail. He mined the king's memory to add to his own considerable knowledge of the relationships and grudges that add complexity and to a commonwealth.

As they talked, Ira and other Mighty Men came in. When David finished his recitation, they looked expectantly at Benaiah, who was studying the firepan. Finally he spoke. "I don't know for sure—I'll need to nose around on my own— but my gut feeling points to a conspiracy. The very dumbness of the jealousy issue and the way people rose to it… Somebody saw a molehill and decided to build a mountain. If I had to guess who, I'd say Sheba *ben* Bicri."

David sagged in his chair. "Again?"

Benaiah shrugged. "His mark is all over it. He's shrewd and inventive and goes for the big plan. We haven't seen the last of him."

Later, when Ira told Abigail of Benaiah's judgment, she was quick to concur. "Yes. Of course. How obvious, now you mention it." She shook her head in admiration. "That Benaiah. Worth a thousand camels, even when he's half dead. And I believe Absalom is involved, too, perhaps through the concubines, but he may have a direct link to Sheba." She noted Ira's look of alarm. "I know that won't set well with my lord the king, but I feel the boy has great mischief in him. He merits watching."

Abigail's intuition was right. "Who said that?" David growled. "No, don't tell me. Abigail, wasn't it?"

"Yes, my lord. Your wife," said Ira. "And I respect her judgment. She's been right on more matters than I can count in years past."

"Well, she's not right this time." David took a bite of bread and said with a full mouth, "There's absolutely no connection between Sheba and Absalom."

14

We come now to the fourth pivotal point in David's life, which came at a time, as Solomon describes it, "When winter rains decamp, when flowers scatter sweetness across the golden land. Sing, Asaph! Coo with doves, smell the almond blossoms. It's spring, Asaph. Spring!"

David had a cold.

Maacah urged him to take care of himself. "You've got a capable commander; let him fight the war. Stay here and be king."

Abigail could be depended on to disapprove of any advice Maacah might give.

Joab had things to say about wives and kings and colds before going off to Rabbah to renew the fight with the Ammonites.

The world of an Israelite king is a web of spiritual devotion and conquest and fortification and government.

The world of his wives is children and clothing and household management.

The interface between these worlds is the king's bed. The king's bed can also be the interface between the forces of spring and winter, of life and death.

David heeded Maacah. He ate well, slept late, took long naps. On the far 'end of the cold, he rose and stretched and strolled out on the roof terrace. Tough, heat-resistant plants ringed the perimeter of this outdoor room, with more succulent, flowering varieties softening the interior. A private garden; a place for reflection, for prayer. He checked the sky. The dull red ball near the horizon had yielded to the cooling breeze of evening, which was gathering spring's redolence as a maid gathers flowers. Fragrant arrows from a myrtle tree below found their mark in David's heart. Doves relayed ardent messages one to another. He closed his eyes in surrender to the insidious sweetness of an enemy every bit as artful as Ammonites.

When he opened them, his eyes fell on naked beauty in the bathing pool of the courtyard next door. Slowly, sensuously, a woman poured water over the alabaster of her skin. David sank behind the hedge plants to watch.

The woman, protected from ground-level view by two maids and a bit of shrubbery, sat on linen with her feet in the water. She scooped a pitcherful and handed it to her maids. Twisting her head slowly from side to side, she arched her body under the luxury of coolness on a hot day. She was, perhaps, seeing to her monthly purification. After toweling her dry, the maids slathered oil on her skin. *That's not the way to do it*, muttered David. Because of his cold, he hadn't been near a woman for several days, and someone was playing a lute downstairs.

Without disengaging his eyes, he snapped his fingers in the direction of his sitting room. Smoothly, quietly, his personal servant Joram appeared on the terrace. Slightly older than David, Joram had great skill in anticipating the king's thoughts and needs. Even more to the point, he had impeccable discretion. David nodded toward the courtyard. "Who is that?" he said.

Joram studied the view, a slight twitch on his mouth. "The house of Uriah the Hittite, my lord. Presumably, that's Uriah's wife, the daughter of Eliam." That made her Ahithophel's granddaughter.

"Ah!" was all David said.

Uriah the Hittite. A *Gibbor*—Mighty Man. The man who had backed Joab in the taking of Jebus. "Flame of *Yahweh*." His name said it—a man honorable, courageous, willing to take on the noblest effort or the most menial task for the sake of God's chosen. A man with a beautiful wife. David sighed. Abigail had talked about this woman, how lonely she was. Her name...Bathsheba...yes. Bathsheba the Beautiful would be lonely again tonight, for her Hittite husband was far away, holding up his end—whether noble or menial—in the siege of Rabbah.

The sun went down; light spilled from Bathsheba's house, and a lamp traveled from doorway to pool across the thickening gloom. Bathsheba finished her ablutions, pulled on her robe, and withdrew. David remained on the roof; the lute continued to play.

"Would you like something to eat, my lord?"

"No...yes. In my room...and perhaps later. Food for two. Wine, fruit, whatever you can find. And...the woman next door. No rush. Whenever..." David spread his hands vaguely.

With the slight lift of one eyebrow, Joram bowed and went out.

He returned two hours later, after the palace had settled into silence, with no one in the hallways to observe a woman who didn't belong there. At the doorway of the king's suite, he propelled Bathsheba through. She hesitated in fragile beauty until David, responding to her scent, looked up. She had dressed carefully for this first impression, with arm and ankle bracelets and a nose ring just visible behind her face covering. She was clearly nervous, but at the same time aroused and hungry. She had come to David with everything she would have provided for Uriah, had Uriah cared.

David reached out an appreciative hand and drew her in. "My lady Bathsheba, your name is like perfume. Welcome to the chambers of the king." He walked her around the spacious room, warm with wall and table lamps, rugs, bouquets, and banners. He took her to the terrace, pointed out her own house—not mentioning the bathing pool—and other landmarks around the walled city. When her trembling lessened, he settled her on a pile of cushions and signaled Joram for food.

The servant first poured nectar from an infusion of fig blossoms, then laid out bowls of dates and figs and apricots, followed by curds, roasted leeks, and choice morsels of lamb. Spiced wine followed. David handled Bathsheba in practiced fashion. He talked gently at first, then playfully, and soon had her laughing.

The actual presence of the king overwhelmed her more than she had anticipated. Larger and older than Uriah, his body had the leathered toughness of a mature warrior. His celebrated muscles, now bracelet bound, had definition even under the soft robe that covered a purple tunic. A gold chain hung from his shoulders, and rings ornamented his scarred hands. The bush of his red hair, held in check by a gold headband, framed the heart-melting blue of his eyes. Everything about him spoke of power, but a power reined by gentleness. Despite herself, Bathsheba continued to tremble.

When they had eaten and she seemed more relaxed, David reached for his great lyre and rearranged his own cushions to better face his guest. Lamplight glinted off burnished almug wood as his fingers explored the ten-stringed instrument. He began to sing, softly at first, "A Dove on Distant Oaks."

> Come to my garden, my sister,
> Come gather myrrh and spice;
> I have eaten my comb and my honey;
> I have drunk my wine and my milk.
> Eat, O friends, and drink, O lovers.
> The dove far off in the clefts of the rock,
> A dove on the distant oak.

Bathsheba picked up the familiar words of the second stanza and sang tentatively with David.

> How beautiful you are, my darling!
> My dove, my perfect one;
> Show me your face, O jewel of my heart,
> Let me hear your voice;
> Your voice is sweet,

> *Veiled eyes are doves,*
> *A dove on a distant oak.*

She had a dusky voice and musical sense and sang with passion. He was bewitched. They went through the entire ballad a second time, eyes locked on each other. When the song ended, David continued to thrum almost awkwardly as though not quite sure what to do. Then with great care he set aside the instrument and moved toward her, kneeling by her cushions to lift the smoky veil. Her eyes, dark and wide with fright, hardly dared meet his. With infinite gentleness, his hand stroked the thick, wavy hair he'd admired from the terrace a few hours earlier, now woven with pearls. His fingers traced filigreed earrings against her cheeks and followed the line of jewels along her fine, straight neck. Bathsheba's eyes took on desperation, her mouth opened in a frantic effort to breathe under the weight of a desire she'd never before known.

David lifted her effortlessly and drew her toward his bed of silk. The unfairness of wifely deprivation rose within her, ironically making way for contradictory sensations. She was out of place. This was not happening. For an instant she almost tried to stop the process, but then David was on her.

When his desire had been satisfied, David settled beside her. She lay on the king's bed, laughing and crying under the amazing incongruity of it all.

Some hours later she made her exit, accompanied by the imperturbable Joram, who had waited outside the king's sitting room. The air was balmy, but it might have been winter, for all her nerves knew. In what was left of night, she would huddle on her own hard bed and hug to herself this one drink of love she was ever likely to have.

Writing this chapter of David's life has been awkward for me for many reasons, not least of which is the necessary telling of intimate details. I would like to clarify the origin of this information. Bathsheba did not tell me directly, although she did talk about it with others. My wife, who had access to assorted queens and servants and maids and court gossip, was particularly helpful in the difficult task of piecing it together.

In the midst of this less-than-enjoyable task, I was struck by two crowning ironies. First, for David, well-practiced in the art of lovemaking, this episode was no different, than countless others—except for one tiny shift: he had made love to another man's wife and thus planted a seed of death, not of life, when he lay with Bathsheba. Second, the soldier who best kept the spirit of holiness the king insisted on was himself cuckolded by the king.

15

Hanun king of Ammon was stupid, but with a thick, towered city wall and a virtually impregnable citadel to hide in, he could afford to be. Though his northern allies had evaporated the year past, and though his army was less than robust after this spring's encounter with the Israelites, he still had significant advantages. Abundant winter crops lay safe within his walls, and Rabbah at the head of the Jabbok was not called "City of Waters" for nothing. He could afford to wait until the lions tired of prowling and went home. Patience was now Hanun's weapon of choice.

Patience, though, is a double-edged sword. Joab had won the first round, but now, with no Ammonites venturing forth for him to fight against, he, too, turned to patience and laid siege to Rabbah.

"But we're not just twiddling thumbs, my lord." The runner, newly arrived in Jerusalem, shifted nervously under the king's sharp questioning. "Slingers go at it every day. Firebrands work well, too. Such a blaze was going when I left. A siege is a siege, my lord. It goes slowly, but Rabbah will tumble—of that much I'm sure."

360 *Eleanor Gustafson*

In addition to these weekly reports, David kept busy with plans for the temple and his inventory of materials. He sat for hours in the olive grove across the Kidron Valley, envisioning the temple, tall and gleaming, with two great pillars facing him. A fit place for the Name of the Lord. He pictured the inner sanctuary and Most Holy Place. Gold on every surface—the walls, the altar of incense, the table for the bread of the Presence, lampstands, dishes, tools, the very wings of the cherubim on the Ark—all gold.

"Asaph, I can see it, I can feel it. Carved cedar and olive wood. Pomegranates, lilies, palm trees. And instruments. Harps and lyres—all overlaid with gold."

"A lot of gold, my lord," I said.

"Yes, but I've already got almost enough. I still need bronze for the pillars and their capitals. And the laver. A huge basin— a sea, if you will—resting on the back of bulls."

"My lord, may I live to see this temple with my own eyes, instead of yours!"

"You will, Asaph. You're young. You'll buttress my son while he builds the temple. Ha! A bull supporting the king. What do you think of that, Asaph?" He nudged my arm, and we both laughed. With hardly enough flesh to cover my bones, I had never been likened to a bull.

Gradually, though, our conversations took on a different flavor, almost like milk beginning to turn. I was scarcely aware of it at the time, being caught up in the privilege—and pride— of being one of the king's close friends, privy to temple plans. Our talks ranged from lofty considerations of God to a discussion of insects that can ward off starvation but not make you throw up.

I became aware of his talking a bit too heartily, especially on such topics as kings' rights and prerogatives. His devotion began to pale. Always, his love for God had made up the fabric of his life, flowing out in psalms by day and meditation by night. But now his piety seemed forced, though his prayers and offerings and holy-day observances never faltered. He worked at justifying his absence from battle, though no one who had seen the physical ravages of the previous year's campaigns begrudged his decision to mind the war from home, at least until things settled down.

They didn't settle, though, for a long time. In fact, on a day early in the month of Sivan, Mephibosheth *ben* Jonathan, to whom David had without exception been kind, came to me, pale and shaken. The king had stormed from an inner room and had knocked him down. Had it been an accident or Mephibosheth's clumsiness, he could have understood. But this was no accident. More than Mephibosheth fell in the sweep. Jars and furniture up and down the hall suffered the king's rage. Even a slave boy at the far end had his nose smashed against the wall.

"What set him off?" I asked. "Do you know?"

"No, not...really."

"But you know something."

"Only that someone was in the room with him. No one I recognized. A servant, I think, but not ours. After it happened, I just stared after the king, expecting him to turn and say, 'I'm sorry. Are you all right?' But he never did. It's not like him, Asaph."

I shook my head at the mystery. "No, it's not. This, on top of..." I tried to pass it off. "If I see him...we sometimes chat right after morning songs. I'll try to find out. But you're right, Mephibosheth. It's not like him."

Neither I nor anyone else could discover what was wrong. David's rage evaporated quickly, as usual, but he kept to his rooms. When he did come out, he talked to no one. He sat alone or walked the hills north of the city. Benaiah wasn't happy with that. "I'm responsible for you. I'll get someone to tag along, someone discreet."

The word *discreet* set David off. He gathered himself as though to flatten Benaiah, who reflexively pulled his knife but just as quickly sheathed it and danced away. David backed down too, looking ashamed.

"My lord," said Benaiah gently, "what is it? You're in trouble."

David closed his eyes, but only for a moment. In a move that surprised Benaiah, he kissed the guardsman, then held him at arm's length. "Thank you...and I'm sorry. It's...a bit of a knot, easily loosed. Don't worry. I'll be all right." His blink transformed his eyes into aureoles of kindliness. In his latter years, this particular eye movement always communicated benevolence, never hostility. His anger, though, was marked by a complete absence of blinking, and both friend and enemy knew the implications of a steady gaze.

Benaiah remained uneasy. "Someone will go with you, but with orders to keep his distance."

The king shrugged peevishly. "If it makes you feel better." He turned to go, then hesitated. "There is one other thing you can do. I'd—uh—like a firsthand report from Ammon. Will you send a runner and ask for Uriah's return? He's a good man and tells things straight. I'd like his assessment of how the siege is going." David looked anxious.

The request was easy enough, but Benaiah's fertile mind sorted through implications.

Uriah and Joab were likewise surprised by the summons. Runners were sent to the king weekly, if not more often. Were the reports incomplete or unsatisfactory?

The king greeted Uriah warmly in his upper aerie. "You seem in good shape, Uriah. Sieges may be boring, but fewer scars— eh?" He studied the warrior's dark good looks, his long, straight nose and separated eyebrows. He wished fervently that those eyes were less serious and more used to smiling.

"You're looking well, too, my lord the king. Better than when we left."

"How's Joab holding up? He hates sieges. The men in general? Please tell me everything. Runners report only what they're told, but you have an officer's perspective. Thank you for coming."

They talked and laughed through supper. David thanked him again for making the trip, then led him to the door. "I suppose you stopped at home on your way here."

"No, my lord." His eyes took on the burning passion that had so unsettled David when they first met. "Your business is my first obligation."

"Well, your duty is completed. Now you can go home. Go down. Wash your feet. Take your ease with your beautiful wife. You're a good man, Uriah. Ira tells me that you're one of the few *Gibborim* who still do target practice. I value that— your integrity and loyalty, your excellence as one of my Mighty Men. Go home now; forget war for a night or two."

Almost as soon as Uriah left, David sent his servant Joram after him with one of the king's own armbands as a gift, along with select portions from the king's table to enrich the couple's evening together.

David himself slept well for the first time in weeks. A good thing, for sleep was scarce in succeeding nights.

"What do you *mean* he didn't go home?"

"Just that, my lord. He slept with the servants at the palace entrance."

"I find that hard to believe," snapped David. "Send him up here."

David found cordiality difficult, especially when he heard Uriah's reason for not going home. "The Ark and the armies of Judah and Israel rest in tents in a foreign land; my master Joab and his troops camp in open fields. Why should I enjoy a comfortable home and a beautiful wife while they fight the enemies of God and His kingdom?"

Uriah—*flame of Yahweh.* A spiritual wildfire was hardly what David needed right now. He suppressed his anger and with only slight discomposure said, "All right. Stay one more day, and tomorrow I'll send you back with a message for Joab. But eat with me again tonight. Laughter is a pleasure even a loyal soldier can enjoy."

Laugh they did. Joram, at David's instruction, kept Uriah's cup well filled, and by evening's end the *Gibbor* was quite drunk. "Take him home, Joram. *See that he gets there this time.*"

Uriah, however, his eyes glowing columns, would go no further than the servants' rooms, and Joram could do nothing about it. Given the unpleasantness awaiting his return to the king's chambers, Joram wished that he could have shared quarters there with Uriah.

After a long night for both servant and king, David was ready in the morning. He did not see Uriah again. Joram himself had the unhappy task of delivering the fateful message the warrior was to carry to Joab. Joram later said, "The scroll seemed almost too heavy to carry. After giving it to him, I had to bathe before returning to my duties."

I can give no details of Uriah's arrival at the siege camp outside of Rabbah. Joab refused to speak of the matter, even long afterward, and no one else had a taste for it, not even Eleazar, who would say only, "I knew right away." Uriah obviously delivered the king's scroll, and Joab obviously read and obeyed it. But what went through his mind is pure conjecture, and I'm forced back to my own perspective, the facts as I myself saw them.

Five days after Uriah's departure, I happened to be with David, discussing a school for musicians. Looking back, it seems the height of folly to have been speaking of such things at such a time, but of course I knew nothing of the context, only that the king was out of sorts and paying little attention.

The arrival of the weekly runner interrupted us. David ordered him in. "You don't mind, do you, Asaph? A siege report—five minutes, maybe."

"Of course not, my lord. Would you like me to leave?"

"No. A trivial report."

One might as well have called Moses' parting the waters of the Red Sea trivial.

The report was somewhat out of the ordinary in that an actual battle had been fought outside the city walls. The occasion of the skirmish was in itself embarrassing. A band of Ammonites had sneaked out and decimated the platoon that was supposed to guard against such tactics. The guerrillas were driven back in the end, but not without cost. The very act of forcing them through the gate made Joab's men targets for sharpshooters on the wall, and a number of Israelites fell.

David was furious. "Does Joab have the brain of a sheep? No one in his right mind sends men directly up to a city wall." David stopped pacing and positioned his nose within an inch of the runner's, whose back was already pushing through the wall. "You tell Joab—"

"My lord—" The runner buckled under the king's tirade. "I...Joab....My lord, Uriah the Hittite...is dead."

David froze. His face, still inches from the runner's, underwent such a rapid array of changes that I became alarmed. "My lord!" I said, rising from my chair. My voice seemed to release him. He backed away from the runner, who sagged even further in relief, then moved to a window.

I was stunned by what was happening. Before I could formulate any sort of hypothesis, David turned with a measure of composure and said to the runner, "I'm...sorry to hear that. And from the look of you, I'm guessing Joab is upset, too. Tell him I...understand. The sword devours this one and that. That's the way with war. The marvel is that any of us live. Tell him...to keep pressing Hanun the king, to keep fighting till the city is destroyed. Now, buck up." He brushed dust from the young man's tunic and steered him toward the door. At the last minute he held his arm. "Have you told anyone else... about Uriah?" His voice was tight.

"No, my lord. My orders were to speak to you."

David nodded and pushed him along, then turned to me, eyes empty and spectral. He tried to smile and sat down as though we would carry on as before. I formulated an excuse, but he seemed unwilling for me to leave. Was death too staggering a companion to commune with alone right now? Finally, after a weak attempt to get back to the music school, I stood resolutely. If he could reshape the runner's fear of David into a window on Joab's mind, I could do something similar. "My lord, I can't allow your interest in my school project to keep you from your responsibilities concerning Uriah. This has been a severe blow, and if I can do anything to help in such a time..."

Raw fear welled in his eyes, but he managed a gracious farewell as I took my leave.

I would not return until nearly a year had passed.

Less than two weeks after the news of Uriah's death, after his wife had completed her time of mourning, Abigail appeared at my house. David and Bathsheba had married, she said, in a small, private ceremony. "'Out of consideration for her feelings,' he says. *Her* feelings." She looked away to hide her own emotions, and brooding fragments of some dreadful theme seemed to pluck at her soul.

Abigail turned and faced me squarely. "Asaph, I will tell you something else. A prediction. A royal birth will take place at the time of the latter rains. I am as sure of that as I am of anything."

Scarcely six months away. I frowned, unable to make the numbers come out right. Which wife was pregnant? My wife, who knows such things, would surely have told me.

Abigail saw and almost smiled. She leaned toward me with a hand on my arm. "Your wife will know and explain...sooner than you think."

With a rush, the whole affair suddenly crystallized. I must have gone red or pale—I don't know which. Abigail squeezed my arm, then left with great sadness, saying, "I thought I had done with Nabal."

I can write only superficially of my emotions in the months that followed. I excused myself from official duties, Heman agreeing to come from Gibeon to fill in. Devastation, anger, confusion, shame, stupidity. How could I have been so close to David—in the very room with him when he received news of Uriah's death—yet not put it together? He despised Joab's ruthlessness, yet was himself ruthless when it suited his own purposes. The man that I respected most in all the world—God's man, God's chosen sovereign—how could he have done it? How could he go on? He married her, appeared with her in public, seemed happy in her presence.

My anger turned on others, as well. Yes, I'd been slow to catch on, but now that I knew, life could never be the same.

What about those who seemed not to know? Or who knew well enough but said nothing? Hardly anyone did more than shrug as though to say, "That's what kings do." But adultery is adultery, even for kings. The Law says, "If a man commits adultery with another man's wife, 'with the wife of his neighbor'"—the irony of that—"both the adulterer and the adulteress must be put to death." I'm not suggesting that the king and Bathsheba should have been executed. Don't misunderstand me. As with the jealousy test, such severity is seldom carried out these days, and never on kings. But why hadn't Abiathar… well, I knew why Abiathar didn't speak up. Zadok, though. He wasn't afraid of the king. I finally became calm enough to confront him.

After hearing me out, he drew a long breath. "Asaph, I know it's neither reason nor excuse, but I'm only a chief priest, not high priest. It's not my place to call the king to account. The thing is wrong; you know it, I know it. The king knows it. He knows he's more than just a *melech* king. He's *hamelech*, king of kings, if you will, ruling in the fear of God. This dazzling sin of his has cut off not just his own legs, but the legs of the kingdom, the nation's sovereignty, its covenant with God. That's the horror of it all. And everything seems normal on the surface. That's what you're complaining about. But I'm guessing there's a royal battle going on inside him. The covenant God is his judge, Asaph, and if I were you," he said, a hint of a smile in his eyes, "I wouldn't stand too close to *Hamelech David* in a thunderstorm."

Uriah had on David's armband, the gift he'd been given, when he died. I had more than one occasion in succeeding years to think on that.

I meditated, too, on the supreme irony of Uriah, *flame of Yahweh*. Had he known or guessed that his wife was pregnant? He was certainly intelligent enough to put two and two together. Yet he would not do the one thing that would get David off the hook, and his very bravery and zeal became David's weapon to destroy him. A man of gallantry, ready to die for his prince's honor, he died instead by his prince's hand.

Then, too, Uriah was a man of consummate self-control, whereas David's discipline was eroding. David, who had refused to kill Saul, even when no one denied his right so to do, held sexual pleasure more dearly than the life of one of his Mighty Men. Alas, those who practice self-denial often become thorns to the self-indulgent.

Abigail could attest to that.

16

The longest year of David's life was half over in terms of time; the full weight of anguish was still to come. But that too must be qualified. Public anguish lay ahead, but, from the start, the inexorable rise of floodwaters in his soul must have been even more terrifying. Having stepped from the familiar pitfalls of ordinary, bumbling misdeeds to the stony, surreal landscape of deliberate sin, he had to learn how to eat, breathe, walk, and talk in this harsh, new climate. And the tide crept higher.

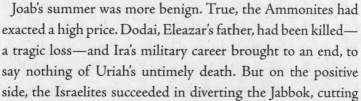

Joab's summer was more benign. True, the Ammonites had exacted a high price. Dodai, Eleazar's father, had been killed—a tragic loss—and Ira's military career brought to an end, to say nothing of Uriah's untimely death. But on the positive side, the Israelites succeeded in diverting the Jabbok, cutting off Rabbah's water supply. Capturing the city was then only a matter of time. Joab briefed the weekly runner two days ahead of schedule.

"Tell this to David," he said, none too cordially. "Tell him, 'I've got Rabbah in check, water cut off. If you want a hand in this, get out here and help. Otherwise, the city gets *my* name.' And tell him to find me some good officers. For one reason or another…" Joab paused significantly, "the summer's been hard on generals."

The runner was left to figure out a diplomatic translation.

David was not pleased by the invitation. If he'd been in poor shape for war at the start of the season, he was even worse off at midsummer. He took note of Joab's threat, however, and decided that plucking the military plum out of his commander's hand was worth the effort. He set Amasa to mobilizing the militia.

On their arrival at Rabbah, the newcomers found the veterans held together with little more than war grime. A sour sort of grimness had settled into their souls. Few pleasantries were exchanged with the incoming troops.

Joab's initiatives had indeed softened Rabbah. Court and military officials were hoarding the trickle of water, leaving little for rank-and-file soldiers and none for commoners or villagers. Thirst draped its black tongue over the walls.

When David and his reinforcements mounted the final attack on the city and broke the bars of the gates, they discovered an even greater horror inside. Charred bodies of children stacked around the idol Molech told of the desperation that had driven parents to lay their own screaming children on the glowing arms of the god whose bowels were fire. Even that could be understood, given the desperate circumstances. But when they reached the massive citadel itself, they found in it an evil no one could comprehend: infants ripped from their mothers' bellies for Molech's embrace. "This is Hanun's doing," snarled David. "Hanun and the men of Ammon will pay!"

The military counsel awaited David's orders. He was mean-eyed, full of bile. "Ammon has been a stench in God's nostrils from the time of Moses. Do to these vipers what you will. Saw them in half, hack them to pieces with their own axes, run harrows over them. Fire the brick kilns. Let Molech's hot breath devour the men of Ammon. Nothing is too cruel for the likes of them. *Let God's wrath fall on Ammon!*"

Abishai looked at Shammah. "Our splendid monarch seems a bit viperish."

Shammah drew his sword. "Yes. If nobody minds, I'll do it quick and clean."

Amasai had the satisfaction of killing Hanun and placing his crown on David's head. Crafted of gold and precious stones, its weight threatened to drive David's head into his shoulders. "I don't believe I'll wear it home," he said. But while it rested on his head, he stared down Joab with grim satisfaction.

The longest, most expensive war of David's career was finally over—the last great war of his life.

As Abigail had predicted, Bathsheba gave birth "prematurely." Aside from the midwife and Abiathar, who circumcised him, few others had an opportunity to see and comment on his precocious size. A beautiful baby though, by all accounts. Named Boaz after his great-great-grandfather, he had a particular charm that set him off from others: a dimple when he smiled, a softness that clutched your heart to the point of tears. This was according to my wife; I myself never saw the child.

By the end of the rainy season, David had begun to relax, to become his old self. He threw parties during barley harvest and once again became the bard of old. He slaughtered countless animals in sacrifice for burnt and sin and fellowship offerings—all, ostensibly, in thanksgiving for his new son. He even wore Hanun's crown the whole distance from the palace to the Tent—no small feat—and there gave it over to Abiathar amid great rejoicing.

I kept my distance. When David came to the Tent for morning or evening sacrifice and the singing of prayers, I found occasion to talk with other musicians or busied myself elsewhere. Only once did I inadvertently encounter David. I probably turned assorted shades, but he did nothing more than touch my arm with wistful compassion before going his way.

Bathsheba was an enigma. I blame her as much as David for his moral lapse. She had no business accepting his invitation. Surely she knew that David was not simply being neighborly. She didn't even dress modestly, according to Joram. She could hardly have made herself more provocative, he told me, and, over the years, Joram had squired many women in and out of David's apartment. Such an unworthy consort for a king. A concubine, perhaps, but not a queen.

But whatever I thought of her, Bathsheba quickly became David's favorite wife and remained so for the rest of his life. Not only did she possess that fragile beauty that so affected David, she complemented his musical gifts with her warm, rich voice. She was intuitively attuned to David on other levels, as well, and knew how to keep him at her side. She had

practiced on Uriah with little effect, but David's responsive-
ness nourished her native gifts. No one would ever call her
clever or wise, but her intelligence on handling a man matched
any woman's in the kingdom.

The two, of course, had discussed the implications of their
liaison. Both knew the penalty for adultery, and fear kneaded
Bathsheba's imagination. But David assured her that kings
could pretty much do what they wanted. Even her father
and grandfather had come to accept the situation. After all,
a whole year had gone by. What could happen now? David
could breathe again. The nations that had challenged Israel
had all been put down. He had installed his trusted friend
Shobi, son of Nahash and brother of Hanun, in Rabbah to
govern the territory. Spring had rolled around again with no
wars to go off to. He had the temple to occupy his thoughts,
and for that he was grateful. The project provided hours of
diversion from his own private fears, his own nightmares, the
ache deep in his bones that not even Abigail's hands could
have massaged away. He chose not to think about Abigail.

All was well, all was peaceful—until the day Nathan the
prophet fell over a sheep.

Nathan, too, had been having bad nights. He had thought
long about a safe way to approach David. If he'd been uneasy
about the Lord's word concerning the temple, a positive message for the king, how could he deliver a tirade about wife
stealing and husband killing? The words themselves, let alone
the probable consequences, seemed to choke him. Any king
guilty of such doings would hardly tolerate a prophet auda-
cious enough to point them out.

In his mind he tried one tactic after another. Finally, urgency burned so powerfully that he had to face David, ready or not. He delayed only long enough to oil his hair and face. His eyes—coal-fired craters in his skull—he could do nothing about.

He could not walk to the palace; the Spirit drove him headlong, a wild turbulence that scattered men and animals from his path. An unfortunate ewe, confused by the approaching whirlwind, leaped directly into his path. Both went down. The ewe scrambled to her feet and ran off bleating, but the prophet sat still and looked curiously after it. *The Lord is my shepherd, the Lord is my shepherd...* With a soft smile, he stood and walked serenely into the palace.

David's greeting was warm, if not altogether tranquil. Although he had not avoided the prophet in past months and had in fact purposely invited him to assorted court functions, he was understandably nervous in his presence. Today, though, the seer seemed relaxed and as pleasant as his nature could allow. David called for refreshments.

As food and drink were set before them, they chatted about the temple. "The Name of the Lord and the Word of the Lord are bound together," Nathan said. "Where the Name is, the Word is. And glory. As when Moses first set up the Tent."

"Yes," said David. "The cloud of glory filled it. No one could enter. Nathan, do you think glory will fill my son's temple?"

"Humph. The only glory fit for a man-made structure is the beauty of holiness. The temple will be no sounder than the people who worship there. When soundness goes, the glory will go."

David shifted uncomfortably and moved to a safer subject. At a suitable lull, Nathan leaned forward. "My lord, I have a matter I'd like to bring before you, if I may."

"Certainly." David felt the knife at his belly, but he nodded encouragingly.

"It concerns two men in a town not far from here, one rich with cattle and sheep, the other poor, his only treasure a small ewe lamb. So dear was this lamb that it lived in his tent, shared his food, even slept in his arms—as precious as any of his children."

David settled back, expansive with relief. "Do I know these men?"

"Possibly, my lord."

"The poor man was bottom-rung herdsman for the wealthy landowner. His tent was scraggled, mean, his kids half starved and toothless."

David's eyes narrowed. "I think I see where you're going. If the landowner is wealthy, why isn't he paying a living wage?"

"Worse than that," said Nathan, leaning forward. "One evening a traveler came by the rich man's house looking for a place to stay the night. The landowner bade him welcome— perhaps not enthusiastically, but he did his duty. The traveler would have to be fed, and this posed a problem for the householder. The hour was late, his closest sheepfold far off. He did have prime lambs right behind the house, but they'd been set aside for sacrifice—and to impress the high priest."

David raised an eyebrow and smiled.

"While he stood scratching his head, he saw his bottom-rung herdsman walk by carrying his lamb, his youngest daughter with him, presumably heading home to a thin supper. 'Aha!' the landowner said to himself. 'Just the thing! I can keep my sacrificial stock and won't have to trouble myself to fetch an animal.' He hurried out and demanded the orphan lamb. The poor fellow pleaded, of course, but the rich man knocked him down and wrestled the lamb from his arms, the little girl screaming in terror the whole—"

David whacked his chair and exploded around the room. "As the Lord lives, that man will pay! Nathan, you were right to tell me. Four times over he'll pay for that lamb, and he deserves to die! I can't imagine such a thing. Not an ounce of pity!"

Nathan stood, and an eternity passed between his leaving the seat and standing so tall his head seemed to graze the ceiling. His swirling robe inscribed judgment on the air; his eyes incinerated the heart of the king.

Every hair on David's head stood straight.

"*You are the man!*" Nathan thundered. "This is the word of the Lord."

David stood frozen before this furnace of wrath. He did not move, yet the distance between the two men grew by a mile, two miles, and the prophet's voice came as from a distant mountain.

"'I delivered you from Saul,' says the Lord; 'I gave you his palace and women, had you wanted them. I made you shepherd over Israel and Judah. Was that not enough? I would have given more. Yet you lifted your heel against me and did what was despicable in my eyes. You stole the beloved lamb of Uriah the Hittite and then killed Uriah himself with the sword of the Ammonites.'"

The entire two-mile room began to rotate, with David at the center. Nathan was circling, faster and faster, his words beating on David's head.

"This is what the Lord says: 'Since the sword fits your hand so well, the sword will continue as your bosom companion, never departing from your house. Calamity will come, not from far-off enemies, but from your own palace. Your wives will be taken by a man close at hand. He will lie with them in broad daylight. What you did in secret, I will emblazon across the sky for all Israel to see.'"

In the silence that ricocheted off that terrible voice, the spinning slowed, leaving David with only the thinness of his shadow to lean against. He dropped and lay crumpled, face down with his hands protecting the back of his head. A servant started in with more food, but a glance at the floor and the residual flame licking off Nathan's face sent him running. Nathan stepped to the door for a word with the guards, who were whispering apprehensively, then reentered and sat quietly on a cushion near David.

Was it one hour or ten they remained that way? Neither David nor Nathan could say afterwards. How long before sin of that magnitude is reamed out of a man's heart? Nathan did not interfere; he simply sat with his flaming sword sheathed—and waited.

Oddly, David did not weep. Tears wouldn't do for that sort of sorrow, he told me later. An occasional tremor passed through his body, but otherwise, he remained silent.

Finally, without moving, he spoke. "My father..." His voice struggled through the gravel of repentance. He tried clearing his throat. "My father, I have sinned against the Lord. I am...

ready to die. I bear the sin of us both. Please, my father, may
she be spared?" He lifted a blotched face to the prophet in
pleading.

Nathan bent to David and put a hand on his head. He said
gently, "The Lord has taken away your sin. You will not die."

Those words. *The Lord has taken away your sin.* The taste of
honey. The fragrance of lilies. The comforting touch of a shepherd's hand. *Hoo.* What the trumpet of doom could not accomplish, the whisper of forgiveness did: David's heart broke.

Nathan explained gently that though he would not die, his
sin was not without consequence. "The secret is out. Already
the Lord's enemies are talking and have nothing but contempt.
That damage can't be undone, and there'll be further repercus-
sions. But before that"—he hesitated—"the child Uriah's wife
bore will die."

Every muscle in David's body convulsed. The child whose
eyes could melt a stone. The pet lamb of his bosom. The innocent, sweet-natured victim of lust. David thought of the
charred little bodies in Rabbah. Was that atrocity any worse
than his own? He lifted himself to his knees and his face to
the Lord, his voice choked and gravelly.

> *Have mercy on me, O God.*
> *Blot out my transgressions.*
> *My sin burdens me as a camel weighed down.*
> *I know my transgressions;*
> *I cannot escape them.*
> *They stare me in the face.*
> *It is you I dishonored;*
> *Against you only have I sinned.*

Only you can take away my sin,
Heal my bones.
Flick blood on me with hyssop and make me clean;
Wash me till I'm snow.
A clean heart, O God,
And have mercy.

You are the man! Four words. Words that shattered David's protective armor and left him with tiny shards under his skin. Never again would he walk comfortably.

But they also brought relief, as though an evil, shadowy man within him had been felled by an arrow. Though his spirit agonized, the heart of the matter was settled with four words.

David's only request was that Bathsheba not be told of the infant's coming death.

Word of David's humbling raced through the palace. Abigail had little to say on learning the whole story, much of which she had already discerned. "David managed to stay alive through thirty-five years of warring, only to trip at the midpoint of life. At least when he fell into the wrong bed, God didn't allow him to lie comfortably."

Inwardly, she was appalled. Adultery was one thing; murder was quite another. She hadn't thought him capable of such an act. And what of her own hand in the tragedy? She'd seen it coming, but "principle" had cut her off from doing any good. Relegated now to the same inactive status as Michal, she who knew him best could no longer apply her love and devotion to draw him toward righteousness.

David talked at length with Ira, whose leg had been mangled at Rabbah. "Joab's loss is my gain," David said. "You dressed my wounds all these years; now you can dress my soul." He also talked to Hushai and Benaiah but not to me. I was not ready.

Actually, David badly wanted to talk with Abigail. She would understand about the inner shadow. She would bear him up for the impending sentence. She would say the right things about his cruel treatment of the Ammonites and cauterize the guilt that festered his heart. But oh, the fearful lengths pride will go to protect position and reputation! I cannot help but wonder if the coming disaster could have been averted if they had spoken their heart's pain to each other.

Nathan was relieved. David was not Saul; he was indeed the king after God's own heart, and God's grace could heal such a man. The kingdom would stand.

For one week, David's world waited in numb silence.

For reasons known only to himself, Joab chose that particular time to return to David the armband the king had given Uriah before sending him off to die. Uriah had worn it proudly—almost defiantly, some said—in his last battle. With uncharacteristic drama, Joab described his discovery of Uriah's body, an arrow through his neck. The fallen *Gibbor* was facing the city wall, his own arrow nocked and ready to release. Joab and Ittai removed the gold band and other effects and buried him with extraordinary honor.

Had anyone but Joab told the story, David might have grieved openly under the double burden of a wound reopened and the death of a valued officer. But with Joab almost licking his chops in anticipation of such a show, the king bore the knife in stoic silence.

Even so, Joab went home satisfied—and unconcerned about his own hand in Uriah's death. Why did he give the order in the first place? If Uriah had been a common soldier, I could see Joab shrugging and sending him off to die. But Uriah was not a common soldier. He was a Mighty Man, a fine warrior, a dedicated general whose death would devastate Joab's military structure in terms of morale and loss of leadership. So why would Joab consent to such an order?

Some have pointed to the obvious, which he, of course, did assert: a king decrees; underlings obey. But in light of Joab's previous behavior, it's a thin reed. Others have pointed to the water-shaft scramble for Jebus and the key role Uriah played in Joab's triumph. Uriah did in fact save Joab's life at the expense of his own advancement, and Joab was never happily beholden to anyone.

My own conviction is that Joab knew and played on David's weakness just to bring him down to his own level. The man's life supports the theory. His returning the bracelet in the sore moment just after Nathan confronted David is a case in point.

(I, of course, did not learn he had done so until long afterward. The bracelet's significance in my life will become apparent in due time.)

David checked daily on the child Boaz. He spent hours in the room, singing if he cried, making faces for the reward of his bubbling laugh, and watching him sleep. He even insisted on holding him once or twice, his voice rumbling an old lullaby. "*Hoo*, my lamb, my woolly lamb; slumber, little waif of God. *Hoo-ha-ha-ha.*" Seeing her precious child in the rough hands of a man made Bathsheba nervous enough. But snatches of gossip concerning David's encounter with Nathan were also coming to her.

"David, you're frightening me." She faced her husband squarely. "You're acting strangely. Something's going on. I want you to tell me."

David's eyes flickered, but he forced himself to return her gaze. He'd been dreading this moment. He'd gone to extraordinary lengths to discipline his emotions while communing with Boaz. Now he had to face Bathsheba's fears as well as his own.

He led her to their favorite sitting place and held her tightly. "My dearest wife, have I told you today how beautiful you are and that I love you?"

"You're not taking me seriously. You wouldn't say that to Ahinoam or Abigail."

The mention of Abigail redirected his approach.

"I'm sorry. I know you're worried." He sighed. "You've heard gossip. I didn't want to upset you, so I asked that talk be kept from you."

"Talk about us, you mean. About Boaz." She twirled the fringe on David's robe.

"Yes. God revealed our sin to Nathan, and now just about everyone knows."

"The wretch!" Her eyes blazed.

"No. Nathan spoke only to me. Telling others wasn't his business. Servants told, guards...who knows how it got around? But Nathan's business was with me alone."

Her face turned fearful, her body cold. "What did he say? What will happen?"

David tried to keep his voice light. "Oh, I couldn't possibly tell it all, but he assured me of God's mercy and that I would not die."

She relaxed.

"I've prayed for forgiveness, of course, and offered special sacrifices. We're in God's hands. May he have mercy on us."

The first shadow of death made its appearance just a week after Nathan's rebuke. Nothing much. Unaccustomed peevishness, less interest in the breast. He still laughed at his father, though, and David said nothing. The next day, the baby was feverish but hardly what a knowledgeable mother would call ill. Bathsheba began to wail, however, sensing the outcome. David held her without a word, and together they wept.

David considered sending for Abigail. If anyone could save the baby, she was the one. He didn't doubt she'd come if asked, that she would half kill herself as she had done when he was ill. He didn't, however, and though the decision haunted him at the time, he later felt he'd done the right thing; dragging her into his sin and its inexorable aftermath would only have broken her heart and doubled his own pain.

The next-best nurses were summoned, and, after carefully assessing the baby's condition, they assured David that this was a normal childhood ailment. "Go. We'll have him kicking and cooing in no time. Nothing serious."

Reluctant to leave, he laid one last kiss and a hand of blessing on the infant's warm head and turned toward his own rooms, sick dread dragging at his footsteps.

As the days wore on, Joram and other servants became increasingly alarmed over their master. "He scarcely eats or drinks," said Joram. "Got rid of the firepan and sleeps on the stone pad—when he sleeps at all. Nights, days—he prowls and prays. Won't go out, won't talk. Except to Benaiah. The only one he trusts to report on the child."

Time spun its long line, each day, each hour, each minute an independently suspended moment of agony. The end came early on the seventh day. Benaiah came with the news, but, knowing the king's condition, he hesitated in the anteroom. Joram and the others rose from their makeshift beds.

"He's dead?" Joram asked.

"Yes." Benaiah looked nervously at David's doorway.

"How shall we tell him? With him in—"

The croak of David's voice interrupted them. "Whisper in here where I can hear."

The men looked at each other, then edged through the doorway. David, gaunt and haggard, lay on the stone pad. "He's dead." The king's voice was flat, without emotion.

Benaiah knelt by his side. "My lord—"

Eyes shut, David nodded without speaking, without tears. Benaiah gripped the king's hand, tears spilling down his own beard. David opened his eyes and rubbed Benaiah's forearm abstractedly. "Please help me up," he whispered.

He fought dizziness a moment, then plucked at his goat-hair sackcloth. "I'd like to bathe. Lotions, clothes..." He looked vaguely at the servants. "Thank you...."

The men exchanged surprised looks, then hustled to their tasks. An hour later, a much-altered David arrived at the Tent of Meeting. I had to look three times to be sure whom I was seeing. At first I assumed from the look of him that the child must have improved. Obed-Edom, though, having just received the news, drew me aside. Again I gawked in astonishment as the king alternately bowed before the Lord in worship and stood to join in singing and prayer. I was strangely moved. Up to this point, my heart had been hard, even when I heard that the child most likely would die. This is right, I had thought. Just. Life for life. Perhaps if even Bathsheba herself died...

But now the child was dead, David was worshiping, and I was the one weeping.

David returned home and asked that food be brought. While he ate, Joram spoke. "How is it, my lord, that while the child lived you fasted and wept, but now that he's dead, you get up and eat?"

David sipped broth. "Joram, if I've learned nothing else in life, I know God is merciful. He's shown that time and again. While Boaz lived, there was that slim chance. Now he's dead; nothing can be done. I will go to Boaz, but I can't bring him back to me."

When David finished eating, he took a brief nap, then went to comfort Bathsheba. Late in the day, the two of them, directly behind Benaiah, who carried the tiny bundle, led the procession to the place of burial. They had intended the funeral to be small and private, but half of Jerusalem, it seemed, rattled sistrums and ululated in lament.

The days following were difficult. David found relief in sorting through a year's worth of inner conflict. With everything laid open, he could at last articulate his feelings. He sat for hours before the curtain of the Ark, visualizing the mercy of God as it rested between the cherubim.

> *Bathe my heart, O God, freshen my spirit,*
> *But don't throw me away or withdraw your Spirit.*

If sacrifices would please you,
I would bring a hundred—
Bulls, goats, lambs by the thousands.
The sacrifice you look for is a broken spirit;
A broken and contrite heart, O God,
You will never throw away.

I'm reminded of an incident that happened just recently, before David died. I was with the king as he lay on his bed, and I was singing a particular song.

Blessed is he
Whose felonies are forgiven,
Whose crimes are covered.
Blessed is the man
Whose sin Yahweh does not hold against him.

An old man's tears flow easily, but his came from his soul. He wanted to speak, and I leaned close, trying to discern his thoughts. "Bull's-eye," was all I could make out.

"Hits the target," I suggested.

He nodded eagerly.

"Sin *forgiven* hits the target."

His eyes lit, but still he shook his head. Close, but not quite.

"The forgiving grace of God—that's the crux of the matter, the whole of life. *Yahweh saves.* That's what it's all about, isn't it?"

"Yes...yes." His voice creaked, but his face shone as one who had turned in his scruffy deceit and had received back the righteousness of God. "*Yahweh...saves.*" He lay silent a moment, then whispered, "Go on."

When I kept silent,
My bones seemed to waste away;
I groaned all day long.
Then I acknowledged my crime;
I said, "I will lay everything before Yahweh,"
And You erased guilt from my heart.
You are my hiding place;
You will shield me from trouble,
And assure me with songs of deliverance.

When I finished, David was asleep, the peace of deliverance on his face.

Although peace did not come quickly after the death of Boaz, David went to Bathsheba as soon as she was able and lay with her. That very night, Solomon was conceived.

18

As I said, my heart had become flinty toward David during that year, and the rupture affected other parts of my life, as well. So much so that about a month before Boaz was even born, Heman drew me aside and faced me squarely; I knew we were in for a serious talk. Heman has been characterized as bookish, mystical, ethereal, impractical, or artistic, but never direct—not like his grandfather Samuel, who could wither an oak with a single word.

"Asaph," he said, "may I ask what is troubling you? Our brothers are complaining about your ability to concentrate—not mine, for a change."

I closed my eyes, the heavy talons on my shoulders suddenly ripping at my throat. Poison burst forth upon "The Moth," as Joab aptly called him.

"Heman, I know it's wrong, but sometimes I think God should strike him dead."

Heman's eyes widened. "My dear Asaph. Such vehemence! Such retributive...ah...just who is it that you...ah..."

"I'm talking about *Hamelech David*," I replied bitterly, "the mighty warrior, the man God took from the fields to be shepherd over all of Israel."

The eyes became pomegranates. "My dear—"

"Heman, just let me talk. Perhaps then the coals in my heart will burn out."

With a look of distress, Heman sank onto the bench and waved his hand vaguely.

I paced before him. "Heman, the fire began consuming me when my thick head finally got the message: *Bathsheba already had David's child within her when he took her as his wife.* I will never, ever forget the moment of impact. Infidelity...murder. That they would actually *marry* after that! I jumped between wishing David dead and wishing death for myself. King David, the faithful man of God, the mighty overcomer, the avenger of God's enemies—*derelict* at the height of his powers!"

My voice danced at a pitch I could seldom reach. "That glorious, hard-won triumph over the Ammonites. Hollow...empty. A victory more costly than the whole kingdom is worth. How could he have done it, Heman? No, no—" I saw him boggle at a matter so removed from aesthetics. "You don't have to answer. Their baby will be born, life will go on, David will continue to rule—how remains to be seen—but never again will I be able look him in the eye."

The tempest I unleashed on Heman that day lacked one particular motif that Joab, of all people, saw before I did. That he was the one to point it out did not improve my frame of mind, nor did it help me acknowledge it myself.

It was bad enough that Joab often muttered insults at us, calling the Levites such things as "Tent wheezers" and

"Livrites," or that he was fond of describing the high priest as "curd-faced," "string-bearded," and "pillow-bellied." None of that approached the shame I felt during one particular confrontation when Joab closed on me and dug his stubby finger into a wound I had not yet noticed. "Your finest clacks and tweedles in the Tent don't draw the king's eye half so well as one curvy eyelash, do they, A-sap?"

My veins nearly popped, and I sank fingernails into flesh.

Jealous. As I had been jealous of David's friendship with Jonathan, was I jealous now of Bathsheba, of the whole torrid affair that had broken my friendship with David and seemed to leach every bit of righteousness from his heart? I was still sorting it out after the baby's birth and death and the news of Bathsheba's second pregnancy. Even though my heart had been touched by David's appearance at the Tent after Boaz died, the announcement of a coming birth left me feeling even more excluded.

One afternoon as I was thinking on these things, a shadow darkened my cubicle. I looked up and was astonished to see the king himself. He looked like a little boy afraid of a scolding for being where he didn't belong. I knew I should try to put him at ease or at least offer a seat, but I couldn't move, couldn't speak. After an awkward silence, he said with a tone of great sadness, "You are well, Asaph?"

I managed a nod, which encouraged him to plow on. "You've heard, no doubt, that Bathsheba is with child again."

Again I could only nod, my thoughts racing. Why had he come? Why would he talk to me, of all people, about Bathsheba's pregnancy? Just about every emotion conceivable tore through my body. I could see that whatever errand had brought him was becoming intolerable, but still I could not help him or myself.

He looked away, then fumbled at a pouch he was carrying. Hands trembling, he drew forth two scrolls and a gold armband. "I have a...a favor to ask." He handed the scrolls to me. "These are two songs I have written for—"

I think he intended to say, "for you," but he stopped as though understanding that I could not receive them. "They are self-explanatory. I have a double purpose for them. First, I intend to sing them as a public confession of sin, and that would be directed more specifically to you." Again his eyes flickered to mine. I wanted desperately to look at the scrolls, but I couldn't. Not yet.

"The second...is the chief reason I've come." David held out the armband. I took it automatically, but he retained his hold. I almost let go, but the same paralysis that left me dumb as a tree now kept my grip. I looked at him questioningly.

"Do you know what this armband is?" he asked.

My voice finally awoke. "No, my lord," I croaked.

"It's a painful symbol—for me, at least. It will be for you, too, I'm sure. Perhaps...intolerable." Again that great sadness. "I... gave this band as a gift to Uriah...before he left. He wore it in battle, and Joab...retrieved it from his body."

My hand convulsed as though the item had become a viper, but for some reason I did not let go. The horror of what he was doing to me seemed so incredible that my anguished eyes searched his, despite myself. "My lord—" I began, but he hurried on.

"Asaph, I...would like you to hold this armband and the scrolls in trust for my son," he said. "Whether or not you can ever again bear love for me, I want you to instruct my son. I can think of no better mentor. Abigail thinks I'm a poor *abba*. She may be right. But she'll approve of your influence. Please—teach him wisdom. Teach him right and wrong. To walk faithfully and to live out the precepts of God's covenant. These—the armband, the confessions—will serve as bad examples, if nothing else. They'll speak louder than any lessons you could give. I've thought long about this, Asaph. If I could cut myself up as a burnt offering, I would. If it would do anything more than make me sick, I'd grind the armband as Moses did the golden calf when he made the revelers drink the powder. But by putting it in your hands, Asaph, my son may walk a better path."

I was astonished. Dumbfounded. I gaped at him, this time my nerveless fingers dropping from the armband. I can only guess at my appearance, but his eyes interpreted rejection, and with the heaviness of grief he plucked the scrolls from my other hand and thrust them with the armband back into his pouch. Without a word, he turned and left.

For a moment I felt I might faint. My mind was a stone being whirled in a sling in the hand of some powerful outside force. David had reached into the cesspool of my dismay, taken hold of me against my will, and slung me to the top of Mt. Hermon. The air there took my breath away; my feet froze to the mountain's icy mantle. I could see the plain of Jezreel, the Sea of Kinnereth with the Jordan flowing away, the folded hill country. I could see Mt. Zion and the Tent that houses the Ark where the Name of the Lord God of Israel dwells. I could see priests and animals and haulers of wood for the altar. I could see the king walking away from a tiny cubicle outside the Tent. He carried with him my delight and my hope, my recompense for all I had suffered. My very life was vanishing along with the king—and I could do nothing to prevent it.

Did I pray at that moment? I doubt that even an angel with flaming sword could have compelled two words to join together in my mind. Nevertheless, the Lord of grace looked upon me. I believe he orchestrated a small, random event. Had not Abiathar's son Jonathan stumbled when and where he did, the ram waiting in line for sacrifice would not have become spooked, wrenched itself away from its owner, and crashed headlong into the departing king. No damage was done; the king was not hurt.

A minor incident, but watching it happen, I, a stone now red-hot from the unendurable pressure of this meeting with the king, was plunged suddenly in a bath of icy water. I exploded into fragments. "My lord! My lord!" I cried, my feet loosed at last. "Please...what can I...? That you... Why...?" Then I further embarrassed myself by breaking down.

When I opened my eyes, David was before me, himself in tears. We were indeed a spectacle, there in full view of palace traffic and the priests who followed up the ram-and-king collision. I did not care. This chaotic event came underneath me, much like an eagle for her free-falling chick, to becom the balance point of my entire life. For the first time in a year, my heart and not just my voice could sing.

After the baby was born and named Solomon, Nathan came to David with yet another message. Although the name *Solomon* meant "peaceful," said the prophet, God would call him *Jedidiah*—"loved by the Lord." Was this child, born of such a sin-flawed union, God's chosen to follow David as king? He was far down the line of succession, but why else would Yahweh grace this child with a special name?

David requested my presence for Solomon's circumcision, and when the ceremony was completed, the king lifted the wailing baby high, laughing over the Lord's goodness and mercy. Then, more solemnly, he placed the child in my arms. "He is bone of my bone, Asaph, but more than that, he is salt purifying my wound, the seed of God's grace for a harvest that knows no limits. I give this child of mercy to you. From this day on, you will wield the ox goad on his soul."

During David's early years in Jerusalem, Moab and Edom and Ammon had mounted a formidable challenge to his God-given sovereignty. The greatest threat to the kingdom, however, came not from an opposing nation but from an inner flaw within David himself. He fell hard on this stone of stumbling and broke far more than bones. But for now, at least, a thoroughgoing, wholehearted repentance had salvaged the treaty that bound him to *Yahweh*.

"*Your house and your kingdom will endure forever before me,*" God had said—a covenant of salt. "*Your throne will be established forever.*" Heady stuff—a promise that thrilled the heart of *Hamelech David* on the birth of this son, almost as much as when Nathan had first spoken the words.

Promises, though, seemed poor sustenance in the bleak desert years that lay ahead.

Scroll Three

1

David saw it as an excruciating beauty. I found it nauseating, but then, I'm not as accustomed as he to the trappings of retribution.

The drought that spawned the incident started shortly before David's liaison with Bathsheba. It descended on us—a cruel, silent stalker incinerating every green blade and sucking moisture out of winter and summer alike. The loathsome face of starvation leered at every window. The market sat barren; animals added bone to the bleach of the earth. A cloud of well-fed vultures traced its circle of death above Jerusalem.

Abigail did what she could to provide relief for the poor, to the point of going without food herself. This angered David. His tirade, while centered on a wife of the king looking like a plucked owl, was in fact his own anguish over the famine's ever-rising toll. Why was this happening? Was this a part of the "consequences" Nathan had warned of? Nathan didn't think so because of the timing of its onset. Then too, *Yahweh* had forgiven David; surely He would not impose an additional penalty. Any consequences yet to come would stem from David's own actions, not from the hand of the Lord.

After hearing dismal reports from his chief herdsmen, David himself began to fast. He dressed in sackcloth and prostrated himself before the Lord, and at the end of the third day, the answer came but not through Nathan.

The round-faced seer Gad appeared out of nowhere after many years' absence and went directly to the Tent as though he knew David would be there. He knelt beside the supine king, bowed to kiss his ash-covered head, and sat back with a round glow as David raised his gaunt, stricken face.

"I have a word from the Lord," Gad said.

David's eyes flickered between fear and hope, but encouraged by Gad's cheery look, he turned in the direction of the Ark with a word of cautious thanksgiving. He allowed the seer to help him up and lead him into the palace.

"My lord," said Gad when the king faced him squarely, "I have a word, but I will not presume to say whether it is good or ill."

David was not encouraged.

"Bloodguilt." The seer hunched a shoulder enigmatically. "Not yours—not this time. Your predecessor. So says the Lord."

David looked at him blankly.

"Guilt rests on Saul for what he did to the Gibeonites."

David stared. "The Gibeonites." He shook his head, puzzled.

"Yes, Gibeonites, those low-born haulers of wood and water for the priests." Gad went on to explain that these people, an ancient pocket of Amorites, had survived Joshua's invasion of Canaan by pretending to be foreigners. Joshua was upset

when he learned they had lied, but an oath is an oath, a sacred trust. He allowed them to live but insisted they serve the
Tent by hauling the quantities of wood and water needed for
sacrificing. Years later, in misapplied zeal, Saul had tried to
annihilate the Gibeonites but killed off only part. Now this
brutal breach of a treaty had erupted in a pestilent boil that,
for the sake of the land, would have to be lanced.

David closed his eyes with a grimace. The God who was
just was every bit as perplexing as the God who was holy. He
sent for the Gibeonite elders, who heard his explanation with
amazement.

"How can I address this wrong?" he asked.

The elders hemmed and clawed their beards and discussed
among themselves the implications of David's question. They,
of course, had felt the shriveling effects of Saul's sin and had
in fact been crying out to the Lord these many years. That
Yahweh might actually do something to recompense this lowly, disregarded people seemed astonishing.

Finally, the eldest stepped forward. "We've no right to silver or gold, my lord. And killing just any Israelites won't do.
But Saul's descendants...might seven be left? A good, proper
number—seven."

Ahithophel stepped forward crisply. "My lord, Ahinoam's
sons are dead, but Saul's concubine Rizpah had two, plus
whatever sons they've had. His daughter Merab, I believe,
bore a number and his son Jonathan one. Michal, of course..."
He coughed delicately, but the implications for Saul's younger
daughter were clear: had Michal not been barren, David might
well be struggling over his own sons in this matter. David
drew a breath and forced himself to a different concern.

"Mephibosheth will not die," he said. "I will not allow it. My oath to Jonathan overrides any other obligation. The others, yes—seven. A proper number. The blood of Saul's offspring will undo the bloodguilt of Saul."

Abigail was livid when she got wind of the matter—so upset, in fact, that she requested an audience with the king, something she seldom, if ever, did. But David was ready for her. "I know what you're going to say, Abigail. You're horrified that I'd condone this deed—putting seven men to death to save such a small item as the nation of Israel. Do you think I'm enjoying this? Do you think I take pleasure in robbing children of their fathers?"

Abigail normally would have withstood the blast in stiff silence, but the depth of her feeling put fire in her eyes and an edge to her voice. "You may not enjoy it, but you're consenting to it. I would prefer to die myself rather than set my hand to such a deed."

"If it were just my life at stake," said David, "I might sacrifice it, too. But it's thousands of lives. Thousands of thousands. You're forgetting, too, that this isn't my idea—it's God's."

"It's Gad's idea—or God's according to Gad."

"You're questioning Gad's authority? My dear wife—"

"God holds a man responsible for his own sin, not the sin of his father. I don't know where Gad got the idea that—"

"Gad got the idea from *Yahweh*. Look at the massacre of the priests at Nob. Ahimelech wasn't the guilty party; he was a good, righteous man. God was judging the house of Eli, his great-grandfather, who was not a good man. And this matter is even worse, Abigail. It's bloodguilt, and the entire nation is suffering. Can't you see that? I've got to do whatever is necessary to stop the suffering. I can't countermand God's order. You of all people should understand that. You didn't witness Uzzah's demise for merely trying to protect the Ark. If you had, Abigail, you'd have been every bit as angry as I was. I don't understand God, Abigail. *I don't understand*, but I must obey."

With fearful solemnity, David summoned both Abiathar and Zadok, as well as Gad, and in their presence formally committed to the Gibeonites seven descendants of Saul for the healing of the land. Rizpah's sons Armoni and Mephibosheth (not Jonathan's Mephibosheth, of course)—men hardly younger than David—and Merab's five, ranging between twenty and thirty years of age. Joab was given the task of apprehending them; the Gibeonites themselves would wield the sword. As loathe as David was to carry out the dreadful sentence, the famine's relentless toll confirmed the decision.

On a lonely hill in Gibeah, the city of Saul, with sheep and goats looking on, seven representatives of the house of Saul stood trembling as Zadok, the searing sirocco wind billowing his robe, intoned the words of the Law:

> *Do not pollute the land where you are. Bloodshed*
> *pollutes the land, and atonement cannot be made for*
> *the land on which blood has been shed, except by the*
> *blood of the one who shed it. Do not defile the land*
> *where you live and where I dwell, for I, the Lord, dwell*
> *among the Israelites.*

Zadok, who searched each man's eyes before turning him over to the Gibeonites, was satisfied. "My lady, I saw in their faces the clear image of Saul," he told Abigail afterwards. "These were no innocents. Their own swords had not killed the Gibeonites—many had not even been born—but their hands were under Saul's hand as surely as mine is under the hand of David."

There on a hill in the month of Abib, seven sons of Saul were killed and their bodies impaled on stakes before the Lord. Because of the unusual circumstances, they would not be removed before sunset as the Law required, but would remain in place until rainfall signaled the end of the drought and the completion of the Lord's judgment. A penalty, perhaps, more stern than the execution itself. Can a greater ignominy befall the dead than their bodies being exposed to scavengers?

The matter might have ended right there, with everyone turning in on himself and crawling to the nearest patch of shade to wait out God's judgment. But no one had allowed for a mother's love.

As soon as the men of justice had left the hill, Rizpah, mother of Armoni and Mephibosheth, spread a bed of sackcloth on a rocky ledge to watch over the bodies, chasing birds by day and wild animals by night.

Abigail was the first to take food and water to her. David quickly—but gently—put a stop to her ministrations. "I won't have my little skeleton taking nourishment to a fatted calf," he said. "I'll see that the old woman is cared for; it's the least I can do in the face of such an...excruciating beauty." He stared out the window, then turned to rest his hand on Abigail. "Thank you," he whispered in dismissal.

When rain finally fell, he did more than simply bury the bodies. He sent to Jabesh Gilead for the bones of Saul and Jonathan and buried them with the seven in the tomb of Saul's father Kish at Zela in Benjamin.

After three years of misery, the land was healed. Even Abigail feasted in thanksgiving, but never again did she allow more than the barest covering of flesh over her bones.

2

On a rocky hillside overlooking a long slash of valley, Joab, Abishai, and Jashobeam dug parched grain from a sack. The three were only casually interested in food as they watched the activity below. A battle appeared to be unfolding, the troops few and the field of war confined to a barren, rock-strewn area. The combatants were defined by color. The king's sons and retinue, arrayed in purple and polish, moved with stiff choreography against their red opponents, young Levites.

"There's where we went wrong against Saul all those years," grunted Joab. "Should've dressed with tassels and plumes. Makes a picture. At least they're not apt to hurt each other. One of them might hit a camel, but anything smaller... War's just a game for them."

Jashobeam crunched his gums and watched the flailing combatants. "Cousin Jonadab there—Shimeah's boy. Not too bad."

Abishai grunted. "Cousins, servants, slaves—a poor patch of an army. But then, the red boys aren't much, either."

Joab hissed. "*Livrite* kids! A couple of A-sap's whelps and other little saffron plants. All they lack is Daniel, Abigail's eggshell. Picture him trying to hoist staff or spear! In a real scrap, neither side would outlast spit on a noon desert."

Abishai spoke reflectively. "I don't know. Jashobeam's right about Jonadab. A smart lad, maybe too smart. When Amnon becomes king, Jonadab will be beside him, but for good or bad, I wonder?"

"Where's Absalom?" asked Jashobeam. "Don't see him."

"Prince Beautiful? Taking a nap, maybe."

"Absalom—he's no nap taker," said Jashobeam. "Not sure what he's good for, but he absolutely don't take naps."

The men followed the mock battle with interest. Zadok had worked with the Levite boys, and it showed. War was his passion; his zeal had become theirs. They handled weapons reasonably well, and though fewer in number, they mounted superior maneuvers.

With the battle going against the royal army, Joab was caught between disdain and contempt. "Please, somebody do something intelligent!"

Somebody did.

Jashobeam was first to spot him. "There." He pointed. "Coming down that cut."

"I see it," said Abishai. "It's Absalom, all right, but...a *mule*? On that kind of ground? He's crazy!"

Joab watched intently. "Maybe. Maybe not."

"Nobody could get a mule down that cliff," said Jashobeam, "unless..."

"Unless what—that thin crack along the face?" said Abishai. "Impossible. He'd slide down the mule's neck and spatter his brains across the rocks."

"Well," said Joab, "he'll either get the mule down that crack, or the king'll have to work up a replacement son."

"Or he'll turn back when he sees what he's up against."

"Absalom turn back? Now who's crazy?"

Absalom put his mule to the cliff face, and the mule, stepping deliberately, took tentative steps along the diagonal line that appeared too narrow to support even blades of grass. The animal set its feet and slumped backward, but Absalom drove his heels into its sides. This nearly precipitated a flying leap to both their deaths, but the mule scrambled and slid, with Absalom somehow staying aboard. The mule went to its knees, and the men gasped reflexively. Absalom flailed, and he and the animal hung over the abyss for what seemed like minutes until the mule finally gathered its feet and hopped on three legs to the bottom.

Jashobeam's jaw dropped. "Well, walk all over me!"

"What'll he do now?" said Abishai. "Three mule feet is no good."

"Even without a mount," said Joab, "he's primed to hit the *Livrite* flank."

The battle took a significant turn at that point. Absalom remained mounted, even a lame mule giving him an advantage. The Levite boys responded valiantly, but the princely band drove them into a neighboring vineyard for the "kill." The landowner was not pleased.

Abishai and Jashobeam couldn't stop talking about Absalom's feat. Joab shook his head from a contrary conviction. "The kid never fails. That's the trouble. No matter what he does, luck or somebody letting him off makes him a winner. No consequences. Nothing but people kissing his feet. You wait," he went on. "Davi will praise the boy to the skies, without a word about risking his and a good mule's neck for nothing more than a game." Joab spat in a coarse sort of symbolism. "Say what you will," he said, "Saul was the making of King David. The toughest thing most of these cubs have to face is deciding whether to eat barley bread or honey cakes for breakfast. What's going to toughen up the next king?"

"Next king," mused Jashobeam. "Anybody giving thought to Bathsheba's boy? Still in the cradle, sure, but there's talk of him after David."

"With A-sap hovering over him? God help us if he does!"

Absalom, the indisputable leader, though not the oldest of the brothers, had the looks, wit, and politeness to charm the horns off a goat. David was partial to him, but others, too, were drawn by the boy's irrepressible appeal. Absalom knew how to get things done—or how to beguile his way off the hook.

But seldom was he called to account. Even with irrefutable reports of Absalom and his brothers' questionable activities, few were willing to say, "Those boys have a problem." Most found it prudent to ignore their drinking, hurtful pranks, blameshifting, pitting of servants against each other, or drawing of servant girls into their schemes. That was the *minor* mischief. Of more concern were unaccountable pregnancies among daughters of noblemen and servants alike. These things should have caused alarm, but nobody appeared to notice.

Both Amnon and Abigail's son Daniel were twenty-one, but no one ever lumped Daniel in with the other sons. Short like his mother, thin and pallid, he was often sick, sometimes seriously, but David seldom visited him. I believe that both Daniel and Abigail made David uncomfortable; to him they were symbols of failure. Neither wore the face of love he longed for, and he talked with them as seldom as possible.

To my everlasting regret, I did not discover Daniel until the last year of his life. I had seen him often, but always accompanied by Abigail. While he was invariably polite, he revealed almost nothing of his inner self. I had tried to draw him out, but shyness and mistrust kept him away.

A thunderstorm unlocked this fast-barred door. Daniel had come to the Tent to worship, and a storm hit as he was about to leave. Although the palace doorway wasn't far, he would have been soaked. I thought it wise, given his condition, to draw him into my cubicle until the rain passed. Even then he might not have talked to me, but the storm set off a spiritual ecstasy that could not be contained. "Did you see that bolt? It just hung there, a word of glory written on the sky. And the thunder, Asaph! The voice of *Yahweh* roaring above the waters."

He was getting wet by the doorway, but he would not be denied. "Have you ever been blown over by the wind, Asaph?"

No wonder my socially correct questions had fallen flat! "No, I can't say I have."

"I have. Twice. My mother doesn't know about the second time. Sometimes you have to do things even if you know you'll get hurt. The first time it happened on top of a hill. I could hear the wind gathering below. It swept up and when it was right on me I jumped in the air and it took me off the top. I screamed and cried and shouted and laughed. My mother thought I was broken but it didn't matter. The Spirit of God blew on me and I didn't know there was such power. I'd do it again, Asaph. I'd climb that hill even with lightning cracking all around and trees blowing apart. I'd cry out for God to sweep me up and hurl me to Moab. The mighty arm of the Lord! Look at it! Look! The wind and rain and thunder speak the power of God."

Power. Daniel had never possessed power but desperately wanted it. Not power over people. No. He just wanted to hurl himself into the arms of God. And that was only the top layer of wonders wrapped up in Daniel.

The mind that boy had! Plants, stars, the meaning of life and wisdom, the business of apprehending God. I could bring up no subject he had not already considered with astonishing insight.

I sought to interest David in this unexplored treasure. To his credit, he did try to talk with Daniel, but the boy was too awed to converse freely. He admired his father and ached for his approval, but though he was kind and tried not to show his dislike, David never encouraged the boy in any significant way.

After the day of the storm, I took every opportunity to talk with Daniel. I sensed that he wouldn't live long and wanted to mine the depths of his mind and character. While he could still walk, we climbed the olive slopes across the valley. And when he could not push his wracked body for very long, we strolled the palace gardens, his eyes glittering over our mental games. So much to explore, so far to go, but time was running out. *Why* hadn't I tried earlier and harder to unlock the boy's mind?

Perhaps, though, the approach of death was fanning life into flames for Daniel. Perhaps his soul might never have soared upward had his body not been dragged to the ground. And I would have become neither the hearth nor the stoker of this furnace.

I sought to build the boy's sense of worth, which had suffered from almost universal neglect. His mother was, of course, his closest friend and mentor, but under the attention I provided, he expanded like a sponge in water. In that last year, I tried to be the father he never had. And near the end, while he was still alert enough to know me and understand, I gave him the blessing he craved. As Isaac blessed Jacob and Jacob blessed Judah, so I laid my hand on the boy and traced his line back: Daniel *ben* David, *ben* Jesse, *ben* Obed, *ben* Boaz and Ruth the Moabitess, *ben* Salmon—all the way back to Perez, the not-quite bastard son of the patriarch Judah. I did not go into all that, but I did bless Daniel, and for perhaps the first time in his life, he was fully at peace.

Abigail and I held him in his dying moments and closed his eyes. Neither of us had felt it necessary or important to call David in, and the king was not unduly surprised or affected when informed of his son's death. He was moved, however, by the lament I sang at Daniel's grave:

> *O Daniel, you came too soon, too late,*
> *The jewel of your mother,*
> *The gem of your friend.*
> *How the choice are taken away!*
> *Daniel, may the wind of God*
> *Carry you beyond Moab*
> *To rest with your fathers,*
> *With father Abraham.*

I saw Daniel and his brother Boaz once more. I'm not sure when I recognized them, but Boaz showed himself soon after Solomon was born. The same dimpled smile, the same quality of eyes. As I worked with Solomon and began to appreciate both his head and heart, it came to me that *Yahweh* had given Solomon both the sunshine of Boaz and the whirlwind mind of Daniel, forging a choice vessel to sit on David's throne.

3

After her week of mourning, during which David called on her twice, Abigail picked herself up and went back to making bread and soup, as she had done for Daniel in the weeks before he died. Exactly what she did with this food no one was certain. It disappeared, however, and although her Egyptian maidservants would never say, I suspect Abigail continued the charitable work she had begun during the famine.

I had fewer opportunities to talk with her now, and on each occasion I grew increasingly alarmed at her condition. Her life had gone to the grave with Daniel, but a furnace burned within that I—perhaps her closest friend—found chilling. She seemed to be on a vendetta—driven to scale the Jebus water shaft, to capture a fortified city, to drive her personal horde of Amalekites over a cliff. Why? Did she have one more task to complete before joining Daniel? I did not understand such fierceness.

With the help of city elders and a priest, as required by the Law, David judged civil disputes and other judicial matters. Twice a week for up to two hours, the king sat in his carved chair at the city gate with white-bearded elders cross-legged around him. People came from afar seeking justice. This wasn't David's favorite task, but one of the duties of a king was to protect the powerless against exploiters or oppressors, and he took his responsibility seriously. He listened and asked questions and ruled with fairness. People did grumble when lines outdistanced the allotted time, but by and large, justice was done.

Much of the city's activity centered on the broad gateway that tunneled through the shield-hung Millo. With the famine long gone, business was brisk. Intermingled flocks of sheep milled on both sides of the gate, yet a shepherd had only to call *Taa-ho-ho-ho!* to collect his own animals. Heaps of figs, bags of cumin and caraway, bundles of fragrant aloe; caravans— some scruffy, some well-belled; foreign representatives bearing tribute of wheat and barley, wool and lambs; tribal leaders seeking audience; worshippers dragging sacrifices; beggars, soldiers, priests, and Levites. Color, noise, bustle, odors—all played against each other in bracing polyphony.

David's realm was functioning well. A good administrator, he had able men to oversee the complex apparatus of government. Benaiah and his cadre of Kerethites and Pelethites were always at David's right hand, overseeing the king's palace and his personal safety. In addition, competent supervisors were in charge of provisions and supplies. Ezri managed farms and field hands, Shimei the vineyards, and Zabdi saw to the making of wine. Good men all.

And the camelmaster—Obil the Ishmaelite, a small, shrewd-eyed man as irascible as the animals in his charge. No one knew camels better than Obil; no one knew Obil better than David.

Their acquaintance dated back to the wilderness years. The lad Obil had been captured by Edomites. They had just started relieving him of ears, thumbs, and big toes when David rescued the boy, along with his master's camels.

Hardly three months later, the band came upon him again. Again his camels had been stolen, but this time Obil had escaped. Stranded in a wasteland, he had resorted to thieving, and David happened to be close enough to notice. David ran him down and was about to run him through when the missing ear caught his attention. "You!" he roared, shoving the boy to the ground.

Obil did not cower, nor did he plead for his life. He simply stared back with Arabic fatalism.

David thrust his spear into the ground instead of the boy. "Stand up," he ordered.

The boy eased himself up. David studied the new assortment of scars. "What happened to your camels this time?"

"Moabites. Killed my master, left me for dead."

"How long since you've eaten?"

Obil shrugged and said nothing.

David chewed a strand of beard. "I don't throw away what once I saved. And we were once aliens in Egypt. Stay with us until some meat covers your bones, then go make an honest living. Stick to camels; they're healthier than thieving."

A year later, Obil appeared at David's encampment just ahead of Saul's army, to warn him of an ambush along their

escape route. He had a string of camels and somehow managed to keep the animals quiet as the entire rebel band skirted
Saul's line. David never forgot, and in turn, Obil remained
fiercely loyal to his adopted sovereign to the day of the king's
death.

The country, then, was largely at peace, with just enough
challenges to keep the troops exercised. They sometimes went
on what Amasai called "garbage patrols." Despite every effort,
idol worship remained a chronic, detestable practice. The
prophet Samuel had thrown his life against it, but far too few
men could resist worship practices linked with sex. Idolatry
dies hard.

David attacked these practices with power and drama.
"How shall we live if we forget *Yahweh's* most basic law?" he
thundered. "*No other gods; no bowing down to idols or burning
incense to them.* We're not like other nations; we're holy because God is holy. His presence and glory sets us apart from
other people. Even our acts of love are sacred."

All in all, David had good men in place, and his government
worked smoothly.

The complete listing of his administrators can be found in
the annals of the king. My documents, of course, will be entered in due time. Gad, I believe, is also writing up his obser-
vations. Perhaps someday we'll compare notes.

4

David doted on the boy Solomon, still a toddler, and I, too, kept careful watch over him. He was too young to be touched by court influences, and in the minds of his older brothers, Solomon might not even have existed. I thank God for that regularly.

Absalom was the first of the king's sons to marry, a calculated event. His requirements for a wife included beauty and sensuality, but he ruled out a strong, forceful personality like his mother Maacah's. He would not tolerate undue demands for attention. Absalom's wife would serve Absalom, not the other way around.

Absalom's easy camaraderie with his father also paid handsome dividends. David set him up with flocks and herds, a comfortable house, ten fine, imported mules, his own bodyguard—a cadre of fifty men to run before him as befitted a prince. Beauty, valor, personality, talent, a gift for long-range planning: characteristics of a good king.

Unfortunately, his breast was empty of heart and full of guile.

Amnon, though older than Absalom, had not yet married. He had a house and everything a prince could want, except for one thing: Absalom's sister.

Amnon and Tamar had been close from the time they were children. Though otherwise a bit of a haughty peacock, Amnon had been gentle and generous with this sweet daughter of Maacah. She adored her half brother and made presents for him. A beautiful girl, Tamar had the looks but almost none of her mother's stridency. She loved to sing with her father, and not simply to make music. She understood worship. She, along with David, felt the wonder of the heavens and the poverty of human effort before such a God.

Why was she like this? All of David's children should have been so. They'd been taught the way of holiness, their father had poured song on the sponge of their hearts, they had participated in Sabbath and Passover observances, and they were part of the great assemblies on feast and other holy days. Few, though, responded with holy lives. Tamar was an exception.

As he grew older, Amnon had less time for Tamar. He and his cousin Jonadab busied themselves with exploring the ways of adults. They played and fought and connived, full of themselves, full of privilege—spoiled and nasty at best, dangerous at worst.

Tamar, too, was growing, and one day as she sat with the women at one of Absalom's parties, Amnon saw her. His heart fell shattered at her feet.

Oblivious to this devastation, she moved with demure charm among her friends, chatting mostly with other girls. Once, when she passed Amnon, she dropped a teasing word as she had hundreds of times before. Amnon went hot.

"Jonadab, I've got to have her," he said a week later. "Look at me. I can't eat, I can't sleep. I must have her!"

Jonadab looked at him with cheerful dispassion. "I don't know what 'her' you're referring to, but if you can only lie there mewling, you deserve to be sick. What's stopping you? The king's firstborn can have any woman he wants."

"My sister Tamar?"

"Ah!" Jonadab stepped back with a smirk of comprehension. "Tamar the Beautiful. Tamar the Good. Tamar the Untouchable Virgin. That is a challenge."

"Yes, but by everything I own, I'll mount her, and you'll tell me how to do it." His face turned ugly, which made Jonadab laugh even more.

"So that's how it is: you pick the target, and I'm your armor bearer, handing out darts of advice."

"That's the way it is today. Now, come up with something."

Jonadab strode around Amnon's chamber, stroking his beard, his eyes ruthless black beads. He nodded. "You look just awful enough for this to work. Go back to bed. Don't wash or comb your hair. A little ash on your forehead and cheeks..." He dipped into the cold firepan and rubbed his fingers over Amnon's face. "Not too much; mustn't look contrived. Go to bed—No, don't touch your face. It's just right. I'll say you're sick. When your father comes, lie there and look pathetic. It shouldn't be hard under the circumstances. You'll insist that you're not eating, but Tamar might tempt you if she were to come to your chambers and make her heart cakes, maybe... you fill out the rest."

Amnon grinned, clapping his friend on the shoulder. "Jonadab, you just earned—"

Jonadab leaned his swarthy face close, a shrewd gleam in his eye. "The accident of birth ties me to power, my lad. When you become king, I'm your right-hand man, your closest advisor, Number One. Right?"

The plan worked as Jonadab had envisioned. Tamar came to Amnon's house, beautiful in her ornamented virgin robe, full of concern and prepared to bake bread. "My brother," she said, taking his hand, "I'm sorry you're ill. I prayed for you on the way. Our father tells me you asked for heart cakes—the very bread you say tastes like fish scales and bird bones. You must be sick, indeed!"

Amnon smiled weakly. "Ah, my sister! You know how to cheer me." He stroked her hand and played with her fingertips. "I'll watch through the doorway while you grind your scales and bones. Don't take long; I may die before your choice bits reach my lips."

Amnon feasted on her graceful form as she moved to the other room, opened her cloth, and pressed the dough rhythmically. Her hands shaped the loaves deftly and set them on the hot griddle. While they baked she chattered about household gossip she thought might cheer him, flashing smiles in his direction. Getting no response, she rose and moved to the doorway. "My brother, are you all right? The bread will be ready soon. Can I get you something?"

Amnon threw his arm across his eyes and rocked his head from side to side.

Tamar looked anxiously toward the household servants busy with chores, but they avoided her eyes. Perhaps Amnon's personal servant...but he was in another room. The girl tested the loaves. "Ah!" She stood, looking heartened. "They're hot, but if I break off small pieces... I'm coming, Amnon."

She lifted the griddle with her bread cloth and carried it to the bedroom, setting it on the stone floor near Amnon's bed. She took a loaf and tore off small chunks.

Amnon lay with his arm over his face, breathing rapidly.

"There! Doesn't it smell good? This will make you well again. Let me prop you."

Just then, a jar broke in the outer room, and the noise made them both jump. Amnon sat up abruptly, his eyes glittering. "Get them out of here," he roared. "All of them. I can't stand noise!"

Tamar looked at him, astonished, then moved to the outer room. The servants shrugged over the scattered shards and went out the door. She turned back to the bedroom. "I'm so sorry!" she apologized for them. Amnon had dropped back and was again breathing heavily. She bent to her "choice bits." "Take a bite. You'll feel better."

He looked at her. "Heart cake."

She smiled. "Heart cake. Still your favorite, even with bird bones and fish scales."

He opened his mouth obediently for the piece she held out, but as she turned for more, he grabbed her wrist. "Come lie with me, my sister." His voice was hoarse, and a vein in his forehead beat fast.

Tamar froze, the color draining from her face. She forced a smile. "You're teasing me. See? The bread is working. Let go of my arm; I'll give you another piece."

"I don't want bread. I want you. Lie beside me. I have an appetite for one thing at a time. Afterward, we can eat heart cake together. I'll feed it to you."

She strained to get out of his grasp. "Don't. Please don't, my brother. Don't do this to me. It's wicked! Please—let go!"

"I won't let you go. I've been sick with love since the day of Absalom's party."

Her eyes widened. "You're not sick at all. This was a trick to get me here."

"I am sick. I haven't eaten all week. And only you can make me well."

Tamar struggled and twisted with sharp cries. Then she stopped, panting. "*Think*, Amnon. Think what you're doing." Her voice trembled. "What you want is wrong, before God and before all Israel. And what about me? A virgin daughter of King David. How would I survive such disgrace? Think of the consequences, Amnon. Please think!"

"I think about what I want. *And I will have it!*"

"Then you are a fool, and I pity you. Stop, Amnon! Listen to me. Listen! Maybe you could speak to the king, and he would let us marry. Surely that would be better than—Amnon, you're hurting me! Stop!"

She shrieked as Amnon forced her to the bed. He fastened his hands around her throat until her shrieks turned to choking. Then, he kissed her flailing, struggling form until he could contain himself no longer.

His passion spent, Amnon lay beside her, his gasping almost seemed to be sobs. Suddenly, in a fit of rage, he threw himself off and pushed Tamar to the floor with his feet.

Her sobs were the groans of a woman in labor. With only a quick, desperate move to cover her nakedness, she huddled on the hard stone with nothing but woe to cling to.

Amnon kicked her again. "Shut up!" he roared. "Get out of here!"

"No! Look what you've done! You can't just throw me away. You've killed me; will you now leave me unburied? You have to take care of me, Amnon!"

"Let the king take care of you. Or brother Absalom. I hate you! I detest you! Don't come in my sight again!"

"No, no..." She sobbed uncontrollably.

Amnon rose to his knees, looking toward the outer room. "Nadab! Come here!"

His personal servant entered and bowed before his master with scarcely a glance at the distraught girl. Amnon spoke sharply. "Put her out of the house, Nadab, and bar the door."

"No! Amnon, please *listen!*"

"Get her out. Now!"

Nadab dispassionately tried to raise Tamar against her determined efforts to sink to the floor. Finally, he lifted her frenzied body and deposited her, not ungently, outside the courtyard gate. The bar thunking into place sounded to Tamar like a beheading she'd once inadvertently witnessed.

Not far from where she lay, a small pile of ashes, most likely from her bread fire, sent up a thin line of smoke. Tamar crawled to it and grasped a handful, the shooting pain of a tiny coal giving grim satisfaction. With poignant ceremony, she ground the ash into her hair, then tore her virgin dress. Her voice rose in a keening wail. "*Ai!* God have mercy on me!"

She staggered to her feet and began to run blindly, weeping loudly.

Word sped quickly to Absalom, and he captured her with his arms. She could say nothing but "Amnon! Amnon!" It was enough, and Absalom's eyes became stone—hard and gray and remote and impenetrable. His words, though, were carefree and comforting: "Hush. *Taa-ho-ho*, as Father says. It's all right. He's your brother; it's a small thing." But Absalom's eyes ranged across the earth, across the years. In that instant something inexorable was set in motion.

He took her to his home where his wife cared for her, but no amount of washing could erase the lurid stains that encamped behind her eyes.

Tamar remained there, desolate, her only comfort a niece born and named for her, who, in the end, turned out to be the lone survivor among Absalom's four children.

David heard the news almost as quickly as Absalom and was furious, but his response was mostly smoke. He hauled Amnon out of bed and breathed brimstone into his gullet. When the young man's legs buckled, he tacked his blistered body to the wall and kept on until his voice grew hoarse. That was it, though. Amnon had clearly broken the Law; he had brought shame to the king and to Israel, as well as to his half sister. He should at least have been severely punished or restricted in his activities. If David had flogged him or commissioned someone else to do it, perhaps... perhaps... But he didn't, and the poison began to seep.

Absalom said nothing one way or the other about the affair, to Amnon or to anyone else. He simply waited.

5

David was in pain. He'd taken a fall, not in battle or by attempting some great feat, but simply by tripping over a dog and tumbling against a stack of mud bricks in the market. The bricks buried him, but the greater pain came from the laughter of children too young to know about kingly dignity. His pride, as well as his body, had been wrenched.

"I don't suppose..." he said wistfully when he got inside. "No, probably not. Find me the next best, then. I hurt."

An hour later found him lying facedown on a padded table in the cool, dark, massage room. A shelf close by held an assortment of oils, ointments, and spiced wine. Underneath were jars of hot and cold water. A familiar room, one that David visited frequently. Unfortunately, he could never predict how good a massage he might get, even at the hands of regulars. He lay grimacing over the prospects.

His thoughts blocked out the rustle of preparation. The fall had been embarrassing. He'd walked out with Zadok, who was heading back to Gibeon and his Tent responsibilities there. The two threaded the market jumble, drawn by a "needle" of

Kerethites and Pelethites. "Benaiah won't let me off the road to pee without at least six men dancing attendance," David had grumbled.

"You sneaked up on Saul in the cave," said Zadok. "An enemy can do the same to you. Benaiah's doing his job, and I thank God for that."

"So what could come of walking through the market to see you off?"

At that instant the dog had taken refuge between David's feet.

David sighed and stirred on what felt like a bed of rocks. An attendant put a cup of warm liquid to his lips. He sipped appreciatively, glancing to see which of his three massage slaves he should brace himself for. The Nubian tended to be most consistent, but this wasn't he. The newest one—an Edomite with muscles like bronze bowls—was good but hurt him the most. The figure now over him, as tall as the Nubian but only half as broad and with no discernible muscles, pressed David's head to rest under a hot, wet towel. The spiced wine began to work, and sounds of stirring, pouring, and whispers retreated through the folds of more hot towels.

Still, the market scene descended on his mind like an unnerving hail of sling stones. They laughed, he thought. *At me, who loves children.*

A number of hands turned him groaning to his back. All but the head towel was removed, and he felt something wet and warm, almost hot, being molded to his body. An odd smell—familiar, yet different. What was it? He clawed at the towel on his face, but his hands were quickly imprisoned. One glimpse, though. *Mud—black Salt Sea mud.* That was it. *From*

En Gedi. When all but his head was encased in the muck, the table covering itself was pulled up and over, and he became a hot cocoon.

The head towel was then removed, and warm, oiled hands worked his face and eyelids. His muscles relaxed deeper still.

When the heat became almost unbearable, the shadowy masseur signaled for the mud to be stripped off. A cool-water rinse and toweling was followed by deep kneading with scented oil. Strong, ministering hands pursued the contour of every muscle to the source of its pain and scoured away residual pebbles of mortification. The king slept.

When he awoke the room was empty except for a slave who held his clothing in readiness.

He said little the rest of that day, waving off inquiries concerning his fall. When I talked with him the next day, he seemed unable to describe the experience or to say how it affected him. "It seemed...like God's hands on me, Asaph. The pain in my body meant nothing. My spirit was being worked on, strengthened, prepared for...for what, Asaph? What is to come? And who was it? Someone tall, which rules out Abigail. I thought of her right away. I don't even know if it was a man or a woman. Hoarse whispers—could've been either. The hands, though...I don't know...."

Something else shook him a few days later: a gift for Bathsheba—an elegant, gold-ornamented robe exactly right for her coloring, her build, her personality. No one knew where it had come from; no one knew who had made it. David found it in his apartment, wrapped in fine linen, fragrant with myrrh, aloes, and cassia, with only the designation attached. Although he roared up and down, no one could say. This time he did go to Abigail but was told by a stiff, crusty servant that she was unwell and could not be disturbed.

Unwell, indeed. The next day she died.

David was thunderstruck. Why hadn't he been told she was ill? Obviously, anyone could discern from looking at her that she'd been wasting away for some time. She hadn't appeared for meals, but that in itself was not unusual. During Daniel's slow demise and her time of grief, she'd kept to herself. She had not appeared in public, and even I had seen her only a few times since Daniel's death.

Under the king's direct questioning, her servants did admit to having been cowed into not telling of her condition, but that neither explained anything nor placated the king. He wept inconsolably both during the funeral procession and the hours following, tossing stones into the air.

"It was her, Asaph; it had to have been. Who else would do that?"

"What is it you're speaking of, my lord?"

"The massage. The robe. I looked at the robe, on the inside... not the right shoulder seam like mine, but the left. Bathsheba would stand at my right hand; that shoulder would be next to me. One thread. Just one thread, that's all. Not her initial like with mine, but one red thread. Did she hope I wouldn't find it, or that I would? And the mud massage. It had to have been her."

"But you said the person was tall."

"Yes, but you know as well as I, Asaph, that Abigail could grow eight inches if she put her mind to it. I don't know how she managed, but those were her hands; I know that now."

"Maybe she stood on something."

David didn't answer and just stared into his mind. "Less than a week before her death. *How could she do it?*"

Tears came to my eyes. "She was a strong woman, my lord," I said. "Hands trained on countless loaves of bread, her heart conditioned through—"

"—through putting up with me; you don't have to say it, Asaph. Abigail of all women could do a full-body mud casing and massage the week before she died."

"She did have helpers. You saw them."

"Yes, but when you're in pain you don't care about helpers."

"Did you ask...? No, you wouldn't get answers. Looming torture wouldn't persuade Abigail's servants to open their mouths. I'm surprised they admitted to anything at all."

"That's what it took—the threat of a beating. They'd been with her more than twenty years—the Egyptian slave girls Dodai gave her when we first went to Ziklag. But there must have been allies. If you ever find out who they were, Asaph, let me know."

I never found out.

Why would she make such a robe for Bathsheba? Was it the last selfless act of a giver? Her inner need to demonstrate love? Her belated stamp of approval on the marriage? Or was it the only way Abigail could legitimately "get back" at David and rub salt into his guilt? Was it her way of expiating her own resentment?

Whatever her motive, she died as she lived—her own person, taking care of the needs of her husband before her own, not being a nuisance.

To my gratification, David fully understood his loss and mourned deeply the death of his third wife, the first of them to go.

6

A shadowy figure, face obscured, dragged two protesting animals through the newly opened palace gate
and to the sanctuary.

Barefoot Levites prepared for the day's activities. They filled
the laver, checked the wood supply, and readied themselves
to serve the priests. Two musicians bent over a harp that was
chronically out of tune. I had pronounced a death sentence on
it, but they wanted to try one more trick to tighten the pegs.
Outside, yawning gatekeepers of the third watch reported to
replacements who would continue in unceasing patrol around
the sanctuary enclosure.

The early arrival presented his ewe lamb and goat for guilt
and thank offerings, along with sifted flour, oil, salt, and a
half-hin of wine. He noted with satisfaction that Abiathar
was dressed as a regular priest, not as high priest. A scheduled
priest was ill, and Abiathar would take his place at the altar.
Was this, after all, the man's priest of choice? He waited at the
entrance while Abiathar prayed, washed his blood-blackened
hands and feet at the laver, and sacrificed the daily ritual lamb.
The harp and cymbals sounded, and a priest blew the silver

trumpet. The rest of those present—a poor patch of a choir that day—sang as Abiathar laid the butchered pieces with his own burnt offering on the fire that never went out, along with grain and drink offerings.

When early worship was completed, the priest checked the two animals for defects. The man, eyes averted and head tucked to the side, confessed to human uncleanness, then muscled his lamb to the altar and laid a hand on its head. After slicing its throat, he held the animal until its blood filled Abiathar's silver basin. The priest then sloshed the blood on diagonal corners of the altar and poured the remainder on the drain at the base. With quick, sure movements, his assistants skinned the animal, reserving the hide for the officiator. Only the fat and kidneys of a guilt offering were burned.

The grain offering of consecration came next. The priest took a handful of flour and oil, seasoned with salt, to burn with incense as a sweet aroma before the Lord; the remainder would go to the priests. Wine, too, was poured before the Lord.

The second animal was similarly sacrificed and presented before the Lord, the fat burned, and the meat placed in a pot. This time the priest would fork out a portion for the worshiper to eat. The priests and Levites would eat their portion later, but the entire fellowship offering would be consumed in the consecrated courtyard.

As the offerings progressed, a second worshipper came in. The high priest greeted him effusively. "My lord Absalom! You're out early. May the Lord bless you this fine morning."

The prince bowed affably to Abiathar and to those assisting him. He had brought only a fellowship offering, his portion of which he took to the north curtain of the courtyard where the other man squatted. There they talked on two different levels—one an audible, getting-acquainted sort of chatter, the other a cryptic exchange that seemed to indicate some prior acquaintance. Absalom was the first to leave the courtyard.

The conversation struck me as odd, for I was behind that curtain trying to locate Ethan, whom I'd heard had just arrived to help plan for the Day of Atonement, only a week away. Absalom's voice I recognized, but not the other.

David's ill-fated affair with Bathsheba had humbled him before the Lord, and now his undeniable love for her above all other wives and concubines weighed heavily. "If the Lord had taken Bathsheba instead of...it would've been hard to bear, but I could understand it. But to still have her *and* her sons— she's pregnant again, Asaph, did you know that?"

Blessings not deserved. No wonder he was blinking.

"It's almost worse this way. I know pain and loss are a warrior's lot. But *grace* on a self-inflicted wound... Who can stand such a burning?"

Mercy received at the hand of primal love. Many point to David's moral lapse as the cause of far-reaching woes, and while that may be true, I saw him grow because of it. The cheapness in his heart melted and reconfigured into a reaching, pulsing hunger for God. It could even be said that *Hamelech David* reached his spiritual apex in this time of humiliation. There's no limit to the height of greatness to which God can exalt a man whose heart bends low in repentance.

David's contrition spoke through his most moving and personally revealing psalms. "Bless the Lord, O my soul" is a

diamond shaped by mercy's fire, the love song of a foul-heart-
ed sinner to a God who pardons.

> *Bless the Lord, O my soul;*
>> *all my inmost being, praise His holy name.*
> *Bless the Lord, O my soul,*
>> *and forget not all His benefits*
> *Who forgives all your sins*
> *and heals all your diseases,*
> *Who redeems your life from the pit*
>> *and crowns you with love and compassion,*
> *Who satisfies your desires with good things*
>> *so that your youth is renewed like the eagl"s.*
> *As high as the heavens are above the earth,*
>> *so great is His love for those who fear Him.*
> *As a father has compassion on his children,*
>> *so the Lord has compassion on those who fear Him;*
> *For He knows how we are formed,*
> *He remembers that we are dust.*

David's psalms were sometimes highly structured, sometimes random colors painted across the soul, or sometimes
what I call "attack poetry." You think you know where it's going, then suddenly you clutch the dagger in your heart and
dissolve in tears.

New forms, new concepts of worship fascinated him. He'd
call me, Heman, and Ethan together and talk music and in-
strumentation. The new temple was always on his mind, and
he wanted to develop an appropriate service for future use.
He'd try out different positionings for singers and trumpeters,
new liturgies and antiphonal singing between choir and worshippers. On one occasion, he amassed four thousand voices

with such breathtaking effect that he urged me to make such a festal choir an annual event in the future temple.

Worship became David's lifeblood. A man who knows thirst desires to drink constantly. "Sometimes," he said to me, "I want to rip the curtain from top to bottom, to expose myself to God in the raw there between the wings of the cherubim, as does the high priest on the Day of Atonement. The fountain of life is behind that curtain, Asaph. Yes, I know what would happen, but there are worse ways to die. I see that now, and I think Uzzah would agree."

Absalom returned with an extra gift for Abiathar, something he often did. "Did you know that fellow who was here when I came this morning?" he asked in an offhand way. "I thought I'd be first, but he beat me."

"I didn't pay much attention," said Abiathar. "I'd just gotten here myself. I'm trying to think...do you need to know? I could—"

"No, no. Just curious. He said he was from the hill country. Didn't ask his name."

"I should've asked, my lord."

"Not at all. Forget it, Abiathar. Doesn't matter. I hadn't seen him around."

He talked briefly of some other matter, then left with a springy step, whistling the Levites' last song.

Ittai, who knew Philistines better than anyone, warned David. He came with intelligence months before their attack. "They'll try; I'm sure of it."

Joab laughed off the notion. "This isn't Saul's army anymore. Do they think a giant or two will set us atwitter like the old days with Goliath? If Achish were alive, he'd never dress his soldiers in such oversized ideas."

"Just wait," said Ittai.

After that exchange, everyone except Ittai forgot about it. Philistia seemed pliant and trustable—until the day they simultaneously attacked ten outposts along the Shephelah with a vigor that surprised even Ittai.

The fighting was so intense that David mustered the militia to back up Joab.

The question inevitably arose over Ittai's participation in a war against his own countrymen. David dismissed it. "I will never doubt Ittai's loyalty," he said. "When he walked away from the Philistines, he walked toward *Yahweh*. I trust him. He fights with us."

The battles went on day after day, first at Gob, then at Gath. Ittai was invaluable, somehow finding out where the next attack would come. He never forgave himself, though, for David almost getting killed.

The battles exhausted even the most seasoned warriors, not to mention the aging king who'd seen little action since Rabbah. He could still bend the bronze bow, but his aim was not as sure, and a soft belly slowed his movements.

Ittai kept his eye on David, ready to move in if needed. The king appeared to be doing well, trading off weapons with his armor bearers. Then Ittai heard Amasai's horn-like bellow directing his men against a well-organized assault. He slipped around to help beat it back, and when he turned again to locate the king, he was horrified to see David stumbling up-hill alone, a Philistine giant hard on him, taking one stride to David's three. The giant whooped gleefully after the king. David's lungs roared, Ittai bellowed for someone to intervene, and screams of dying men drowned it all.

David went down, whether from a spear thrust or from simply falling. Ittai leaped over bodies, shouting and sobbing, furious at the distance he'd allowed and his helplessness to do anything about it. He ran, heedless of the battle. His armor bearer, trying desperately to keep up, went down, and Ittai, now alone, had only his shield for protection. It was not enough. A blow caught him and sent him under a Philistine chariot. For Ittai, the battle was over.

His cries, though, had been heard. Abishai saw where Ittai was headed and intercepted the giant in several strides—but not in time. As the giant's spear soared, Abishai lined up the stretch and arch of the Philistine's back, and with one savage effort, his own spear found that thin, vulnerable opening between breastplate and belt. The giant went down like a stuck bull, the full weight of his considerable body on the king. Abishai could do nothing about it; the battle was hot. For several minutes he could only protect the spot and whistle for his brother.

Jashobeam was the first to fight his way over, and in a short time, Joab and Amasai, along with Shammah and his men, joined the protective ring. Barking like a ferocious animal, Amasai spurred his men with dire threats, crying in between, "*Yahweh. Yahweh*, save the king! Answer when we call!" The fierceness with which they fought quickly had the Philistines on the run. Eleazar pursued them, and in vengeance, his men cut down nearly every soldier.

Abishai stared at the mess at his feet, not wanting to pull off the hulking body for fear of what he'd find. David's arm, sticking out from under the giant, was not moving. Amasai, blood coating his body, dropped to his knees and continued to demand a miracle. Jashobeam stepped forward. "I'll get him off; you tend Davi," he said, bending his muscle to the bulk at his feet.

After the body had been removed, Abishai took a big breath and knelt to the job. Blood and dirt covered the king, and his condition was hard to assess. The giant's spear lay diagonally across his body. "At least it's not through him," muttered Abishai. "Look at the size of it!" He scraped off blood with the edge of his hand.

Amasai checked the armor and found the entry hole. "Grazed him, from the look of it. Get his breastplate off."

"He dead or alive?" said Jashobeam. "It don't look—"

"Dead," said David into the mud that coated his face.

The Mighty Men whooped and danced and slapped backs.

"Don't...jiggle me," said the king. "Don't even touch...every rib... Leave me...six weeks. Can't breathe, can't move."

Ittai's injuries were more serious than David's, but learning that David was alive was the medicine he needed. "Bless *Yahweh*, O my soul!" was all he could mumble.

On the slow trip home, the generals talked. In the foothills, they came to David, who was grimacing in the shade. Eleazar had been appointed spokesman. "My lord the king," he said, "we've decided you're through fighting. Your life's too important—to us, to the nation."

David tried to straighten, anger overriding pain. "What do you mean? I'm not even sixty. Saul was fighting in his seventies."

"Yes, and he was killed, wasn't he?" said Eleazar. "That's just the point. You're the lamp of Israel, and we want to see that you stay lit."

"Besides," said Abishai, "we're not asking; we're telling. From now on, you will not lead the army of Israel. Period. That's our job."

"Keep the lamp shining," said Amasai. "That's all we ask."

S heep shearing was my father's favorite festival. As an orphan, he'd been sent out to tend sheep and goats. Life had been harsh for the boy, but when shearing time came each spring, he feasted and drank and sang and played, gleaning enough pleasure from those few days of abundance to see him through a year's worth of privation.

Absalom owned a number of scattered pastures on which he grazed his herds. At the appointed time, his shearers would travel from place to place, and a feast would appear at each site. This year, however, the king's son arranged only one celebration, at a rustic settlement nestled against Mt. Baal Hazor on the border of Ephraim, to which shearers, herders, and close friends were invited. He extended a special invitation to his father and his father's advisors, knowing full well that the king would decline. A shearing feast is fun for the young and rustic but hardly an important appearance for a king of Israel—especially one whose ribs still hurt abominably.

"Thank you, son. I'm honored that you'd ask me to sing. But did you count the extra cost if I showed up? It's not just me, you know. Benaiah and his fellows would hover, and your mother would have choice words if she were left out—she plus forty maids and slaves." David's eyes blinked merrily. "Thanks, but we'll keep life simpler for you this time."

Absalom bowed. "I'm sorry you won't come, Father. I was counting on it. But if I can't persuade you, will you allow the crown prince to come in your stead?"

David stiffened, and the blinking stopped. "Amnon? You want Amnon to attend your feast? You haven't said three words to him in two years. Why are you asking him?"

"*Abba*, it's a party. I've invited mutual friends—all kinds of people. It'd be rude to leave Amnon out. And like I said, as firstborn, he'll represent you. He sings pretty well. He can do some of your favorites."

David studied this son, now number two after Daniel's death, but saw only ingenuous pleading. Finally, he sighed and tousled the young man's head. "All right, invite Amnon. May the Lord make you all merry—and at peace with one another." With the latter words, his hand closed on the thick hair, and he tipped his son's head back, voice and eyes hardening. Though Absalom's eyes widened, he did not flinch. When his hair was released, he kissed his father and bowed low before jogging out.

The party was everything Absalom's resources could produce. His holdings in Baal Hazor included a rambling house with a large, tree-shaded courtyard. He had lined up singers, musicians, dancers, storytellers, the finest wine, bowls of fruit, platters of deer, gazelle, roebuck, and choice fowl. Nine of the king's sons—from Amnon the oldest to Adonijah's brother

Nepheg, who was barely twelve—had arrived on their mules and were greeted with pomp and awe. Amnon, uneasy about how he might be received, soon relaxed. His brother had kissed him with at least a show of warmth, and while he said little after that, he saw to it that the future king was treated as such by other guests.

This sat very well.

After much wine had been consumed and the noise of singing and dancing had risen apace, Absalom brought out the special entertainment he'd promised—a virgin dancer dressed like and bearing a striking resemblance to his sister Tamar (who was not in attendance). Silence fell over the courtyard, and there, against a lush backdrop of new-leafed trees and sweet-smelling vines, a single lute throbbed with passion and ardor. The young woman lifted her arms and began to dance.

The herders and shearers became bug-eyed as they watched the girl's demure, graceful movements. Amnon became transfixed. Her beauty was undeniable, and she appeared to be dancing just for him, turning first toward him, then away. Circling and twirling with soft elegance, she kept her eyes on the young man's face, which went alternately white and damp with perspiration. The wine he had drunk beat in his temples. He swayed uncertainly, unable to take his eyes off the maiden.

Absalom moved quietly behind him, taking advantage of his brother's focus. He drew people away from Amnon one by one until the crown prince and the dancer were alone in the mesmerizing circle of music.

As the dance reached its sensuous climax and Amnon had joined her steps, Absalom nodded to the guardsman beside him. The man stepped toward Amnon, then stopped, apparently struck by the consequences of what he was about to do. Absalom thrust him forward. "Go! This is by my order, nothing you need answer for. Backbone, man, backbone!"

Just then, Amnon awoke to his isolation and whirled around. The guardsman came at him, no longer ambivalent. In his mind, it was clearly Amnon's life or his own. His eyes held no doubt which it would be.

The virgin dancer saw, too, and fainted soundlessly at Amnon's feet. Amnon, reflexes slowed by wine, thought only to pick her up as a shield for himself. By this time, guests were screaming and shouting in panic. The guardsman reached around the maiden and left his dagger in the prince's side. The maid dropped from Amnon's arms, and Amnon fell writhing on top of her. "No!" he screamed. "You can't do this!"

The guardsman grabbed black hair with one hand and sword with the other, settling the matter.

By this time, everyone assumed that all the king's sons were doomed. The remaining princes knocked over tables in a rush for their mules. Jonadab ran with everyone else, thinking Absalom had gone mad. A hundred yards away, however, his brain connected Amnon with Absalom's sister Tamar, and he nailed the air in anger. He spun around as though to go back, then thought better of it when he recalled that Absalom's guardsmen would be bristling with spears.

By the time he reached the palace, his fury had turned pragmatic. Amnon was dead; Abigail's son Daniel was dead; Absalom was next in line. Perhaps his crime was not so heinous, after all.

He found the palace in an uproar after the early report that all of the king's sons had been targeted. David was on his face, crying, "Twelve sons! Twelve! *Why* did I let them go?"

Jonadab took in the scene and knelt at the king's side. "My lord, not all dead—only Amnon. Because of Tamar. Absalom's been plotting this for two years. I should have seen it."

The king raised his head. "Absalom is alive?" he asked with disbelief.

"Yes, my lord. He's alive, and your other sons. Only nine were there, anyway. Not the little ones. Only Amnon is dead."

Joab did not join the mourning. He and Eleazar and a dozen men took off for Baal Hazor but were back by evening. The king was with Ahinoam, so Joab sent for the manservant Joram. "Get David out here. I need to talk to him."

Joram opened his mouth but closed it after noting Joab's swiveling left eye.

David came to the great room, eyes bloodshot, ashes covering head and clothing.

Joab got right to the point. "Absalom took off, apparently alone. With everything else planned to the last grape, he probably stashed supplies along a squirrelly route to his granddaddy's in Geshur. My guess is he'd be hard to ferret out, but say the word and I'll go after him. I'll find him, if I have to chase him to the top of Mount Hermon."

David rubbed his face. "Joab, I've lost two sons today. That only one is actually dead is beside the point. If I go after Absalom, he'll have to be killed. I can't do that. As Jonadab said, he had reason for what he did. Enough that he's banished himself. Maybe his grandfather can do with him what I haven't been able to." He sighed. "Two sons gone; two wives to comfort. I can't bear any more right now."

Joab helped himself to a handful of figs.

Even today, a stranger would never guess that Jonathan *ben* Abiathar was related to the high priest. Prominent ears, yes, but Jonathan had none of his father's rabbity eyes or weak chin. He was a chatterer but didn't blather—not like Abiathar, who could talk a jackal to the ground. Instead, Jonathan shared the virility and chutzpah of his buddy Ahimaaz, who bore the marks of his father Zadok, the fiery chief priest at Gibeon. The day when the king's sons and young Levites engaged in mock battle, the two young men had come close to reversing the effect of Absalom's daring flank attack on the Levite "army." "Your instincts were right on," Zadok told them afterward. "You just lack experience. I'm proud of you both."

Now in early manhood, the two were older, stronger, and certainly brasher. One day, nearly three years after Amnon's death, they cornered Hushai, who was just leaving the palace. They bowed before him.

Hushai batted them playfully. "What are you two up to? I see schemes."

Ahimaaz spoke. "You're the king's friend."

"Ah! I see. The king's friend might get something out of the king. Is that it?"

The pair grinned.

"Go see Ahithophel," said Hushai.

"Us? Talk to Ahithophel?" Ahimaaz spun tight circles around Hushai.

"Then just go talk to the king—but do stand still in his presence."

"Sorry." Ahimaaz stood still and fidgeted instead. "There's still Ahithophel."

"Yes. One way or another, you have to deal with Ahithophel."

"Well," said Jonathan, "David likes you. He needs Ahithophel, but he likes you."

Hushai laughed. "That may be. However, the kingdom would get on very well without me, but without Ahithophel... What's this bee you want put in the king's ear?"

The two looked at each other. "Ahimaaz wants to train under either Ittai or Amasa," said Jonathan.

"You don't want much."

"We're not asking for Joab or Abishai."

"How prudent. Why just Ahimaaz?" Hushai looked back at Jonathan. "Are you already superior to Ittai and Amasa?"

"Zadok agreed to take me on. He thinks I'm pretty good, but he'd expect his son to be better than good. And this way we can teach each other what we learn."

Hushai sighed. "I'll see what I can do. You better pray for David's good humor."

Several days later, David sat with me in his private room, eyes closed, forehead on his hand. Finally, he looked up with a sigh. "Asaph...will the pain ever go away?"

I opened my mouth, hoping an answer would come, but he went on.

"It's hard enough losing valuable men. Asahel, Dodai...then my wife, my son Boaz, my son Amnon. And my son Absalom might as well be dead."

I was sorry he didn't think to mention Daniel.

David had a standing order for news concerning Absalom. He sent messages to his friend Barzillai in Gilead. "If you go up that way, or anyone you know..."

Barzillai himself was too old for such travel, but his friend Makir, benefactor of Jonathan's Mephibosheth before he came to David, was younger. On two occasions, he went to King Talmai's court in Geshur and spoke with Absalom. "The young man seems well, though bored," he wrote. "A fine-looking man, David, but God sees the heart better than I. I'm sorry to give so sketchy a report."

After such communiqués, David would ricochet between exhilaration and lethargy. Joab became alarmed. With David's attention drawn northward, his administration was unraveling. His counselors and officials were doing their best, but when leadership loses focus, decay sets in and enemies get cocky. Always, always, lions prowl the realm, waiting for that moment of inattention.

Sheba was frequently seen with Absalom, but it is impossible to reconstruct their conversations. From what I could learn, they walked and talked alone, although a servant overheard a discussion on how much loyalty to Saul still existed in Israel. Were the two men sizing up the northern tribes even then? The essence of history may rest more on the odd scrap of conversation, such as, "I've seen Jonadab. He's working on the king," than on earth-shaking events.

Working on the king. He was indeed. Daily. Jonadab sighed over life without Absalom. He kept reminding David of his son's talents and of Amnon's despicable act, hinting boldly that if David had responded properly to Amnon's crime, none of this might have happened.

Eleazar expressed surprise that the king didn't lop off Jonadab's swarthy head for such insinuation.

Joab grunted. "Time to get Absalom home. Davi won't get back on track until we do."

David was not the only one feeling out of joint. I was writing bits of a psalm, but snakes kept getting in the way. Water snakes. In the end, I altered the image to sea monsters, the great leviathan, but snakes kept slithering through my consciousness.

10

Something's got to change, Abishai. Three years we've been slogging this tar pit!" Joab turned from his brother and curled into himself.

Abishai grunted. "Well, do something. He's ignoring Bathsheba, even, and that puts a burr up everybody's back. When she's not in his lap, she's a snake, and everyone tastes her venom. Then she says he doesn't want her because he's tired of her clothes and she has to buy from every passing caravan. The whole palace will be glad when David and Absalom sort this out. What do you plan to do?"

"I'll think of something."

"Humph," said Abishai. "Make it a woman—other than Bathsheba."

Joab stared at him with the hint of a smile. "A woman." He swung off with a spring in his step.

He was away three days and came back looking satisfied. A week later, he went to the inner room where David was finishing his evening meal alone. "Behaving so badly that nobody'll eat with you?" he asked.

"Get out."

"Our ever-cheerful monarch." Joab sauntered toward the window, snatching up a rib on the way. He chewed thoughtfully while staring into the dusk. Suddenly, with a slight twitch on the corner of his mouth, he turned back to the king and began a rambling account of Ahimaaz's initial tutorial with Amasa. "Amasa sized him up, then proceeded to kill him by inches. Ran him, tumbled him, broke his sword in pieces, threw spears at him, hauled him by his new-mown beard. Finally, when the boy was a lump of sobs, Amasa said, 'You'll make a fine warrior one day. If you still have the stomach for it, I'll work with…'"

He trailed off as Joram appeared at the door. David looked up peevishly. "My lord," said the servant, "a woman seeks audience with the king."

"I'm eating, Joram."

"Yes, my lord, but she's walked all day just to see you."

"Give her a coin; put her somewhere. I won't see her today."

Joram stood firm.

"What is it, Joram?"

"My lord." He coughed. "I have a certain amount of judgment concerning—"

"This woman I should see. All right, I'll see her, but take the mess away first."

While Joram tidied the room, Joab continued around the interruption. "So Amasa walked away. But when Ahimaaz pulled himself up, you could see the faint shape of a man under all the blood. Whether he'll—"

Joram reappeared with a woman dressed darkly, a sackcloth veil on her head. A pair of penetrating green eyes met David's.

She was not young, nor was she small, but something about her brought Abigail to mind. The king rose, and the woman bowed with her face to the ground. He helped her to a seat.

"My lord the king," she said, her voice low and unaffected, "this is not the hour I would choose to come with my petition. I started from Tekoa early enough but was waylaid by the very troublemakers I came to speak with you about."

"Please tell me your trouble, my lady."

The woman drew a breath against nervousness but then raised a forefinger. "Before I begin," she said, rummaging a sack at her side, "I brought a small gift—a toy for the little ones." She withdrew a charming doll that rattled with soft sibilance.

David was touched. "I think even Solomon, as big as he's become, will like this. And the little ones..." He scrutinized the plaything, then gave the Tekoan a blinking smile. "Thank you," he said. "You are kind. Now tell me your story."

The woman bowed. "Your servant is a widow, my husband being dead several years now. I had two sons, but they were quarrelsome—born that way, it seems. My husband could not... Anyway, on the fateful day, the boys went out to plow. And there in the field with no one to interfere, they got into another argument. This time the younger pulled off a piece of the plow to strike the older and...killed him."

She looked at David, her chin up and under control. David was pleased with what he saw: a well-framed, freckled face, green pools alive with intelligence, and laugh lines that grief could not erase. He said unaffectedly, "I'm sorry."

The woman nodded. "Grief enough." She straightened her back, and again David thought of Abigail. "But now the clan is demanding that I hand over the remaining boy for blood revenge. My only son now, the only live coal left me, the end of my husband's line—he being dead with neither name nor descendant."

A moth flirted with the lamp flame. The woman's eyes followed its death-defying swoops as she composed herself. "I could bear this, but the simple truth is that the clan cares more about the inheritance than in seeing justice done. They've actually spoken—in my presence—of vengeance as the way to get rid of the heir. What would you take that to mean, my lord? This morning, they tried to stop me from appealing to you. That's what delayed me. Knowing how fair and impartial you are, they had good reason to wish I wouldn't." She sighed. "But, my lord, I had to come. What other recourse do I have?"

The king, who had listened attentively, stirred. He reached out and compassionately helped her to her feet. "Go home in peace. I'll issue an order on your behalf."

She looked at him, grateful, but she stood still. "My lord the king, this is a nasty business at best. They could still make trouble. And I don't want your intervention on my behalf to bring slander back on you."

David smiled. "That's not likely, but if anyone suggests it, send him to me."

"Thank you, my lord. An oath, perhaps, for my son," she asked hesitantly, "that the Lord God will keep them from carrying out vengeance?" The appeal in her eyes and voice was irresistible. David took her hands.

"My lady, as surely as the Lord lives, not one hair of your son's head will fall to the ground. Does that give you peace of mind?" He smiled.

The woman smiled back, but now she appeared even more ill at ease. She glanced toward Joab, sitting cross-legged in the corner, then forced herself to look straight at the king. "Just one more word, if I may, my lord?"

"Speak."

"My lord..." She hesitated and then straightened, a waggish look in her green eyes. "My lord, you've exempted my son from blood vengeance for the sake of the family line, but the king has not done the same for his own son. You haven't brought him back. My lord, hear me." She leaned forward. "Water spilled on the ground can never be recovered. Death can never be reversed. But a banished person need not be cut off forever."

Her words now poured forth. "I came here because I was afraid. I thought, *Perhaps the king will deliver me from those wanting to take away our inheritance*. And now I'm not afraid. My lord the king knows good from evil. May the Lord God be with you." She bowed again with her face to the floor.

The king watched her, a bemused look on his face. "Stand, lady," he said gently. "Stand and look at me."

She did as directed, her own laugh lines becoming prominent.

"I will ask you a question, and I want the truth. Joab is behind this. Isn't that so?"

Her eyes gave her away. "As surely as you live, my lord the king has the wisdom of an angel. No one can turn right or left from—"

"Stop! Enough of the charade," he said, not unkindly. But when he saw Joab rocking with satisfaction, the blink went out of his eyes. "Bring him back, then. But not to me. To his own house. Absalom must not see my face."

Joab bowed before David. The king turned to the green-eyed lady. "You were used. Does that bother you?"

The woman pondered a moment. "My lord, I offered myself to *Yahweh* first, then to my lord Joab to help straighten the king's throne before we all get a backache. I pray that what I did proves wise in your eyes and in the eyes of the Lord God of Israel."

I prayed the same prayer many times in the two years that followed. Now I wonder: What if Absalom had not been brought back? Might things have been different? Was his return necessary for the "consequences" predicted by Nathan? I don't know. I only know that Joab had mixed motives for having him back, not least of which was his preference for Absalom over the rumors that Solomon might eventually ascend the throne. He would have done anything to prevent that.

Joab's regard for Absalom continued to rise over the next two years—until the night his barley crop went up in flames.

"You burned my grain!" he barked at Absalom. "What did you do that for? And don't deny it. If you're going to order a field torched, you ought at least to pick a man without a gimpy leg. Your servant was seen."

"I won't deny it at all," said Absalom easily. "I wanted to get your attention."

"Get my attention!"

"Yes. I sent for you twice, quite civilly, and you didn't think it worth your while to respond. The third time I knocked a little harder."

"So that's it." Joab leaned away from the prince, his eyes squinting. "Well, my lord Upstart, you want to see the king, and I don't think that's smart. That's why I didn't come."

"I will see the king, and you won't have a say in the matter. The king is my father. I came back to Jerusalem at your bidding, but for all that's happened here, I might as well have stayed in Geshur. I will see the king, and if he deems me guilty, then it'll be up to him to put me to death."

In the end, five years after Absalom killed his brother Amnon, Joab led him into the king's presence. Seeing David's conflicted face, Absalom put his face to the ground and said only, "*Abba!*"

In that moment, the cloud of anger, fear, and dread that had hung over David evaporated, and he knelt to erase the sting of rupture. He murmured brokenly, "My son, my son! Absalom, my son! My heart has longed for you. We shall—we must be at peace."

Absalom kissed his father, but the only tears came from David's eyes.

11

Heman, Ethan, and I were sitting in the palace courtyard one sultry day. We were working out alternate tunes for some overused psalms, such as "How Blessed We Are When Brothers Live in Harmony" or David's miktam, "Keep Me Safe, O Lord, for I Hide Myself in You." We were discussing the tune "The Death of the Son" when a ruckus in the street sent us to the gate. There we beheld fifty runners in purple tunics and plumed headgear carrying banners and gold shields. Trumpets sounded; the men sang and shouted as they ran with precision and skill. We three musicians looked at each other. Where had they come from? Why here in the middle of Jerusalem?

The answer followed the runners: a gold and silver chariot and a hot-blooded team. Absalom, in uniform, waved and threw gold pieces to children. The chariot bore down on the runners, but as onlookers screamed, the unit split apart with programmed precision to allow passage. The chariot turned with a flourish, and the men, now reversed and again in front, trotted back toward the city gate.

Abiathar came from the Tent and stood gushing with admiration. I looked at him in surprise. He told of talks they'd had, gifts he'd been given, Absalom's daily worship—which, I had to admit, I could attest to. Still, the high priest's unqualified approval did not set well. Absalom shouldn't have gotten off so easily after deliberately murdering his brother. For that matter—and more on God's doorstep—why should he, a murderer, stay healthy and strong, untouched by ills that plague most God-fearers? Does a pure heart not matter? Absalom was treading slippery ground, to my way of thinking.

Later we learned that Absalom was also using the city gate for his own purposes. He rose early and mingled with people. "Where are you from? How are you faring? Do you have a problem you are hoping the king will address?" And he'd look on them compassionately. "You do have a claim here—no doubt of that. But getting to see the king..." He'd cluck and shake his head. "He's so busy these days. If only I..." Again, compassion. "So many folks with valid cases, so little done for them. If I were a judge in the land, things would be different. I'd see justice done—swiftly!"

More often than not, those who had come to complain to the king would turn around after this chat, satisfied they'd been heard or sure they'd never see the king. But before they left, Absalom would squeeze their shoulders and then, as though on impulse, kiss them.

Four years of this built a storehouse full of goodwill for the heir apparent to David's throne. David saw only that his "difficult" son was comporting himself well.

Ahithophel's eyes were seldom merry in those days, particularly when Solomon was mentioned. I never learned why.

The boy was, after all, his great-grandson. Did he still resent David's affair with his granddaughter?

One particular conversation with David in this regard touched off a rare clash between the two men. Ahithophel had lined out his long-range report—thorough and detailed in every respect. At the end, he sniffed affectedly and said, "This projection does presuppose the ascension of Absalom to the throne—at the proper time, of course."

David's eyebrows shot up. "Oh?"

"Yes, my lord. I am, of course, assuming—"

"Assuming. Ahithophel, as much as I love Absalom and think highly of his capabilities, I'm assuming nothing at this point. It's much too soon."

Ahithophel's well-manicured beard twisted with just the slightest show of annoyance. "Perhaps, then, the rumors concerning...*Solomon* are true." The slight hesitation and emphasis revealed a hostility he tried to cover by moving quickly to another detail of the plan, but David's eyes narrowed.

"What rumors?"

"My lord?"

"What rumors about Solomon are you talking about?"

"I speak of your stated desire to make him king, my lord."

"My stated desire... The boy is ten years old! Why would I even think of making him king? Where did this come from?"

Ahithophel stiffened his dignity. "I cannot say for sure, my lord.... Perhaps Asaph, among others—"

"Asaph? The sun rises and sets on the lad for Asaph, but rumors about his becoming king..."

Ahithophel nodded. "As I thought, my lord. Hardly a wise option. The succession will go as is customary, with Absalom—"

David exploded. "Enough! I have not said Absalom will be king; I have not said Solomon will be king. But neither have I said Solomon will not be king. I can make Japhia king if I want to—or any of my sons."

"My lord, the matter of birthright, of proper succession—"

"My first two sons are dead. My third son killed his brother. Do I want a murderer—"

"With justification, my lord. The sordid details—"

"I know the sordid details. If rumors are going around about Solomon, I want them stopped. Rumors can castrate a king. And I'll have no more disparaging remarks about the suitability of Solomon—or any of my sons, for that matter—to be king. *I will decide who will become king.*"

David's wrath had subsided by the time he confronted me with Ahithophel's hint that I might have started the rumors. I had to admit that, while I had not actually said that the king favored Solomon, others might have put that slant on my words. I told him I'd always felt deep down that Solomon would be king. To bolster the point, I called the boy to me and catechized him for his father. By the time David left, he too was impressed by the child's intelligence and insight, as well as the warmth and joy of his nature. He kissed Solomon and searched his eyes. He saw his own broad, open face made even more handsome by the dark sensuousness of Solomon's mother. "Yes, Asaph, we have a gem here; you are nurturing him well. His mother, of course, is on your side, and what Bathsheba wants, Bathsheba usually gets."

"Whooee!" Ahimaaz walked backward toward his friend Jonathan, his eyes on a nearby exchange.

"What is it?" asked Jonathan.

"Amasa getting drawn and quartered by the brothers Joab and Abishai."

"That's hardly new," said Jonathan. "They're always on him."

"They call him irresponsible," said Ahimaaz, "but he just comes at things differently from what you'd expect. He could be a top general, but they'll never give him the chance." He studied the receding dust storm. "You know whom he gets on with, don't you?"

"Whom?"

"Absalom. Absalom butters him, builds him up. David does, too, for that matter. It's mostly the brothers. He's kin, but they still hate him. Absalom treats him differently. He spends time, asks questions about military organization, jokes with the soldiers. They like him. A lot. I don't know—that Absalom..."

"Enough already about Absalom," said Jonathan. "Tell me what you learned from your 'top general' yesterday."

David's reconciliation with Absalom gave him opportunity to get to know his first grandchildren. Three beautiful boys and a girl, who was named after her reclusive Aunt Tamar. Joy turned to mourning, however, when an epidemic carried off all three boys within a single week.

Absalom took it hard. David tried to comfort him. "There'll be other sons. You're young; your wife is young. Go to her. Console her. She needs you right now."

But Absalom did not lie with his wife. Instead, he drove his chariot, alone, wildly, up and down the country. Somewhere during this odyssey, he met with Sheba and Jonadab. What they did or talked about, no one knows, but one visible outcome of their meeting was a monument to Absalom erected in the King's Valley because he now had no son to carry on his name.

In retrospect, I see Absalom's parades and his strange twisting of tragedy into personal glorification as the first tremors of the approaching earthquake. Unfortunately, these omens stirred little more than astonishment at the time. Even I was too busy with petty Levitical matters to pay much attention.

12

Not long after Absalom returned home to erect his monument, Sheba started on his own circuit of the ten northern tribes. He sat in remote tents drinking countless cups of milk, or in huts of tribal leaders drinking wine. These visits produced a strange bonding between brooding, restless northerners and this unknown hawk whose talons, though simply scratching backs now, promised to seize for them future treasures beyond calculation.

The protocol of hospitality took most of his time: the exchange of kisses and expressions of peace, washing of feet and anointing of oil, the obligatory eating and drinking, and endless entreaties to stay the night. His actual business at each place was conducted in a matter of minutes, and when he left, his hosts set off to spread the latest hints and whispers, the hard glint of Sheba's eyes reflected in their own.

A man by the name of Shimei, who lived in Bahurim just over the hill northeast of Jerusalem, made his annual pilgrimage to a hilltop in Gibeah. Small, fierce, outlandish, he sat under a tamarisk tree, wrapped in sackcloth and a long, white beard, sifting handfuls of dust over his head. His beaked nose lifted skyward, and his eyes squeezed out gall to baptize his moaned lament:

> Your glory, O Israel,
>   lies slain on your heights.
> How the mighty have fallen!

The ugly, turreted stronghold of Saul was now used only for storage and administration. The officials who worked there had watched this strange sight for years but still paused to marvel at Shimei's unyielding loyalty to the house of Saul long after the king's death. Yes, he was of Saul's clan, but his sense of loss went deeper than blood. The glory of Israel had been sheathed in Saul and his strong sons. Now, Saul, Jonathan, Malki-Shua, Abinadab—all were gone. Esh-Baal's death reeked of villainy, as did Abner's. One must consider, too, David's hand in the death of Saul's two sons by his concubine Rizpah and five grandsons by his daughter Merab—a man of blood ruling a kingdom of blood.

Shimei's shoulders hunched and his chest sank as the pain within became a hot coal, blown white under the wind of sorrow. The force of his hurt uncurled his torso and burst forth in a bellow of rage.

With his foot on the bottom step, the secretary in charge of royal storehouses paused to look at the contorted figure, then shifted his tablets of inventory to the other arm and continued up the stairs.

Ahimaaz was nettled. Amasa had canceled on him again—this time without even sending a message. After waiting nearly an hour for his military mentor, the young man decided to hunt him down. But Abishai hadn't seen him, nor had Benaiah or Eleazar. *All right*, thought Ahimaaz, *I'll ask his wife. She can at least tell him I'm angry.*

But the general was not home. He was away for an indefinite period and would not be available for lessons any time soon.

This did not improve Ahimaaz's temper, and he kicked rocks. One of the missiles clipped the leg of a dark-haired man in front of him. "Ow!" said the victim of the young man's frustration.

"I'm sorry," said Ahimaaz. "I was just...kicking."

The man rubbed his calf, eyebrows slouching dangerously, then moved on.

Ahimaaz recognized him: Amnon's friend Jonadab, lately attached to Absalom. Unlikely he'd know Amasa's whereabouts, but why not ask?

To his surprise, Jonadab laughed. "Don't bother looking," he said. "A waste of time."

"You know where he is? His wife said he'd gone off but couldn't say where."

"Not likely she could. And I'll say even less."

The hackles rose on Ahimaaz's neck. "You know, but you won't say?"

"Exactly. Now, if you'll excuse me, I will forgive your attack and tend to my business."

Mechanically, Ahithophel touched the mezuzah on the doorpost of Absalom's house, spots of color on his cheeks betraying a chink in his usual starched composure. Absalom's wife greeted him, the child Tamar behind her skirts. Ahithophel bowed. Absalom came from an inner room. "I thought you'd be long gone by now," he said.

"I planned to leave this morning, but other matters intruded, and not wanting to leave loose ends—" He coughed delicately. "I expect to stop in Bethlehem for the night and will be home in Giloh tomorrow afternoon."

"You have the guest list?"

Ahithophel pulled forth a small scroll, and Absalom ran his eye down it. "Hm. That's a surprise," he said, pointing to one of the names.

"I thought you'd be pleased."

"And that one." When he reached the end, he continued unrolling as though looking for others. "What about—? Or—?" And he mentioned names Absalom's wife couldn't remember. "I'd expect them to be included."

"I considered them carefully, my lord, but knowing their connections, I thought it best not to invite them."

Absalom shrugged. "I trust your judgment, Ahithophel. The list is perfect. I'll see these people in Hebron. And you. Safe journey, Ahithophel," he said as the older man left.

"All is in order, my lord."

"Yes. At last. The *right* order."

A restless, fragmented patch of melody had fastened onto David's mind and would allow him no peace. Wrapped in an incessant, driving rhythm, it gathered to itself the snarling harmonics of other distractions and annoyances. For one thing, several of the rooms downstairs were being remodeled, the old paneling with its blocky design being torn out in favor of brighter, more pleasing boards of cedar. Abigail had never liked the old paneling. David had defended it, saying it reflected his strength. She'd been right, of course, but it had taken him twenty years to admit it. How desperately he wanted to talk with her right now. Not just about paneling, but about air that seemed dry, stale. He watched the wood being tossed on a pile and wondered that it did not ignite by itself.

The noise, even away from the work area, abraded his nerves, and the tuneless whistle of one of the workers scraped across his own demonic melody.

Ahithophel was away, so nothing seemed right. But David didn't begrudge his chief counselor a break. He had worked far too hard and hadn't seemed himself lately.

And Abishai. Nattering about Amasa. "Where is he? Why did he just drop out of sight? Why didn't he leave word with someone?" Abishai growling in the underbrush wasn't unusual, but right now it annoyed him almost as much as the whistling.

His servant Joram entered and bowed deferentially. "My lord, the cloth merchant you sent for is not available. It seems he's gone to Hebron with my lord Absalom and won't be back for a few days."

"By all that's holy..." David's assault on the nearest table sent Joram a step backward. "Is no one left in Jerusalem? How many went to Hebron with Absalom? Half the city? Zor the elder who sits with me at the gate—why would he trek to Hebron for a party?"

"Hardly half the city, my lord. Obil the camelmaster estimates only two hundred."

"Two hundred! Does Absalom need two hundred to help him fulfill a vow?"

"A vow, my lord?"

"That's what he said. While he was in Geshur with his grandfather, he said that if the Lord took him back to Jerusalem, he'd go worship in Hebron. He was born there, you know, and he wanted to celebrate his thirtieth birthday there. Two hundred men to help him get drunk."

"My lord—"

"Forget I said that. It's mostly dust and the noise in my head. Tell Abishai to look for Amasa in Hebron. I'm taking a nap."

13

David rolled onto his back and flung an arm over his face, conscious once again of dry, sulfurous air. A ruckus at the door had touched off the smell. Joram protested, "No, you can't see him. He's taking a nap." And somebody—Shammah?—was insisting he be waked. He didn't want to wake and was grateful for Joram's backbone in standing up to intrusion. He didn't want to leave his dream, a dream of pain that seemed a sharp sweetness. Abigail had come to relieve the soreness that seemed always upon him. Soreness from countless wounds, from broken ribs, from a sixty-year-old warrior's body. She reached out, fingers dripping ointment and salves. He called for her to come, but something restrained her. The inclination of her body told of her longing to help, but she could not. Oddly, it was Joram holding her back, Joram saying, "You can't see him. He's taking a nap." *Abi...Abi...*

David heard footsteps pounding across the outer room. *So, the fortress is breached after all.*

"David, wake up!" shouted Shammah.

Yes, he'd gotten the voice right.

Shammah shook him. "Absalom proclaimed himself king in Hebron. He has Ahithophel, Amasa, most of the militia, and the northern tribes are backing them."

The giant may as well have thrown snow water in his face. David's chest went tight—or was it just sore ribs objecting to snow water?

King in Hebron…on his thirtieth birthday. David had been king in Hebron when he was thirty.

Shammah was hefting him up, talking unintelligibly, forcing lukewarm goat water into his mouth. Eleazar and Benaiah were there; Amasai ran in, and the room exploded with panic.

David churned through the arithmetic, the number of warriors of Israel who years ago had come to him at Hebron: seventy-one hundred from Simeon, two hundred chiefs and relatives from Issachar, Zebulun, Naphtali, one hundred twenty thousand from east of the Jordan. "He could have half a million," David said.

He caught a whiff of smoke from the paneling burning outside. "We're dead, Shammah."

David glanced around. "Where's Joab? Is he with Absalom, too?"

Joab had, in fact, just come in. His face, for once, was not cocky, but he did not like surprises. "Damn him to Sheol!" he roared. "He's scooped up hundreds of city leaders, and—"

"Two hundred, says Obil."

Joab looked at him. "Two hundred, ten hundred. What's the difference? He's won over all Israel, it seems. Given time, we could muster a big enough army. But time we don't have. He's on his way right now to capture Jerusalem."

"You're sure of this?" asked David.

"Of course I'm sure! He's done his work well. He wouldn't try if he wasn't certain of success."

David was silent a moment, his head bowed. Then he straightened. "All right," he said quietly. "Let's get out. We'll head for Mahanaim."

The palace erupted in chaos. David gave what orders he could, but in the chaos, defeat seemed certain without anyone even setting foot outdoors.

It was Benaiah who saved the day. After a brief session with the guardsmen, he dispersed them with specific tasks to oversee. Jashobeam assigned the heavy work to burly boys, and slowly, under the press of anger and fear, the exodus began.

Panic boiled through the city. Who would be safe from the usurper? Anyone connected with David's administration would most certainly be doomed under the new king. Terror spread like an epidemic, and some abandoned everything and simply sped away. Others stood stupefied.

I, to my shame, was slow to catch what was going on. I didn't know anything was wrong until my son Zaccur staggered in, red of face and with no breath in his lungs. Alarmed, I gripped his arm. "Is it your mother? The king?"

He nodded.

"He's dead!"

"No...Absalom...coming."

"Here? To the—"

"Army...all Israel...against David. He's leaving. Pack up. Go."

He tried to pull away as though to continue his alarm, but I held him. "No! Speak clearly. What's *happened?*"

Just then, Jeiel the gatekeeper blew the alarm trumpet, echoed by trumpets all over the city. I felt the blood leave my face. The courtyard began to spin.

In the palace courtyard, donkeys milled and camels protested. Obil the camelmaster's eyes were inscrutable, but he seemed to be the calmest of anyone. Well-ordered himself, he imparted a semblance of order, and loaded beasts began moving out.

Zadok arrived, having been alerted by his son Ahimaaz, who was seething at Amasa's treachery. "Not only did he suck off the militia, he got some of the standing army, as well. If I could get my hands on him—"

Zadok cut him off. "That's not your job right now. The ark is our concern. And animals for sacrifice. We'll need plenty."

A practical concern faced David. Who, if anyone, should he leave to care for the palace? His wives and children would, of course, go with him. But leaving only servants would be disastrous. Ahithophel's absence cut deeply, and not just because of his disloyalty. He alone could have sorted this mess out.

In the end, he decided to leave ten concubines, plus whatever servants they would need. Their children would go. The women wailed over the edict, but he would not be moved.

He closed his eyes, the pressure beginning to tell. *Absalom, Absalom.* This wasn't happening. It was a nightmare. He was still taking a nap. No, the dream had been about Abigail— reaching, reaching, longing to help. He needed her now as never before. Here, in the presence of his enemies, he needed to hear once more that God would bundle him safely, as the treasures of the palace were being bundled for transport.

"Abigail!" His cry rang through the corridors of the palace.

In a moment of stunned silence, all movement stopped. For an instant, under that familiar summons, Absalom was forgotten.

David closed his eyes and leaned his hands against a wall. His son Ithream moved to his side. Ithream—quiet and steady, not flashy like Absalom, not haughty like Amnon had been. "Come, *Abba*. We must leave now."

14

With the effort a younger man would expend in wrestling a bullock to the altar for sacrifice, Barzillai stood up. His eighty years hung on him like eighty stones. He would not have needed to rise at all; a snap of his fingers would have brought any number of servants to his bidding. But Barzillai stood up because not standing up would be the first step toward death, and he wasn't ready to walk that path. He might need to think about it soon, but not today.

Once Barzillai was on his feet and had taken the first few painful steps, he moved with relative ease. He generally needed little assistance. His son Kimham kept close watch over the old man but discreetly, from a distance.

Barzillai's feet responded to the call of the courtyard with its gnarled, twisted olive trees, myrtle, and vine-hung pools. He never tired of it; it was so different from his utilitarian spread in Rogelim to the north, where he'd made his money. When Kimham and his brothers saw Mahanaim as a lucrative market for their spice, jewel, and rug trade, Barzillai had secured this place for them with an eye toward one day leaving

Rogelim and moving there himself. Trips home were less frequent now and more tiring yet still had to be made. But now, on this day, he followed the brick-lined path, noting fig blossoms or the latest hatch of swallows in the old almond hollow. This, the cool of the evening, was his favorite time. His wealth, the fine food laid daily by an army of devoted servants, his position in the town of Rogelim—none of these could match the elementary pleasure of bird song and fragrance. That deep sense of appreciation was his work, his worship, his crown of life.

Lamps began to glow both inside and outside his sprawling house, like jewels in a century-old setting. He considered contemplating the scene from a nearby bench and was weighing the effort involved when his attention was drawn to a minor commotion at the courtyard gate. The men posted there were talking with urgent-sounding voices. A servant, pottering about the garden—Kimham's eyes, Barzillai suspected—pointed toward Barzillai. Barzillai sighed and turned away from the beckoning bench to whatever duty awaited him.

"My lord, a terrible thing has happened." The runner, still out of breath, gave only a token bow to Barzillai in the rush of news.

"Young man, you need a cool drink. The 'terrible thing' will not be lessened in any way by your death or collapse. Come inside. Some water for your feet, oil for your face. But first a drink."

"But, my lord—"

"Hush. Be still. I'm too old to leap headfirst into panic. I will hear you, but first you will be made comfortable."

The drink stretched into a meal, and finally, after the runner had capitulated to hospitality, Barzillai leaned back on his cushions, his eyes pleasurably crinkled. "If the news is as dire as you say, this may be the last I'll smile for a while, but I give that smile to you. Now, my friend, please allow me to share your burden."

He listened closely without remark until the runner had told the details of Absalom's move and David's flight.

When he finished, Barzillai closed his eyes and said nothing, leaving the runner to wonder if a nap was the next order of hospitality. But with deep sadness, the old man leaned forward to grip his companion's arm. "Ah, such sorrow for my friend David! Such sorrow for me! And for you. I mustn't forget such a devoted messenger." He squeezed the arm again. "He's coming here, you say?"

"Yes, most likely. When I left Jerusalem, nobody knew anything for sure, but Eleazar told me he thought they'd go to Mahanaim and that you would want to know."

"Yes, yes. And we must inform our friend Makir in Lo Debar. Do you know Lo Debar? Just a few miles north, a slight detour...but that's unthinkable!" Barzillai reared back in mortification. "That I should presume... You have already run far. I will send one of my young men. And another, perhaps, to Rabbah to inform Shobi son of Nahash. He'll want to help. You, my friend, will sleep here tonight and welcome David when he comes. Tomorrow sometime, you think?"

The young man shrugged. "It all depends on Absalom."

"Yes, of course. Absalom. We must pray, you and I. Together, we must pray."

David paused high in the Kidron Valley near a vineyard. The rich, warm musk rising from scattered baskets of grapes both comforted and worried him. Insurgencies threaten the wine supply.

From his chair, David gazed down the valley, past the knot of priests and Levites and the river of blood they were producing, to the distant haze over Bethlehem. How far he had come from Bethlehem! But how far did it amount to, in actual fact? A lot of blood, a lot of suffering, a wife dead, one son struck by God, another murdered, a third who died of old age at twenty-one, and now a fourth raising the sword against him. Absalom was somewhere in those haze-shrouded hills. And Ahithophel. Faithful, trustworthy Ahithophel. *Why* had he turned from David to Absalom? And what did it portend for David? Ahithophel at the right hand of the enemy was a dangerous man.

David closed his eyes and tipped back his head.

> *War against them, O Lord;*
> *Fight those who come against me.*
> *Rattle spear and javelin at them.*
> *May those who want to kill me be put down*
>   *in shame;*
> *May those who plot my ruin be turned back*
>   *in utter confusion.*
> *And Lord, consider Ahithophel,*
> *A friend whom I trusted,*
> *A confidant who sat at my table.*

Now he's thrust his heel at me.
Turn his counsel to drivel, O Lord.
May his words turn to ash
in Absalom's ears.

The pain in his heart was distracted by military pomp to his right. As trumpets blew, troops carrying the banner of David marched crisply down the slope and continued up the Mount of Olives, Joab and Abishai in front with the *Gibborim*. Then came Benaiah and his boys, but each of these men had a sizable stone that they brought toward David and piled to form a monument.

David caught his breath at the implication of this gesture. Stones. Stones of remembrance. As Joshua had instructed the Israelites to piles stones from the Jordan river as they crossed into the Promised Land, so Benaiah and his men were marking this "crossing," perhaps in faith that Absalom's rebellious "flood" would likewise be stopped and that they would once again stand here and remember. Tears streamed from David's eyes. *Benaiah*—David's sword and shield, as close as a son. Would that his own sons were as fine as Benaiah!

Last in line was Ittai with his colorful platoon of Gittites. Philistines—some dating back to David's time with King Achish in Gath. They had come over to David, putting their own lives at risk, and now he wanted to embrace them all.

He stood, bringing the platoon to an unmilitary halt. "Ittai, my son, go back. Why should you and your men suffer another exile? I've been set adrift, derelict in God's hands. Stay and serve King Absalom—if he's man enough. May kindness and faithfulness be your crown."

Ittai struggled for composure. This man, this king, had believed in him, had given him a chance to prove himself, had supported him against the advice of kin and military advisors. King Achish had recognized his military ability; David had looked beyond to the substance of his soul.

"My lord the king," he said, his voice uneven, "you're asking me to tear out my heart. How could I abandon you? As surely as the Lord lives, wherever my lord the king goes, whether in life or death, there will your servant be."

He could hold his emotion no longer, and the two warriors clung to each other, a circle of soldiers weeping openly with them.

David gripped Ittai's arms and straightened. "All right, *march on!*"

The ark had been covered for removal and carried by six Levites, two of whom had helped carry it into Jerusalem more than twenty years earlier. Now it rested on a platform of stone near the place of sacrifice.

Zadok had said that we'd slaughter many animals, but the threat to city and kingdom motivated people to give beyond expectation. We started sacrificing when the first exiles descended the slope and did not finish until the last had crossed the valley. I wish I had set someone to counting the exodus. It had to have been several thousand, perhaps even tens of thousands. Two or three hundred in David's retinue alone, plus bearers, herdsmen, tenders of pack animals; five or six thousand military, plus families and attendants; an unknown number of officials who felt at risk from Absalom, and a thousand or more ordinary people who felt safer with David than in their homes. The passage of this horde required several hours and hundreds of sacrificial animals. The priests' ephods were dripping blood before a quarter of the entourage had gone by.

We prayed, we made music. I was glad for specific tasks that held back the bile of fear in my throat. Singing was hard under the utter sorrow that stung my eyes even more than the smoke of sacrifice. Heads were covered. Many in the exodus walked without shoes. Someone told me the king himself was barefoot.

Strangely, I remembered the conversation David and I once had about eating insects to stay alive. Would the king be forced to that state in the coming weeks and months?

Before David left off resting, he summoned Zadok. "May you be blessed, my son, for the work you're doing."

Zadok's eye took in the impromptu monument, but he bowed low. "Your servant, my lord the king."

"The ark, Zadok. I've been looking at it down there in the middle of the river."

Zadok looked at him oddly. "*River*, my lord?"

"God stopped the river's flow for Joshua; He can stop it for me. They crossed the Jordan on dry ground, Zadok."

"Ah!" Zadok studied the monument with a smile of comprehension. "And these are the stones they carried, my lord? More than twelve, I see."

"Yes—more than twelve; far more. Bears and lions after my sheep. Goliath. Saul's spear—in his hand and mine. Ziklag.

Rephaim. Jebus. The ark. God's promise to me. Forgiveness. Faithful warriors like Benaiah, Ittai, Eleazar. I'm not keeping count, Zadok. Stones of God's faithfulness. From the middle of the river, where the water runs deep. This is deep water, Zadok, the deepest yet."

He drew a breath and looked squarely at the priest. "The ark, Zadok. You've served it well. That day when Uzzah…" His eyes turned downhill again. "The ark shouldn't stay in the river. It belongs in Zion, in the place we prepared for it. Zadok, take it back; take it to the Tent. Continue to serve Yahweh there on my behalf. If I find favor in His eyes, He'll bring me back to worship before it; if not, if He says He's not pleased with me, so be it. Whatever He wills."

Zadok seemed about to protest, whether from thinking the ark should be with the king or from wanting to be with the king himself, but he bowed dutifully. "I will do as you say, my lord, provided…" Zadok looked at the king significantly. "If I go back, my lord, Abiathar must stay with you. That's the proper, the safe arrangement for such…for the high priest."

If David grasped Zadok's thinly veiled insinuation, he made no comment. His mind was shifting almost visibly, a familiar glint appearing as he scrutinized the priest. "Zadok—the seer," he said enigmatically.

Zadok cocked his head slightly as though to read the king.

"A seer, a man of peace. Absalom will welcome you in his Jerusalem. Go back, Zadok," the king leaned in closely, "and take Ahimaaz and Abiathar's Jonathan with you."

The trace of a smile appeared through Zadok's enormous beard.

"Bright lads, resourceful, good *runners.*" Except for this cryptic emphasis, the king might have been reviewing a batch of military recruits. "The Jordan fords—I'll wait there till they come."

A flash of teeth confirmed the priest's comprehension.

The king gripped his hand. "You're a good man, Zadok; the man who loves war is, after all, a man of peace. Go now. And take Abiathar with you. He'll be all right. The ark, though— guard it carefully."

15

Hushai, not being a man who walked happily, traveled mostly by donkey. His feet were soft, his body spongy, and God had created donkeys for Hushai's good pleasure.

Today, though, he was afoot. He'd been riding when he left Beth Horon for Jerusalem, but his favorite beast had seemed logy the first few miles, then—suddenly, joltingly—dropped dead beneath him.

Hushai chafed at the turn of events, but the urgency of his journey pushed his steps. He couldn't even dispose of the animal. With much grunting and heaving, he tugged the creature off the path and, with a regretful pat, continued on his way.

Foot misery worsened the misery in his heart. With the news of Absalom's rebellion churning his belly, he was hastening to David. He should have seen the signs. In retrospect, they seemed emblazoned across the sky. The diligence with which Absalom had prepared for this day amazed Hushai. Every move, every meeting, had fulfilled its purpose, and now his time had come. The plum was ripe, and Absalom had his hand out.

Had he picked it, though? Had he reached Jerusalem? Had David already been trampled by his son's defiance? Hushai's heart pounded as he pushed toward the city.

As he reached Gibeah, he came upon a string of food-laden donkeys. The drovers were shouting and whistling, but Hushai paid little attention—until he saw a hawk-nosed old man sitting on the trailing donkey, his voice breathing fire.

"Ziba!" Hushai said. "Is that you?" How many years since Hushai had rummaged through Israel to find this servant of Saul? He had thought the man old then. Yet here he was, still alive.

"Ay, my lord. And who be you?"

"I am Hushai, David's friend. Do you remember when I brought you and Mephibosheth before the king?"

"Aye. A happier day than today, my lord."

"You've heard, then, about David's troubles."

"Why do you think I'm shoving these beasts along the road?"

Hushai hadn't thought the connection all that obvious, but he leaped agreeably to the expected conclusion. "Ah! Food for David, I see."

"Aye. The king should eat a little something at such a time. And the beasts—for him and his wives to ride upon."

A thought suggested itself to Hushai. "An excellent idea. You know, my animal died under me this morning, and I was left afoot. I see one of your beasts has only a wineskin. Since we're both trying to intercept David, might I test the strength of such a superior donkey and ride the rest of the way?"

"Aye. The king's friend is welcome to sit the jenny, miserable though she be." The old man's cheeks puffed with pride.

The hill to Bahurim led Hushai to thank God for the sturdy animal. He could see beyond the village to activity on the Mount of Olives. To get to the top, they threaded through refugees and wailing villagers who were waiting for David, heads covered and garments torn.

Another old man, nose melted by the heat of his eyes, jerked up and down the steep slope of Bahurim as though stitching the town to the hillside. He alone of the villagers was not mourning. The appearance of Ziba stopped his pacing momentarily, but after the caravan passed, Hushai saw him cut around an olive press to a bluff, where he stood like a prophet about to pronounce doom.

When they neared the summit, Hushai slid off his mount and winced as his swollen feet hit the ground. Although he could not see the king, he headed for a protective circle of military personnel near the high place of worship and pushed through.

"Hushai! You've come!" David's voice was hoarse, unsteady.

"I've come, my lord." Hushai bowed. When he stood, David enveloped him. "I'm here," said Hushai, "to ease your flight in whatever way I can. I could go ahead and work out accommodations, I could—"

The king shook his head. "Hushai, as dearly as I love you, you'll be just one more person to feed. But I have something else in mind, something I believe only you can do."

"Anything, my lord."

David drew a breath and glanced away, then looked straight into his friend's eyes. "I want you to go back to Jerusalem."

The hair rose on Hushai's neck.

"Go back and bow before Absalom. Say to him, 'I served your father, and now I'm ready to serve you.' He'll hoist his eyebrows, question you, maybe even laugh, but you'll come up with an answer. *I want you there to thwart Ahithophel*."

The ache in Hushai's feet blanked out. "My lord!"

"You can do it, Hushai. And you won't be altogether alone. Zadok and Abiathar are there with their sons. The lads can relay messages to me." He plowed fingertips up and down his forehead. "It's the only way, Hushai; you're the only one who can possibly make it happen. Ahithophel will size up the situation and give his usual excellent advice. Without you there to counter it, Absalom will listen, and I'm dead. It's as simple as that."

David drew another breath. "The idea came the instant I saw you. God put it in my heart, and He will go before you. Keep saying to yourself, 'The Lord is my shepherd, the Lord is my shepherd.' Hushai, we have no other recourse. We must trust in Him!"

Hushai looked at him for a long time, then bowed again for what seemed like an eternity. He could hear children crying. He heard Joab say hoarsely, "We need time. Just give us some time!" Far overhead an eagle screamed. Hushai rose to squint at the soaring bird. Then, without a word, he turned, kissed the king, and worked his way through refugees and olive trees toward his own personal valley of the shadow of death.

David rode one of Ziba's donkeys down the slope toward Bahurim. Benaiah's men flanked the king's right side, Abishai and Joab the left. The king was frowning.

"Benaiah," he said, "why is it I'm never sure if Ziba's telling the truth? 'Mephibosheth turned against you,' he says, 'so here's two hundred loaves of bread, a hundred cakes of raisins, and another hundred of figs.' Did I do right in giving him Mephibosheth's property, or is the old rooster just posturing?"

Benaiah grunted. "Bread and fruit is a small price to pay, wouldn't you say, for getting Saul's property? But I heard him; he sounded believable. Still, Mephibosheth's not all that bright, and being lame..."

"Well, what I've done, I've done, and—"

He broke off as a stone hit his shoulder. Benaiah vaulted over the donkey's rump and collided with Abishai, whose was likewise shielding the king. More stones rained upon David and his officials. Benaiah dragged him from the donkey and buried him under a dozen large shields.

Above them, on the bluff, a prophet-like figure heaved stones from the pile at his feet and the bag at his side, all the while shouting down curses. "Get away from here, you filthy man of blood! May the wrath of God confound you, may your children be barren, may the path tear your feet!"

Soldiers, led by Amasai, were on him in an instant, but still he railed against David. "The Lord is repaying you for what you did to the house of Saul. The blood you drew from their veins now soaks your own head!"

David pushed from under the protective shields and stood up, shielding his eyes to see his assailant. "Who is it?"

Eleazar worked his way over. "They say it's Shimei *ben* Gera of Saul's clan. A byword in Gibeah. Comes each year to mourn under Saul's tamarisk tree."

Abishai moved in. "Mourn, my foot! He wants his head removed. Give the word, my lord."

"No. Leave him alone."

Abishai spun away in exasperation, then turned back. "You let a dead dog like this curse you? Isn't it enough having Absalom breathing down your neck?"

David turned on Abishai, his eyes blue, thin-bladed knives. "Get away! You sons of Zeruiah don't even speak my language. This man may be cursing because *Yahweh* said, 'Go curse David.' My own son is trying to kill me; why not this Benjamite? Leave him alone. Let him curse. My life is full of stones, but his can't hurt us. The Lord may hear his curses and turn them to good, but may God grind your arrogance in the dirt!"

No one moved. No one spoke. Uncle and nephew squared off, layers of convention falling away from the core of raw hatred that suddenly, unexpectedly defined the two. The thick, black line of Abishai's brow did not so much as twitch in response to David's glare. Nor did David blink. The men surrounding them held their collective breaths. Even the rock thrower kept still. Finally, the tension let go when Abishai—his eyes still locked on David's—whistled a signal to release Shimei.

The old man shrugged free of the soldiers and continued hurling dirt and invectives. "Get away, man of blood! God raised up your son Absalom to your ruin. Go! Go! May you find no rest, not even in Sheol!"

Several months later, when we talked over the flight from Jerusalem, David said, "Asaph, I'm glad she didn't live to see that dreadful day."

I saw his thought. "Do you think my lady Abigail would have chided you, my lord?"

"Oh, no." He sighed. "I would have had to carry her bodily out of the palace. I can see her: back straight, chin tipped up, every inch in control. 'You go along, my lord,' she'd say. 'I'll handle Absalom.'" He laughed wryly. "And who knows? Maybe she could have." He sat silently a moment. "Bathsheba was furious with her that day we left."

"With...?"

"I called out in my need, and so she was jealous of Abigail. A dead woman, Asaph! Perhaps, though, anger was good that day. It kept her from thinking of what lay ahead."

"Why would she be jealous?"

Pain twisted David's face. "Shadows, Asaph. Shadows never leave her alone."

16

Hushai made it through the city gate only minutes before Absalom himself entered in a spectacular show of triumph. Cheering crowds lined the way. Hushai wondered if they had been conscripted and positioned for the occasion, but with a sinking heart, he realized that most were ordinary folk genuinely happy to have a new king. All David had done for them seemed to have faded from their minds, and the implications of a scheming monarch who feigned godliness were not yet visible. Absalom had plowed his ground well.

Hushai wanted to give Absalom time to settle in before seeing him, so he decided to look for Jonathan and Ahimaaz. He found neither but did locate Zadok. "The boys are in En Rogel at the foot of the valley," said Zadok. "They're too well-known to risk coming here, but we have a trusted servant girl who can deliver messages. When you have something to send, come to the Tent to pray. I'll take it from there."

"Good." Hushai drew a deep breath and looked toward the towering pile of stone and cedar that was the palace. "Zadok, pray for me."

Pray for me. His heart pounded wildly. How could he do this—the biggest, most consequential act of his life? David's life, the kingdom, and the future of Israel all hinged on this afternoon's performance.

It was important that he be one of the first to welcome the new king as though he had remained here in Jerusalem. He had hurried to arrive ahead of Absalom, and no matter how his feet hurt, he dared not grimace or otherwise show signs of a journey.

The Lord is my shepherd, the Lord is my shepherd...

He thought of the superb acting of the woman Joab had primed to speak on Absalom's behalf. Now her shoe was on his foot; he must act superbly on David's behalf.

He took several deep breaths and strode toward the door of the palace with a show of eager confidence.

Caleb and his wife Acsah were having an argument. In a way, quarreling helped relieve the sickness that gripped their bowels. The king had abandoned his throne. He had passed through Bahurim, passed the courtyard of their house, looking old and tired and anxious. Acsah had so wanted to step out and say, "There, there," that Caleb had to physically restrain her.

Now, though, she was indignant. "I will go to Shimei. I will tell him to grow up!"

"Grow up?" said Caleb. "Shimei's an old man!"

"Years have nothing to do with growing up. Has he grown past his pride in being kin to Saul? Can he see who Saul really was? Does he really know David? Someone needs to tell him, and if you won't, I must!" Acsah lowered her plump body to a bench, but the thrust of her elbows spoke her mind.

"My dear—"

"Don't 'my dear' me! His behavior…imagine a man of any age heaving stones and curses at the king of Israel—and getting away with it! Only a humble man would say, 'Leave him alone.' Only David—" And here Acsah pulled up a handful of robe and wept into it, though not for long. She sat up, and her eyes, normally as soft as figs, blazed fire. Pulling her shawl over her head, she stood and faced her husband. "You're a man of peace, you say, and don't want to confront Shimei, so unless you hold my body and risk God's wrath, I will confront him in his house." She looked defiantly at him, spots of indignation on her cheeks, then swished toward the door.

"No." Caleb seized her arm, and she lifted it as though to jerk away. "No," he repeated. "I will go. If a man of war can overlook such an insult, then a man of peace can confront the insulter. I will go."

"Just give us some time!" Joab had said.

Hushai pushed through the exuberant crowd of guardsmen, courtiers, cronies, and elders of Israel and strode familiarly into David's throne room. Jonadab was there, as were Amasa, Ahithophel, and the malcontents whose carping treacheries had for years been thorns under David's skin—all clustered in this place of power. The wisps of disloyalty that David had merely felt now seemed a thick, noxious cloud, the shape of which took Hushai's breath away.

He moved quickly to the throne, to the bush-haired figure that seemed as out of place as a slave. He bowed low. "My lord the king. Long live the king!"

Absalom froze, the silver wine bowl halfway to his lips. Then he leaned forward. "You! What are you doing here?"

"I bring my formal greeting, my lord. Why should I not be here?" He smiled in what he hoped was his usual jocularity and wished his knees would stop trembling.

Absalom leaned toward Ahithophel. "What do you think of this, Chief Counselor? The king's friend has abandoned the king."

"You, my lord, are the king," said Ahithophel, bowing in his clipped way.

Hushai made himself smile at Ahithophel, though he admitted later it was perhaps the most difficult part of the entire encounter. "He's quite right, my lord. The man who sits the throne is the king, not the palace chamberlain."

At this, Absalom choked on the wine and had to have his breath pounded back.

He's drunk, thought Hushai. "My lord! Are you all right?"

Absalom sat back, still chuckling. "No wonder my father liked you. But you've abandoned him. Is this the way you show love to your friend?"

His moment of truth—or deception—had come. Absalom was looking hard at him. Ahithophel was looking. The circle of swords was looking. *The Lord is my shepherd...*

"My lord the king, my heart and my knee bow to whomever *Yahweh* and the people here have chosen to be ruler of Israel. His I will be, and with him I will remain. As I served the father, so shall I serve the son." Again he bowed low and remained thus in the silence that followed.

Absalom shifted uneasily. "Well, Ahithophel. What do you think of our implausible subject?"

Hushai closed his eyes and held his breath, hoping the clanging of his heart could not be heard in the long moment of Ahithophel's hesitation. If a sword was going to fall in his direction, he preferred not to see it coming.

Ahithophel finally spoke in a studied manner, "In my experience, my lord, implausible subjects sometimes prove invaluable."

"Ha!" said Absalom. "There, Hushai. You may rise, invaluable servant to the new king! Here! A cup of wine for the invaluable servant!"

Hushai tried to ease into the revelers' hilarity. He had made it safely thus far; how now to extricate himself? He jumped at the sound of his name.

"Hushai!" shouted the upstart king. "Come hear this. Tell me what you think. You're on the ground floor of a new kingdom, did you know that? Ahithophel has just begun to tell me what to do, and do you know what he says? He says I should lie with my father's concubines. He left them here, you know. Did you know that, Hushai?"

"He left them here? All of them?"

"All ten. Ahithophel says it will make me a stench in my father's nostrils. Sometimes a stench is a good thing to be, Hushai, and this is one of those times. Now, go make yourself invaluable, Hushai. Set up a tent on the rooftop below my father's 'eagle's nest.' I want all Israel to watch me become a stench."

Hushai forced a grin and bowed quickly to cover its lameness. On the way out, he seized a competent-looking steward carrying more wine. "Come with me," he snapped. "I have a job for you."

That night, Hushai lay in the little cell Zadok had provided, staring through a dark, dry cadence of insect song. He could have requested his usual room in the palace, but the thought brought bile to his mouth. What he had done this day, what he had seen...

He closed his eyes and thought of David. Where was he tonight? It wasn't likely he had reached the fords. Thousands of people, their baggage, and an old king would be slow going. Would that he were over the river and safe in Mahanaim. Absalom would not be drunk tomorrow, at least in the morning. He'd be ready for action, but what shape would his action take? How could Hushai find out? How could he shape the action to benefit the king? He would certainly need his wits in the morning, and staying awake would not sharpen them. "*Just give us time!*" He scrunched his eyes tightly, trying to will himself to sleep, but insects continued to scratch the night, and sleep paid him no mind. He prayed, he sang, he reviewed the old days.

> *Be merciful, O Lord, I'm in distress;*
> *I'm weak with sorrow;*
> *Grief is twisting my body.*
> *Turn Your face to me your servant;*
> *Save me, O Lord.*

Finally, in the few hours before dawn, a peace and Presence descended upon Hushai in a precious moment of rest, beginning with a message in his heart:

> *Be still, Hushai, be still.*
> *With Me, weak is strong.*
> *In the shelter of My presence*
> *I will hide you from the intrigues of men.*

Hushai was jolted awake by a shaking. "Absalom is calling for you! Get up!"

Raw terror replaced sleep in his eyes.

"On your feet, man," said Zadok. "You've got three minutes to brush your clothing and wash your face. Up, up; I'll help you."

How he did it he could never say, but within five minutes he strode into the throne room as though he'd been awake for hours. The room was nearly as full of cronies, elders, and guardsmen as yesterday, though the noise had diminished.

"Ah, Hushai," said Absalom. "You slept well, I trust? Let's see, you're on the second floor...on the east, is it? I need to get oriented. It's *my* palace now."

"I slept well, my lord, thank you."

"Have some fruit, Hushai. A bowl..." He pulled off a bunch of grapes and handed them to his guest.

Hushai received them and hoped his knotted stomach would tolerate this bit of politeness. He noted with dismay that Absalom seemed none the worse for yesterday's drunken orgy. Ahithophel, standing behind the fruit, bore an air of disquietude. Everything about him was in splendid order—a robe striped and layered and finer than Absalom's, his sculpted hair and beard, rings that adorned his slender fingers. His face seemed composed, but something about him led Hushai to believe he was not as happy as Absalom to see "the king's former friend."

"Now Hushai, we need your opinion. Ahithophel here has told me just how to defeat my father, and the plan sounds good. His advice is always right." Absalom nodded with a sort of reverence, then spit his grape seeds through a chance ray of sun. "But still, I'd like to scratch through your mind, Hushai. What do you think we should do?"

This was his test. How could Hushai pull the right advice out of the air? *What had Ahithophel said?* He could feel his face tighten, and he reached for another grape. This one could choke him, but he had to eat it. *Lord...*

He swallowed hard, seeds and all, but before he could say anything, Absalom went on. "Ahithophel says to muster twelve thousand and set out immediately. My father David is not the man he was, so attacking early while he's vulnerable would undo him. A quick, clean strike, killing only the king and his guard. The people with him will flee and eventually come back to me. Done. Just like that. What do you think, Hushai?"

An excellent plan, thought Hushai. *If Absalom buys it, David is dead. What can I possibly say that would counter it? He's watching me. Ahithophel is watching. He knows. Maybe both of them know. They're bears; I'm the lamb caught in the—*

Hushai straightened and replaced a budding smile with a studied look. "My lord, with due respect to Ahithophel's wisdom"—he bowed toward the counselor—"I must disagree this time. You know your father as well as I in this regard. He's a born fighter. His *Gibborim* are fighters, fiercer than she-bears robbed of cubs. In every hamlet up and down the country, minstrels sing their exploits. David didn't become king by someone pasting a crown on his head. No, he earned it—the hard way. Those years in the desert, running from burrow to burrow: do you think he's forgotten those lessons? Not likely. Even now, he's tucked in some cave, and you'll run the legs off your twelve thousand trying to find him. And suppose he attacks first? What then? Getting your troops slaughtered right off is hardly the way to launch a kingdom. People, even the bravest of soldiers, will fall away in terror."

Hushai dared not glance at Ahithophel, whom he was sure could see the tremble of every thread covering his body. Absalom, though, was listening well, and Hushai paced up and down with contrived confidence.

"No, my lord, I'm afraid going out before you're really prepared would be disastrous. My advice is this: go from north to south and collect a real army, an army outnumbering the stars in the sky and the grains of sand on the shore. And don't just send them out under your fine general." He nodded toward Amasa. "Lead them in battle yourself. You're an excellent warrior, your father's son. I still hear songs about you descending the cliff on the mule. Lead the troops, my lord. We'll overwhelm him. If he runs to a city, we'll pull it down until not one stone is left on another. David and his men will be dead; his son will sit straight and squarely on the throne. A new day has come!"

Here Hushai punched his fist upward, then bowed low—and prayed.

The entire room held its breath, then exploded with cheers and slaps on the back. Absalom himself shouted, "Yes! Yes!" and hauled Hushai to his feet. Only Ahithophel stood silently and stiffly.

When the din settled, Ahithophel stepped to Absalom's side and said, "A word, my lord."

Hushai crunched his jaw into an obscene grin and continued to shake hands, trying not to pay attention to the conversation two feet away. The whole scheme could still go into the slops jar. He could not hear Ahithophel's studied presentation, but his spirits rose when Absalom burst out, "Nonsense! Look what he did yesterday. Would he have set up the concubines if he were still in my father's pocket? You yourself told me the act of mounting the king's women would confirm my claim to the throne. I became a stench, Ahithophel, and Hushai made it happen. You're wrong this time, old man. Hushai's got it right, and you don't like that. Get used to it: things will be different around here."

A servant girl worked her way down the valley against the tide of sheep, goats, and tradesmen. With a basket full of round loaves, she eased out of the jostling traffic into the peace of the little village at the junction of the Kidron and Hinnom Valleys. En Rogel, a few dozen houses clustered around the fuller's well, had its own backwater commerce, but traffic from yesterday's political turnover now flowed around it.

The girl, neck craned in search of a certain gateway, bumped into a man who was crossing the street. "I'm sorry, my lord!" she said, retrieving two errant loaves. As she bent, a small scroll slipped from her basket. The man caught it, glanced at it, returned it to the flustered maid, and continued on. A few feet farther, however, he stopped and reversed direction so he could see through the gate the girl had entered.

Two men in the courtyard welcomed the girl. "You have a message, Mara?"

Another loaf fell as Mara extricated the scroll. With a wink, one of the lads snatched it and took a bite. He said, "Read it, Ahimaaz."

Ahimaaz scanned it quickly, then read:

> *Ahithophel lost the first scuffle, and I've bought the king a little time, but sooner or later when the farce begins to unravel, common sense will prevail and they'll be on him. David must not dally at the fords. He must cross as quickly as possible and get to Mahanaim. I can't stress it more strongly: speed is of the essence. Go quickly. Give David this word.*

"Well! There's news at last!" Ahimaaz looked up, but his friend was staring across the street. "Jonathan?"

Jonathan popped the last bit of bread into his mouth, gave the girl a coin and a shove toward the gate, and pulled Ahimaaz toward the house. "We've got to move quicker than even Hushai's thinking. That was Jonadab across the street."

17

My dear wife,

I write this, my sincere apology, for the unfortunate but unavoidable inconvenience my action will bestow upon you. You have borne much over the years and have seen well to my household. Your husband and sons rise up and call you blessed. I trust you will make the necessary adjustment to an altered life and routine with minimal perturbation.

I have sought to minimize the shock to your person by assuring the following:

1. There will be no blood or other unpleasantness to unsettle you.

2. The discovery of the deed will not fall to you.

3. You will be spared from making weighty decisions at a time when you may be in an awkward state. I have seen to every detail, leaving nothing untended.

I believe all is in order. Eliam, our firstborn, will, of course, assume charge of property and livestock. He being capable and orderly, and the shift of

proprietorship should be of no major consequence to
him or to you, beyond the inevitable though distasteful
flurry of residual sentiment.

A word about the circumstances leading to my action.
I have made few errors of judgment in my life.
Contrary to what you may hear, my advice to Absalom
concerning an immediate attack on a weakened and
vulnerable David was not one of them. If the new king
had followed it, David would be dead this day and
Absalom firmly settled on his throne.

My most serious lapse in judgment lay in not
recognizing the new king to be a fool. He has the
personal and organizational ability to manage a
kingdom such as David established, and his youth
and energy give him a definite advantage in holding it
together. He has, though, neither the inner discipline
nor the spiritual capacity of his father. That he has
functional discipline can be denied by no one. His
patient, methodical approach to long-term problem
solving was one of the aspects of his character that
attracted my attention. Perhaps I was lulled by his
overtures of friendship, the hours we talked about
the affairs of the kingdom, his deep interest in my
perspective and assessment. He listened; he seemed
to care; he acted upon my advice. Unfortunately, that
sense of mutual understanding did not last beyond the
concubines.

Another error of judgment lay in underestimating the
efficacy of David's prayers. Hushai's "advice" to muster
a large army before attacking David, while a stunning

performance, was patently transparent; even a fool
should have seen through it. I conclude, therefore, that
no advice of mine, however sterling, would have had
sufficient power to breach the wall surrounding the
Lord's anointed.

That Hushai, normally a meek and unpretentious
man, should even dare appear before Absalom speaks
strongly of his devotion to David. I envy the former
king his possession of such a friend—an inestimable
treasure.

Will David regain the throne? The odds are against
it. Joab is nearly as old as the king and no less a
toad than he's ever been. The Gibborim, while still
formidable, are likewise past their prime, and few
young warriors even approach their stature. The
question, then, remains: Can enough goodwill be found
in Israel to mount an army capable of prevailing over
Absalom? For me, however, the issue is moot. I would
not have you think that I chose this way to avoid the
king's wrath and eventual execution. No, this is purely
a matter of honor. There was nothing left for me but to
saddle my donkey and head for Giloh.

May the Lord bless you and keep you, my wife; the
Lord shine His countenance of grace and peace upon
you.

A shepherd discovered the body of Ahithophel hanging from
a tree an arrow's arc from the eastern edge of Giloh. The tree
stood atop a sharp rise facing not toward his home in Giloh,

nor toward Hebron to the south, nor north to Jerusalem where his hopes lay dashed; his last window on life looked toward the wilderness crucible to the east from whence flowed the gold that became King David.

18

"Oh, Caleb, what do you think?" Her round face stiff with worry, Acsah studied her handiwork to make sure she hadn't overlooked some little thing that might draw attention to the well in their courtyard.

"It looks fine to me," said Caleb. "The cloth covers everything, the grain looks normal. I could fetch another basketful, if that would help."

"No, it wouldn't look right. Maybe an empty basket, like we were— Oh, no! Here they come! There...the top of the hill!" Her hands flew to her face, patting a new layer of terror in place.

Her husband looked at her sharply. "Calm down, my dear, or you'll give us away. Look composed, even if you don't feel it. Be still, now. Go take a drink."

"No." Acsah drew herself up with deep breaths. "My face is red, isn't it?"

"Quite red. Perhaps you should dab water on it."

"No, I'll grind grain—a hot job—excuse enough for looking red. Be still, boys," she whispered loudly toward the grain-covered cloth. "They're coming."

A dozen guardsmen jogged downhill to the mud-brick village of Bahurim and halted at the first courtyard. Within they saw a domestic scene: a middle-aged man bending to a sheaf of wheat in preparation for threshing, and a plump wife vigorously thumping her pestle, hoping the men would not see she'd forgotten to put grain in it.

"Peace to you," said the leader. "Men of Absalom here. We're looking for two young men."

Caleb straightened slowly. "Two young men, you say. Do we know two young men, Mother?" He turned to his wife.

"Yes, we do. More than two, actually. Which two are you hoping to find?"

The soldiers looked at each other. "Jonathan and Ahimaaz, the priests' sons."

A look of concern came over Acsah's face. "Are they lost? Sneaked away from lessons, did they? Boys will do that, you know. And priests' sons...their folks must be worried. I know when my boys—"

"No, ma'am, not lost, but it's important that we find them. I thought you might have noticed boys running—"

"Oh, *those* boys!" said Acsah, clasping her hands. "Why didn't you say so? We saw them, didn't we, Caleb? We saw them running as hard as they could."

"You saw them, my dear. I was threshing."

"Yes, it must have been I who saw them. I even went to the doorway to look, and they were still running. I didn't go after them, but I did see them cross the brook at the foot of town. I had grinding to do, so I didn't—"

"Thanks, ma'am." The leader nodded, and the men continued downhill. Over the wall, the couple heard, "Think they're leading us on?"

"Sillies like that? You should live so long."

Two hours later, after the soldiers had passed on their return to Jerusalem, Jonathan and Ahimaaz crept stiffly from the well and kissed the couple. "Splendid job! Superb!"

"You're wet and cold. I'll stoke the fire and—"

"No time. We'll tell the king what you did. You'll be remembered."

Night was falling as they reached the fords. They were taken directly to the king, who read Hushai's message and gave immediate orders to cross the Jordan.

"Stay with me," he said to the boys. "Right now, your life is goat dung in Absalom's eyes. God has brought us this far; the cloud and pillar will lead us on."

> *How many have risen against me, O Lord?*
> *They're not telling me.*
> *Joab talks with Abishai, Eleazar with Shammah*
> *and Amasai, but they don't talk to me.*
> *I don't control my army.*
> *I'm helpless...but not hopeless.*
> *If Absalom's thousands were here—*
> *   now—on every side,*
> *I know you'd sustain me.*
> *Arise, O Lord! Save me!*

During that long, dreadful, nighttime march from the lower ford of the Jordan to Mahanaim, the incessant cries of terrified children seemed to Joab like an invisible hornet that he couldn't bat away. Children in war were seldom a factor for him. When his troops entered a conquered city, its inhabitants shrieking and wailing, he assigned the mop-up task to other officers and simply removed himself. Here he had no place to go.

On top of that, along with keeping the king safe, he somehow had to pull a sizeable army out of territory suddenly hostile to their cause. *Strike their jaw; break their teeth, O Lord*—Joab's most well-worn prayer.

He knew his men, though. He'd always prowled the ranks to learn of special capabilities. Now came payoff time. He asked for this soldier or that, dispatching each to a particular clan or trusted militia leader.

A small, hawklike figure hung around the fringe of this deployment, an almost invisible presence until Joab was about to send a runner to an influential man who lived far to the south. As though waiting for this moment, the shadowy hawk glided across the darkness and bowed low before Joab. Joab yanked him up in anger. "Who are you and what do you want?"

"O most worthy general." The figure tried bowing again, but Joab's ivory-handled dagger flashed in his free hand. The man stood impassively as though impending death was little more than a sudden change of plans. A single earring glimmered in the dim, circumjacent light.

"Wait!" said Amasai. "It's Obil."

Joab growled and shoved the camelmaster to the ground. Amasai helped him up.

Obil bowed a third time. "What is it, Obil?" he said. "Speak quickly."

After the obligatory bow toward Amasai, Obil spoke. "My lord and masters, I will carry the message to Hotham the Aroerite. I will travel down the Arabah on my fastest camel. The Negev is my mother's breast to me. I will drink in Hotham's tent and in the tents of others who would fight for my lord the king. May my skin be flayed from my body if I return with fewer than four thousand warriors."

Joab relieved his headache with a string of curses. Amasai drew the little man to safety and said, "What you say is good, Obil. The Lord may be in it. I'll talk to Joab and tell you what we decide." But Amasai felt a sudden, surprising resistance in the scarred and dented body. He put his hand on the Arab's shoulders and looked him straight in the eyes. "I know what you want, Obil. Trust me. Ready your camel. You'll have your chance to sing for David's well-being as he sang for yours. Give me half an hour."

Amasai's conference with the Three—Jashobeam, Eleazar, and Shammah—followed by a more heated discussion with Joab and Abishai, finally brought grudging approval of the plan. He jogged to the already mounted Obil, and within seconds the camelmaster was a swift-moving shadow against the sandstone cliffs.

The night seemed interminable. The children stopped crying, whether from exhaustion or resignation, but Arabah wildness had everyone on edge. David walked now and then to stir his blood, but as the long march wore on, the cold, strange noises of night began twisting his thoughts.

We went too far, missed Mahanaim.
I see bulls of Bashan. Or are they lions?
O God, I'm water poured out, bones out of joint,
   heart like wax.
I'm a dry, cracked potsherd.
Dogs nip at me, stare at my bones.
Do they want my clothes, my life?
Abba, I'm afraid.
I want You close to me;
O my Strength, come quickly...help me.

Dawn dissolved the terrifying shapes into nothing more threatening than wild donkeys. They pushed on through grotesque, deep-carved bluffs that protruded into the river valley. Now only those who couldn't keep up rode donkeys. David himself refused to ride. "Are my feet poorer than anyone else's here?"

As day brought oppressive heat to the Arabah, David began to sway. Still he insisted on walking. "I'm sleeping, Benaiah; don't bother me." Benaiah positioned two burly guards on either side to steady the king's dreams.

In mid-afternoon, David tried to shake off a dream rising out of the shimmering haze: camels ornamented with chains and medallions, donkeys, a flock of sheep, men talking peaceably with Joab and his officers.

As they came close, two men slid from their animals and a third struggled from a chair. The three approached David, whose eyes lighted in recognition. "Barzillai!" he cried. "And Makir! Shobi! Here in this forsaken place?" He kissed and patted them in disbelief. "You've come in my need—friends precious as water in the desert." He looked from one to another and embraced them again. "You've come so far!"

"Not so far as you think, my lord," said Shobi. "The Jabbok River is straight ahead. Once we reach the ford, you're almost to Mahanaim."

David closed his eyes wearily.

Makir took his arm. "Come, my lord. You will ride now. Barzillai has a chair."

"We knew you'd be hungry, as well," said Barzillai. "We have—" he pointed toward the lead camels. "There's bedding and water jars and bowls, and to put into the bowls"—his finger continued along the line—"barley, beans, lentils, honey—the little ones will like that—cow cheese….Ah! A fire's going. A good meal in your belly, my friend, and the ascent to Mahanaim will seem as nothing."

Tears streamed into David's beard during this inventory of friendship.

Barzillai, though, in a flurry of chagrin, threw up his hands. "Oh, but I've made it sound like this was all from me. Not so, not so! Shobi brought sheep, and Makir—"

"Never mind what Makir brought," said Makir. "Enough that God has brought David safely through the Arabah. You will find rest in our homes."

Late that night, with David and his wives bedded in Barzillai's gracious villa, the sons of Zeruiah and the Three, along with Amasai, sat in the cool of the courtyard with Makir, Shobi, and Barzillai's son Kimham, who distributed a mountain of pillows to the grateful generals. "You fellows look dreadful," Kimham said. "I thought the king was haggard, but you're worse. Such responsibility, such...dedication." He sighed. "I won't keep you long, but a quick word before you sleep may give us a critical advantage. We want authorization to help raise an army. We've got the operation already in place. We just need a word from you to set it in motion."

Joab stared at him with eyes that were dying embers.

"We don't want to usurp authority or undermine your own plans, but..." Kimham's voice trailed off as the *Gibborim* continued to stare in stupefaction.

Shobi coughed uncomfortably. "Perhaps this is not the best time."

Silence shimmered around the lighted lamp, gradually seeping into the dim soul recesses of the exhausted *Gibborim*.

Tears rolled down Joab's cheeks. "Thank you," he whispered hoarsely, then struggled off his cushions and stumbled into Barzillai's garden.

19

I was disappointed when Zadok told me the king had instructed him to return the ark to Jerusalem and that I would return, as well. In my anger, I almost turned to follow David. *He needs me*, I thought, but something else said, *How presumptuous!* Far from helping, I would hinder, perhaps by hoarding one of the precious donkeys. That, or the ignominy of falling from exhaustion and being stuffed under a broom bush with water and a thin bag of grain. No, I did well to give up my whim.

As it turned out, I was of some small use to Hushai during his ordeal. Word of Ahithophel's suicide sent Absalom into a brief, towering rage, but he soon sent for Hushai and appointed him chief counselor. Hushai tried to plead ineptitude, old age—anything—but Absalom would have none of it, and Hushai found himself with a foot on either side of an ever-widening chasm. I met him stumbling through the courtyard in obvious distress.

"What am I to do, Asaph?" he asked.

I wanted to comfort him and draw him to my cubicle to talk, but I considered who might be watching and listening. Guards were everywhere. I wiped concern off my face and suggested he do the same, wave casually before walking away, and then to make his way to the Tent when it seemed safe.

That was the first of many conversations. Hushai had the unenviable task of advising Absalom against David without actually doing harm to his banished king. I made a few suggestions but mostly listened while he weighed various approaches. "I can stall only so long, Asaph," he said. "I can say the army isn't large enough yet, but the bigger it gets, the harder it will be for David to defeat. And can Joab pull together an army? I'm appalled by disloyalty everywhere. Sheba is doing incalculable harm. The whole of Israel seems against David! Where can he get enough warriors to fight the entire militia?"

Where, indeed? That was the question in Mahanaim. The Kimham-Makir-Shobi trio produced several thousand soldiers, some of them Ammonites. "The government you established after defeating my brother was like sunrise after a storm," Shobi told David. "My people are grateful."

Many of Joab's emissaries had done well, also, and a slow, steady trickle of men appeared at Mahanaim. Not enough, though, and as word of Absalom's buildup reached the Jabbok Valley, tension mounted.

Hushai wanted advice. The king and his officers talked and decided that time outweighed Absalom's buildup. "Whatever you do," said David in a return communiqué, "don't arouse suspicion concerning your role. You're of inestimable value right now—a friend in the enemy's bed. You're doing what you can; God will take care of the rest."

The Mighty Men trained new recruits and even young boys for a last-ditch stand around the king. "We're not much in numbers," said Abishai, "but skill has won battles before. Right now it's our first, our last, our only hope."

David prowled and watched these training sessions but also engaged in staff duels. Eleazar became suspicious. "What are you doing?" he asked.

"We've got a war to fight, don't you know?"

Eleazar shook his head. "Uh-uh. *We're* fighting the war; you're back here praying."

David drew himself up fiercely, and the warrior of song and legend flashed out, taking Eleazar's breath away. The past weeks had shrunk the king's paunch and toughened him; the old glint was in his eye once again.

But Eleazar shook his head. "No, my lord," he said regretfully. "Who is Absalom after? Not the army, not the *Gibborim*. If most of us died, it would mean nothing. It's you he wants. You're worth ten thousand *gibborim* to Absalom—even more to us."

Shammah moved close. "My lord," he said, "we want you here to deploy the reserves as needed."

David bristled at this obvious sop. He knew the "reserves" would be the old, the injured, the painfully young. He was an old king commanding mere odds and ends. But after a moment, he took a breath and bowed low. "Where would I be without you? I will do...whatever seems best...."

David launched himself into structuring the troops, appointing officers over units of hundreds and thousands. Despite Joab's protest, he divided the army into thirds, with Joab, Abishai, and Ittai as equal commanders. "Flexibility will help balance numbers. You'll see I'm right when you get out there."

The numbers were stacked against them. From all reports, Absalom's army numbered in the hundreds of thousands, David's in the tens of thousands.

Amasa was a capable general, which even his cousins had to admit. He, of all Absalom's officials, saw the folly of waiting and kept pressuring his king to move out. Finally, when Hushai could see nothing to be gained by stalling further, he seconded Amasa's plea. "Yes, my lord the king, it's time." *And may Yahweh have mercy on us!*

Absalom was well north before word got to David, putting everyone off balance at the start. "He's coming through Ephraim, not the Arabah, and will cross the Jordan below Adam maybe tonight. He'll most likely attack from the south," said the scout.

"No!" roared David. "That mustn't happen! We've got to draw him to ground of our choosing. The hills north of here, the Forest of Ephraim. Ravines, precipices, trees—our kind of landscape."

Joab almost smiled. "Right. Let's move out. We'll be on him at first light."

Zadok had appointed Abiathar's son Ahimelech as priest to David. He now stood at the gate of Mahanaim before the assembled troops, a nervous but persuasive fervor upon him. "Hear, O Israel! Today...you go to battle...against your enemies." He spoke the ritual slowly and with far more passion than his father could have called forth, igniting a fire that quickly engulfed the pitifully small army.

The men raised their hands and sang praise to God.

Ahimelech continued. "Do not be fainthearted and do not give way to panic. The Lord your God...goes with you...to give you...*victory!*"

An explosive shout, far out of proportion with the size of the army, swallowed the last word, and the troops set out on what could well have been their last march.

David had a word for the men as they passed by the gate in units—first Joab's, then Abishai's and Ittai's. David's life hung on the outcome of this battle, but the price of victory was foremost in his mind. "*Please*—for my sake, be gentle with my son, with my son Absalom." Ittai gripped his hand, shaken by the warrior-father tension that was tearing David apart.

Jonathan and Ahimaaz, far back in Ittai's ranks, felt the tension, too.

20

When David's tripartite army came upon them, the rebel forces were fording the Jordan River. It was late afternoon—not the time to mount an attack. The three commanders lay atop a bluff, aghast at the horde below. Almost without end, ranks of well-equipped soldiers, each with its own string of donkeys, hauled themselves up the broad, sloping bank and moved off to await further orders. The sight itself was reminiscent of the mock battle years ago, with its banners and plumes and burnished shields. This lavish display was Hushai's idea, I later learned, one that appealed to Absalom's vanity and at the same time squandered a fair amount of time. Joab muttered thoughtfully, "Can an army dressed in cobwebs put down a rebellion?"

Ittai stared below. "Will they camp here tonight, do you think, or go on?"

The other two remained silent. "I think they'll stay," Joab said at last. "They won't head up the ravine to Mahanaim; that would be suicide—any time of the day. Steep, rugged, too easily defended. And it's late. They could go farther before dark, but I think they'll opt for an easy bivouac—that broad, dry shelf, perhaps." He pointed. "Right below where we want to fight them. If they camp there, we'll have time to get in place and change their mind and direction; if not...we make do. Davi was right: with three armies, we can surround them—*if* they stay."

Joab pulled back from the overlook. "Here's the plan. Abishai will move up river beyond the army, keeping to the underbrush. Ittai will position himself about even with Absalom. At first glimmer of light, both attack—Ittai first on their backside and right flank, taking out as many as possible before they get their eyes open. When it gets hot, head for the hills. Then Abishai strikes the left flank quick and hard, but they'll be ready, and you'll have to dance off fast. Follow Ittai to the hills, but dawdle, like you really don't think they'll bother coming after. Careless, defenseless."

They stared at him.

Joab muttered grimly, "Small armies use mice to bait the fox. They'll follow...to the hills where we want 'em. I'll stay at the Jabbok in case they don't like mice." He fell silent, studying the activity below. "Dog's head!" he muttered. "Absalom—there by his mule." He pointed. "That hair makes an easy target. When the chance comes, aim at the fur ball."

Absalom did bed down on the river shelf, allowing David's armies to establish position. In the morning, as men and animals began to stir, Ittai made his first furious strike from the rear, wiping out an entire battalion. When Ittai took off, Abishai rose out of the Jordan gulch with equal fervor, but with the surprise factor gone, he could inflict only half as much damage before the rebels mobilized effectively. Nevertheless, the attackers had dented the behemoth and could head into the hills with no small satisfaction.

Amasa pounced at the bait, as expected. Joab watched the rebel general disappear behind the hills, a swarm of chariots and foot soldiers tight behind. Joab held back until Absalom set out on his mule, surrounded by his elite cadre, before biting into the confused mass of supply personnel and animals left behind. His was the more dangerous position of the three. If Absalom turned to fight or Amasa suddenly remembered his king, Joab would be hard-pressed to get to the others, but the rebels danced to the *Gibborim's* tune and disappeared in the wooded hills.

Once there, the advantage of numbers over experience began to lessen. Amasa performed well, as Ahimaaz had predicted, but he lacked his cousins' toughness and experience in fighting from rocks and caves, from bush and tree. Then too, he was saddled with a king who had no real battle exposure yet insisted on orchestrating troop movements.

David's men, on the other hand, were comfortable with their leaders and their place of battle. Using the landscape as a weapon, they lured whole regiments to ravines or precipices where they could be easily slaughtered. Absalom's chariots were useless, and most were abandoned. Nevertheless, sheer numbers mocked even these advantages. In addition, David's army no longer had young versions of Jashobeam, Eleazar, or Shammah, who in their prime could take on hundreds at a time.

Benaiah and his men were supposed to defend David at Mahanaim. The king, though, couldn't see manpower going to waste and sent most of them join the conflict. They came on the scene as pressure on the smaller army was mounting. Abishai's chewed-up men cheered them on sight, but though formidable, the Kerethites and Pelethites too were swept on the rocks by the rebel wave.

This is madness, thought Benaiah after being separated from his men. Wiping an arm across the veil of blood on his face, he clambered to a high point to look around. David's armies were fighting well—better, perhaps, than ever before. Given the circumstances, they were well-deployed and well-organized. But no matter how many rebels they killed, more kept pouring in. An even greater concern was that they were being pushed off their chosen battlefield to smoother terrain where Absalom's chariots and lesser-skilled warriors would have the advantage.

Benaiah was about to leap back to the fray, ready to die in defense of his sovereign, when a fast-moving mass behind and to his left caught his eye. He stood frozen, first in fear that Absalom had circled around, then in astonishment. Whatever army was rising from the Arabah carried the banner of David!

He turned and whistled a signal. Eleazar looked up. Striding uphill in response to Benaiah's frantic beckoning, he, too, studied the strange army that had both horses and camels attached. "It's Obil!" he shouted and leaped up and down, arms waving. "Ob-illl!"

"With seven or eight thousand warriors!" Benaiah shouted to the men below.

His boys, with a quick cheer, fought with renewed strength. The tide began to turn. With Obil's help, they moved the fight back to rougher ground, and the forest once again began to claim its rebel victims.

Absalom came to grief in a thick stand of oak. After accounting for what he thought were all the enemy forces, he separated himself to check on the overall battle. Cresting the hill where Benaiah had stood, he happened upon one of Ittai's battalions. Wheeling his mule about, Absalom raced toward the relative shelter of a nearby wood. The Gittites, beyond exhaustion, could only lean on their spears, gasping and cursing, as he disappeared among the trees.

Ahimaaz, too tired to curse, threw himself to the ground. He looked up, mildly surprised that the puffy clouds overhead cared nothing about the battle. When the signal came to move, he rolled to his side and waited until his companions had left the hill.

When finally he stood, his eye caught movement to the left. A mule, saddle empty, emerged from the trees and galloped down the ravine. With a glance toward his fellows below, Ahimaaz jogged to the wood and crept cautiously through the trees. He could hear what sounded like screams but couldn't separate the sound from battle noise. Soon, though, shrieks and curses led him to a sight worth ten caravans of treasure. There was Absalom *ben* David, *ben* Maacah, dangling from the branches of a huge oak, his thick, russet, vainglorious hair tangled in its branches. He twisted and struggled and wept but could do nothing to extricate himself. His hands could reach the limbs, but he could not hold himself with one hand long enough to sort out the snarled hair, and sudden, inadvertent drops brought screams of anguish. He kept feeling around his body for a knife, but the initial jerk had sent his weapons flying.

Ahimaaz stood dumbfounded and unsure. He looked at his own bloodied sword. He could run it through Absalom, cut him down and then run him through, or cut him down and give him a head start.... None of the ideas appealed to him. He wished Jonathan were there. Absalom hadn't seen him yet, for which he was grateful. Eye contact carried obligation, and he didn't yet know its shape. He crouched low and worked his way to where he could run again.

A short way from the wood, he froze defensively at noise just over the brow, but it was Joab and his armorbearers, moving up for their turn on the hill. Ahimaaz ran to the commander and grabbed at his attention. Joab, trying to hear his Cushite bearer through the rasping of the exhausted men, shook him off, but Ahimaaz continued pulling. "Absalom," he cried, "in the trees!"

Joab almost cuffed the boy, then stiffened, hand still raised. "What did you say?"

"Absalom—in the woods over there, hanging by his hair."

"Hanging by— Alive or dead?"

"He's alive! I saw him. His hair got—".

"You *saw* him? You saw him helpless in a tree and didn't kill him?"

"Of course I didn't kill him. I should kill the king's son?"

"Well, you just lost ten shekels of silver and a warrior's belt. That's what I promised to whom ever did him in."

Ahimaaz's eyes widened, but he shook his head. "I thought of killing him, but...the *king's son*! You heard David.: 'Go easy on Absalom,' he said. He said that, and to my way of thinking, killing Absalom isn't exactly going easy. I heard it, and ten or even ten thousand shekels wouldn't be enough to make me go against it. And even if I had, if David found out I'd done it, you'd be the first to step away and leave me to dangle. Don't deny it!"

Ahimaaz couldn't believe what he was saying—he, the lowly son of a priest, defying the Commander in Chief. Joab paid no attention. "Out of my way. No. Show me where he is, and God help you if he's not there!"

But he was, mostly pulp by that point. The armorbearers stared, as Ahimaaz had done. The irony of thick hair, symbol of strength and virility, bringing down "Strong Man Absalom" was not lost on them. Joab might have taken time for mockery, but because the priest's son happened to be watching, he took three javelins from the Cushite bearer and thrust them home. Then, nodding to the rest of his men, he stood back and watched them attack like so many jackals until the writhing body grew still.

With a foot in the pool of Absalom's blood, Joab blew the long blast of victory.

Benaiah, coming on the scene at that moment, lurched into a tree under a vicious wrench of emotion. He saw not Absalom's blood on the ground but Abner's, and Joab's words echoing through the hollow gateway, "*I will walk in your blood!*"

21

Ahimaaz pounded around trees and boulders, counting the inches gained on the Cushite in front. Joab's slave, whose speed had made him chief armorbearer, had been commissioned to bear the good and the bad news to David—to Ahimaaz's disappointment. That Joab had allowed the lad to follow was due mostly to the commander being too tired to argue.

Suddenly, Ahimaaz stopped. *This is crazy. This may be the direct route to Mahanaim, but you couldn't find a rougher way. The Cushite has long legs, but I have brains.*

He had brains, and he knew the countryside. He made an about-face and dropped toward the Jordan plain. Once around the headland, he could again nose uphill on a less alarming trail. If his calculations were correct, he'd end up in front.

But that meant he'd get the king's big question. It was one thing to report the kingdom safe and quite another to tell David his son was dead. What would he say? Maybe the Cushite should get there first, after all. No, God had shown him how to win this race; he'd take whatever came. Something would come to mind.

He ran along limestone cliffs above the Jabbok ravine, glorying in his speed. As he topped the knoll above Mahanaim, his heart leaped to see the Cushite scrabbling up the slope to his left, a hundred yards behind. The distance grew between the runners. *Am I*, Ahimaaz wondered, *as fast as Asahel?* He wished he could test it out. He'd developed a style of running that marked him, even from a distance. No one he knew could keep up with him, and the only reason Joab hadn't sent him in the first place was the implication of the message. "This is good news to you," Joab had said, "but it won't be to the king. More than one man has lost his head over his perception of good news, and Zadok's son won't be immune. If it's reward you're looking for—"

"No," Ahimaaz had said. "I just want to run. I'll take my chances with the king."

Joab shrugged. "Well, run, then." He turned to the business of burying Absalom.

I'll take my chances. Brave words at the time....

Mahanaim was a fortified city, a safe city with towers at each corner, but the main gateway served as the primary watchtower. A stairway inside the gate led to an upper chamber and continued to the roof, from which watchmen could see the surrounding villages. They could see beyond the Jabbok River to the south, the Jordan Valley to the west, and the hill country that stretched northward. On this day, David had posted one of his men to stand watch.

David sat in the broad passageway, his eyes riveted on the northwest approach to the city. Servants brought food and drink, which the king largely ignored. Ira was there, trying to boost the king's spirits. Mostly, though, David kept a lonely vigil—face drawn, eyes haggard, knuckles raw from chewing them.

The sun completed its arc, and the king's anxiety grew. "Why isn't there news, Ira? You'd think—"

A cry from overhead brought David to his feet. He hurried through the outer gate and peered up. "What is it, Ezra? What do you see?"

"A man running along the bluff, my lord."

"Alone?"

"Yes, my lord."

The king turned, his fists clenched triumphantly. "A lone runner, Ira. It must be good—"

"Ho," the voice called again. "A second runner, this one overland. Also alone."

"Still good news; it's got to be!"

"The first comes like the wind. Zadok's son, I'd guess. No runner like him."

"Even better. A good lad, Ahimaaz; a good lad. He brings good news!"

Ahimaaz hauled himself up the last slope, shouting, "All is well!" He collapsed before the king in what he intended as a bow and gasped, "Praise be to the Lord...your God! He's... delivered up those who raised their hands against...my lord the king!"

"Praise God! Praise God!" breathed David, pulling Ahimaaz to his feet, mopping sweat with his own mantle. "But my son—is the young man Absalom safe?"

Ira knew instantly from the drop of Ahimaaz's eyes. He knew, too, that the boy would lie.

"My lord..." Ahimaaz's gasping took a sudden turn for the worse. "My lord...the confusion. You just...wouldn't believe. Everyone...I couldn't tell..." He sagged with relief as the Cushite runner hauled himself to the gate.

The king's face went rigid. "All right, Ahimaaz. Let's hear Joab's man."

The Cushite bowed. "My lord the king... Good news of deliverance. The rebellion has been put down, the revolution... over."

"Yes, yes. So Ahimaaz says. What of Absalom? Is he safe?"

The Cushite bowed again, and Ira wondered if no one would give a straight answer. But the slave said, "May all the enemies of my lord the king be as that young man." He remained straight-faced, and Ahimaaz marveled: the king's sword was inches from the king's right hand, and the messenger's neck stretched invitingly.

But David simply stopped breathing. His intensity froze; he might have become a statue. Then, slowly, in fragmented unreality, he turned and mounted the steps to the upper chamber. The sounds that came from deep within him were neither words nor groans but the outgrowth of pain that forty years of life had scraped raw. Saul's jealousy and rejection; the years of being hunted in the wilderness; false accusations; disloyal friends; famine; God's wrath over his affair with Bathsheba; the death of three sons and a wife; this son, so dear to him, so full of promise, a traitor and usurper of his kingdom; the long, dreadful flight; his naked ignominy paraded before the entire nation. And now..."O my son Absalom! My son, my son

Absalom! If only I had died and you had lived. O Absalom, my son, my son..."

Ira sent Ahimaaz back to warn Joab. "Tell him this isn't the time for celebration. Our men did the impossible and deserve the highest praise and recognition, but not now. Not while the king is grieving."

Joab was furious. "Pig-brained!" he said of Ira's advisory, but it was too late. Word had filtered to the soldiers, and the army's return to Mahanaim the next day seemed more in shame than triumph. They crept into a city that was wailing with the king and slunk into corners to sort through the meaning of what they'd done.

Joab, though, with fire in his eye, went straight to Kimham's house. Bathsheba saw him coming and tried to deflect him with words of appreciation, but he ignored her and pushed his way into the room where David lamented Absalom.

"Enough!" he thundered, and the walls shook.

The rocking stopped, sistrums fell silent, and the room went deathly still. David, clothing torn and ash-ground face swollen with grief, simply stared at Joab.

The commander strode to the king's chair, snatched his sistrum, and sent it rattling against the far wall. "Do you know what you're doing? Thousands of men are out there in the camp," he said, pointing behind him, "men who saved your life. They saved the lives of your sons and daughters, the lives of your wives and concubines—for what they're worth now. Do you care? No, you humiliate your warriors. You hate those who love you and lament those who hate you. Your Mighty Men, officers, slingers, and archers went out to die for you—it seemed *that* impossible. Jashobeam was hit hard. He'll never fight again. Ahithophel's son Eliam—"

Bathsheba let out a tortured cry. "My father *dead?*"

Joab spun around. "He might as well be." Again he faced David. "They mean nothing to you—no more than dogs in your sight. You'd be happier if Absalom were alive and the rest of us dead, and I suppose that includes yourself. Don't think for a minute that Absalom would have had any sentimental feelings toward his father if he'd won this war. And he well could've won it. Even with Obil's reinforcements, the outcome was far from sure. A freak accident! That's all it was—God's hand, if you will—that's how Absalom was brought down."

David leaned forward, his eyes thin columns, and in that moment made a decision that would ultimately cost yet another life. He said nothing of it, however, and his voice when he spoke was rapier sharp. "If I've been informed correctly, it wasn't God's hand."

"Yes, I killed Absalom. No one else had the stomach for it. God hung him up by his insufferable vanity. None of us would have thought of that. I just finished the job. The men of Israel turned tail, and your men came back here, the kingdom in their hands. The least you can do is get out there and say 'Thank you.' If you don't, I swear by God that not a man will be left here by nightfall. You think Absalom's death is bad. If the army leaves you here, everything else that's happened from your youth till now will seem as nothing. Think about it."

David did think, fury being a powerful stimulus to thought. Initially, it all centered on Joab's chronic ruthlessness. First Abner and Achish, then his part in Uriah's death, and now Absalom. But then his thoughts moved to Jashobeam and the tragedy of losing his services. He thought of Ittai, of Hurai and Elhanan who had brought him water from Bethlehem. He thought of Eleazar and Shammah and the years of close companionship. Joab was right, of course, and David hated him for it.

David rose and went to his room. In little more than an hour, he reappeared, washed, combed, and dressed in blue, purple, and scarlet—the finest of Abigail's robes. Every inch a king, David walked the entire distance from Kimham's house to the gateway of Mahanaim. His men heard the trumpet fanfare of victory and scrambled to come to him just before sunset. Line by line they passed by. Six young men bore a litter, on which Jashobeam lay more dead than alive. David knelt beside the old warrior. This mightiest of his *Gibborim*, who had once killed eight hundred in one encounter, reached a horn-hard hand to his sovereign's beard. "Davi," he whispered, then closed his eyes.

David leaped to his feet, his fists thrust into the golden sky, his grizzled head tipped back. "You are my body," he roared before the assembled troops, "my blood, my life. *I will not forget this day of victory!*"

Joab wasn't entirely accurate when he said that David's men had returned from battle with the kingdom in their hands. Nothing is ever that simple. In truth, the situation was delicate. A would-be monarch—even one seated for thirty years—could not simply muscle his way to the throne. Both Saul and David had been anointed long before the people had actually made them their kings. God calls; people eat the bread and salt of ratification. Absalom understood this and had carefully laid his base of good will.

The northern tribes of Israel fled from battle and went home to fight among themselves over David's suitability for leadership.

"He's too old," said some.

"But look what he did," said others. "He drove the Philistines out of our towns; he defeated the Arameans and the Ammonites. Yes, his son looked good, but now Absalom's dead; why shouldn't we get behind the victor?"

Sheba, having lost his second groomed champion, made a barely discernible shadow in these conversations as he slid from tent to tent, planting reasons to search for another king.

During this time of indecision, David fidgeted. Reports came in, and the northern tribes seemed better disposed toward David than his own people, who were still trying to sort out friend from foe in Jerusalem.

Finally, he sent Jonathan and Ahimaaz with a message for the elders of Judah. "Ask them what's holding up my return to Jerusalem. The Israelites seem to want me; why should my own brothers hedge on the matter? Tell Zadok and Abiathar to light a fire under them. And you," he said, turning abruptly to Ahimaaz, "tell Amasa I want to talk with him. He made a bad move with Absalom, but he's a good general—and a nephew I don't utterly detest." David's jaw jutted westward. "May God strike me down if I don't make Amasa commander in place of Joab!"

What David had decided in secret was finally out, and Ahimaaz's eyes became ripe figs. The implications of what he'd just heard David say—publicly, before advisors and officials, before Barzillai's son Kimham, before Benaiah, and before a handful of Mighty Men—took his breath away. *Joab* to be replaced by *Amasa*, a traitor who should rightly be killed instead of rewarded? Eyes still wide, Ahimaaz bowed and said, "Yes, my lord!" and grabbed Jonathan to begin the long jog.

The high-priestly prodding worked well. Within days, a delegation arrived with an official invitation. "The hearts of the men of Judah are as one in this: Return, O our king, to your throne in Jerusalem."

Within the hour, Joram began to pack.

The trip back, at least the first part, was as relaxed and comfortable as their flight had been miserable. Half of Mahanaim accompanied David to the southern ford. Barzillai rode his chair next to David's, but because of the old man's deafness, the two only smiled and nodded. Enough, though, for friends.

When they arrived at the ford near Gilgal, they halted in astonishment at the horde of people on the far side, some of whom had crossed over at sight of the king. These were friendly people; David saw this from Benaiah's guard who was greeting them and slapping backs. Yet, when the ropy shanks of his old gadfly Shimei, with what seemed to be an army of Benjamites, beat the water to froth and scrabbled up the bank, his head spun. Shimei was about to attack as he had at Bahurim, and the guards were just watching. Was that a bag of rocks under his cloak? David steeled himself at the little man's approach.

The goat-beard scarecrow threw himself before the king's chair, hands to his forehead. "Your servant Shimei *ben* Gera," he said. "O my lord the king, erase my guilt from your mind; forget my outrage the day my lord the king left Jerusalem. Woe is me, for I have done wrong in your sight, but today— today I come as firstfruits of the whole of Israel—the first to welcome my lord the king."

David got out of his chair to give himself a moment to assess this strange performance. "Dog pee!" muttered Abishai at his side, sword at the ready. "He cursed the Lord's anointed; let his head be firstfruits."

At this, David's inclination made a sudden, explosive shift in Shimei's favor. "Get away!" he roared at Abishai. "You and your bastard brother—my enemies from this day on. No one will be put to death today. These Benjamites have come to welcome me back as king of Israel, but you can only think of murder." He shoved Shimei roughly with his foot. "Get up, old man," he said. "You won't die, at least not today—I swear this by all that's holy."

Saul's old steward, Ziba, appeared, too, with fifteen sons, twenty servants, and obsequious, hands-on-forehead bowing. He offered to help get everyone and everything over the river. Coming as Ziba did on the heels of the Abishai blowup, the king's greeting was cool at best. Not seeing Mephibosheth anywhere, David was satisfied, at least for now, that he'd done right by the steward on the way out.

Mephibosheth did appear, though—suddenly, silently, after Ziba had been set to work. David fought the bile already high in his throat. *Another traitor with an eye to his neck.* He looked terrible—unwashed, untrimmed, his crippled feet dirty and bloodstained. His wife was with him, looking equally pathetic and carrying a small boy. He crept forward and bowed meekly before the king.

David, despite his ill humor, was touched. "Mephibosheth," he said softly, "why didn't you go with me? Why did you remain with Absalom?"

Mephibosheth looked up, aggrieved. "My lord! Look at me. From the day you left, I have been as you see. I was away when I heard about Absalom's rebellion. I gave the order to have my donkey saddled, hoping I could catch up with you. Then they told me what Ziba had said about me, and I dared not follow. I've been in mourning ever since." He looked full at the king's face, tears in his eyes. "When I think of what my lord the king has done for me…I deserved nothing but death, but you gave your servant a place at your table. You spared me from Gibeonite vengeance. You've been like an angel of God to me. But now—whatever pleases you, even if I die. I have no more appeals."

David grimaced in frustration. Why could he never sort out the truth with these two men? Mephibosheth seemed sincere, and Ziba was a consummate dealer. Still…

"All right," he said at last, "I gave your land to Ziba, but now the two of you will divide it." He lifted his chin defiantly against the weight of uncertainty.

Mephibosheth bowed again. "My lord, let Ziba keep it all. The important thing is my lord the king is safe."

David grasped his arm. "Half is yours once again—yours and your son's. I'm glad you stayed true to me, Mephibosheth." But as he spoke, a dissenting inner voice said, *Why, if he stayed true, did you give him back only half the land?*

Mephibosheth's family made their slow way back across the river, leaving David perched on a lump of injustice and wondering if Jonathan himself had spoken the words.

The farewells began. David could not persuade Barzillai to continue on with him. "No," the old man said, his eyes crinkling. "I'm eighty. How many years left to wait on you in Jerusalem? You don't need a fogy who can't see much and can't tell good food from bad. And I'd have to sit on your lap to hear you sing!"

David laughed. "Come, come! Eighty's not old. Look at Moses. He hardly got started till he was eighty."

"Ah, my friend, when you're eighty, we'll see how eager you are to play Moses! No, I'll go back and die in my own town. My daughters will look after me. Kimham, though…" He reached a trembling hand toward his son, whose eyes gleamed eagerly. "Take him with you. A fine man and worth six of me."

Parting was hard. Both men knew they would not likely see each other again. "I cannot tell you…" David began and could not continue.

Barzillai whispered brokenly, "Sheol's but a short stroll for us both; your fathers and my fathers wait there. Perhaps—" He broke off and smiled. "Perhaps they—and we—will know each other in that day. Until then, my friend…"

When did the mood shift begin to show itself? At first, as the caravan lumbered up the long incline from Gilgal to Jerusalem, men from all Israel came alongside, excitement growing with the size of the crowd.

Then suddenly, inexplicably, everything changed when a large knot of Israelites, as peevish as a wet lion, pushed forward. "Why weren't we told about this? You men of Judah are sneaking David home as though Israelites don't matter!"

"Of course you matter," said David's advisor Jonathan soothingly. "But the king is from Judah—reason enough to bring him back. Why are you upset? We're not getting anything out of this. We don't eat out of the king's larder!"

Some Benjamites joined the group, thrusting out elbows, chins, forefingers, and heels. Amasai prowled uneasily. "This is a setup," he muttered to Benaiah. "Who's behind it?"

"Huh," said Benaiah. "We should have to guess? It's definitely organized and growing by the minute."

A tribal leader from the north stepped forward. "Judah is one tribe. We're ten and have the greater claim. Should we allow one tribe to hold ten in contempt? We were first to talk of bringing the king back. You couldn't make up your minds, so—"

"You talked first, but we acted first!" bellowed a Judahite.

As the furious interchange went on, Benaiah got his men around the king.

Just then, behind the men of Israel, a trumpet sounded the signal to withdraw from a field of battle. Everyone whirled around to look. There on a rocky elevation, sun shining hard on his scarred cheek, stood Sheba *ben* Bicri, sustaining the final blast. Removing the trumpet from his lips, he shouted, "We have no share in David, no inheritance in Jesse's son! To your tents, all men of Israel!"

Maacah had not gone to Mahanaim with David. She was not well, and the trip might have killed her. And as Absalom's mother, she alone of David's wives and concubines had not been a symbol of conquest. She also hadn't stayed in the palace but went to Absalom's house instead, where her daughter Tamar, Absolom's sister, was still living. Her daughter-in-law, along with the child Tamar, had been there, too, but only until Absalom took over the palace. His mother and sister had been invited, but they'd chosen to remain at the house. I had stopped by occasionally to offer whatever comfort and assistance I could and was appalled at the decay of this once-proud woman. She had lost teeth as well as shape, and the unbearable tension of loyalty divided between husband and son had brought on a palsy that played its grim staccato over her body and spirit. Little remained of her former fire, and I pitied her particular tragedy.

Tamar, on the other hand, had remained strong throughout the ordeal. While she, too, had been divided between father and brother, her own personal ruin had given her perspective and patience, and she had been able to support her mother as needed.

When word arrived of the final outcome of the battle, both women had responded predictably: Maacah had collapsed with drama and pathos, while Tamar, after seeing to her mother's immediate needs, had gone to the Tent to worship.

As David made the final ascent to Bahurim and the Mount of Olives, I joined the welcoming host from the city that helped ease the sting of Sheba's treachery. He was disappointed not to see Hushai, but he kissed me and held me in a gratifyingly long embrace. As soon as I saw that he was well—in fact, more fit than he'd looked in years—I asked about Solomon.

He waved vaguely. "Back there somewhere. Hunting bugs under rocks. You know how he is."

David paused at the monument of stones Benaiah and his men had erected. With tears in his eyes, he sank to his knees and bowed low. "I will remember," his whispered.

When Zadok told him of Maacah's condition, David immediately went to his wife, perhaps to bring her back with him to the palace. She clung to him, and both wept afresh, but she was clearly not up to an impromptu move. Within a week, however, she did move back, and this time Tamar went along to care for her mother until she died a year later.

Hushai, with a boyish grin and a retinue of faithful servants, greeted David at the palace gate. In that exuberant ecstasy between the closest of friends—especially in light of Hushai's heroic performance—years seemed to drop from David, and I felt compelled to turn away and seek solace in Solomon's delight at being with me once again.

The palace, under Hushai's oversight, was in excellent condition. Some repairs had been necessary after Absalom, but these were hardly noticeable or—in the removal of a wall hanging I'd particularly despised—a decided improvement. The concubines waited for the king in near panic. Under the best of circumstances, a king's mistress could expect love and service only as long as her beauty lasted. These women, though, had been defiled; what would become of them? Yet David went to each in turn with thanks for managing the palace in his absence, listening, comforting, and finally explaining what must be done. They could not stay at the palace, but he would establish a house where they could live as protected widows with every reasonable want supplied for the remainder of their lives. He gave each a kiss and a straight look of love and regret, then resolutely turned them over to the chief eunuch. He never saw them again.

Amasa was the next order of business. Absalom's general entered the throne room guardedly, mistrustful of Ahimaaz's tittle-tattle about pardon and elevation to commander in chief. He did know of David's loathing for Joab and that this was not the first time Joab had been shown the door. But he also understood his cousin's ruthless fondness for power. David's whimsy might rest, after all, on Joab's chicanery.

But Joab was not in the room, and Amasa took heart. David got right to the point. After a *pro forma* lecture on loyalty and mistakes of judgment, he gave his orders. "You are now commander in chief of both the militia and the standing army. We face a national crisis. I want you to muster the men of Judah to go after Sheba. He wouldn't have made his move if he didn't have men behind him. Get seventy-five thousand or more; have them assembled within three days. And be here yourself. Is that clear?"

"Yes, my lord." Amasa bowed.

"Time is critical. *Don't* make Absalom's mistake." He looked hard at Amasa.

The general took on an injured air. "My lord, by all that's holy, I told him—"

David waved placatingly. "I know. You weren't listened to, nor was Ahithophel. Only Hushai here had the voice of an angel."

Hushai snorted. "More the voice of Balaam's donkey. It was God who spoke. Like Ahithophel said in his note, any dolt should have seen through the ploy. Give credit where it belongs."

David moved Amasa toward the door. "Speed, Amasa— God's and yours."

Ahimaaz could have told David that punctuality was not Amasa's strong point, but the king learned that himself when Amasa failed to appear within the three days. After fretting half a day, David called for Abishai. "We've got to move. If we wait longer, Sheba may do even more damage than Absalom. He's plowed ground for years, and from every intelligence, the whole of Israel is his flock of sheep. You take over Joab's men; Joab goes on the tradesmen militia."

Abishai's mouth twitched. "The overripe fruits."

"You got it. A challenge for his leadership. But Abishai—get Sheba before he holes up in some fortified city."

Both Abishai and Benaiah were nervous about Joab's reaction to David's ruling, but he merely shrugged and tapped his own armorbearers, including Naharai and the fleet Cushite.

The elite corps that had been Joab's arms and legs for so many years wasn't happy about this change, and their grumbling stopped just short of ugliness. It wasn't that they disliked Abishai—they respected him as second only to Joab himself. But loyalty in the military is a mysterious commodity as important as the size and skill of any given unit.

David's army, then, grumbled its way to the great rock at Gibeon where they spied Amasa approaching with a disappointingly small force—barely fifteen thousand. Abishai halted, and Joab came up beside him. "Not many," Joab said, "but a fair replacement for my toadstools. They had trouble climbing to the rock here. We'll send them home."

Abishai studied the approaching general. "Just who's in charge now?"

Joab's left eye circled, but he said only, "It'll work out."

Amasa drew near, and Joab went forward to greet him. As Joab stepped over a protruding rock, his arm caught his ivory-handled dagger, and the knife clattered to the ground. With a smooth movement, he retrieved it with his left hand, then reached with his right to grasp Amasa's beard. "Cousin! You've come at last. Is everything well? We were worried."

They exchanged kisses. Then Joab's beard hand tightened, and his well-practiced dagger wrenched upward in the belly opposite. With scarcely a sound, the rival for Joab's position dropped out of the contest, intestines oozing onto the ground.

It happened so quickly that only the nearest soldiers saw. All of these—even Abishai—stood dumbfounded, caught between the unreality on the ground and the casual chatter still going on behind. Joab wiped his knife with studied care, then signaled the Cushite to remain by the body and keep things moving. He put trumpet to his lips, and the march resumed.

The Cushite had his hands full. The shock of seeing the slain general brought everything to a crawl. After trying to hustle the army along, he finally dragged Amasa's body off the road, covering it with his cloak. Then the lines moved freely, with most men unaware of the assassination until they camped that evening. Half the night was spent in talk. The military structure was back to normal, but "normal" now had a strange taste.

The trek through the rock-strewn hills of Benjamin caused concern about what they might be up against. A number of clansmen had followed Sheba—the start of what Joab feared might be an immense army. But as they pushed north, opposition amounted to little more than name-calling and rock throwing.

North, always north. Sheba was not hard to follow; few along the way tried to deceive them. Finally they neared the border and found, as David had feared, that Sheba had holed up in the fortified city of Abel Beth Maacah on the river plain in Naphtali, not far from the city of Dan.

Joab surveyed the city with Abishai and Benaiah. "A single wall, but well made; strong gate. It'll be a job."

"We can handle it," said Abishai. "A ramp there," He said, pointing. "Trees for rams, good elevation to shoot from. It'll take time, but we'll dig the jackal out."

Battering corps worked one gate and an old, weakened section of the wall. The defenders were able to pick off a number of attackers, but Abel Beth Maacah was no Rabbah, and a breach was inevitable.

Looking on was a woman of the city noted for her wisdom. She was the quiet sort, choosing not to speak her piece until long after the intentions of the invading army were clear, and the slow work of constructing a siege ramp had neared completion. It was then that the wise woman took matters into her own hands. The sun had set, the warriors were tired and bloody, the defenders thankful for one more night of safety. As both sides trudged toward food and rest, a woman's voice sounded from atop the wall.

"Please listen to me!"

Joab and Abishai whirled around, while three thousand archers reached for one more arrow.

"My lord Joab!" the voice called.

Joab signaled his men to wait. "What is it you want?" he called to the woman.

"Are you Joab?"

"Yes. What do you want?"

"I want to know what you want." She spoke slowly and distinctly. "People used to say, 'Go to Abel for wisdom,' and that usually settled the matter. We're a peaceful people, mothers of the faithful in Israel. Yet here you are, trying to destroy us. Why do you want to swallow *Yahweh's* inheritance like a lion swallows a hare?"

Joab and Abishai looked at each other. Was it possible the inhabitants didn't know why the city was under siege? Was no one even aware of Sheba and his followers?

"Not us!" shouted Joab. "Destroying innocent people is furthest from our minds."

Amasai choked and had to turn away.

"We only want one man. Sheba *ben* Bicri lifted up his heel against David and against the kingdom. Hand over that man, and we'll be gone by noon tomorrow."

In the twilight, they could see the woman turn to confer with someone.

"One man?" she called. "That's all you want?"

"That's all. Give us Sheba, and we'll leave."

Another small silence, and the woman spoke again. "Can you wait a few minutes until we find him? What does he look like?"

The brothers shook their heads in disbelief. "A man of some fifty-five years," shouted Joab. "A sword once parted the left side of his beard. You may not see his eyes this time of night, but beware: they cut deeper than a knife. And take whatever time you need to find Sheba *ben* Bicri. We've waited a mere thirty years."

The woman stepped down, and for nearly an hour, they heard little but owl conversation and antiphonal cries of "*Hoo-ha-ha-ha!*" over scattered sheepfolds. But as the waning moon rose orange over the distant river, a stir within the city brought them to their feet. Shouts and cries followed by cheering gave notice that something was indeed happening. Within minutes, a male voice probed the darkness. "My lord Joab! We have the head of Sheba *ben* Bicri. How will you find it in the dark?"

Abishai turned to confer, but Joab replied immediately. "Wrap it in white cloth. The moonlight will tell us where to look. If it is as you say, we'll leave you in peace."

It was as the men of Abel said. Within this bastion of peace, the predator who had nipped David's flank for thirty years was brought down. With a final blessing on the city's wise woman, Joab dismissed his troops and headed home, comfortable once again in his cloak of command.

24

No one knows just why he did it, but I have a theory.

David's order to count the fighting men of Judah and Israel was so out of character that even Joab went nose to nose with him over it. "You want *me* to go through the whole country just so somebody can write impressive numbers on your scrolls? Are you out of your mind?"

"No, I'm not out of my mind. I need to know this. And since you haven't quite taken over the throne, I'd appreciate your obeying my order."

A vein in Joab's forehead pulsated, but he backed off and walked around the room. Noting dismay among the Mighty Men in the room, he halted once more. "Consider what you're doing, *Hamelech* David." The title dug. "You have rest from your enemies. You've extended and secured your borders. Every man of us can sit in peace under his fig tree. What more do you want? Still bigger armies?" He moved to within inches of the king's face. "Numbering the fighting men is—*sin*." The word fell like a loathsome toad. "Ask your *Gibborim*, if my saying so doesn't suit. Judah and Israel have enough on their heads after their frolic with Absalom and Sheba. Maybe that's what this is about, after all. God wants to get back at the nation, so he lets you wallow on a dung heap called pride to justi—"

David hurled himself from his chair with a force that put Joab off balance. *"Don't talk to me about sin and pride, you bloated pig!* You'll do what I order, and you'll see that the Mighty Men do it, too." The king's hand inched toward the dagger in his belt as though wishing desperately to use it, but the battle remained at eye level until, with a venomous glare, Joab peeled away and stalked out.

None of David's counselors favored the census and said so in an array of colors, but David would not be moved. For whatever reason, he'd made up his mind, and that was the end of it.

I've thought long about the matter. At first, I, too, thought it a matter of pride. But in reviewing the preceding months, I uncovered possible clues.

After David's return to Jerusalem following Absalom's defeat, he was subdued and introspective. He continued to mourn, though he did so quietly. Only once did he refer to Absalom or indicate how he felt. We had been talking about the coming Passover, and I had remarked about the shortage of unblemished lambs. "Every one I look at," I said, "seems to have a torn ear or slashed wool." I was about to make a joke of it, but the king grew solemn and said, "My lamb had no blemish. Not a mark on him, from head to toe. And his hair...he never liked to trim it, you know. 'I'm like Samson,' he'd say. 'My hair is my strength.'" David sighed, then said, "A perfect lamb..."

He was quiet a moment, then incongruously brought up his contest with Goliath. "A silly, cocksure boy, full of brash, noble words. I was young and strong and loved God passionately, but I didn't know much about him. And I hadn't ever failed."

Someone had said that about Absalom, but I couldn't remember whom.

He looked at me, pain dulling the watery blue of his eyes. "Was Absalom any cockier than I? If God was able to work his will through me, why couldn't he have done so with Absalom?"

The answer was obvious, but I said nothing.

The silence lengthened until David began to sing.

> Trust in the Lord and do good;
> > Dwell in the land and enjoy safe pasture.
> Delight yourself in the Lord
> > and He will give you the desires of your heart.
> I was young and now I am old,
> > yet I have never seen the righteous forsaken
> > or their children begging bread.
> They are always generous and lend freely;
> > Their children will be blessed.

I closed my eyes. This tiny act of worship sketched in clear, deft strokes the vast difference between father and son. The poignancy of the moment tore my soul. This was not the heart of a man who sought to puff himself up by numbering his troops.

Then, too, he had become almost obsessive about the temple his son would build. Which son that would be didn't seem to trouble him. Adonijah *ben* Haggith was next in line, followed by Shephatiah *ben* Abital, should anything befall Adonijah. I, of course, hoped that somehow Solomon would rise to the top. "In building the temple," said David, "my son will finish my task as Joshua finished Moses' when he conquered the Promised Land. Worship, Asaph, high, holy worship, is the lifeblood of a nation. Without it, the temple might as well house idols."

With the help of Nathan and Gad, we envisioned temple worship. I, along with Ethan and Heman, would oversee two hundred and eighty-eight musicians. Priests, Levites, and singers would serve in rotational divisions for temple duties— duties that would require four thousand instrumentalists and four thousand gatekeepers. The scope and thoroughness of David's planning—to say nothing of his vision—was beyond belief.

"From the city wall," he declared with seeming irrelevance.

We looked at him.

"Be sure my successor protects the temple. All that gold... the wall will need to be expanded, you know, to enclose the temple."

Where was he going with this? Where, exactly, did he see the temple located? Obviously outside the present wall.

"I can see that new wall with a thousand, maybe two thousand singers on top, worshipping *Yahweh*." The rest of us looked at each other in breathless shock.

The stockpile of precious materials grew along with Solomon. A budding man by this time, he loved to scramble among the heaps of gold and silver and bronze in the storehouses. David noted with satisfaction that the value of these goods mattered

less to the boy than did their beauty—the spicy scent of cedar, the luster of precious metals, the individuality of jewels.
One day as they studied David's temple drawings together,
Solomon drew his finger down the great pillars. "They're so
big! They should have names, *Abba*."

"Oh? What would you call them?"

"This one would be Asaph, and this one Boaz."

David sat silently, his arm tight around the lad. His voice
was husky when he spoke. "You've made two people very happy, son, whether or not it works out as you say."

David had already appointed metalworkers for the temple.
He had lists for everything: the weight of gold for lampstands
and tables and altars, the weight of silver for dishes and other
articles. As each piece was finished, it was placed in a new
storehouse, and at that point, David began to worry. Guards
were posted, of course—almost as many as around the palace
itself. But he worried less about petty theft than about the
safety of the entire city. His insistence on a new wall indicated
a more pervasive fear. And this, I believe, is what prompted his
bizarre decision to number the troops.

The security of Jerusalem became obsessive, driving him
past prudence. If Joab had not been the first to point out possible sin in the matter—had it been Amasai or Ira, say—David might have listened to reason. The true source of David's
damning pride in the business of numbering stemmed from
his fierce determination never to bow before Joab's advice. He
would not listen to reason, and the wheels of disaster began
to turn.

D avid was given a specific amount of time to contemplate the hazards of not trusting God to protect Jerusalem: nine months and twenty days, to be exact, the time required to complete the census. One day during that time, he asked me to read from the Law, "where it talks about census taking."

I fetched the scroll, *These Are the Names,* and found the place.

> When you take a census of the Israelites to count
> them, each one must pay the Lord a ransom for his life
> at the time he is counted. Then no plague will come
> on them when you number them. Each...is to give a
> half shekel, according to the sanctuary shekel...as an
> offering to the Lord.

"And that's it?" he asked.

"No, I believe there's another word that ties census taking to the army." I took the scroll called *The Lord Spoke* and read the beginning.

> The Lord spoke to Moses in the Tent of Meeting
> in the Desert of Sinai on the first day of the second

> *month of the second year after the Israelites came out*
> *of Egypt. He said: "Take a census of the whole Israelite*
> *community by their clans and families, listing every*
> *man by name, one by one. You and Aaron are to*
> *number...all the men in Israel twenty years old or more*
> *who are able to serve in the army. One man from each*
> *tribe, each the head of his family, is to help you."*

For the first time, David looked plainly worried. "I may have done it wrong, Asaph. For one thing, we're not collecting the tax for the Tent. Then, tribesmen aren't doing the counting— just Joab and his men." His eyes grew large and anxious. "Remember the Ark?" he whispered.

Remember the Ark! Who could forget? That debacle came from just such inattention to detail. My gut feeling, though, recognized a difference. Moving the Ark to Jerusalem was a good, wise thing to do; counting the fighting men of Israel and Judah without the Lord's specific instruction was not, and niggling over counters and taxes missed the point. I couldn't say this out loud, but as the months passed, David got the message on his own.

The death of Eleazar at the Tent in Gibeon was the first nail in David's flesh, the firstfruits of what was to come. This closest, most beloved of David's warriors, second only to Jashobeam in heroic exploits, had taken ill, gone to the high place to make sacrifice, and collapsed over the animal he had just slain. Ira, who broke the news, had to repeat it several times before David would accept it. *Eleazar!* His shield, his right arm, his heart and mind. Warm, ugly, caring Eleazar. How could he be gone? After that, nothing could persuade David to travel to Gibeon for any amount of sacrificing.

The arrival of the prophet Gad was unsettling, as well. The seer came infrequently and unexpectedly but, unlike Nathan, was invariably cheerful. I always loved to hear of his arrival, for he spent much of his time with us musicians, and we were always the richer for it. I enjoyed just looking at him—his round, chinless face; mirthful eyes the color of fresh-baked bread; skin the color of honey; and bony arms that stuck out from his round body. God's sunbeam in a straw basket! Gad seemed to have no particular message this time for David, but his very presence set off ominous overtones in the king's heart.

When Joab and his men finally reappeared, David could hardly bring himself to face them. He sat stricken as they reported their zigzag course through all the tribes. As they read them aloud, the numbers lay like jagged rocks on his soul. "Eight hundred thousand able-bodied men who can handle a sword in Israel, five hundred thousand in Judah. There, my lord the king, a fine militia to feast upon. *May it stick in—*"

Benaiah stepped in front of Joab with a sword not visible, and Joab broke off, bowed curtly, and left.

David himself left soon after and went straight to the Tent. Under a protective cover of dust and ashes, he lay prostrate before the Lord.

> *Look at me, O Lord.*
> *Look on this fool with Your great compassion.*
> *A sin that seemed no bigger than a gnat*
>   *is now a scorpion.*
> *Against You alone have I sinned*
>   *and done this foolish thing in Your sight.*

> *Lord God of grace and mercy,*
> *Take away the guilt of Your servant.*

Gad was sitting cross-legged in the king's outer room when David arose next morning. The seer was smiling as usual, but David's heart turned to ice.

"Go." Gad waved airily. "Wash. Dress. I'll wait."

But David moved toward him warily. "Why are you here?"

"A bit of breakfast first. Then we'll talk."

"No. We'll talk now. You have a word from the Lord."

Gad looked directly at David, eyes not wavering, then sighed. "Bad news always tastes better after breakfast."

"Speak!"

Gad popped to his feet and bowed. "My lord the king, you have three intolerable choices. Which of them would you prefer: three years of famine across the land, three months of hot pursuit by enemy swords, or three days under the sword of plague? None of these are happy prospects, my lord, but that's the way of sin. Gnaw on them, if you won't have breakfast, and let me know so I can answer the Creature who woke me out of a dead sleep last night." His words and tone were light, but his eyes held fathomless love and compassion, and David could only fall to his knees.

Gad prepared to withdraw, but David pulled himself up, eyes red and face white. "My heart is so full of distress that I can no longer think. No man could choose among those judgments. I can choose only to fall into the hands of God, rather than man, for His mercy is great. I have no other recourse...."

He dropped to his knees and lifted his arms imploringly. "*Oh, that God would wear the face of love!*" His shoulders, grown narrow and old, bent low and heaved under soundless sobs. Gad lay his younger, stronger hand on the king's head, then withdrew from the room.

The plague started across the river to the east of Jerusalem. It entered on a hot, dry sirocco from the desert and traced the route that Joab and his census takers had taken to the north, turning westward to the Great Sea, down through the northern tribes, through Judah to Beersheba, and finally back toward Jerusalem.

David and the elders were beside themselves with grief. They lay in sackcloth in front of the Tent, then went to the city gate, which finally had to be closed against the hordes of people irrationally hoping for a measure of safety within the fortress.

David took the elders to his rooftop terrace to pray over the city, and there they saw it. Their eyes, hooded against the searing wind, had been sweeping the northeast quadrant of their circle of prayer, over the Mount of Olives, and past the road to Bahurim. When they looked north, David's face turned to chalk, and the elders cried out in terror and fell on their faces. As in a dream, David pushed past the greenery edging the terrace and gripped the balustrade so tightly the skin on his hands broke open. "My Lord!" His voice ranged through creaks and rattles in just those two words, and for a moment, no other sound would come out. He sank to his knees but could not take his eyes off the apparition hovering above Mt. Moriah.

"Is it gone?" asked one of the elders through chattering teeth.

David didn't answer. "My Lord!" he shouted with all his strength. "Can You see me? Can You hear—?" The vision moved almost imperceptibly, and David's heart thudded in such a powerful response that he clutched his chest. He struggled on. "Look at me! It was I who ordered the fighting men to be counted, I who sinned, I who did wrong. O Lord my God, let Your sword fall on me and my family, not on these poor sheep." His hand took in the prostrate forms behind him and the whole of the city, as well. "Let them go. Remove the plague from them. O Lord God..." He sank down, sobbing, his legs no longer able to support him.

How long he lay crumpled he couldn't say, but suddenly Gad was shaking him. "Get up!" he commanded, his voice still jovial. "What did you see?"

David badly wanted to laugh. He wanted to say, "No wonder you couldn't sleep!" Mirth was inappropriate right then, but still he felt like laughing. Perhaps if he giggled, the angel would catch him up with that dreadful sword and flip him like a plaything, over and over. This Angel of Death had brought down how many thousands in three days? Perhaps he was not so far removed from life, after all.

In reality, David didn't have the strength to laugh. Gad pulled him up and half carried him indoors, past the elders, who were still on their faces. "You saw him," Gad said. "Did he speak?"

David shook his head.

"Well, he did to me. I heard the Lord's voice say, 'Enough! Withdraw your hand!' That's all. And that's when the angel appeared on Mt. Moriah. Big, wasn't he?" He grinned. "How'd you like a sword like that? Makes Goliath's look like a tooth scraper."

David no longer felt like laughing. Perhaps the angel had moved on. How much of human cheer was dependent on angels?

"Come," said Gad, "you're to go to Mt. Moriah, to the threshing floor of Araunah the Jebusite. You're to build an altar there. Come, man; stand up. Pull yourself together. I'll resurrect the elders. If you don't get over there, Araunah will turn to yogurt."

Araunah was already yogurt. The looming apparition that seemed part fire and part jasper had caused him and his sons to forever forswear their Canaanite roots.

When Araunah saw David, the elders, Abiathar and other priests, plus a contingent of guardsmen, he crept from behind a heap of grain. His sons remained buried. He fell before the king and clutched reflexively at the straw-covered ground.

David's voice was far from steady when he greeted the Jebusite. "We saw the Destroyer, too. We saw the line of death drawn across your threshing floor. And here I must build an altar before he erases the line and the plague sweeps us away. Will you give me your threshing floor, Araunah? I will pay for it, of course."

The old man dipped in pathetic eagerness. "It's yours! *Take it*, O lord the king! Take what pleases you. What else do you want? Oxen for sacrifice...where'd they go? Even they saw it!" His eyes took on the rabbity look of Abiathar. "They won't of gone far. And wood. The threshing sledge. And wheat for the grain offering. Fine wheat. I *give* it to you, my lord the king. Not a shekel for it will I take."

This seemed like the start of reverse bargaining, but no one could misinterpret the Jebusite's sincerity on this occasion.

Anything that would ward off another visitation was already a bargain, in his mind.

David shook his head. "No, I will pay. In full." He closed his eyes, an incalculable weight of sorrow adding measurably to the burden of his years. He looked again at Araunah. "I will pay," he said more firmly. "This must be my offering, not yours. Can I give to the Lord something not mine, an offering that costs me nothing?"

With an anxious look at the sky behind him, Araunah accepted David's six hundred gold shekels. At Araunah's command, his sons crept from their lair to pursue the frightened oxen and prod their reluctant return.

Meanwhile, David paced the hilltop as though measuring the land, his color returning and an added glint to his eye. For the first time, he saw a connecting thread, albeit thin, between the current calamity and his temple dream. He directed the placement of stones for the altar on a particular spot, as though this, too, had been lined out by the angel. When the reluctant beasts appeared, all was ready. Abiathar slew the first ox and prayed over it, David the second, and the priests butchered and heaved heavy pieces of burnt offering onto the sputtering fire of the altar.

While the priests worked on the second ox, David cried to the Lord.

> *O Lord, do not rebuke me in your anger*
> *or discipline me in your wrath.*
> *For your arrows have pierced—*

He stopped abruptly, eyes popping open. He felt the familiar tingle of the ephod, the dangerous smell around Uzzah as he lay dead after touching the ark, and the incongruous sensation of strength and well-being that the Angel of Death had left on him. David dropped to the ground, writhing against a new immanence of holiness—and just in time. Was it lightning? Was it God's own hand? Whatever it was, it reached down, and in seconds, the meat of those great oxen was reduced to ash.

The plague was over. David had been forgiven. That much was clear. "I can think of less frightening ways to communicate pardon," said Gad afterwards. "If God could write notes to Moses on stone, a little scroll for you shouldn't have been a problem."

David was a new man from that day forward. The vision, the altar, and the fire from heaven all pointed in one direction: *The temple was to be built on Araunah's threshing floor.* He knew that as well as he knew his wives' names. The great irony lay in his own sin becoming the catalyst for such a revelation. The glorious temple he envisioned would stand as a monument, not to Law and death and tears but to grace and mercy and laughter. It would stretch far beyond his few remaining years to generations untold. "'Decide whom you want to serve'— Joshua's words, Asaph. 'But as for me...'" He pulled himself from the chair and stood tall, eyes glittering across the years. "*I will serve the Lord.*"

26

As large as my basket of scrolls has grown—three baskets, actually—I have the feeling that I've captured only the bare outline of David's life. I've said almost nothing about the great celebrations full of feasting and singing and dancing; or the nighttime solemnities, processing to the Tent with lamps and flutes and song; or the times of holy introspection, of fear and awe before a God who touches people with death and laughter, all in the same breath.

I've all but ignored David's parental family and his early years among large and capable brothers and sisters. I've said little of his parents' deaths and of the passage of his siblings.

I could probably write another entire account of warrior-king logistics: how he scheduled time with each wife and concubine and managed to keep them happy most of the time; the farm and livestock system that stocked the palace and fed the army; offensive and defensive arms, the making of even one war's worth of arrows, supply depots around the country; the education and religious instruction of his children; Sabbath observance; and on and on. So many areas of inquiry, so little time to record them all.

I have tried to portray David as the first national leader in centuries who truly understood Israel's holy destiny. An unparalleled *gibbor*, a mighty warrior who fought only in the name of and for the honor of God, he freed the nation from its enemies, completing the task begun by Moses and Joshua. He also drew tribal factions together—an even more daunting task. The nation of Israel, a land flowing with milk and honey, was finally beginning to look and act like the treasured possession God had claimed through Abraham and redeemed from Egypt.

Especially close to my heart was David's recovery of the worship of God that had become tarnished during the dark days of the judges and of Saul. He gave the Ark a temporary home and drew up plans for a permanent one. To his son, he left a great body of psalmody, along with an extraordinary model for worship and the Levitical organization to administer it.

In the public realm, he was a true shepherd, leading his flock along safe pathways to green pastures and quiet waters. He administered courts of justice, developed commerce, and appointed superintendents of agriculture and animal husbandry. His personal guard and standing army were second to none.

He was *Hamelech* David, Goliath of Goliaths, his throne too large for ordinary sovereigns to sit on without their feet dangling disgracefully short of the floor. Even Solomon, gifted as he is, is not like his father, and already I see some of the father's weakness in a vessel not half so tough or expansive. And who after Solomon will measure up? His firstborn, Rehoboam? While I may be least among the king's seers, I feel the world will wait long until one comes along who is truly large enough to sit comfortably on that throne.

David's final years were peaceful. For one thing, Abishai died, and David mourned him eagerly. Two more of his wives died, as well—Amnon's mother, Ahinoam (David's second wife), and Haggith, mother of Adonijah. Some say she was the last restraining influence on her feckless son, for David never interfered with his activities, even after the lessons of Amnon and Absalom. The king still maintained a routine with his remaining wives and three new concubines, though much of it, I suspect, was show and comfort. *Age decrees: men are gelded by degrees.*

The love of his heart remained Bathsheba. Whatever her intellectual shortcomings, she had been a satisfying, undemanding wife. She of the smoky eyes and fluid personality could snuggle into the jagged contours of David's imposing individualism, and the illicit blaze that flared that fateful night so long ago did in fact weld a bond of love that remained strong until the king died.

Solomon, of course, remained David's pride and joy, and I cannot count the times he commended me for building a "strong tower," a son he could be proud of.

By the time Adonijah made his play for the throne, David was scarcely able to make decisions. Adonijah, like Absalom, adorned himself with chariots and men to run before him and was incensed when few bothered to look. He presumed that his roguish, toned beauty, his velvety voice, and his grasp of kingdom affairs would impress others as much as he impressed himself. Popping knuckles, though, draw the wrong sort of attention.

The day came when people had to pay attention. A crown appeared on Adonijah's head, and the most unlikely collaborators—Joab and Abiathar—had put it there. This relationship was, of course, strictly pragmatic. Joab would as soon step on Abiathar as claim his friendship. But Joab needed a high priest to fulfill the Law's requirements for kingmaking, and Abiathar was more pliable than Zadok.

Nathan turned things around. Matters at the time were touchy in the palace. With David in bed and sinking out of competency, Bathsheba mourned the failing power of her charms. He had not asked for her in over three weeks. She did little to hide her feelings, becoming frowzy, puffy, and sallow, but nobody cared. David's favorite wife no longer counted for anything. If the king was too busy dying to see to her needs, why should the people she'd walked over for twenty-odd years feel sorry for her?

Nathan, though, saw in Bathsheba a means of breaking into the king's deathbed agenda. He had her brought to him, and with his usual charm and tact, said, "You look like a rotting grape. Take off that purple rag and make yourself presentable—no, make yourself beautiful. You snared the king once; do it again. The challenge is greater this time, and the stakes are higher, so dress as though your life depends on it—because it does."

Bathsheba's eyes widened, her mouth forming an all-encompassing question. Nathan spun her around and thundered, "Go! Dress! I'll tell you later what to say."

Bathsheba dressed, and by all accounts it was her finest hour, perhaps her moment of destiny. She flowed into the king's chamber with the command of a queenly, well-seasoned harlot.

She got his attention. Her scent spoke to him, and his eyes, if not his body, sat up.

After they had communed and the time was right—again, Bathsheba's fine art—she knelt beside his bed, an age-stippled hand between hers. "My lord," she said, "didn't you tell me your son Solomon would be king after you? Didn't you say that?"

David stroked her tinted cheek and murmured absently, "Yes, yes. I did."

He was not paying attention.

"But my lord, behind Solomon's back—behind your back—Joab and Abiathar have set up Adonijah as king." The name *Joab* earned her a flash of animation. "I'm told they're sacrificing every calf and sheep in the city, and if the son of Haggith does become king, what will become of Solomon? What will become of me?" The sword at Bathsheba's own neck pricked open a well of tears.

David leaned to comfort her, and just then Nathan entered and confirmed Bathsheba's report. In moments, the king was galvanized, and he summoned Zadok and Benaiah. Feeble though David was, they took him to his throne, where he sat with little propping. Servants scurried to light wall sconces, but the room seemed stuffy, unused, empty of life. David spoke in a surprisingly strong voice. "Set Solomon on my mule and take him to the spring Gihon. There Zadok and Nathan will anoint him king over Israel. Then blow the trumpet and start the shout, 'Long live King Solomon!' Bring him here and place him on my throne to reign in my place. And," he added irritably, "get air or spices in here. Where's Abigail when I need her?"

Benaiah whooped. "Amen for the new king! As *Yahweh* has been with my lord the king, so may he be with Solomon. May his throne be even greater than the throne of *Hamelech* David." He bowed, then looked into the king's face, eyes wet. David reached out a trembling hand and gripped Benaiah, long and hard. "Leave the mule to the others, Benaiah, and take me back to bed."

While this was going on, Adonijah was busy with his own coronation festivities—until Joab jabbed him. "Shut up a minute. A noise from the city. Listen!" He held his breath, body stiff as from a dagger touching his belly.

As they listened, the high priest's son Jonathan jogged into view. Jonathan, now in full manhood, had demanded the privilege of informing Adonijah out of anger over his father's treachery and a delicious sense of irony.

Adonijah motioned. "Come, son of Abiathar! A good man brings good news. Already they're celebrating in town; we can hear it. Is word spreading that I'm king? Or are you looking for your father?"

"No on both accounts," Jonathan answered, breathing hard. "David just made Solomon king. You haven't a chance, Adonijah," he told him, "even with Joab and my father. A consummate team, don't you think? Run to the Tent, Adonijah. Solomon might let his brother live—for a day or two."

Adonijah turned white and Abiathar even whiter. They both looked at Joab, but the general, again relaxed, rolled his eyes and shrugged fatalistically. In that moment, Adonijah knew he'd lost his gamble. He took off in a dead run and headed straight for the Tent of the Ark to claim sanctuary at the altar.

He did stay alive until after David's death—until he asked Bathsheba to intercede for the hand of Abishag, David's beautiful young bed warmer, under the premise that he who mounts the king's consort mounts the throne. That brought both him and Joab down at last, as I recounted in my first scroll.

The day before David died, he called me to his bedside. "Asaph, my friend." My heart leapt at the word. "So busy, yet you came, and on such a cold day!"

I smiled under the oppressive warmth of his bedroom. Abishag, his beautiful attendant, replaced cooled footstones with hot ones.

"You're looking well today, my king," I said, grasping at straws in the presence of death.

"Humph! A man whose remaining time...is numbered in hours can't be said...to look well. Don't waste breath. I need... two things, Asaph: a listening ear...and a writing hand. Will you grant these?"

"My lord, you know I'd do anything for—"

He waved me off impatiently but lay in silence, looking at me with a certain sadness, wishing, perhaps, for simpler footing?

My heart pounded at this unforeseen opportunity. Might I sweep aside protocol on the occasion of death? I looked around. Abishag had left the room, and the guards outside were not peering through the lattice as they sometimes did.

I leaned in closely and dared to clasp his hand. "David, my... friend!" My voice was unsteady in this first speaking of his name in his presence. Could he hear my whisper? Was the tremor in his hand or mine? I waited with a sense of panic.

For what? Was I expecting him to leap out of bed and embrace me as he might have Jonathan or Hushai? Or did I simply want him to say he loved me, that I was indeed his friend? It was enough that he returned my clasp, that he didn't call Benaiah to throw me out. He lay with eyes closed, seemingly content with my company.

After a few moments, guttural rumbles creaked into speech. "Forty years, Asaph. A long time...to be king. I've known you long. Hours...talking, making music, writing songs for each other."

My heart swelled; I gritted my teeth to stay the tears.

He cleared his rattling throat. "But what has life amounted to? I've worked, fought, sung, made love...ruled, lived in a palace. But *why*, Asaph, why so blessed? My sins...moving the Ark...Uzzah. And Uriah...good *gibbor*, bad husband. I loved her, Asaph. Bathsheba—always, always the face of love. Not like Abigail. God could have taken Bathsheba instead of Boaz, but he didn't." Sadness gathered in his face. "He took Boaz, he took Amnon, he took Absalom... And what of Adonijah? Abigail was right—they weren't handled well. They had...too much, too early.

He lay there a moment, sifting through shadows. "The foolish numbering," he went on. "And Joab. Honorable men...murdered, and I did...nothing." His voice dropped to a tormented whisper. "I *needed* him, Asaph; do you see that? My sword, my throne. We didn't need chariots; we had Joab and Abishai. I've told...I said, 'Put him down, Solomon.' Benaiah will back the boy. Benaiah's stronger than I. He'll have the gumption to drag him from the altar, if it comes to that." He lay quietly for a moment. "That's where he'll go, you know. If all else fails, he'll climb the altar steps. A fox, twisting, doubling back." His face twisted with loathing. "Joab—"

"My lord, more cheerful things to talk about?"

David tried to sit up. "Old soldiers make mistakes," he said as though stumbling upon some missing treasure. "Old soldiers make mistakes; he said that!"

"Who, my lord?"

"Joab. When four hundred Amalekites and their camels escaped from Dodai. And I said to Joab, 'You'll remember those words.' He's made his mistake, Asaph; now make him remember. Tell him—" He collapsed back and closed his eyes.

Abishag came with a drink and another change of stones. As she went out the door, he pointed a shaky finger and said, "Adonijah'll want her, you know. And he'll use a mouthpiece— the king's mother, perhaps... Don't speak of it now. Just remember who told you."

He stared at the ceiling. "These things haunt me, Asaph. I tell them to no one—not to Ira nor Hushai. If Abigail were here... Tell me, Asaph. Have I become...like Joab?"

"No, no, my lord! Not in any way."

"Do my confessions burden you?"

I leaned forward and pressed his hand. "My lord, I only wish I had words—"

"Words, Asaph. In our youth, they were gold, but old age...a man's *heart*—that's where the sum of his life rests." He turned his plangent, watery eyes on me. "Tomorrow is Passover. You know, I was a lamb to be slaughtered in those wilderness years. Later, my own lamb...taken from me. I asked a child's Passover question, 'What does it mean?' Tell me, Asaph, what *does* it mean?"

The question startled me. My mouth opened ineffectively, but he went on. "It means, Asaph...the angel of death passed over me. Not in battle, not during the plague, but...passed over *my sins*. Forgiven, Asaph. That's what Passover means. I see them, Asaph." His eyes probed the ceiling.

"Your...sins, my lord?"

"Kings. A forest of them from the stump of *abba* Jesse. I'm running with them, trying to keep up...." His voice seemed charged. "My bronze bow. I can pull it without my arms shaking. The arrow goes true, arcing toward a king with the face of a lion, a king more splendid than...Solomon at his coronation. He's...on a mountain, wet with dew. Asaph, Asaph, can you see? The king is...*me!*" His eyes blazed with atonishment. "Me, young again. Strong as a lion, yet holding a...Passover lamb." Tears spilled from David's eyes; his breath came in rattles and gasps.

From the outer room came laughter—Abishag flirting, perhaps, with guards and chamberlains, doing what youth demands, weaving her vibrant melody into the symphony that inevitably and without mercy modulates to the wintry passion I was hearing from this toothless, liver-spotted, slack-stringed harp.

"Me," he went on, "but not me. My son...yet somehow my Lord. *And this king...wears the face of love.*" His voice became a constricted whisper. "Asaph, it's *Abi's* love, after all! Her name...'As a father loves,' *so she loved me.* I was blind to her kind of love, but I see it now...I *see* it." Again, those anguished breaths. "And *Yahweh knows* me, everything about me, yet... *loves me still.* Asaph, what can I do? What can I say? Who can bear such love? *Abba!*" Thrusting a palsied hand upward, David cried hoarsely, "My bronze bow. Take it! My best, my only thing..." If a shrunken, dried-up corpse could cry, it would make sounds like those that came from David's chest. My stomach knotted at the hearing of it.

Whether dream or vision, I became alarmed and pressed his hand. "You must rest now. I'll come back tomorrow." I thrust my hand under his pillow to raise his head, then stopped as my hand struck something hard. I pulled out a small, lumpy, linen sack. "What's this, my lord?" I said, feeling the bag. "Rocks—under your pillow?"

"Stones," he murmured. "Five stones..."

I frowned, trying to think. He had often bent to pick up a stone, perhaps an odd habit of warriors. And as I look back through my scrolls, stones seem almost a metaphor in his life. But these—five stones. Five...*smooth* stones? I opened the sack and examined them. "My lord, are they connected with... Goliath?" I felt silly asking the question, but to my surprise, he closed his eyes in assent. "These stones...killed...?"

He shook his head. "No...no." He took one of the stones and held it familiarly. "After Nathan, after Boaz, I picked them up...to remind me—"

"Of victory instead of shame?"

His head rocked sideways. "No. Goliath was first, but...many victories followed."

"Goliath to Sheba, and everything between."

"No...small stones...to remind me...God uses weak things—stones...half-grown he-goats...broken, wayward kings—to conquer giants, vast armies. What was I against Absalom? Only Hushai's wit saved me. I hold the stones and feel... not my power...but God's. Keep them, Asaph. The power is there, but only for those who know their own weakness. Will Solomon know? If he doesn't know in the end, get them back. Take them, my friend, take them!"

His urgency spent, his frame seemed to disappear under the cover. "A few more words, Asaph. These," he said, tapping his chest, "from the heart. You must write...."

"Tomorrow," I insisted. "You'll be more rested."

"Tomorrow is a mist. Write."

What could I say? I readied my parchment.

Slowly, haltingly, he gave it out, and tears troubled my eyes.

> *The final word of David ben Jesse,*
> *a man lifted up and anointed by God,*
> *Israel's singer of songs:*
> *The Spirit of the Lord spoke through me;*
> *"When a king rules righteously in the fear of God,*
> *he is like sunrise on a cloudless day,*

> *Like brightness following rain*
>   *that brings grass out of earth."*
> *God did an amazing thing:*
> *He made a covenant with me,*
>   *secure in every way*
> *To establish my salvation*
>   *and grant my every desire.*
> *But evil men are like thorns,*
>   *gathered for destruction with a tool of iron;*
> *Burn them where they lie.*

"A thorn, Asaph. He's a thorn, but...Solomon's tool of iron... will consign Joab...to fire."

Each breath was labored. "Go, true...faithful friend. Speak my name once more...in blessing. I shall not...hear your voice again."

I fell to my knees, sobbing. "David...my *friend.* Oh, David..."

When I rose to go, I heard his whisper, "King...that is lion... that is lamb. *Abba,* I love you." But then the shadow of his old roar carried to the door of the room. *"Abi...I need you!"*

Addendum

List of Characters by Categories

(Parentheses designate fictional names, not fictional characters)

Kings (and their Families)

Saul, first king of Israel
>**Ahinoam**, Saul's wife; her sons:
>>**Abinadab**
>>**Malki-shua**
>>**Esh-Baal**, also called Ish-Bosheth
>>**Jonathan**
>>>**Mephibosheth**, crippled son of Jonathan
>**Rizpah**, Saul's concubine; her sons:
>>**Armoni**
>>**Mephibosheth**

David, king of Judah and Israel
>**Michal**, wife and daughter of Saul

Ahinoam, wife
>   **Amnon**, son

Abigail, wife
>   **Daniel**, son, also called Kileab

Maacah, wife
>   **Absalom**, son
>   **Tamar**, daughter

Haggith, wife
>   **Adonijah**, son

Abital, wife
>   **Shephatiah**, son

Eglah, wife
>   **Ithream**, son

Bathsheba, wife, former wife of Uriah; her sons:
>   **Boaz**
>   **Solomon**
>   **Nathan**
>   **Shobab**
>   **Shammua**, sometimes Shimea

The mothers of the following children of David are not specified:

Ibhar, Elpelet, Nepheg, Elishama, Eliphilet, Elishua, Nogah, Japhia, Beeliada, Jerimoth

Achish, king of the Philistines

Hiram, king of Tyre and friend of David

Nahash, king of the Ammonites and father of:

    Hanun, who succeeded him

    Shobi, governor appointed by David after Hanun

Hadadezer, king of Zobah in Syria

Talmai, king of Geshur, father of Maacah, grandfather of Absalom

Military personnel

Joab, commander in chief:

    His armor-bearers:

        Naharai

        A Cushite

    The Three

    Jashobeam

    Eleazar, son of Dodai

    Shammah

      Abishai, chief of the Three but not one of them

Mighty Men (selected from the Thirty)

Benaiah, chief of the Kerethites and Pelethites, David's bodyguard

    Amasai, chief of the Thirty

    Amasa

    Asahel

Dodai

Elhanan

Hurai

Ira

Ittai the Gittite

Uriah the Hittite

Zebadiah, son of Asahel

David's Retinue

Shammah, Abinadab, Nethanel, Eliab, David's brothers

Jonathan, David's uncle and counselor

Ahithophel, chief counselor, father of Mighty Man Eliam and grandfather of Bathsheba

Joram, personal servant (fictional name)

Obil, camelmaster

David's Friends

Barzillai of Rogelim

Kimham, his son

Caleb and **Ascah**, couple in Bahurim who hid the king's messengers (fictional names)

Hushai, friend, counselor

Shobi, son of Nahash, king of Ammonites

Makir of Lo Debar, who befriended Jonathan's Mephibosheth and the fugitive David

David's Enemies

Abner, who fought against David after the death of Saul (more adversary than enemy)

Cush, a man of Benjamin named in the title of Psalm 7

Doeg, chief herdsman for Saul who betrayed David and slaughtered the priests of Nob

Jonadab, David's troublemaking nephew

Sheba, led a rebellion of Israelites against King David

Shimei, Benjamite gadfly

The Priests

Ahimelech, high priest at Nob, father of Abiathar

Abiathar, high priest under David, served at the Tent in Jerusalem

Jonathan, son of Abiathar

Zadok, priest at Gibeon, high priest after Abiathar's defection

Ahimaaz, son of Zadok

The Levites

Jeiel, the gatekeeper

Uzzah, son of Abinadab at whose house the ark rested for many years after its capture and release by the Philistines

Obed Edom, along with his sons kept the ark after Uzzah's death

The Levite Musicians

Kenaniah, head Levite in charge of singing
Asaph
Heman
Ethan

The Prophets

Samuel
Nathan
Gad

Hebrew Terms Used in the Narrative

Abba—Father. (Technically an Aramaic term found only in the New Testament, but I have chosen to use it because of its familiarity and similarity to *Ab* or *Abi*, the Hebrew word for father and David's nickname for Abigail.)

Ben—Son of.

Cherem—The devotion of things or persons to the Lord, often by totally destroying them.

Gibbor, gibborim—Warrior(s). The capitalized form refers to David's elite corps of Mighty Men.

Melech—King.

Hamelech—*The* king, equivalent to "high king."

Yahweh—Jehovah, Lord, the "I AM."

About the Author

Eleanor K. Gustafson has been publishing both fiction and nonfiction since 1978. Her short stories and articles have appeared in a number of national and local magazines. *The Stones* is her fourth novel.

In many of her stories, Eleanor explores the cosmic struggle between good and evil in light of God's overarching work of redemption. A graduate of Wheaton College in Illinois, she has been actively involved in church life as a minister's wife, teacher, musician, writer, and encourager. She has enjoyed a variety of experiences, from horses to house building, all of which have helped bring color and humor to her fiction.

She and her husband live in Massachusetts, where he teaches philosophy. They travel extensively, spend time with their three children and eight grandchildren, and enjoy camping at the family forest in Chester, Vermont.

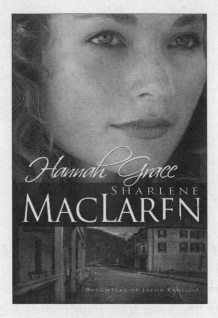

Hannah Grace
Sharlene MacLaren

Hannah Grace, the eldest of Jacob Kane's three daughters, is feisty and strong-willed, yet practical. She has her life planned out in an orderly, meaningful way—or so she thinks. When Gabriel Devlin comes to town as the new sheriff, the two strike up a volatile relationship that turns toward romance, thanks to a shy orphan boy and a little divine intervention.

ISBN: 978-1-60374-074-6 ♦ Trade ♦ 432 pages

WHITAKER
HOUSE

Long Journey Home
Sharlene MacLaren

Single mother Callie May is still nursing emotional scars from an abusive marriage when a handsome but brooding stranger moves into the apartment across the hall. In spite of his attractiveness, pastor Dan Mattson has problems of his own—he abandoned his flock and turned his back on God following the deaths of his wife and baby daughter. When Callie's ex-husband shows up to wreak even more havoc in her life, Dan comes to her defense—and faces his own demons in the process. Will Dan and Callie allow God to change their hearts and mend their hurts so they can take another chance on love?

ISBN: 978-1-60374-056-2 ♦ Trade ♦ 400 pages

WHITAKER
HOUSE

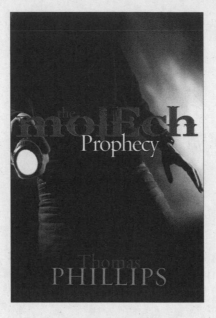

The Molech Prophecy
Thomas Phillips

Former gang member Tommy Cucinelle thought he had left his old life behind when he became a Christian. That's why he's surprised when his pastor asks him to use his discarded "skill"—finding people who don't want to be found—to locate the church secretary after she mysteriously disappears and the church is vandalized. Tommy's investigation brings him face-to-face with unpleasant memories from the past that threaten his new identity, but inner turmoil is soon the least of his worries....

ISBN: 978-1-60374-055-5 ♦ Trade ♦ 336 pages

WHITAKER
HOUSE

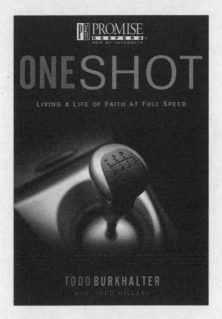

One Shot
Todd Burkhalter

You have one shot at this life. One shot to make it count. If you don't make the most of it, you risk wasting your life. What story will your life tell? God designed your life to be lived with purpose, passion, and direction. Your life was intended to mean something. In *One Shot*, author Todd Burkhalter challenges men to live a life of adventure and significance. True risk always begins in the heart. By understanding who you are in Jesus Christ and who He is in you, you can experience the adventure, meet life's challenges, and live a significant life of faith at full speed.

ISBN: 978-1-60374-071-5 ♦ Trade ♦ 208 pages

WHITAKER
HOUSE

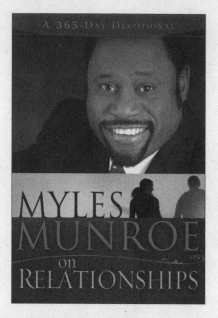

Myles Munroe on Relationships
Dr. Myles Munroe

Can you fulfill your purpose in life and have harmonious, thriving relationships? Best-selling author Dr. Myles Munroe says you can. In fact, the two can only be achieved together. *Myles Munroe on Relationships* reveals how God's purpose for you is the key to your fulfillment—especially in your relationships. Dr. Munroe shows you how to discover your true purpose in life and offers practical and biblical advice for developing relationships of all types. Discover God's design for men and women and start building strong, productive, loving relationships today.

ISBN: 978-1-60374-070-8 • Cloth • 384 pages

WHITAKER
HOUSE